What Reviewers Say About Nell Stark's fiction:

"In this character driven story, the author gives us two very likeable and idealistic women that are without pretense. The growth these two experience from their involvement in an important cause, as well as the friendships that they make throughout the year, is moving and refreshing. Kudos to the author on a very fine book."—*Curve* magazine

"*Running with the Wind* is a fast-paced read. Stark's characters are richly drawn and interesting. The dialog can be lively and wry and elicited several laughs from this reader…the discussions of the nature of sex, love, power, and sexuality are insightful and represent a welcome voice from the view of late-20-something characters today. The love scenes between Corrie and Quinn are erotically charged and sweet."—*Midwest Book Review*

Visit us at www.boldstrokesbooks.com

By Nell Stark

Running With the Wind

Homecoming

everafter

by

Nell Stark and Trinity Tam

2009

EVERAFTER
© 2009 By Nell Stark and Trinity Tam. All Rights Reserved.

ISBN 10: 1-60282-119-4
ISBN 13: 978-1-60282-119-4

This Trade Paperback Original Is Published By
Bold Strokes Books, Inc.
P.O. Box 249
Valley Falls, NY 12185

First Edition: October 2009

Credits
Editors: Cindy Cresap and Stacia Seaman
Production Design: Stacia Seaman
Cover Design By Sheri (graphicartist2020@hotmail.com)

Acknowledgments

The act of writing may be solitary, but every piece of writing is a collaboration. We are indebted to Radclyffe for sowing the seed of this idea years ago and for giving us the opportunity to publish this book. We'd like to thank all of the good people at Bold Stokes Books—Connie, Lori, Lee, Jennifer, Paula, Sheri, and others—for helping to put out and market quality product year after year. Cindy Cresap's editorial expertise was instrumental in improving this project from a promising draft to a polished narrative, and Stacia Seaman's careful fine-tuning of the manuscript is very much appreciated.

Dedication

For the ones who kept stitching each of us back together,
when everything seemed to be falling apart.
You know who you are.

valentine

CHAPTER ONE

It was a perfect evening for romance. The early October air was refreshingly crisp after a warm afternoon, and wisps of cirrus clouds the color of cotton candy wafted slowly westward before a gentle breeze. Even the omnipresent car horns sounded musical, somehow. I slipped my right hand into my pocket and rested my fingertips on the surface of the suede box nestled inside. It felt soft and warm, like a living thing. I had to work at keeping my lips from curving up. It might be safe to walk around Midtown Manhattan sporting a full-blown grin these days, but the Lower East Side was still a different story.

Even so, how was I supposed to stay staid and serious when tonight was the night—the night when I would propose to the love of my life? The smile broke free after all as I thought of her. Alexa. Quick-witted, silver-tongued, tempestuous Alexa—graceful as a dancer, with hair the color of smoldering ashes. My love. She was probably just leaving her Torts class now. I liked to imagine Alexa in class—sitting in the second row, focused intently on the professor, occasionally raising her hand to ask a question or volunteer an answer. But right this moment, she would be walking quickly down the steps of NYU's law school, hurrying toward the bus stop in her eagerness to get home for dinner.

I always cooked on Tuesdays. While Alexa was slammed with back-to-back classes, I only had Anatomy in the morning, leaving me ample time for both studying and playing chef. I enjoyed cooking and liked to experiment. But even on Tuesdays, I didn't usually go so far as to make my own fettuccini and vodka sauce from scratch. And I certainly didn't make a habit of running out to the liquor store with the intent to buy an expensive bottle of champagne. Tonight was no normal Tuesday. Tonight was going to be one of the best nights of my life.

I turned right on Avenue D and walked for a few blocks, past the projects on my left and a variety of small, ramshackle stores on my right. Alexa would be on the bus by now. The bus ran right past the Niagra, where I had bartended last year. Where we had first met, almost ten months ago. I could remember that night so clearly, still: something—a change in the air, an electricity—had prompted me to look up when she entered at the front of a group of already-intoxicated women. She was wearing deep red leather pants that precisely matched the color of the cloud of hair framing her face. Tiny sequins in her silver tank top shimmered slightly as she moved toward the bar. Toward me. I remember her gaze dropping first to my name tag and then lower, an unseen hand caressing the swell of my breasts before moving back up, ghosting over the hard muscles in my upper arms and finally coming to rest on my face. She flushed, but her voice was steady.

"Valentine," she said, holding out a credit card. Her nails were that same shade of deep burgundy. "Seven lemon drops, please. And one Coke."

My fingertips slid over hers as I took the plastic. It was an unconscious move—she was irresistible. With an effort, I turned my back to run the card, taking careful note of the name beneath the VISA logo. Alexa Newland. "Would you like me to keep it open?" I asked over my shoulder.

"Yes, please."

I poured the Coke first, before getting to work on the seven shots. When I glanced back at her face, our eyes met. Hers caught the light like finely cut emeralds. Suddenly, it was hard to catch my breath. I remember shaking my head slightly, nonplussed at the force of my attraction. Beautiful women came into this bar all the time, and I flirted with them adeptly. Sometimes I took them home once my shift was over. None of them had ever made me feel like this—dizzy and winded after the briefest of exchanges. Fighting the vertigo, I broke eye contact. That's when I noticed that she was sipping on the soda.

"I don't trust a woman who doesn't drink."

Her thin eyebrows lifted at my challenge. "Why is that?"

I answered while expertly coating the rim of each shot glass with sugar. "Not indulging in a simple vice implies that you're saving yourself for something much more extravagant."

Alexa laughed. It was a beautiful sound, clear and ringing. "It's obvious that you don't know me."

I poured the shots, filling each precisely to the rim. "I'd like that to change. Let me take you out to dinner. Tomorrow." In my three months of work at the Niagra, no one had ever turned me down. But when I returned my attention to Alexa's face, she shook her head.

"You're very smooth. But no, thank you."

The rejection twisted in my gut, but I managed to pull off a nonchalant shrug in the process of arranging the glasses on a small tray. "All right." I smiled at her as she took the drinks. "Enjoy your night."

I remember enjoying the slight crease that appeared across the bridge of her nose at my apparent lack of disappointment. I could tell what she was thinking: that I was the consummate player, fickle and hotheaded. But she had judged too quickly, failing to bank on my capacity for patience. There was no reason to push right now. I had her name. This wasn't over.

I smiled again at the memory of how Alexa had put that patience to the test, making me pursue her for almost two weeks before finally agreeing to a date. Two weeks of waking early each morning to wait for her in the hall outside of her first class. I came bearing a venti cappuccino the first day, and learned that she had given up coffee in college. Every day thereafter, I brought chai lattes. She was reticent, but I was persistent. And now, I was about to ask her to make an honest woman of me.

Would she say yes? I wasn't certain. Technically, I was rushing into things—we hadn't even celebrated our first anniversary yet. I wasn't opposed to a long engagement, if that was her preference—years, if necessary. I just needed her to know that I meant it whenever I said "forever." And I wanted her to be mine—not my girlfriend, but my fiancée. I wanted my ring on her finger.

I was so deep in thought that I almost passed the liquor store that was my destination. A tall, burly guy wearing a leather jacket and knit cap loitered a few feet away, smoking the last inch of a cigarette. I shouldered open the door and walked in quickly, hoping that his smoke wouldn't cling to my hair or clothes. Normally, I would take pleasure in browsing the selection, but this time, I headed straight for the portly, balding man hunched on a stool behind the cash register. He looked up tiredly at my approach. His name tag dubbed him Stan, and the manager.

"So," I said, extracting my beat-up leather wallet from the back pocket of my jeans and withdrawing every last bill inside it. I tossed them down onto the grimy counter top. "I just cleaned out my checking account, and I have…eighty-seven dollars. Oh!" I jammed one hand into my left jeans pocket to fish up some change. The coins clinked against the glass. "And forty-nine cents."

"Good for you?" Stan offered. He was looking at me warily.

I rocked back on my heels, picturing the common room of the small, fourth floor apartment that I shared with Alexa, as I had left it just a few minutes ago. Miles Davis was playing softly through my desktop's speakers. The plain wooden table that we had chosen at a secondhand furniture store last week was now covered by a white silk cloth and decorated with a pair of crystal candlesticks. A trail of rose petals—plucked by hand—started from the front door and circled the table before leading into the bedroom. There was only one thing missing.

"I need the best bottle of champagne I can get."

Stan sighed and stiffly got to his feet. He shuffled around the counter, gesturing for me to follow. I trailed behind him obediently, watching as he paused halfway down the second aisle and selected a bottle two-thirds up the shelf.

"J Schram, 1999. Eighty-six dollars and ninety-five cents."

I took the bottle from him and turned it over in my hands. J Schram, I remembered, was served at the White House whenever a new president was inaugurated. It wasn't the $475 per bottle Dom Perignon that my father liked to serve at his parties, but it was fancy enough to drive home my point to Alexa.

"I'll take it." I tried to keep my mouth closed and play it cool, but the words came out anyway. "I'm proposing to my girlfriend."

"Congratulations." Stan's voice was monotone as he slipped the bottle into a paper bag and shuffled my bills into a neat pile. His fingers were ringless. Had he never found someone? Not for the first time, I contemplated how easy it would have been to miss Alexa that night at the Niagra, so many months ago. I had been there by chance, subbing for a coworker. By all rights, we should never have met. I shuddered at the thought and reached into my pocket once again to stroke the box reverently, as though it were a talisman. She had to say yes. She just had to.

"Thanks," I told Stan, grabbing the neck of the bottle with my free hand. The clock behind the counter read 7:46, and Alexa's bus was due in at 8:00. I had just enough time to put the champagne on ice and start boiling the noodles. I hadn't prepped a dessert—not of the conventional variety, anyway—but in extremis, there was most of a pint of strawberry Häagen Dazs in the freezer. I smiled faintly as I imagined us lounging naked in bed, feeding each other ice cream in the early hours of the morning.

Outside, dusk had faded into twilight. I retraced my steps past the shuttered storefronts emblazoned with graffiti. Still focused on the daydream, I automatically threaded my way around the piles of garbage bags heaped on the edge of the sidewalk. How would Alexa want me tonight, in the wake of my proposal? What would her mood call for? Would she want me to be slow and sweet, tenderly compelling her to succumb to the gentle strokes of my fingers? Or would she want me to take her, hard and fast—to unveil the full force of my desire and claim every inch of her? Or perhaps…perhaps I would simply remain on one knee to bury my face between her legs and let my tongue slip-slide across her warm, wet heat.

I was so caught up in the fantasy that I didn't register the sensation of someone walking close behind me until I had to pause at the first cross street. Suddenly anxious, I forced myself not to look over my shoulder. I quickened my pace, silently berating myself for not running this errand during the daylight. Parts of Alphabet City were becoming gentrified, but this wasn't one such section. Petty crime and drugs were still a problem, and—

Shit. The footsteps were no longer even with my own. They were faster. I tried to tell myself that the person behind me was simply in a hurry, but my instincts knew better. A hot rush of adrenaline flooded my body, bringing me to the balls of my feet. There was an all-night supermarket two blocks ahead, dingy but well lit. I could make it. My stalker wouldn't dare try anything if I reached that corner.

I clutched the neck of the J Schram tightly and balled my right hand into a fist in preparation for a sprint. This would not happen. I would not be a victim. Not tonight of all nights—not when the noodles were drying next to the sink and the freshly made sauce was simmering on the stove. Not with Alexa's ring in my pocket. No. Fucking. Way.

I ran. In a burst of speed that would have earned praise from my high school track coach, I leapt forward, put my head down, and pumped hard with both arms. Gravel scattered beneath the soles of my Doc Martens. I pushed off from the pavement explosively, focused on the goal…only to be shoved sideways into a narrow alley between two buildings before I had taken more than a few steps. I landed hard on my left side, grunting as the impact knocked the wind from my lungs and the bottle from my hand. It shattered in a spray of glass shards and fizzing liquid. Barely two inches from my face, a torn garbage bag leaked pale fluid. The smell of rot was overpowering. Choking on the stench, I tried to scramble to my feet. Scream. I had to get my breath back and scream. Someone would hear me.

But before I could open my mouth, a hand, rough with calluses, clamped over my face. I tried to jerk away, but another arm snaked below my ribs. The sharp scent of tobacco chased away the odor of rot as my assailant pressed me tightly against his body. My sudden shock made me momentarily passive. It was him. The man who had been smoking outside the liquor store. He had been lying in wait.

He was breathing heavily into my ear, and I could feel him hard against my lower back. Panic turned to refusal. No. I would not be mugged. I would not be raped. I would not be killed. No. Alexa's face was clear in my mind's eye, and the edges of the box in my pocket dug hard into my right thigh. I imagined again the subtle weight of the platinum band in the palm of my hand, its round diamonds winking mysteriously up at me in the softly modulated light of the Tiffany's showroom. *Etoile*. The ring was precious and elegant and beautiful. It was meant to sit on Alexa's finger. Where she was concerned, I believed deeply in destiny. Nothing would come between us—not ever.

I bit down hard on his middle finger. He yelled hoarsely, caught off guard just enough for me to twist free of his restraining embrace. I took off again toward the open mouth of the alley, planting my right foot down hard as I skidded around the corner…but a sharp pain blossomed in my hamstring and my leg gave out, on the edge of freedom.

I crumpled to the ground and stared disbelieving at the knife protruding from my jeans. Its handle was glossy and black. I hated it desperately. Closing one palm around it, I grit my teeth and pulled, managing to fling the weapon out of my body. The knife's clatter against the asphalt was drowned out by the rasping scream that escaped my lips, gushing from my throat as the bright red blood flowed from my leg. God, it hurt—but with the agony came another rush of adrenaline, bringing the edges of the night into sharp focus. Clarity returned in the form of a single imperative. Run.

The sound of slow footsteps approaching galvanized me. I had to get up—to get up or die here. Bracing myself on both hands, I pushed up hard with my left foot, only to fall back to the ground under the weight of my useless right leg. Immediately, I tried again, but he was already looming over me, face obscured by the shadows. He raised one hand and a flash of color caught my eye—something reptilian slithering across his knuckles, briefly illuminated by a thin sliver of light before he cut off my second shout with a vicious backhand to my cheek, so hard that my head slammed against the pavement.

Pain exploded behind my eyes, dazzling my vision with glowing specks as bright as the diamonds in Alexa's ring. *Get up. Get up, Valentine.* The thought belonged to someone else. It seemed important, but when I tried to raise my head, a wave of nausea forced my jaw open in a wrenching gag. A heavy weight settled on my thighs. Someone groaned in the distance, low and tortured.

And then another bolt of agony, this one lancing through my shoulder, hot and sharp like lightning. The world was blood. I could feel it leaving me all in a rush, pulsing past the lips of the wound in time with my heartbeat. It hurt too much to turn my head, but if I moved my eyes to the right I could just barely make out the dark pool gathering against the darker asphalt. So much blood. I was going to die.

Weakness pervaded my body, insidious and totalizing. I could only twitch feebly as a cold hand slipped under my shirt, palming my stomach and pushing up the fabric. *No,* I tried to say. *No, I am not yours. No, I belong to her. Alexa.* I needed to apologize to Alexa, but one of his hands closed around my throat while the other pushed up my shirt and his mouth was cold and wet on my sensitive skin like the tongue of a snake and it hurt…oh God, it hurt.

All lights were fading. I could feel them being extinguished, one by one—the stars and the street lamps and the cheerful squares of yellow that checkered every skyscraper. Gone. The curtain fell. Darkness like a gun barrel, black as my father's mercenary soul, narrowing to swallow me—the darkness of dead things underground. If I called her name, would she follow?

My lips moved silently as red ribbons anchored my body to the earth. *Follow me, Alexa. Bring me back. Marry me, Alexa, marry me please I'm sorry I swear I meant forever but I waited too long to tell you and now you'll never know.*

Mercifully, the pain receded then, leaving me beyond all sensation.

CHAPTER TWO

For the thousandth time since leaving my apartment, I checked my reflection in a nearby storefront window while waiting for a crosswalk light to change. The verdict was the same as it had been a minute ago: my three-button, pinstriped suit, fresh off a Brooks Brothers rack, set off the crystal blue of my eyes and together with my spiky blond hair, completed the image of the dashing young man I was constantly being mistaken for. I had flirted with the idea of going to a bespoke tailor, but that would have necessitated dipping into a bank account that I'd sworn not to touch except in extreme need. And while impressing my date tonight was imperative, it was just as important that Alexa be attracted to me for my own merits, and not because my father is Edward Darrow, Secretary of the Treasury, whose net worth (according to CNN) is at least 650 million dollars.

The suit I was wearing was still an extravagant purchase for someone who was about to revert to student status, but it had been bought with my own money, earned and not inherited. That made all the difference, as far as I was concerned. Mostly, I just hoped that Alexa liked the way I looked in it.

I crossed the street quickly and began checking the numbers on the buildings. Getting close. I twirled the single flower that I held delicately between two fingers and silently chided myself for being nervous. There had been many dates, and many women, before this one. By all rights, I should be operating on autopilot. But there was something about Alexa—something powerful and more than a little frightening—something that made me want to break most of the rules that I'd imposed on myself when I turned eighteen. I had already bent one by getting us a dinner reservation at Stella's.

As long as I was being honest with myself, I had to admit the facts: first, that Alexa Newland was under my skin; and second, that way deep down, that's exactly where I wanted her to be. Which was a new feeling.

When I pulled my attention back to the increasing numbers to my right, I realized that I'd gone half a block too far. I retraced my steps and ended up at a brick house, squeezed between a convenience store and a florist. When I rang the bell for apartment 2B, a dog on the first floor began to yap.

The wait lasted forever. Doubt crept into my gut and tied knots there. I raised my hand to ring the bell again just as the door finally swung open—and then my jaw dropped, because Alexa was standing in front of me in a strapless black dress that fit her body like a sheath, and her glossy hair was catching the city lights, and if tonight ended without at least a kiss I knew I was going to die.

I knew I was going to die. Strength had deserted me, borne on the streams of wet that pulsed from my leg, my shoulder. My heart was racing—I could feel it pounding against my ribs—and I tried to tell it to slow down. But when I felt him push one cold, clammy hand beneath my shirt, I begged it to stop beating entirely.

I knew I was going to die. But not fast enough. His mouth followed the trajectory of his hand, leaving a wet trail of saliva across the faint ridges of my abdominal muscles. When I shuddered, he laughed against my skin.

"Please," I tried to whisper, but gagged on the blood trickling into the back of my throat. Coughing was excruciating. I turned my head to the side and retched sour bile and blood. Undeterred, he laughed again.

"Someday, Valentine," he crooned. His voice was disturbingly soft, almost melodic. "Someday you'll appreciate the beauty in this."

He was insane. I had just enough time to realize it before his teeth sank into the meaty flesh under my right arm. I screamed as his mouth tugged at the wound. The pain was paralyzing. Directly above my head, a fire escape twisted sinuously, dancing in the neon lights of a nearby storefront. Black specks floated at the corner of my vision. I didn't fight them. I didn't want to be awake anymore.

But then another arrow of pain lanced through me—a blinding meteor across the welcome darkness, jerking me back into consciousness. Above the pulse pounding in my head, I could hear the heels of my shoes dragging against the pavement. A car door opened, and then another. One of his hands pressed against the wound he'd made with his teeth as he pushed me into the vehicle. The dim, too-distant lights of the supermarket faded in the wake of another wave of agony. I gasped for air and inhaled the sharp odor of newly cleaned upholstery mixed with the scent of stale cigarette smoke.

When he shoved my legs against one of the seat backs, white heat lanced up my spine and my vision swam again. So much, it hurt so fucking much. He knew my name. How did he know my name? Was this about my father? Or was it something else? Would they come after Alexa next? Please no, no, not Alexa—

The car's engine roared to life. My pain was ebbing now, its angry fire fading as the darkness returned. I felt empty. Hollow. Numb. *Why did it have to be tonight?* I asked him in my head. *Why are you doing this? Where are you taking me?*

"Where are you taking me?" Alexa asked as she took my outstretched hand.

To my bed, sang my body, sparking at the sensation of her palm sliding against mine. Our fingers entwined effortlessly.

"I told you," I said. "It's a surprise." I tugged lightly, drawing us down the front steps. As I scanned oncoming traffic for a cab, I wished, absurdly, that I had arranged to have a limousine waiting. What was it about this woman that brought out the extravagant in me?

Shaking off the unsettling thought, I flagged down a taxi and gave the driver an address in Midtown while opening the door for Alexa. Once we were settled inside, I felt bold enough to reach for her hand again. "Tell me about your day."

Alexa shrugged. "It was uneventful. I was in class."

"Well then," I said, trying for once in my life to sound like my mother, "what did you learn at school today?"

She laughed. It was a good sound, throaty and rich. "Do you really want the boring details?"

"The details wouldn't bore me. I had to take a class on the

intersection of law and social psychology one semester, and I found the law part fascinating."

Alexa crossed one leg over the other and shifted on the seat to lean closer to me. "You know...at first, I thought you were lying about your degree."

"You did? Why?" This was intriguing. Especially since she looked a little chagrined. It was a cute expression on her.

"Well, people with a master's in counseling psychology aren't usually bartenders."

"Alexa Newland!" I exclaimed, pretending shock. "You are a snob."

"Pot, kettle," she singsonged.

"Low blow. Just because I have the snob gene on both sides doesn't mean that it's expressing."

Her face became serious and she covered my hand with hers. "Just so we're clear: in no way am I here with you tonight because you're Edward Darrow's daughter. I'm sitting in this cab because," and here she smiled, "you wouldn't leave me alone, and I owe you for two weeks of chai."

I blinked, taken aback by the sudden change in trajectory. I'd had plenty of experience with women who were interested in me only because of my last name, and she had exhibited none of the indicators. Hell, if I hadn't kept after her for two solid weeks, we wouldn't be sitting here right now. So why did she feel the need to explicitly mention that she didn't care about my family's fortune or political connections?

She must have noticed my surprise, because she quickly hurried to clarify. "I just didn't want you to ever have a moment of doubt that I might be gold-digging. I made it here from small town Wisconsin entirely on my own steam." Her shrug was self-conscious, but elegant even so. "Sometimes I think my mother believes I'm a changeling."

I smiled and angled my body toward hers, wanting to ease the tension I could feel in the tight press of her fingertips against the back of my hand. Hopefully, I could convince her that she didn't have to prove herself to me.

"Well, just so we're clear: I'm glad you're not after my money, because while my grandfather did leave me a hundred-eighty-million-dollar trust fund, I can't touch a penny of it unless I marry a man."

Her jaw dropped. "Are you serious?" When I nodded, she rested her free hand on my thigh. The warmth of her palm soaked through the light wool and into my skin. "That is...awful."

"That money comes with a lot of baggage that I'd rather not deal with. I'll do fine on my own. And believe me, there are still plenty of perks that I enjoy." I tried to make my voice sound mysterious. "As you're about to discover."

At that moment, the cab pulled over next to the curb. I paid the driver, hopped out, and hurried over to Alexa's side. "Shall we?"

She looked around in confusion. I didn't blame her. She was looking for a restaurant, and there weren't any in sight. Struggling not to betray my excitement, I led her toward a nondescript black door between two high-end clothing boutiques. When I rang the bell, an intercom crackled to life.

"Good evening," said a male voice. Alexa turned toward me, clearly puzzled. I grinned.

"Valentine Darrow and Alexa Newland," I said.

"Of course. Thank you."

The door opened. When I gestured for Alexa to precede me, she raised her eyebrows and smiled faintly. She was intrigued. Good.

"Welcome to Stella's." The voice belonged to a middle-aged man wearing a tuxedo. He shut the door silently behind me and then led us down a long hallway lit intermittently by tall, thick candles set into wall sconces. At one point, Alexa looked over her shoulder, as though checking to make sure I was still there. I had a feeling that the expression on my face was bordering on smug, but here, it was hard not to be.

When the corridor emptied out into the dining room, the host paused. Alexa gasped quietly. I moved to stand next to her, daring to thread one arm around her waist, and wondered what impressed her the most. The crystal chandeliers? The elegant, three-tiered fountain that took up the center of the room, ending in a stone basin populated by large, orange koi? The immaculately attired band playing jazz music on a dais?

"Your table is this way," said the host. He directed us to an alcove, out of sight of the musicians but with a perfect view of the fountain. "Enjoy your meal."

I pulled out a chair for Alexa. She looked bemused, but didn't try *to stop me. Once we were both seated, she reached for my hands and squeezed hard. I let my thumbs gently caress her knuckles, enjoying the sight of her so clearly excited. A light flush had settled high on her cheekbones, and her eyes were glittering. Coming here had been the right thing to do—I had no doubts now.*

"This is incredible," she breathed. "What is this place? Where am I?"

Where am I? The ground was hard and cold. Wind howled somewhere above me, and a drop of moisture landed on my cheek. I was outside, and it was starting to rain. But I had been in a car, hadn't I? Had I? I tried to open my eyes, but pain roared through my head at even the slightest movement. Concussion—a bad one.

I could do nothing but lie still. I lay there forever with the night sky wheeling around me. There was the cold and the pain and the keening of the wind—nothing else. What if the memories I had of my life, what if they were a dream, and this was the reality? What if Alexa had been only a figment of my imagination? What if I had always been like this, broken and bleeding and utterly alone?

Or perhaps I was dead, and this was hell.

And then I heard them—low in the distance at first, but rising in pitch as they approached. Sirens. They sounded like church bells on Easter morning. It didn't matter that they might be a mirage, or perhaps even another, crueler aspect of my eternal punishment. The sensation was one of buoyancy—of rising up, like a bubble climbing from dark depths toward the surface, and sunlight. Hope.

The world was blinding. I closed my eyes immediately, taking shelter from the devastating brilliance. The air tasted dry and smelled like disinfectant. Steady beeps rose over the whirring hum of some kind of machinery. I lay on something soft and warm, and I was very, very thirsty. Why was I in the hospital?

Oh no, Alexa. Was she here, too?

The thought propelled my shoulders from the hospital bed. But as soon as I moved, the pain came down like a giant fist, cracking my head open. I groaned over the ringing in my ears.

"Oh my God, oh my God, doctor, nurse, someone—please—she's awake!"

It was my mother's voice. Very slowly, I turned my head to the left and forced myself to confront the dazzling light. After a few agonizing moments, the world swam into focus. My mother was wearing a navy suit and matching hat. The hat had a feather in it. Diamonds glinted at her earlobes and neck. They hurt my eyes. She was looking down at me and squeezing my hand.

"Valentine, Valentine, can you hear me? Oh, sweetie, I've been so worried—"

I tried to speak, but nothing happened. I swallowed painfully and tried again. "Mom."

She burst into tears and held my hand against her cheek. I focused on taking slow, even breaths, and gradually, the pain in my head receded to background noise. While my mother fussed over me, I tried to remember. Why was I here? What had happened?

I could remember Monday night. The double-whammy of a Physiology presentation in the morning and a Neuroanatomy test that afternoon had fried my brain. When I got home and told Alexa about my day, she dragged me to the couch. We spent the evening watching zombie movies and eating popcorn and making out like teenagers.

We went to bed. We made love. I could recall in vivid detail the way she had moved under me, the sound of her calling my name, the peace I'd felt as I curled myself around her afterward. But I couldn't remember anything after that. Not a damn thing. Panic welled up from my gut, and the tempo of those steady beeps increased.

"Mom," I croaked. "What happened to me?"

My mother blotted the skin under her eyes with a tissue. Her mascara was streaking. "You were..." She paused, and her grip on my hand tightened. "You were mugged, Valentine. He—he stabbed you."

Mugged? Stabbed? I started to shake my head, then stopped. "Where? When?" I could hear my heart racing on the monitor. How could I have forgotten all of that? How much time had passed?

My mother looked frightened. "Can you really not remember?"

"No," I whispered. Where Tuesday should have been, there was nothing. Nothing between falling asleep wrapped around Alexa and waking up here. Panic clogged my throat. How badly was I hurt?

"Tuesday night," my mother was saying. "They found you on Canal Street, near the bridge."

I could move my fingers and my toes, but was afraid to try anything larger. Canal Street? Near the Manhattan Bridge? Why would I have been down there? Had Alexa been hurt, too? Desperate for information, I sucked in too deep a breath and started coughing. My ribs were on fire and my throat was aching. I gripped the handles of the hospital bed hard, trying to still the spasms that racked my body.

"Where—" I gasped, when the fit had past. Blinking away the tears, I looked up into the concerned face of my mother. "Where is Alexa?"

When she hesitated, I felt the world start to disintegrate. Despair loomed like a tsunami, dark and inevitable. Oh no, God no, no, she couldn't be— But then my mother sighed sharply and pursed her lips.

"Downstairs. Waiting in the lobby."

I saw red. My hands were suddenly claws, digging into smooth metal. The threatening tide turned to vapor in the face of my anger. What kind of mother had the heart to do a thing like that? *How dare she? How fucking dare she?*

"I promised to tell her when you woke up," she added, as if that somehow made it acceptable for her to have denied my lover—whom she had met on more than one occasion—access to my bedside while I fought for my life.

"How long?" I grated.

"Three days." Her words were clipped, her tone superior. In that moment, I hated her.

"I want her here. Now."

"Valentine—"

"I'm awake, God damn it. Call her."

"You need to talk to the detective who has been here every—"

"Later. I need Alexa now."

"I'm afraid I don't have her—"

"Six-four-six. Five-five-five. One-three-one-three. Now call her, or I'll find someone who will."

She extracted her cell phone from the bowels of her navy purse and slowly dialed the number while I lay trembling with rage and adrenaline. I strained to hear Alexa's voice through the tiny speaker poised next to my mother's bejeweled ear.

"She's asking for you. Room 803," was all my mother said before hanging up the phone. She rose from the chair and smoothed her suit regally. "I'll be back tomorrow," she said, not quite meeting my gaze.

"Fine." I was too angry to trust myself with more than a monosyllable. Once she had gone, I stayed focused on the door, fractals of anticipation blooming in my stomach. A bank of windows stretched out horizontally to the left of the door, but the blinds were pulled. I cursed at them under my breath as the seconds stretched out interminably.

The faint sounds of a commotion trickled under the door. "Hey, slow down!" someone called. I smiled. That, at least, didn't hurt. And then the door crashed open, and Alexa was standing in the threshold, fists clenched at her sides. In three days, she had noticeably lost weight. Shadows partially encircled her wild eyes, and when she saw me, she gasped.

"Alexa." I meant for those three, perfect syllables to tell her what my appearance obviously didn't—that I was going to be fine. But my voice broke in the middle, and the next thing I knew, she was next to the bed and her arms were awkwardly wrapped around me and she was kissing my forehead, my cheeks, my lips.

"Val Val oh sweetheart thank God I was so scared…"

I breathed in as deeply as I dared. Her familiar, beloved scent eased the ache in my head and the dryness of my throat. I ran my fingers through her silky hair, savoring her nearness. Alexa, my touchstone. As long as she was with me, I could get through anything. Even this.

"I'm sorry," I whispered. "So, so sorry."

"Shh, love," she said, resting her head next to mine on the pillow and lightly caressing my cheek with one finger. "It's not your fault."

I leaned forward slightly to touch her lips to mine. "No, I mean, I'm sorry about my mother. I wish to God that I'd thought about power of attor—"

The sound of someone clearing his throat made me pause. I looked past Alexa's shoulder at a pale, slender man wearing a white coat and khaki pants and holding my chart. A pair of tinted, horn-rimmed glasses partially obscured his eyes. He was staring at me with an unnerving intensity.

"I apologize for the interruption," he said. His voice was accented lightly—French, I thought. "I'm Harold Clavier, Valentine, the doctor who has been monitoring your progress. How are you feeling?"

Alexa raised her head and turned toward the doctor, but continued to crouch next to me, my hand enfolded in hers. I was thankful—I needed to be touching her.

"I'm not really sure," I told him. "My head hurts. I'm thirsty. What else…what else is wrong with me?"

"How much do you remember?" he countered.

Fear must have shown in my face, because Alexa leaned over to press a gentle kiss to my temple. Her tenderness made me want to cry with relief. "Nothing," I whispered.

He cocked his head slightly, like a bird. "Nothing?"

"If she says nothing, then she means nothing," Alexa snapped. "Now what did he do to her?"

I brought our joined hands up so that I could stroke my cheek against her knuckles in a paltry attempt to soothe her. Alexa was fire, through and through. Even so, she usually did a better job of reining in her temper—in front of complete strangers, anyway. She was at the end of her rope right now. Because of me.

"You have two cracked ribs and a serious concussion," Dr. Clavier said. Despite Alexa's outburst, he looked unruffled. "You were also stabbed twice, once in the leg and once in the shoulder. You lost a great deal of blood, and required two transfusions, but you'll fully recover from both injuries with a little physical therapy."

Stabbed. Again, I shied away from the word. How, how could I have been attacked without remembering it? My brain knew the answer, of course—head trauma compounded by post-traumatic stress disorder. I wasn't sure what frightened me more: the thought that I might never remember, or the prospect that I would start experiencing flashbacks.

"When can she go home?" said Alexa.

"Probably in a few days. Maybe a week." Dr. Clavier was staring at me again in that unnerving way. Expectantly. "Because of your head injury, I want to be more cautious than I otherwise might."

"How long before my memory comes back?" I had my own guesses, but I wanted to hear his.

"Impossible to say. Perhaps within the next few days. Perhaps not for months." He replaced the chart on its hook near the foot of my bed. "I can recommend some excellent therapists, if you'd like."

"Okay." Alexa squeezed my hand, and I squeezed back. A knock at the door made me look up quickly, only to be dazzled by a flash of searing pain behind my eyes. Blinking against the sensation, I focused on the newcomer.

She was a striking woman—almost as tall as I was, and a little stockier. Jet-black hair fell to her shoulders. She wore a dark pantsuit, and a gold shield was clipped to her belt. When she turned to face Clavier, I could make out the slight bulge of her shoulder holster beneath the jacket. The detective, obviously. She carried herself like a soldier. A thin man with short, sandy-colored hair followed behind her. He wore his badge prominently on the lapel of his sport coat.

"I'll be back tomorrow," said Dr. Clavier as the detectives approached my bedside. The woman glanced curiously at Alexa, but held out her hand to me.

"Detective Devon Foster." Her grip was firm but not painful. "And my partner, Detective Jared Wilson. Your mother called me a short time ago to let me know that you were awake. How are you feeling?"

"Lucky to be alive," I said.

"She's in a lot of pain," said Alexa simultaneously.

"And you are?" There was no meanness in Foster's voice—only curiosity.

"Alexa Newland. My girlfriend."

"It's a pleasure," Foster said, shaking her hand, too. "I can only imagine how awful you're feeling right now, Valentine, so I won't take long."

"Do you have any idea who did this?" Alexa asked. Her tone was beseeching.

"No, ma'am. Not yet. But we're working on it." Foster regarded me intently. "Can you tell me what happened?"

"I wish." I swallowed again in an effort to draw some moisture into my parched throat. "I can't remember anything about Tuesday. Nothing at all."

The detective nodded. "You were found on Canal Street, near the Manhattan Bridge. Any idea why you might have been down there?"

"No. I can't think of any reason."

When she sighed in clear frustration, my hands clenched into fists. I wanted to help, damn it. How did she think I felt, unable to put the pieces of my own life together?

"When you go out, what do you usually take with you?"

I frowned at the change in approach. "Wallet, keys, and cell."

"It seems likely that this was a mugging, then. We didn't find anything on you."

"I already canceled your cards, sweetheart," Alexa reassured me, reaching over to hold my hand again.

"There's been a rash of very violent muggings over the past six months." Detective Wilson spoke up for the first time, his voice a smooth baritone. "The other victims...haven't pulled through."

A sudden wave of exhaustion blindsided me, threatening to pull me under. The adrenaline was fading. My eyes closed involuntarily.

"I want to remember. Just...can't."

"I understand," Foster said.

It felt so good to hide from the light. My head hurt less. Her voice sounded far away, as though I were underwater.

"Please give me a call if you think of anything, remember anything."

I tried to open my eyes, but couldn't. "I'll be sure that she does that, Detective," I heard Alexa say. Then, footsteps. A door closing. Quiet.

"Tired," I mumbled. "Alexa."

"I'm right here, love," she said. She squeezed my hand again. She was so warm. "I'm not going anywhere. You sleep."

The darkness behind my eyes was tinted with streaks of red. I knew they were the lamps in my room, filtering through the thin skin of my eyelids. They didn't look like lights, though. They looked like blood.

Thirsty.

CHAPTER THREE

Does it hurt, love?" Alexa asked from behind me as I limped slowly up the stairs toward our apartment. Despite the help of a cane on loan from the hospital, I had to momentarily put weight on my bad leg each time I ascended another step. Whenever I did, it felt like someone was twisting a jagged screw under my skin. I was already nauseous and sweating, and I had half the stairway left to go.

"It's not too bad," I said.

"Just take it slow."

I fought back a retort about how I couldn't exactly do much else. Alexa had barely left my side for the past five days. She had braved hospital food, sleeping in a chair, and my mother's nastiness to be there for me. She didn't need me snapping at her. So I ascended slowly, painfully, focusing on how good it would feel to be home.

When I finally reached the landing, I was shaking. Sweat was dripping into my eyes and off my chin. Alexa carefully reached around me to unlock the door and push it open, and I gratefully stepped inside.

A brittle cracking sound stopped me in my tracks. Puzzled, I looked down. They littered the floor, shriveled and deep, deep red— almost black. Rose petals.

I remembered.

I remembered kissing Alexa good-bye as we parted ways that morning. I remembered hurrying out of my Anatomy class and immediately heading uptown, toward Tiffany's. I remembered holding the ring in the palm of my hand and watching its diamonds glitter. I remembered blasting my cheesy 80s music playlist while making fettuccini. I remembered realizing, early in the evening, that I had neglected to get champagne. I remembered descending the stairs, walking out into the crisp night, shoving my hands into the deep pockets of my leather jacket…but afterward, nothing. Nothing—like a light switching off in a windowless room.

"Oh, no," said Alexa. She moved past me and dropped her duffel bag next to the coffee table. Her voice was saturated with contrition. "Oh God, Val, I'm so sorry. I didn't think—I should have come home to clean this up."

Grief knocked the wind from my lungs as I imagined Alexa walking into the apartment a week ago, the scent of roses rising beneath her feet. I could see her standing exactly where she was now, surveying the elegantly set table for two—only in my mind's eye, she was smiling. Had she called my name? The smile would have dissolved into a frown when I hadn't answered. Had she thought that my absence was part of the surprise? Or had she phoned my cell right away? How long had it taken for her to become frantic?

I took a deep, shuddering breath. It must have sounded like a sob, because she turned toward me, pain and worry shadowing her eyes. I don't know what she saw, but she was at my side in a second. Her arms were wrapped around me, holding me up.

"What is it? Are you in pain? Val? You're trembling—"

"I can remember," I whispered. She tightened her grip on me. My ribs hurt, but it would have been worse if she had let go.

"What, sweetheart?" she said in a too-measured voice. That meant that she was freaking out, but trying to keep it from me. Which never worked. "What do you remember?"

"Tuesday. The day." Despite the throbbing of my leg, I turned awkwardly in the circle of her arms so that our bodies fit together. "I wanted us to have champagne. I ran out just before you got home…"

"What then?" Against her will, fear leaked into her words.

But I still couldn't see anything else. Trying made my head hurt, and I leaned down just enough to rest my cheek on her shoulder. "Nothing."

She didn't say anything for several minutes—just stroked my back very gently until I finally stopped shaking. I wasn't going to tell her about the ring. It was gone anyway—stolen by the mugger, along with my wallet and cell. I couldn't have cared less about the credit cards, and my phone was easily replaced, but when I thought about his bloodstained fingers touching Alexa's ring—God, I wanted to fucking kill him. I trembled again, this time out of rage.

"You're chilled," Alexa murmured. "We should get you into bed." Her hand crept up to play with the short, fuzzy hairs on the back of my neck. "But first, we should call the detective."

"I still don't remember something that will actually help."

Alexa tugged gently on my hair, urging my head up so that she could meet my gaze. "She told us to call if you thought of anything," she reminded me. "Let her decide what's useful and what isn't."

When I nodded, she leaned in and pressed her lips to mine. I wrapped my good arm around her waist and lost myself in the tenderness of her mouth. The soft strokes of her tongue against mine melted away the pain, the fear, the frustration. There was nothing more powerful than this—than us. Suddenly desperate for the feel of her skin, I slipped my hand under her sweater to rest my palm in the warm hollow of her lower back. The tenor of the kiss changed immediately—she groaned into my mouth and used her hand at the back of my neck to urge me closer. This moment wasn't about desire, or even love. It was need that drove us, need that inspired the insistent thrusts of her tongue and the hard clutch of my fingertips against her muscles.

We might never have stopped if I hadn't felt the drop of moisture on my cheek. Not mine—hers. I tried to pull back, but at first she wouldn't let me. My shoulder protested as I raised my left hand to cup her face, but I ignored the flash of pain. I held her gently but firmly, lifting my head just enough to take in her frightened expression and the tears that streamed from her eyes. She wouldn't look at me. I thought about what I would feel like if our places were reversed, and even the hypothetical terror was enough to steal the breath from my lungs again.

"I'm sorry," she whispered. She was staring hard at the splash marks on the floor where her tears had landed. "I know this isn't what you need from me right now. I'm sorry."

She was wrong. I was next to helpless—bruised and broken, haunted and scared. There wasn't much I could do except hold her, but I could do that. I wanted to be strong, and in this one small way, I could be.

"Don't you dare apologize," I breathed into her hair and let the words bubble up from the well of emotion that she had opened inside my soul, only ten short months ago. "I need you to need me. When I imagine how you must have felt...God, baby, it would have destroyed me. You've been a rock. But you can't be one all the time. It's okay. I love you. It's going to be okay."

Gradually, her quick, hitching breaths became slow and deep, and her body softened against mine. After a few minutes, she raised her head. Her eyes were red-rimmed but clear. Back in control of herself, she regarded me steadily.

"I know you're exhausted. Why don't you rest on the couch until the detective gets here? I'll call her right now."

"Okay." I leaned forward to lightly kiss her cheek, determined to be an obedient patient. Still, when she handed me the gray, foam-handled cane, I couldn't help but grimace. Before last week, I had been able to run a mile in under seven minutes without even pushing. Now I could barely walk.

Sighing, I hobbled around the table toward my side of the couch. As I passed the opening to the kitchen, my nose wrinkled. The skillet of vodka sauce was exactly where I had left it, covered on the front left burner. On the counter nearby was a plate piled high with homemade noodles. I limped close enough to the sink to witness the green and purple mold that had wrapped itself around the thick strands of fettuccini. The sauce probably looked even worse. The sharp odor of decay was a far cry from the aroma of basil and shallots that had filled the air when I'd last stood here.

"...appreciate it, Detective," Alexa was saying. She snapped her phone shut as she came up behind me and rested one hand on my waist. "What are you—oh. That is gross."

"Looks like somebody's science experiment," I said around the lump in my throat.

Alexa moved, placing herself directly in my line of sight to the stove. She kissed me again, smoothing one thumb over the dark circles under my right eye. "Whatever you had planned for that night—thank you. It was...it was going to be beautiful."

She had no idea. Forcing myself to smile a little, I let her lead me over to the couch. When she asked if I needed anything, I asked for some water. Incessant thirst had been plaguing me since I'd woken up—no matter how much I drank, my throat was always parched. After draining the glass, I leaned my head back against the cushions. The sounds of Alexa cleaning up the kitchen were soothing. As my eyes drifted shut, I wondered how long it would take me to get back to normal. And how I was ever going to make up all the work I had missed from my classes. And whether I would ever be able to banish the fear that some kind of awful memory would resurface.

Mercifully, a knock interrupted my thoughts. I watched enviously as Alexa jogged to open the door. Running was one of our favorite things to do together. I wouldn't be able to join her for months now.

"Please come in, Detective."

Foster was dressed more casually today, in khakis and a blazer. I had the chance to watch her unobserved for a few seconds as the two of them chatted briefly, and was surprised to find that she pinged my gaydar. It wasn't that she looked queer per se, but that the way she looked at Alexa was...appreciative. Then again, Alexa routinely turned the heads of straight women.

I was working on getting to my feet so that I could shake the detective's hand properly, but she waved me off. "No no, please. Stay put." When Alexa pulled over her desk chair, Foster thanked her and sat. "How are you feeling, Valentine?"

Alexa curled herself into my side and reached for my hand. Foster's gaze flickered between us, and an unfamiliar wave of possessiveness crashed over me. I momentarily tightened my grip on Alexa's fingers. *Mine.* What was it about the detective that pushed my buttons?

"I'm improving, but slowly," I said, working to keep my voice even. "Apparently my memory is improving, too."

"So I hear." Foster withdrew a pen and a small notebook from one pocket. "Did you have a flashback?"

"Sort of. As soon as I set foot in the apartment, I could remember what I'd done on Tuesday, up until a certain point." I told her everything then, except for the part about picking up the ring at Tiffany's. "Errands uptown," I said instead. She was particularly interested by the end of my narrative.

"The last thing you remember is leaving the apartment," she double-checked. I nodded. "Where would you have gone to get the champagne?"

"Not sure. There are several stores around here that sell alcohol." My palms had begun to sweat, and I knew Alexa could feel it. She stroked my knuckles with her thumb.

Foster frowned. "So you wouldn't have gone to the intersection where you were found? Canal Street, near the Manhattan Bridge?"

"I was in a hurry," I said, reliving the moment when I had realized that I'd forgotten to buy a suitable dinner drink. "I wouldn't have gone all the way down there."

"You're certain?"

"Yes." I shifted nervously. The ache in my leg and shoulder was getting sharper. Time for more pain meds. "What does that mean?"

"I'm not sure," she said. "Possibly that your assailant moved you—either before or after the attack."

"Why would he do that?" Alexa asked. Her voice trembled a little.

"I don't know." She put away her notebook and got to her feet. "I appreciate the phone call," she said, looking me squarely in the eye. "I know this must be difficult, but every piece that you remember—no matter how minor—could be important."

"Thanks for coming so quickly, Detective," Alexa said, also rising.

Foster smiled. She looked several years younger when she smiled—less an experienced warrior and more an eager cadet. And she had nice teeth. "Please, call me Devon. Both of you."

Something inside me snarled. I wanted to reach for Alexa, but she was too far away. What was wrong with me? I wasn't a jealous person by nature. Foster hadn't even done anything provocative, and I was still reacting like a Neanderthal. And God, I was thirsty. Maybe that was it—being constantly parched had frayed my nerves. That, and being mugged. And now apparently kidnapped.

"Good night," I managed to say as Alexa opened the door to show her out.

She locked and chained the door as soon as Foster had stepped over the threshold. "How are you doing?" she asked, returning to her spot on the couch. I ignored the question, still grappling with the unfamiliar rage churning deep within my chest.

"She has the hots for you. I can see it in her face."

Alexa snorted. "Bull."

"Not so. She gets this hungry expression whenever she looks at you. I recognize it from my reflection."

Alexa shifted, half kneeling over me. She cupped my face in her hands and kissed me tenderly, soothing away my tension. "You are the only one I want. Now, let's go to bed."

"How about a shower first?" I countered. I hadn't had a real shower in over a week. I felt disgusting.

"Okay."

She kissed me again before heading for the bathroom. I limped back into the kitchen, refilled my glass, and gulped down more water along with two pain pills before slowly making my way to the bedroom.

Alexa was waiting by the bed, naked. I froze, drinking her in. Deep red curls swirled around the contours of her tan shoulders. Her breasts were high and small, in perfect proportion to her slender torso. Nestled between her slender, shapely runner's legs, her neatly trimmed patch of hair beckoned to me, calling up my blood. Making me ache.

I wanted to devour her.

"Let me help you with your clothes," she said.

I took a few faltering steps forward. "I need to make love to you."

When she laughed, I realized that I had surprised her. Had she truly expected me to be so distracted by my own ordeal that I wouldn't want her? Nothing was more important, more necessary, than us. Nothing.

"Please."

"Val," she said, lifting the hem of my shirt and working it gently over my injured arm. "I love how you want me. And I need you, too. But it's too soon."

Desperate to touch her, to hear her call my name as she came for me, I shook my head. "It's not. You can sit on my face. I won't move anything except my tongue, I swear."

It was her turn to freeze. The color rose in her cheeks, and her eyes darkened. "Jesus Christ, Valentine."

"Let me." A whisper.

"No." She threw back her shoulders and reached for the hem of my pants, her touch brisk and efficient. Not the touch of a lover, but a nurse. "Not tonight."

Defeated, I let her finish undressing me. Disappointment sapped me of what little energy I had left. Silently, I shuffled toward the bathroom. How, how could she deny us this? Never was I more alive than when we were together, skin to skin. I needed to feel alive again. I needed to take her—and in taking her, to find myself.

In that moment, the ache of my need eclipsed every other pain. Even the thirst.

Alexa paused to adjust the water temperature before beckoning me into the shower. I hissed as the spray touched my stitches. It stung. But after that initial twinge, the drumming of the hot water against my dry skin vastly outweighed any lingering discomfort.

"Don't be angry with me," she said as she began to touch me, washing my body gently with a bar of soap. "I almost lost you, Val. I almost lost you."

The tremor in her voice broke my heart, and I reached out one hand to stroke the curve of her hip.

"You're in bad shape right now," she continued, her voice low and intense. "All I want is for you to get well. And I'm afraid that if we make love right now, I'll hurt you. That's how crazy I feel inside."

This I could understand. I had felt it myself sometimes—a need so powerful it was almost frightening. I'd never realized that it was something we shared. The surge of relief made me feel a little dizzy, and I threw out my good arm to brace myself against the tile wall.

"Being apart from you is the only thing that can really hurt me," I whispered over her head as she bent to wash my legs. Her hands on me felt so damn good. "But I understand. And you're right—I am a mess. I can wait a while, if that will make you feel better."

Alexa gently spun me to face the spray, her kneading hands moving slowly up my calves. "I love you. Don't ever doubt that I—what the hell is this?"

"What?" She had paused her ministrations near the top of my rib cage. I could feel her quick breaths against my damp skin. When she pressed in gently with her fingertips, I winced. "That's tender. Is it a bruise?"

She didn't answer. I twisted my head around to try to catch a look—either at the spot, or at her. "Baby? What is it?"

"It looks like…like a bite, actually."

My stomach fishtailed and my pulse sped up. "A bite? He fucking bit me?"

Alexa rose and pulled me close. "I hate him," she whispered.

"Yeah. Yeah, me, too." I was trembling again, and I couldn't stop. This was insane. A violent mugging I could at least understand. It was awful, but comprehensible. But what kind of psychopath bit someone?

My balance wavered as a sickening wave of dread punched me in the gut. "You're sure…the doctors were sure he didn't…rape me?"

"Oh God, Val." Alexa's grip tightened. Her hands were shaking, too. "They said he didn't, sweetheart. They sounded really certain."

"Okay." I tried to get my breathing under control. "I want to go to bed now."

She toweled me off as gently as she had washed me, then turned down the covers. I slid beneath the sheet and pulled the blanket tightly around me. If I thought about him sinking his teeth into me, I was going to fall apart. My own teeth were chattering.

Alexa reached for me immediately, wrapping one arm carefully around my waist and pressing her face to my good shoulder. "Are you cold?"

"Don't think so," I stuttered. "Just don't feel so good." I didn't want to be this weak, but I had no idea how to stop panicking.

As always, Alexa had my cure. She rubbed my stomach lightly while pressing tender kisses to my jawline, my cheek, the corner of my mouth. She didn't speak—she didn't have to. Her touch calmed me, easing the tightness of my muscles and settling my stomach. I needed her. I needed her so much.

"Close your eyes, sweetheart. Don't be afraid. I'm going to hold you all night."

"'Kay." Fatigue pressed in on me, dark and heavy. There was no reason to resist—not with Alexa wrapped around me. She pillowed her head on my shoulder and sighed into my neck.

The sound of her pulse followed me into sleep.

CHAPTER FOUR

The thirst consumed me.
It was a bottomless abyss, the eternity of deep space. Essence of need.

In the dead of night, it demanded that I fill myself with Alexa. It compelled me to reach for her—to claim her, to hurt her if I had to. To make her mine. She was soft and yielding, yet the craving remained.

I am become Thirst, that great emptiness.

The need was a goad, bright and hot. It crawled down my spine, making me desperate to possess her. Wild in the throes of urgency, I thrust into her, forcing her back into a perfect arch. When I twisted my hand, she called out my name. Sweat beaded up along my hairline and dripped into my eyes as I fucked her mercilessly. Her head thrashed against the pillow, snarling the elegant fan of her crimson hair. I gave her everything I had. It should have been enough.

It wasn't.

I needed to take. The impulse was undeniable, irresistible. Inevitable. It rode me hard, forcing my mouth against her neck. She smelled sweet, like the memory of sunlight. Beneath my tongue, her pulse raced. It sang to me, a Siren.

My teeth sank through the layers of her skin, cutting through the vessels below. She screamed, flowing around my hand as her blood burst across my lips and dribbled down my chin. I raised my head, spattering droplets in a fine shower across the crisp, white sheets, finally at peace.

I woke suddenly, the horror of the dream jerking me into a sitting position, and hissed in pain when my shoulder and ribs protested the movement. Swallowing was agony—my throat felt dry and cracked. I reached for the glass on the nightstand, only to find it empty.

"Val?" Alexa's voice was gritty with sleep. "Sweetheart? What's wrong?"

I faced her. When she mimicked my position, sitting up with her back to the headboard, the sheet slid down to pool against the slight swell of her stomach. Her skin glowed in the predawn light. The remembered sensation of my teeth ripping into her—of how right it had felt—warred with my terror and disgust at the impulse. I leaned in toward the pulsing artery in her perfect neck before I knew what I was doing, only to jerk away when she reached for me.

"No!" I scrambled out of the bed as quickly as I could, ignoring the spasms in my leg. "Stay away from me."

Her face crumpled. "But—what happened, love? Did you have a nightmare?" She threw back the blankets and easily covered the distance between us. Desperate to keep her at arm's length, I thrust my empty glass toward her.

"Please."

She frowned, but went into the bathroom to grant my request. I sat on the side of the bed, trembling. I felt so weak, but that passed for normal now. The disturbing thing was the pulse of arousal that beat between my thighs. And I was wet. Jesus. Just how fucked up was I? What kind of person got aroused by a dream of tearing out her lover's throat? Hell, what kind of person had those dreams to begin with?

I rested my chin on my sternum and took slow breaths until she returned. When she handed me the full glass, I unclenched one of my fists from the tangle of sheets and gulped the water down. Still, my throat burned.

"More?"

I forced myself to drink the second glass slowly, but it too did nothing to appease the thirst. What was happening to me? Yes, it made perfect biological sense for my body chemistry to be out of whack, since I'd lost so many fluids. But this…how could this kind of craving be normal? Was this part of the PTSD? Was I going insane?

"Please, Val." Alexa's voice was higher than usual. She was on the edge of panic. "Tell me what's wrong. Do I need to call the hospital?"

I shook my head, still afraid to touch her. She had sensed my uncharacteristic need for distance and was awkwardly perched on the windowsill. Beyond, dawn was spreading over the city. The light should have been comforting.

"It was a nightmare."

Alexa took a step forward before stopping herself. "About the—"

I shook my head once. My brain was still imprinted with the delicious, horrifying memory of my teeth slicing through her skin. "No."

"Tell me?"

"I can't," I whispered, battered by confusion and exhaustion.

She didn't—or couldn't—resist the impulse any longer. When her arms came gently around my waist, I stiffened. But when, after a few moments, the only urge I felt was to rest my head on her shoulder, I relaxed in her embrace.

"Let's go back to bed," she murmured.

I let her guide me under the covers, lying quiescent as she tucked the blankets under my chin. When she snuggled in close, I didn't try to stop her. But I did turn my head away from the delectable expanse of her neck.

She fell into sleep immediately, her even breaths puffing against my shoulder. But I stayed awake for a long time, watching the daylight creep closer, until fatigue trumped the sharp ache in my throat.

❖

The distant sounds of Avenue C filtered through the windows as I sat on the couch, cradling my Neuroanatomy textbook in my lap. A full glass of water sat on the coffee table, untouched despite the fact that my thirst had not abated. It was of no use—drinking liquids nonstop all day hadn't done anything except make me have to get up every fifteen minutes to visit the bathroom.

I was alone for the first time since waking up in the hospital. I alternated between enjoying the peace and jumping at every harmless noise. The dream had haunted me all day, making me wary around Alexa. She had debated not going to her evening seminar, but I had urged her to go. Being afraid to touch her made my stomach ache.

I was obviously being silly. Then again, maybe I was just acting like a trauma victim. Was I expecting too much of myself? Creepy dreams were probably par for the course. I had been through hell, after all. My psyche was going to have to deal somehow. I cringed at the thought that any minute now, I might start remembering exactly what had happened to me. Part of me—a very big part of me—wanted to live in ignorance. But the rest of me knew that until I remembered, I would be afraid. I made a mental note to call Dr. Clavier tomorrow to get his therapist recommendations. Clearly, I needed to talk to a professional.

A few seconds later, the buzzer rang. My heart began to pound and a thin layer of sweat broke out across my palms. I forced myself to get up and walk to the intercom next to the door, silently berating my autonomic nervous system. If my attacker wanted to find me in order to finish the job, he wouldn't ring the damn doorbell. Would he?

"Hello?"

"Valentine, it's Harold Clavier. May I come up?"

I frowned at the coincidence. Think of the devil and he shall appear. "Of course." I buzzed him in, but when he knocked on the door, I didn't take the chain off before opening it. When I peeked through the crack, my anxiety faded into a background murmur. It really was him, in a long, black wool coat. I undid the chain.

"This is a surprise, Doctor," I said. "Can I get you anything?"

"No, thank you." He sat in our threadbare armchair, and I took my place on the love seat. "I was on my way to the hospital and thought I'd make a house call to see how you're recovering."

On his way to the hospital? I didn't envy him the night shift. "This is above and beyond, really. Thank you for dropping by."

It had only been a day and a half since I'd last seen him, but I had forgotten just how unnerving his stare was. Did the man ever blink?

"So?" he prompted.

I grimaced. "The headache is pretty much gone, but I'm still very weak. I expected to feel at least a little stronger by now."

"And the incisions?"

"Fine. No signs of infection."

"How is your appetite?"

At that moment, my throat throbbed painfully. Out of instinct, I reached for my water. "I'm eating fine. The strange thing is that I can't stop feeling thirsty, no matter how much I drink. I've probably had over a gallon of water today, and I still feel parched."

He steepled his fingers beneath his chin. "Interesting."

"Do you have any idea what might be causing that?" I asked, hearing the note of desperation in my voice. "Any idea about what I can do to fix it? It's really uncomfortable—painful, even."

"Yes, I imagine so." He sounded distracted, but pulled a business card out of his coat pocket and handed it to me. "It will be helpful to run some additional tests. Come and see me on Wednesday at this address. This is my second office, in Midtown. Not the hospital."

I took the card from him. "Do I need to call to make an appointment?"

"Come at three thirty. Does that work for you?"

"That's fine. Thank you."

"And how about psychologically?" he asked. "Any memories resurfacing? Violent dreams?"

My heart sped up again. Dreams. Why had he asked about violent dreams? I took a futile sip of water and pulled myself back under control. Maybe because violent dreams were normal after a violent attack. Jeez. I really needed to give my neuroses a break.

"Memories, no. Dreams, yes. Actually…you offered me a list of recommended therapists. I'd like to take you up on that."

"Of course. I can give you several names on Wednesday."

"Thank you."

He got to his feet. Interview over, apparently. I started to rise, but he held out one hand to stop me. "Don't tax yourself—I'm sure that your leg is still very sore. I can see myself out."

"Okay. Thank you for taking the time to make a house call." I smiled, but he only nodded in return.

"Good night, Valentine," he said, halfway through the door. "See you soon."

When it clicked shut behind him, I got up and refastened the chain. So much for me not taxing myself. I went back to the couch and flipped open my textbook again, determined to at least finish this chapter before Alexa got home. But instead of seeing the words, all I saw was his expression after I had told him about my bizarre excessive thirst. His face hadn't really betrayed emotion—it never did, as far as

I could tell—but for one split second, I could have sworn that his eyes sort of…gleamed. It was the way my cousin looked when he won a hand at poker; the way my father looked when he talked about his latest financial conquest.

Triumphant.

❖

I was going out of my mind.

I had barely slept last night. Fear of my dreams and for Alexa's safety had made me twitch awake every time I felt myself descending into a deep sleep. Once she had left for class, I collapsed back into bed and crashed for three hours, before being wakened by the burning ache in my throat.

It was getting worse.

Now I stared at myself in the mirror—at the dark bags under both eyes, at the gruesome stitches in my shoulder, at the fine tremor in my hands—and felt disgust. The fear was ruling me. It was taking me over and eating me up, because I kept feeding it. It was winning because I was letting it.

No more.

I went back into the bedroom and pulled a sports bra over my head, wincing as one of the straps caught on a stitch. My NYU sweatshirt was next, followed by a windbreaker. I limped to the front door and frowned at the cane propped against the wall nearby. I didn't want to take it, but I was about to try walking a distance much farther than I had since being injured. Sighing through my teeth, I grabbed the cane, limped out the door, and made my slow, painful way down the stairs.

I was afraid of two things: what might be causing this awful thirst, and the horrific memories that were waiting to resurface. I couldn't do anything about the former until my appointment tomorrow. I could, however, do something about the latter. I could retrace what my steps might have been, willingly putting myself in the path of places likely to jog my memory. Willingly subjecting myself to the terrifying truth. But at least it would be my choice, my timing. At least I would be in control.

I paused for a moment outside the red door of my building, leaning heavily on the cane. Stairs were a bitch. When I felt a little stronger, I took off limping down the sidewalk, past the familiar row of walk-ups. At the corner, I debated whether to turn left or right on Avenue D—there were stores that sold alcohol in both directions. Deciding on right, I hobbled past the 24/7 supermarket. Across the street, the projects rose into the sky like accusatory fingers. Hunching my shoulders against the dread that churned in my gut, I peered furtively down every new block, expecting at any moment to be bombarded by memories.

I hated feeling this way. Alphabet City was my neighborhood. It was Bohemian still—wild and unkempt, queer and unapologetic. I loved it. Had loved it. Now, it frightened me.

When I reached the first liquor store, I paused. No epiphanies, not yet. Would going inside help? Maybe. And we were out of Jameson anyway. I might as well make myself useful while out on this fool's errand.

The bell tinkled lightly as I stepped inside. The store smelled musty and a little dank, like an ill-maintained wine cave. I shuffled in the direction of the whiskey aisle, past the watchful eye of the manager on duty. His beer belly made me glad that I mostly stuck to the hard stuff.

In the act of grabbing a bottle off the shelf, I looked around the store. It was familiar to me—I'd been coming here occasionally for almost a year now—but no dark memories stirred beneath the surface of my psyche. So much for taking back control of my life. Sighing, I limped up to the counter and awkwardly fished for my wallet. Maybe the Jameson would help my throat.

"You're back," said the manager as he scanned the barcode on the bottle.

I blinked at him. "Sorry?"

"Did she say yes, or what?" He scoffed, taking in my battered appearance. "Or did she beat you up?"

Realization struck. My God. This was the place. He had been working here when I had come in, two weeks ago. I could feel the blood draining from my face. How was it possible that this perfect stranger remembered a part of my life that was still barred to me? How many of the blanks could he fill in?

"That night. Do you remember what I bought?"

"Sure, yeah," he said, looking at me as though I'd gone crazy.

"Show me."

Shrugging, he came out from behind the counter and led me halfway down the champagne aisle before pausing to extract a bottle two-thirds of the way up the shelf. "J Schram. 1999."

He held the bottle out to me. I didn't take it—not this time. But I remembered the triumph I'd felt as my fingers had closed around the smooth, dark green glass. I remembered dumping the contents of my wallet onto the counter, and confessing to an uncaring Stan that I was on the verge of proposing to my girlfriend.

The memories were coming back. God help me.

"What the—"

"Have to go," I choked. "Sorry." I staggered for the door, desperate to breathe the cool autumn air. Once outside, I lurched into the graffiti-covered brick wall. Catching myself, I leaned hard against it, forcing it to bear my weight as I gulped fresh air into my burning throat. The veil had been torn away. Oh God. I had thought I could do this, but what if I couldn't? What if the next thing I remembered was him, hurting me?

Only a few minutes ago, I had been fighting to reclaim my memories. Now, I fought against them. My cheeks were tingling. I was hyperventilating. Calm down, I had to calm down. Deep, slow breaths. Foster—I had to call her. To show her where. Not Canal Street. Here. It took me three tries to navigate to her name on my new cell phone and hit the Call button, but I finally managed.

"I'm flashing back," was all I said.

"Valentine. Where are you?" I could hear her snapping her fingers at someone.

"Avenue D and Fourth. The liquor store."

"Don't move." Her voice was strong and steady. My head was spinning—I was still breathing too fast. "Stay exactly where you are. I'll be there within minutes."

"Yeah."

"Do you want me to stay on the phone with you?"

I considered it for a split second, before the memory of how she had looked at Alexa flashed over my vision, tinged in red. Hell no. I hung up.

In the ensuing minutes, I tried to make my mind blank, afraid that if I dwelled too long on what I had just remembered, I'd trigger an avalanche. My fingers twitched toward my phone. Alexa. Maybe if she were here, I wouldn't feel so afraid. It was so tempting to hit speed dial—she wouldn't blame me for pulling her out of class. But even as the thought crossed my mind, I clenched my hand into a fist. No. Alexa was my rock, not my crutch. She was already playing catch-up this semester because of me. I could be strong. I could.

A dark car pulled up next to the curb, its tires screeching. Detective Foster jumped out, closely followed by her partner, who I hadn't seen since that first day in the hospital. Wilson. I stopped leaning against the wall and drew myself up to my full height, ignoring the ache in my leg.

"Are you all right?" Foster's voice was crisp and professional, but her dark eyes were shining with a fierce excitement. I was the key to the fucking city as far as she was concerned—the only known survivor of this criminal's spree. I was going to be indispensable to her quest to take him down.

The knowledge was calming. It gave me strength. I wasn't helpless—not totally. "I'm fine."

"Okay." She turned to Wilson. "I'll stay here. You question whoever's working in there."

When he nodded and went inside, her attention returned to me. "Can you tell me what you've remembered?"

"I came here on Tuesday night, shortly before Alexa got home," I said. Foster whipped out her little black notebook.

"What time?"

I frowned in thought. "Must have been about quarter to eight. On my way in, I noticed a man hanging out…" I looked to the right and pointed. "Over there. He was smoking."

Foster paced over to the spot that I had indicated and crouched to examine the ground. Even from here, I could tell that at least a dozen cigarette butts littered the sidewalk. "Can you describe him to me?"

I took a deep breath and focused in on that particular memory. "Pretty tall—at least six feet. Burly. Wearing a knit hat and a leather jacket."

Foster's pen was a blur against the white page. "What happened after you noticed him?"

This, at least, was the easy part. "I went into the store, chatted with the manager for a minute, and bought a bottle of champagne. Then I left."

"And then?"

"I don't remember."

"You would have gone directly home?"

I thought about it for a moment, before recalling that I had been in a hurry inside the store. "Yes."

Foster jerked her head toward the direction of my apartment. "Let's retrace your steps. We'll take it as slowly as you like."

When a fresh layer of sweat broke out on my palms, I told myself not to be a coward. I didn't want to remember, but I needed to. Leaning heavily on my cane, I fell in beside the detective. I kept my head down as we walked, not wanting to look over and see sympathy—or worse, pity—on her face. We were paused at a cross street, waiting for the light to turn green, when I had the sudden urge to look over my shoulder. Foster started to cross, but turned back when I didn't join her.

"He followed me," I said, fighting down panic.

"The man loitering outside the liquor store?"

"Yes." The memory was growing clearer now, even as I shied away from it. I hunched over my cane, looking across the street at the blocks ahead. Remembering how I had increased my pace, first, but when he had done the same—

"I started running," I said, feeling an echo of the hard clench of my leg muscles, just before that initial burst of speed. "But he was too fast. He…he knocked me down. I think."

I was trying to keep my voice steady, but the brand-new memory of being knocked to the ground was making me tremble. I could remember the sharp pain as my body hit the ground, and the sound of glass shattering.

"He knocked me down," I repeated. "The bottle broke."

"You're doing great," Foster said. "Let's keep going, to see whether we can find that spot." She squeezed my elbow lightly. I trembled again, this time at the effort it took not to knock her hand away from me. The urge to hit her blazed down my right arm, sudden and fierce.

What the hell?

Fortunately, she moved off down the sidewalk. I followed a few feet behind her, glad that she couldn't see my face. Where had that impulse come from? Was I finally becoming unhinged? Thirst pulsed in my throat, and weakness tugged at my limbs. I wanted to go home, and it felt so far away.

"Valentine," Foster called from halfway down the block. Her

voice was low and tense. She stood in front of an alley between a dry cleaner's and a deli. I swallowed hard. Was that it? The place where he'd caught me, beaten me, cut me…bitten me? I approached reluctantly, dreading the new memories about to be jarred loose.

The alley was narrow and deep and smelled like urine. Shards of glass littered the asphalt, catching and reflecting the few rays of sunlight that managed to penetrate the gloom. Foster was crouched near the mouth of the alley, inspecting the ground. Where she pointed were dark stains.

Bile filled the back of my mouth when I realized that the stains were blood. My blood. I swallowed hard, waiting for the memory to blindside me. One heartbeat. Two. Three. Nothing. I could feel Foster's expectant stare on my face, but I kept staring at the spot where I had been bleeding out. I shuddered at the thought, but the memories remained at bay.

Relieved, I turned away. "Nothing."

Foster stood straight. She looked disappointed. Seeing that unhappy little frown on her face made me want to hit her again, and I clutched my cane hard.

"I'd like to go home now," I said firmly. I still had a few hours before Alexa got back. Maybe I could sleep a little more. "I'll call you if I have any more flashbacks."

She paused in the act of pulling out her phone and gave me a nod. "That's fine. Thank you. I mean it. Thank you. This can't have been comfortable for you."

I shrugged. Her pity was only stoking the bizarre rage that was still seething under my skin. I had always been short-tempered, but this kind of unwarranted aggression was totally unlike me. Tomorrow's appointment with Dr. Clavier couldn't come fast enough. I really needed to talk to someone professionally.

"I'm going to call for a CSI unit," Foster continued. "I'll let you know what we find out."

"Okay. Thanks."

I hobbled away. A minute later, I was wishing I'd asked her for a ride back to my apartment. There were only a few blocks left to go, but despite having eaten only an hour before, it felt like my blood sugar was in the basement. What was going on with me? Why wasn't I improving?

Any day now, I told myself, gritting my teeth at the effort it took just to put one foot in front of the other. Any day now, I would start feeling better. Healthier. Stronger.

Yeah. Right.

CHAPTER FIVE

A re you sure you don't want me to go with you?"
I paused in the act of pulling on my jacket, Alexa's plaintive tone wrenching at me. I looked across the room to where she was sitting on the couch, books and notes spread out all around her. She wore a long-sleeved NYU shirt and black sweats, and her hair was up in a loose ponytail. She was stunning. And she looked unhappy. I couldn't stand that.

As quickly as I could manage it, I was standing in front of her. She wrapped her arms around my waist and rested her head against my stomach.

"Babe," I said quietly. "It's not that I don't want you to come with. But you have an exam in two days. All I'm going to do is step outside and hail a cab. I'll be fine. Back before you know it."

She nodded, her face rubbing against my shirt. Her movements pulled the fabric up a bit, and before I could blink, her lips were tracing my navel. Oh God. Desire shot through me, sweet and piercing.

"Alexa," I groaned, cupping the back of her head and pulling her more tightly against me.

"You feel so good, Val," she murmured against my skin.

My body had become molten under her touch. The ache between my thighs mirrored the burn in my throat. I needed her so badly—needed her to fill me up. I didn't realize that I had spoken the words out loud until I felt her fumbling with my belt buckle.

"Sweetheart," I breathed, reaching down to still her hands. She swatted mine away. "Alexa…baby, look at me." When she finally did, my resolve trembled.

Then I remembered the dream—how good it had felt to rip out her throat while thrusting into her with my hand. How hard I'd been throbbing, and how wet I'd gotten. I was so fucked up right now. If I surrendered to her seduction, God only knew what I'd end up doing to her.

I took a shaky breath, resisting the urge to push her away. "I have to go."

Fortunately, she pulled back of her own volition. The distance between us was agony. "I know. I got carried away. I'm sorry."

"Don't be." I managed a smile and couldn't resist trailing my fingers along her cheek to one corner of her mouth. "See you soon, okay?"

She kissed my fingertips. "Be safe."

I limped down the stairs and out the door, then turned toward Avenue C. To distract myself from thinking about the dream, I thought about how good it would be to have this thirst issue under control, once Clavier figured out what was wrong. While most of me was apprehensive about what kind of condition—or pathogen—might be causing it, the med student part of me was morbidly curious.

Fifteen minutes later, I was standing in front of a tall, concrete building bordering the East River. It wasn't a very hospitable place. Its only noticeable windows were three stories up, and they looked more like medieval arrow slits. In fact, the whole structure felt like some kind of modern day fortress. But this was the address on Dr. Clavier's card, so I took a deep breath and shuffled into the revolving door. I hated revolving doors. As a child, I had been afraid of them. Now, as an invalid, they were a pain in the ass.

The door opened onto a lobby, furnished in the Art Deco style. A bank of elevators was set into the wall on the right. A turnstile to the left of the receptionist's desk blocked casual access to the rest of the first floor. The receptionist was a woman—tanned, thin, and blond. I caught her appraising glance, but wasn't even remotely tempted. I didn't go for the waifish look, for one thing. For another, Alexa owned me. The memory of her lips against my stomach made my throat burn.

"I'm Valentine Darrow, here to see Dr. Clavier," I said.

She typed some kind of query into her computer, and the attached printer spat out a plastic card imprinted with a bar code.

"Room 317," she said, her fingers, adorned with bright red nail polish, grazing mine as I took the card. "This will open it for you."

Hi-tech. Impressive. "Thanks," I said, turning toward the elevators.

The third-floor corridor felt like something out of a *Star Trek* episode. Light from fluorescent lamps glittered off the metallic walls and floor. The air smelled of disinfectant, and my palms began to sweat as I flashed back to the hospital. Unlike the hospital, though, this place was silent. Creepy. I rolled my shoulders in an effort to shake off the weird feeling and slid the card beneath the infrared scanner glowing redly on the wall. It was like swiping my savings card at the grocery store, only much less mundane. The door slid open.

This was like no physician's waiting room I'd been in before. Yes, it held an examination table, a desk with a computer on it, and a rack on the wall containing a stethoscope and a blood pressure cuff. But there was also a small conference table surrounded by four chairs, and strangest of all, a lab bench, complete with pipetting equipment and what looked like a really nice microscope. I debated between sitting in a chair or perching on the examination table and decided for the latter. The trademark crepe paper crinkled beneath me, and I had to fight the urge to kick my dangling feet like I had when I was a child.

Instead, I leaned back on my elbows and started to daydream. Dr. Clavier would come in, draw some blood, run a few tests, and discover that I had some kind of minor chemical imbalance, like a mild thyroid problem. He would prescribe a pill. Within days, the weird thirst would go away and I would start feeling stronger. He'd direct me to a really good therapist—maybe even a psychiatrist, who could prescribe some meds that would help with my anxiety. If I could stop being so afraid, I'd be able to focus enough to get caught up on my schoolwork. The nightmares would disappear, and the thought of making love with Alexa wouldn't frighten me at all.

The door opened. I sat up straight as Dr. Clavier entered, wearing a white lab coat, black slacks, and those same tinted glasses. "Hello, Valentine," he said, setting what I assumed was my chart down on the desk. "How are you feeling today?"

So much for small talk. Clavier was a good lesson in how not to build rapport with my future patients. "Pretty much the same as Monday," I said. "Except thirstier, if that's even possible."

"Mmm. I'd like to draw some blood in order to run a few tests."

I rolled up my left sleeve without needing to be asked, surprised that he didn't have a technician to do this kind of thing for him. He applied a tourniquet and unwrapped a needle and syringe before gently grasping my elbow with his left hand. His fingers were cool against my skin. I watched as he inserted the needle deftly into my vein. I expected him to try to distract me with a question, the way nurses usually did, but he remained silent.

"Let's take a look," he said, once two vials were full and a Band-Aid was covering the small puncture wound. He gestured toward the microscope. "I'll just be a moment."

I watched him remove a sterile eyedropper and slide from a drawer under the lab bench. He added a drop of my blood to the slide and affixed it to the microscope stage, then he peered into the lens and adjusted the focus. I gripped the examination table hard, watching for some kind of reaction. But he had none.

After a moment, he stood, withdrew a cell phone from his pocket, and pressed one button before replacing it. Then, he walked to his desk, leaned against it, and crossed his arms over his chest. My heart was pounding against my rib cage as I tried to decipher his lack of expression. What the hell was wrong with me? Why was he being so…abnormal? Usually, physicians frustrated me with their forced friendliness, but Clavier's laconic style was brutal.

"You have been infected with a parasite," he said finally. "A very rare parasite, called *Plasmodium sitis*."

There was no truly effective preparation for hearing bad news about your health. Despite having known that something was wrong with me, I freaked out. My autonomic nervous system went crazy, dumping adrenaline into my system and making me want to run for the door. I dug my fingers even harder into the metal edge of the table, willing myself to calm the fuck down. Most of the parasites I'd ever heard of were treatable. I just needed to not panic, so that I could get all the details from Clavier.

"I've never heard of that one," I said, willing my voice not to shake. He actually smiled a little. How the fuck could he be smiling?

"Most people haven't."

"What does it do and how do we treat it?" I asked, in as business-like a voice as I could muster, even though what I really wanted to do was punch that smiling mouth of his.

"*Plasmodium sitis* is a fascinating little creature." His voice had dropped slightly, and had a musical quality to it. He wasn't looking at me, but at the microscope—as though he could see my blood sample from his desk. "We've been studying it for decades and still don't understand it fully. Put simply: it is a blood eater."

My brain was in hyperdrive. The only way to keep myself from panicking was to fall back on rational thought processes. "It eats blood. Like…like the malaria parasite?" But even as the question left my mouth, I knew I was barking up the wrong tree; my symptoms were nothing like those of malaria.

Clavier shook his head. "It does consume hemoglobin, but the mechanism is completely different. And this particular parasite is very, very greedy—it not only feeds off red blood cells, but from elements in the plasma as well. Most disturbing of all is its viral behavior."

"Viral behavior?" The fear was starting to win. Parasites are multi-celled organisms. Viruses are genes covered with protein. Apples and god damn oranges.

"*Plasmodium sitis* is so very thirsty," Clavier explained softly. He sounded like he was talking about a lover, not a pathogen. "It has a use for almost every component in the bloodstream. It alters human DNA by injecting part of itself into T-cells and modifying the cytokines that they release. These new cytokines still act like the carrier pigeons of the cellular world, but instead of sending messages about an immune response to other cells, they pass along the same alterations made in the first. A domino effect, if you will."

"Jesus Christ." I was shaking now. This fucking thing was inside me, changing me. I couldn't think anymore. I could barely breathe. "What the hell is it doing to me?"

At that moment, the door opened. The woman who entered was so impossibly beautiful that she momentarily distracted me from my full-blown panic. She looked to be in her mid-thirties and wore a dark red pantsuit that I knew had been designed with her specifically in mind. Tall—though not quite as tall as I—and slender, she carried herself like a queen. Raven black hair cascaded down her back, falling to her waist, and her eyes were the color of rain-dampened slate. I had the truly bizarre impulse to hop off the table, get down on one knee, and swear fealty to her. And then I noticed her companion—a hulking man who looked like his muscle-bound torso had barely fit through the doorway. He was clearly a bodyguard. His carriage reminded me of Penn, my father's chief of security: strong, confident, capable of breaking a man's neck without the slightest hesitation or remorse. Whoever she was, she didn't need me if she had someone like him.

"Good afternoon, Harold," she said in a husky alto. She took one step toward me, extending her hand. Her skin had a rich, olive tone to it. "And Valentine Darrow. A true pleasure."

"Um," I said. And instantly hated myself.

She laughed. "Helen Lambros. You must call me Helen."

"Hello," was all I managed. Her touch was cool against my sweating palm. The part of my brain still capable of functioning on a rational level was wondering who she was, and why she had so cavalierly joined a private conversation between my physician and me.

"Valentine and I were just discussing the parasite," said Clavier. His tone was distinctly deferential.

"Ah." Helen took a seat at the conference table, crossing one elegant leg over the other. Her bodyguard leaned in one corner of the room, bulging arms crossed over his massive chest. "Please," she said, gesturing toward me. "Continue."

"Ever since you were infected, the parasite has been changing your DNA," Clavier explained. "Some of these alterations are beneficial. You will discover that your senses are slightly sharper and your endurance greater than in the past. And already, you have stopped aging. The other changes, however, can be troublesome. The parasite reacts poorly to sunlight, and will make you more sensitive. But most significantly of all," and here he exchanged a meaningful glance with Helen, "you must drink blood in order to replenish that which the parasite consumes."

Silence reigned in the room. I leaned forward, blinking hard in my total and utter disbelief. I wasn't going to age? I had to drink blood? "What?"

"Two days ago, you spoke to me of your unquenchable thirst, Valentine. Your body is not craving water. It is craving blood."

I laughed, because this was fucking psychotic. I didn't care who the hell was sitting at this conference table, and what kind of crazy charisma she had going for her—Clavier was a nut job, a quack, and I was getting the hell out of here. Now.

"Thanks ever so much for your professional opinion," I sneered as I limped toward the door. How much more ridiculous could this get?

Was he part of some kind of crazy religious sect or something? How had I gotten caught up in this bullshit?

But when I pressed down hard on the door handle, it wouldn't engage. I tried again—nothing. I spun around as quickly as I could, struggling not to betray my sudden terror. Trapped. Fuck.

"I know this is difficult to believe, Valentine," Helen said in her bewitching, melodious voice. "But Dr. Clavier is only giving you the medical facts."

When I scoffed at that in a show of bravado, he pointed toward the microscope. "See for yourself."

What else could I do? He was appealing to logic. I was in training to be a doctor. The results would speak for themselves. And besides, I was shut up in here, at their mercy. I could either throw a futile tantrum, or follow orders.

I turned slowly and walked to the back of the room, trying not to let them see just how frightened I was. A cabinet door opened and shut behind me, but I didn't look back. I perched on the stool that Clavier had vacated and pressed my eye to the lens. With a few slight twists, the slide came into focus. My blood. The red cells were most abundant, of course, while the larger white cells were much more infrequent. For a moment, I was captivated by the complex beauty of it—so many components, all working together in harmony. To keep me alive.

And then I saw the parasite.

It had a half-moon shape, like a scythe, and it was in the process of devouring a red cell from the inside out. My God, I thought, watching the monster effortlessly eat through the cell's membrane. It was reproducing in there. And when the cell burst...

My stomach pitched and rolled, and I clutched hard at the table edge to keep myself upright. That thing and the thousands of others like it in my bloodstream were incontrovertible proof that something was terribly wrong with me. Unless—and the shock of this revelation turned my knuckles white—unless this wasn't my blood. What if this was some elaborate ruse? Sure, I'd been watching him as he made up the slide, but not closely enough to see through a sleight of hand.

I ripped off the Band-Aid and opened the drawer in the same movement, yanking out a fresh slide and squeezing the tiny hole in my arm as hard as I could. A drop of blood welled up and I caught it on the glass. I looked over my shoulder, certain that the big guy would be two-thirds of the way across the room by now to stop me from exposing the lie...but they were all where I had left them, watching me. Expressionless.

Snarling, I discarded the old slide and snapped the new one into place, but when I peered back into the lens, the same horror awaited me. I slumped. Clavier wasn't lying about the parasite. Could he be telling the truth about everything else? I didn't want to believe it. How was I supposed to take them at their word when they were talking about the stuff of thriller novels and horror films? Vampirism? Eternal youth? One thing I knew for certain: that thing inside my blood was killing me, not making me ageless. And how the hell had I been infected in the first place?

A sudden suspicion made me lurch to my feet and stagger toward Clavier, despite the blinding surge of pain that radiated up my thigh. "You! Did you do this to me? Put this in me? In the hospital—did you?" I was eye to eye with him now, but no matter how close I got, he refused to take a step back. His preternatural calm infuriated me, and I clenched my right fist, finally surrendering to the violent impulses that had been plaguing me all week—

At that instant, an aroma filled the room: sweet, tangy, metallic. My head whipped around and saliva flooded my mouth. My throat spasmed, the burn so intense that I couldn't help but cry out. Behind me, Helen was squeezing the contents of a bag of blood into a mug.

A bag of blood.

My brain was repulsed. The idea of drinking that was anathema. It was sick, twisted, wrong. Perverted. But my body took a step forward, and then another. Tears leaked down my face as the fire in my throat blazed hotter than it ever had. My gaze was locked on the cup. I wanted it. Needed it. The scent wafting up from it was...heavenly.

"You are starting to understand, aren't you?" Helen said quietly. My brain demanded that I stop moving, but my body continued its slow stalk toward the table. "The parasite is making you immutable and stronger. Though you can be killed, you have already ceased to age. But it demands blood in return. For the rest of your existence, you will crave it—crave it like nothing else on earth."

Alexa, my brain howled. *It's Alexa that I crave, Alexa that I need. More than what is waiting on that table, more than anything.* But my legs continued to move. The urge to lash out at Clavier had been completely subsumed by the impulse to gorge myself on the contents of that mug.

"Drink," Helen ordered, taking a shallow sip before holding it out to me. I stood before her, breathing hard, hands trembling. My eyes were transfixed by the small movements of the viscous fluid as it sloshed gently against the ceramic walls. Need spiked through me, crackling under my skin, white and hot. It reduced me to instinct. I had to feed.

I snatched the cup from Helen's hands and tilted it to my lips. As the first thick rush hit my tongue, my brain screamed in revulsion. But for the first time since I'd woken from my coma nearly two weeks ago, the thirst eased. I drank and drank, tilting both my head and the mug to catch every last drop. When it was empty, I set it onto the table and licked my lips. My throat throbbed greedily. The fire was slightly muted, but still present.

"More." It was a demand, an imperative. My rational thought was bound and gagged. I channeled the will of the parasite.

"Yes, more. You will always want more." Helen's long, low laugh began to wake me from the feeding-induced haze. The aftertaste lingered on my teeth, my tongue, a so-sweet hint of copper. "What you just consumed has barely taken the edge off. Cold, preserved blood is a poor substitute for that taken from the source."

I blinked and shook my head. Coming out of the thirst-induced fog felt like waking from a lucid dream. I looked at the mug on the table. I had drained it. The hairs on my neck stood straight up, but otherwise, my body refused to react. It was satisfied. Sort of. And my nausea had disappeared. "The source?"

"Bagged blood will not sustain you," Clavier said, stepping forward to dispose of the remnants of the bag. "Only blood taken directly from a live human is truly nourishing."

My brain rebelled again, and without the enticement of that rich aroma to distract me, the panic returned full force. "You want me to kill people? Just to...to get a fucking meal?" Oh God. How the hell had this happened? What was I going to do? I had to go to the police. To turn them in. And myself. I would starve without blood. The parasite would destroy me—I'd seen that for myself. But did that even matter, if I saved countless lives?

"Of course not," said Helen. Once again, her silky voice silenced my gibbering internal monologue. "We don't countenance murder. It is quite possible to take enough blood for your needs without harming the donor."

My brain, racing a mile a minute, was on to her euphemisms. Suddenly, the bite mark on my side made perfect sense. He had infected me—bitten me to gorge himself and in the process, transmitted the parasite. "Taking blood" was violent. There weren't any "donors"— only victims. Like I had been. But I wasn't innocent anymore. Now I was part of the problem.

My head was spinning. This was just too fucking much. I sank into one of the free chairs around the table.

Vampires existed.

And I was one of them.

"Who are you?" I whispered.

Helen rested her palm on my hand before lightly brushing my knuckles with her crimson-tipped fingers. The scrape of her nails against my skin sent shivers up my spine. "We call ourselves the Consortium," she said. "Here in the City, we have many resources. All of them will be at your disposal." She paused in her relentless stroking to squeeze my hand. "You deserve a full explanation, Valentine. And you will get one."

Alexa. The thought pierced through my anxious confusion and I looked down at my watch. I needed to get home to her. But what the hell was I going to tell her? Would she believe me? Would she be afraid? Would she leave me?

"Alexa…my girlfriend will start to worry," I managed to say. "I have to figure out how to—to tell her about…this." I rubbed at my temples. How the fuck was I going to do this? "Can I come back? For the explanation?"

Helen's fingertips migrated to my chin. She raised my head so that I was forced to meet her gaze. Eternal, she had said. I wondered how old she was, and shivered.

And then she spoke the most terrifying words that I could imagine.

"You must realize, Valentine: Alexa is in danger. From you."

CHAPTER SIX

The car moved slowly down Second Avenue, caught in rush hour traffic. I stared out the window at the lights of St. Mark's, winking cheerfully at me in the gathering dusk. Almost home. I wanted to beg the driver to turn around. I couldn't do this. But I had to. I had to.

My teeth sank through the layers of her skin, cutting through the vessels below. She screamed, flowing around my hand as her blood burst across my lips and dribbled down my chin. I raised my head, spattering droplets in a fine shower across the crisp, white sheets, finally at peace.

The memory of the dream was paralyzing—ice in my veins, frozen tendrils ripping into my heart and slicing it to pieces. Even the simple thought of Alexa's blood set my thirst ablaze, even more potent now that it had a focus. Of course I wanted her in that way, too. It made perfect sense. I needed her heart, her mind, her body. And now her blood.

The pain was debilitating. Clutching at my stomach, I leaned forward and rested my head between my legs. My thoughts were spiraling like Yeats's falcon. The sickly sweet smell of the car's air freshener was cloying. If I vomited now, it would be blood. More, I needed more. Needed Alexa's—no. Not Alexa, not ever. So I had to do it. Else, I would destroy her. I bit down hard on my bottom lip to stifle a sob.

Oh God, I begged silently. *Turn my heart into stone so I can survive this.*

I shut my eyes. Behind them, my last conversation with Helen and Clavier played out, tormenting me.

"You must realize, Valentine: Alexa is in danger. From you."

At the words, my chest constricted painfully. Every untainted cell in my body protested, but the truth lay in those infected by the parasite. The dream flickered in my memory, dark and sinister. I had torn out her throat in my imagination, days ago. How long before my body's need overruled my brain, my heart?

"No," I whispered. "Oh, no." I turned my gaze on Helen. I could barely hear my own voice over the sound of blood rushing through my ears. "What can I...how can I keep from—"

"You must let her go," she said.

I stared at her in disbelief, the utter absurdity of the thought overruling every other emotion. Let her go? It wasn't possible. I was hers and she was mine—my love, my desire, my fate. We might not have sworn vows officially yet, but in my head, I had already said them all. For richer or for poorer. In sickness and in health. Till death do us part.

Only now, I was Death.

"It is difficult at best for a vampire to maintain a relationship with a human," Helen said softly. "First, there is the problem of time—the human will continue to age, while the vampire will not. Then, there is the problem of discovery. A vampire must conceal her needs from her human lover, lest that person reveal the secret to others. As you can imagine, Valentine, it is imperative for us to remain in hiding. At least, for now."

She paused, taking in my clenched jaw and listening to my shallow breaths. Her cool hand lingered on mine. "And then there is the problem of thirst. The impulse to feed grows much stronger during intimacy. It is a cycle: sex triggers the urge to drink, and drinking will only sharpen your desire. In a moment of passion, a vampire is quite likely to forget herself. I have...seen it happen."

I caught her hesitation. She hadn't just seen it—she had experienced it. She had killed someone. And I could kill Alexa. While we were making love, I could lose control and rip into her. Just like in the dream.

I slumped in my chair, resting my head in my palms. I was a monster. I had been right to fear being close to her. And I wouldn't continue to endanger her—I wouldn't.

But how, how was I supposed to let her go?

The car that Helen had arranged for me pulled up to the curb in front of my apartment. I didn't reach for the handle. Instead, I looked out the tinted windows at the front door, remembering one night over the summer when Alexa and I had been out until the early hours of the morning, drinking at the Niagra after my shift was over. We had stumbled back home, arms wrapped around each other. Starving for her, I'd been unable to wait. While she was fumbling to get her key in the front door, I had pushed her hard against it and kissed her roughly, greedily. I remembered thrusting my tongue into her mouth and groaning at the taste, whiskey over sunshine. I remembered sliding one hand beneath the hem of her tank top, desperate to feel her. We had been so frenzied that a red-painted splinter of wood had dug into her shoulder, pricking her skin. Chagrined, I had apologized—but she had laughed, rubbing out the single drop of blood between her fingers.

Now, I knew, I would be unable to resist its aroma. I would tear into her and gorge myself.

"Ms. Darrow?" said the driver. Helen had instructed him to drop me off, wait for me to "run an errand," and then take me back to the Consortium's facility, where I would receive my "full explanation." I could live there, she had said. For as long as I liked. Certainly, until I had…adjusted.

I couldn't move. How had everything changed so quickly? Just a few short hours ago, Alexa and I had been on the verge of making love. God, what if we had? What if I had let her take me, only to take her life in return?

"I'm going," I said roughly. "You'll stay, right?"

The driver inclined his head. "Of course."

My hands were trembling so badly that I dropped the key twice before managing to get the front door open. I took the stairs even more slowly than I had that first time after getting out of the hospital. My stomach was turning inside out. I swallowed repeatedly, trying to keep down the bile, which only made my throat throb the worse.

Which was why I was here in the first place.

Once on the landing, I stared hard at the door to our apartment.

Doing this was going to destroy me. Alexa was the love of my life, and I would never recover from pushing her away. But she would never survive if I didn't.

I opened the door. I stepped inside. She was almost exactly where I'd left her—on the couch, surrounded by books. How could everything be the same for her, and completely different for me?

"Val." She looked up, her expression eager. "How did it go? Did he run more tests?" She set down the book that she was reading and got to her feet. "I missed you so much."

I didn't know what to say. My heart was honestly breaking, shattering like a supernova, leaving a perpetual vacuum in its wake. I would be forever thirsty, but not in the way that Helen thought. We'd been planning a trip to Wisconsin—a week-long stay with her family and a side trip to Madison to see her alma mater. I'd never met the Newlands. I wanted them to know how much I loved their daughter— how proud I was to be hers. How dedicated I was to making her happy. Alexa had joked about how bored I'd be in Eau Claire, out in the middle of farm country. But I knew I'd love every second of getting acquainted with her family and her friends. I wanted to know all of her. I wanted to sit next to her mother on the couch, flipping through photo albums and listening to embarrassing childhood stories for hours on end. I wanted to learn exactly how to make Alexa's favorite meal—pork chops and potato casserole—right down to the gravy that she swore was the best in the nation. I wanted to chat up her brothers and sisters, and invite them out to play tourist in New York. I wanted to curl up with Alexa in her childhood bed and listen to the sounds of the night outside her window and feel the past and present coalesce in us.

Now I'd never get that chance.

Alexa started toward me. I flung up one hand. "Stay away from me."

Shock forced her to a standstill. "What? What is it?" Anxiety lent an edge to her voice. I held perfectly still, drinking in the sight of her, desperate to imprint her image onto my brain. I would never hold her again. Never feel the soft brush of her lips against mine, or the heat of her hand inside me. Never again would I twine my fingers with hers as we walked down the street, or cook her waffles on Saturday mornings, or bury my face in her fragrant hair to get through the most frightening parts of a horror film. Never again.

But she would be alive.

When she took another step forward, I shook my head and reached behind my back for the doorknob. "No! It isn't safe."

"What's going on, Val?" she pleaded softly. "What did he tell you? What can I do?"

"I'm leaving." My cheeks were wet. I was crying, and I couldn't stop. She stood less than ten feet away. It took every ounce of my willpower not to go to her.

"What? That's ridiculous!" I watched her hands clench into fists as a visible tremor ran through her entire body. "What the hell is happening here?"

Anger only magnified her beauty. Her cheeks were flushed and her eyes were dark and I wanted to confess, to tell her everything and beg for her help. But I had to be strong. To say whatever it took.

I sucked in a deep breath. "I'm leaving. Things have changed— I've changed. I don't...I don't want this anymore."

"You wanted me just fine a few hours ago!" she protested. "Start talking sense, Valen—"

"Stop!" I shouted. "I can't be with you. I don't want to be with you! Just let me go, God damn it. You can't fix this."

Without waiting to hear her reply, I wrenched open the door and stumbled painfully down the stairs, sobbing in earnest. When I burst out into the late October night, a chill gust of wind blasted me full in the face. I gripped the wrought iron banister to steady myself before limping down to the car. As the front door slowly swung shut behind me, I couldn't keep myself from listening—but no footsteps pounded down the indoor stairs.

She wasn't coming after me. I was alone.

I stumbled into the backseat of the car and shut the door. The driver pulled away immediately. I didn't care that he could hear my choking breaths. I didn't care about anything. I clutched at my ribs, forcing down more bile. The sad thing, the sick thing, was that even having said everything I could think of to push her away, I still had the gall to feel hurt that she hadn't pursued me. She had given up so fast. Had barely even tried to argue. What did that mean?

The same city passed before my eyes—the same lights, the same cross streets. But the whole world felt different. Alien. It was a sensation of floating, as though I were barely tethered to reality. When the car stopped at a red light, I watched a couple cross the street, holding hands, probably on their way to dinner. They were laughing. They made it look effortless. Deep inside my chest, my heart ignited, burning even worse than my throat. It would consume itself soon enough, leaving behind only a pile of cold ash. But no phoenix would rise.

I was twenty-six years old. I was going to live forever. An eternity of experiences awaited me, but the only one I wanted was the one I couldn't have.

My tears had dried by the time the car returned to the Consortium's office. A wave of fatigue crested over me. I got out of the car wearily and paused for a moment, fixing my gaze on the dark smear of the East River. If I walked into it with stones in my pockets, would I drown? How much of all the stories and legends and movies were true?

How was I going to exist without Alexa in my life?

Slowly, I turned and limped into the lobby, but paused just inside the revolving door. What was I supposed to do now? Should I go up to the receptionist and ask to meet with Helen? That didn't feel right. Helen clearly held a high rank in this organization and presumably had far better things to do than to continue babysitting me. But when I glanced toward the desk, the receptionist was gone. In her place was a stiff white envelope with my name written in careful block letters. The envelope contained a keycard and a simple note: *Room 719*. Numbly, I took the card and left the rest on the counter.

The seventh floor was completely unlike the third. Its hallway was covered in carpet instead of tile, and the doors on either side were labeled with both names and numbers. Some of them were open, the hum of computers mingling with the low buzz of voices to create a much less creepy atmosphere than the silent hall of the medical floor. Windows were evenly spaced along the wall, looking into rooms of various sizes: a large chamber filled with cubicles, a narrow room with a single desk overlooking a view of the river, a small antechamber that clearly led to a larger office beyond. I wanted to be curious about who worked here and whether they were all...vampires...but I couldn't find the energy to do more than glance from side to side as I shuffled slowly toward room 719. Going through the motions. I was going to be going through the motions for the rest of my life.

Forever.

Room 719 was a conference room. Helen was there, sitting at a round conference table made out of a very dark and highly polished wood. Her bodyguard was there, too, leaning in yet another corner. A second man sat in the chair next to Helen. He was beautiful, with soft hazel eyes and hair the color of sand. And he was young—in his very early twenties, I was guessing. If that. He was looking at Helen with an expression equal parts adoration and devotion—as though he would walk into the mouth of hell if she asked him to.

I slid my card underneath the scanner and pushed when I heard the click. Remembering how the door had locked behind me last time, I kept my fingers on the handle as it began to close, ensuring that it remained just the tiniest bit ajar. I wanted an out, just in case.

"Welcome back, Valentine," Helen said. "There's someone I'd like you to meet."

I wanted to feel angry that she didn't so much as spout some sympathetic platitude about the hell that I had just put myself through—the hell that would follow me for the rest of my days. I wanted to be enraged that this was happening to me at all: to feel the desire to lash out, to lay blame, to take some suitably dramatic action like punching through a wall or smashing a window.

But I felt nothing. I was numb.

"This is Kyle," she said, indicating her companion. She still hadn't introduced her bodyguard. "I promised you an explanation, and he is here to assist."

Kyle's smile, which he trained first on Helen and then on me, was brilliant. "Hello," I said, extending my hand. He took it in a firm grip. His hand, unlike Helen's, was warm. Was he a human, then?

Helen gestured for me to sit. "I know that this day has been overwhelming for you," she said, modulating her husky voice so that it was low and soothing. "There is much to explain—about the parasite, about our history, about how your life will continue to change. Our records here are extensive, and you will have access to every piece of information that you desire." She turned her attention to Kyle, reaching out to stroke pale fingers through his hair. His eyes closed in pleasure.

"But some things cannot be explained. Some things must be demonstrated." She looked back at me, but continued the gentle movements of her fingers. "You are suffering from malnutrition,

Valentine. I will show you, with Kyle's help, how to become strong again."

The bottom dropped out of my stomach as I finally comprehended the reason for Kyle's purpose. I was supposed to drink from him. To take his blood. My throat pulsed greedily, and I rebelled at the base instinct, mind winning out over body. For now. "No!" I scrambled awkwardly out of the chair and backed toward the door. Thank God I had left it cracked. "No, that's crazy!"

Kyle pulled away from Helen's touch, shaking his head. "It isn't," he said calmly, beginning to roll up the left sleeve of his shirt. "I want this."

I stared hard at him, looking for a trace of fear, but as far as I could tell, he was being truthful. He looked eager, not panicked the way he should be. "How?" I whispered. "How can you possibly want me to—"

From the pocket of his jeans, he removed a small, silver knife. I took another step backward. He was going to cut himself? For me?

"I crave the sensation," he explained as he flicked open the blade. His gaze never left my face. "You may think I'm disgusting, or need help, but it's not like that." He looked to Helen. "And the knowledge that I'm nourishing you…it's a privilege."

She smiled and caressed his cheek. "Kyle wants to give this to you, Valentine. Will you spurn his gift?"

He was young, but not immature. The certainty, the conviction in his voice both chilled and excited me. He was willing, that much was clear. But had he been compelled, somehow? Enthralled? Could real vampires even do that? I had never felt more ignorant in my life than I did at that moment, facing down a boy who wanted to slice open his veins on my behalf.

"I will show you," Helen said, taking my silence for assent. Kyle breathed out a sigh, and I watched the color rise in his cheeks. He poised the blade above his skin and smiled at me. And then he brought it down, expertly opening his median cubital vein. Blood welled up instantaneously, but Helen was there to catch every drop. No sooner had the aroma hit the air than her mouth was over the shallow cut. She cradled Kyle's arm in her hands, cheeks hollowing in a long pull.

He moaned.

It smelled so good. Hot. Fragrant. I didn't even realize that I had moved until I was standing at Helen's side, watching in jealous fascination as she drank. Need twisted my gut, overriding the self-loathing. I had never expected to feel alive again, but in that moment of intense craving, the numbness slid away. Helen's eyes met mine, and after one last pull, she stood. I bent to take her place, trembling with the need to feel the heat of Kyle's blood against the back of my throat.

The door crashed open, jerking my attention away from the ambrosia, toward the unexpected intruder. She was exquisite in her fury, cheeks flushed and eyes dark with emotion. Her crimson hair snapped around her face, and the tendons in her wrist stood out in sharp relief above clenched fists.

I blinked, snapping out of the thirst-induced haze. "Alexa!" Immediately, I turned away from the call of Kyle's blood, daring to hope. She hadn't given up on us, after all. She had come for me. I was a monster, but she was trying to save me.

"What the hell is going on here?" she demanded, looking past me to Helen. I glanced over my shoulder just long enough to see Kyle pressing a handkerchief to the gash in his arm. Helen was sitting next to him again, and she looked…irritated. I shivered.

"What did you tell her?" Alexa pressed. "What sick lies did you convince her of? Are you after her money? Is that it?" When ominous silence greeted her questions, she grimaced and stretched out one hand for me. "You know what? I don't care. Let's go, Val."

I took a step toward her, so very eager to feel her skin against mine after believing that I'd never get the chance again. But there was no way that we could leave. This was no plot, no prank, and I was going to have to explain everything to Alexa. To show her what I truly was. But before I could open my mouth, Helen's bodyguard slid between Alexa and the exit, moving faster than I would have expected. He pinned Alexa's arms to her sides and pulled her against his chest, breaking her hold on the handle. The door slammed shut.

And then, several things happened at once.

I saw red. That brute of a man had his hands on my lover, and he was smirking. Instinct took over, the release of all the rage that was boiling in me, building up since the mugging. I lunged for him at the precise moment when Alexa, who had taken a women's self-defense course in college, stamped down hard on the arch of his left foot. I had a split second in which to be impressed by just how well that move worked, as he shouted in pain and loosened his hold just enough for Alexa to duck under his arms. And then I was shoving him as hard as I possibly could. If he hadn't been off balance, he probably wouldn't have moved. As it was, though, he staggered to the side, tripped over his own feet, and crashed into the conference table, head first.

Alexa slid her hand into mine and I smiled tightly at her. I knew that we needed to have a long talk about many things, but in that moment, we were completely attuned: the perfect team. She jammed her palm down onto the door handle, but it didn't budge. Her hair whipped against my neck as she turned to face Helen—to demand our freedom, no doubt. She smelled so good to me, rich and complicated, like the earth waking up after a long winter.

I followed the direction of her gaze and sucked in a surprised breath. The bodyguard was bleeding from a horizontal gash in his forehead. I took an involuntary step forward at the sight of the red ribbon coursing down his cheek, but stopped in my tracks when he began to convulse.

"Oh, fuck," said Kyle, sounding nothing like the calm, confident boy who had been willing to let me drain the blood from his body. His face was pale and he was out of his chair, backing away from the guard.

Helen snapped her fingers. "All of you. Get in there. Now." She gestured imperiously to her right toward a closet-sized room that I hadn't noticed earlier, just barely large enough to hold one set of shelves and a photocopier. It had a door. I looked back toward the bodyguard and frowned. His body was kind of…blurry.

"Why should we?" Alexa challenged. She was clutching my hand tightly, and her palm was sweating. "What's wrong with him?"

"If you're still here when he makes the change, he'll tear you limb from limb," Helen said coldly. As she stalked into the tiny room, the bodyguard began to snarl. There was no other word for it—he sounded like a rabid dog. Clearly, we weren't safe here. I followed Helen, pulling Alexa behind me.

Once we were all inside, Helen shut the door. Through its small window, I watched the man continue to writhe on the floor. Next to me, Alexa shivered, and I wrapped one arm around her waist. I still couldn't believe that she was here. That I was holding her, as I'd never hoped to do again.

Helen was speaking into her cell phone. "We have a Code Two. Room 719."

I couldn't stop watching her bodyguard. He looked like he was having a particularly violent grand mal seizure. His body contorted wildly, spasmodically, far faster than my eye could follow…and suddenly, where once there had been a man stood a large gray wolf, jaws bared and hackles raised.

CHAPTER SEVEN

No," Alexa gasped. I felt my mouth working, but nothing came out. It was one thing to see a parasite through a microscope. It was fully another to see a man transform into an animal.

"Werewolf," I breathed.

"He is, yes." Helen's tone was brusque. "Your little stunt triggered the transformation. Most Weres find it near impossible to control themselves if they are injured in a violent situation."

I was only half paying attention to her. Alexa was shaking in earnest now, as though she were hypothermic. I had no idea what to say to her, so I gently pulled her in front of me and curled my body around hers. The wolf prowled around the room, growling continuously. On his third pass, he paused to claw at the carpet in front of the door, as though trying to dig his way beneath it. To us.

"Why doesn't he just, uh, turn back?" Even as I asked the question, I couldn't believe the words coming out of my mouth. Werewolves were real. And so were vampires. Jesus Christ. I had a sudden urge to break into hysterics, and bit my lip hard to hold myself together.

Helen's gaze never left the wolf, even when she answered. "It takes a great deal of energy to make the change. Once a Were has transformed, he or she must hunt and eat in order to return to their human state."

I nodded, wondering how the Consortium staff was going to resolve this particular dilemma. Would they tranquilize the wolf and take him someplace to hunt? It was clear from Kyle's reaction that werewolves would happily eat humans, so they'd have to take it someplace remote, wouldn't they?

"How is this possible?" Alexa finally whispered.

Helen sighed in clear vexation. She was probably none too happy with the fact that Alexa was now in on all of these secrets. I, on the other hand, was relieved. Of course, when she finally learned the truth about me, she would probably leave. Who could blame her?

"I am not pleased that you have forced my hand," Helen said, locking gazes briefly with Alexa, who shuddered once in my arms at the ice in Helen's stare. "Then again," she mused softly, her eyes flickering toward me, "perhaps there is something to be gained by this."

Before I could ask what she meant, she was speaking again. "You have just observed the effects of the lycanthropy virus. Darren was bitten, long ago, by an infected wolf. Wolves are the most common, but there are many species of shifters, including other kinds of canines and felines."

Alexa, who had laced her fingers with mine where they rested over her stomach, was squeezing my hands so hard that I thought I might lose circulation. Helen seemed to be deriving some pleasure from her discomfort.

"Valentine, on the other hand, has been infected by a parasite. This parasite feeds on her blood, engendering a biological need to consume human blood in order to survive." She smiled thinly. "You accused me earlier of exploiting her, but nothing could be further from the truth. I am trying to educate her—to show her how to live with an incurable disease."

"Incurable?" The word was strangled, as though it had clawed its own way out of Alexa's throat. I rubbed my thumbs across her knuckles in a lame gesture of comfort as my stomach churned anxiously. Would she leave me, now that she knew?

"Neither the virus nor the parasite can be cured. Yet. But we are trying."

"The man who attacked her two weeks ago," Alexa said hoarsely. "He did this?"

Helen nodded once.

"And he is also a…a…"

"Vampire. Yes. The parasite can only be spread if blood from the donor is mingled with that of the recipient, and it will only survive when the victim's immune response has been drastically weakened in some way. Hence the degree of violence that he uses in his attacks."

I fought back a shudder at the thought of him merging his blood with mine. "Uses?" Alexa stiffened in my arms. "You know that he's doing this serially?"

"Of course," Helen said dismissively. "For some reason, he has decided to go rogue and is endangering us all with his so-called 'mugging' spree. We have been trying to catch him for months, since before the police became involved, but he continues to elude us." She looked at me speculatively. "As far as we know, Valentine is his only victim to have survived the process."

At that moment, the main door into the conference room opened to display a long arm, holding a rabbit by the scruff of its neck. Teeth snapping, the wolf leapt toward the breach—but before he could reach the gap, it had closed again, leaving the rabbit inside. Darren descended on the creature, breaking its neck with one snap of his jaws. I fought down my gorge as I watched him greedily snap up the impromptu meal. Alexa's breaths came shallowly, but she didn't look away either.

"How much blood does Val need?" she asked Helen quietly.

"For now, about one pint a week."

Alexa turned in my arms to appraise Helen. "For now?"

"The parasite is consuming Valentine's blood faster than her bone marrow can regenerate it," Helen said. She met my eyes directly. "It is multiplying, and as it does so, it will begin to change the very nature of your circulatory system. The parasite itself will start to function similarly to your red blood cells. Eventually, your own blood will be virtually nonexistent. At that point, you will need to feed much more frequently than you do now. Six pints a week, at minimum."

I was shell-shocked. My blood was being…replaced? By that thing? I tightened my hold on Alexa as this afternoon's panic returned full force. "I'm dying," I whispered. Alexa reached back to curl one arm around my waist and hook her thumb into a belt loop, trying to get even closer than she already was. She was shaking again.

Helen shrugged delicately. "Not exactly. The process is an echo of both death and resurrection. At a certain point, you will fall into a coma for several days while the parasite undergoes its final metamorphosis. Upon waking from the coma, you will be thirstier than you have ever been. Many of us have also noticed psychological changes. Increased aggressiveness. Less remorse over the feeding process." She cocked her head slightly, watching as Darren's strong jaws splintered the bones of the rabbit as he sought out every bit of meat on the body. "Those of us who are religiously inclined have argued that when the parasite claims your bloodstream, you lose your soul. But such a thing cannot be proven."

Alexa's breaths were quick and shallow. Was she hyperventilating? I was making a concerted effort not to succumb to the terror that was threatening to swallow me whole—to keep my brain focused and sharp in order to understand everything. So long as I regarded this as a medical conundrum and not as my personal problem, I would be able to keep the fear at bay.

One thing in particular wasn't adding up. "Why drink blood at all beforehand, then, if it does no good—if the parasite is only going to supplant my own supply anyway?"

"The thirst is an automatic impulse," Helen explained. "In a sense, the parasite is preparing you for when you have no blood left to give it. You can abstain, but the craving will only grow stronger and stronger, until the urge trumps your will to resist." She glanced wryly at Alexa. "I'm sure that you think it very cruel of me to tell Valentine to leave you, but it was the only way to ensure your safety. She would have hurt you, eventually."

Alexa's trembling stopped as though someone had thrown a switch, and she stepped out of the protective circle of my arms, leaning toward Helen. "You're wrong. She would never—"

"Yes, I would have," I interrupted quietly, arms hanging limply at my sides. "I had already dreamt about it."

When she looked back to meet my gaze, her shoulders slumped. I could see her flashing back to the first night we had spent in our apartment after the accident. To my nightmare. "Don't you see?" I whispered, my heart breaking all over again. "I can't be with you. Not if I'm going to hurt you."

"Bullshit," Alexa breathed. And then, louder, "Bullshit! This is ridiculous, Val. We're in love. We're supposed to work together when things get hard. You walking away solves nothing. There has to be a way to fix this—or at the very least, something that I can do." She turned back to Helen. "Show me how to help her. Please."

Helen flashed her teeth. "You may be the only one who can."

"How?" Alexa sounded as fed up with Helen's cryptic, roundabout way of telling a story as I was.

"There is a slight chance that you may be able to keep Valentine's parasite in check, by offering it another source."

"What?" My voice cracked under the stress as I realized what she was suggesting. "No!" I was absolutely not going to risk Alexa's life by taking her blood. Especially since I wanted to drink from her more than almost anything. I would destroy her. I knew it.

Alexa was frowning. "I don't understand. You just said that Val drinking from other people doesn't stop the parasite from multiplying. What would make it turn to my blood when it's already feeding from hers?"

"It doesn't fucking matter," I said loudly, even though I couldn't help but be curious to hear Helen's answer. "This is a nonissue!"

They both ignored me. "We have observed a few cases in which the parasite's transformation process was halted—for a time—when the vampire in question fed regularly and exclusively from their…mate." Helen appraised Alexa with an evaluative stare. "A few romantics among us claim that it is a mystical process—the power of true love. Our scientists, on the other hand, believe that the phenomenon has something to do with pheromones: that the chemical composition of the partner's blood is, in these situations, more appealing than the blood of the host."

Alexa was fascinated. I watched the emotions sweep across her face like a summer storm: confusion, surprise, interest, determination. At no point did she look afraid. I ground my teeth in frustration.

"You said 'for a time,'" Alexa pointed out. "What's the catch?"

"A human is capable of giving up a pint of their blood each week, but not without a price," Helen said. "Your body will constantly struggle to regain what it has lost. In some ways, your quality of life will diminish: you will feel tired almost constantly, and weak. And you will only be able to sustain giving that much volume for a set number of years. By the time you reach your fifties, you will be struggling to meet Valentine's needs. Eventually you will become too frail to offer what she requires, and the parasite will revert to feeding from her own blood."

"But you've seen it work," Alexa pressed. "Between two people who are romantically involved."

Helen nodded. "One of my colleagues fed exclusively from his wife for thirty-two years before she was no longer able to sustain him."

Alexa turned back to me then, hope illuminating her face. "We can do this, Val."

Her beauty pierced my heart. I looked away, watching Darren the wolf lick clean the bones of his prey. Never had I felt more conflicted. On the one hand, Alexa was telling me that I could have it all: her presence in my life and her blood satisfying my thirst. The mere thought of drinking from her made my throat ache more fiercely than it ever had. But I would hurt her. I would make her weak. She would suffer. I could not, would not do it.

"Didn't you hear what Helen said?" I asked, trying to keep my voice quiet and even, instead of yelling like I wanted to. "You'll be perpetually exhausted. How much energy will you have left for your career? For hobbies? For building a family?" I clamped my jaw down hard when I realized that I was betraying my own grief. We hadn't ever talked seriously about the possibility of starting a family, but in my head, I had seen a child: a girl, with pale hair like mine and eyes like Alexa's. But that dream was lost, now—now that I was a monster.

I kept staring straight ahead as she slipped her arms around my waist and pulled my reluctant hands around her body. Once I was touching her, of course, I couldn't stop. She knew me so well. I pulled her closer and buried my face in her neck. The rhythmic sound of her pulse was soothing and arousing, all at once.

"I'm not taking no for an answer," she murmured against my chest. "You are my family, Val. I need to be with you." She pulled back just enough to look up at me. "You're the one who's always saying that we can do anything together. So practice what you preach."

I stared down at her intently, trying to find a hint of uncertainty or fear. But I couldn't. She meant every word. And suddenly, I knew exactly what I was going to do with the rest of my life. My brain was sharp, my focus formidable. This entire situation was preposterous. I refused it. I would bend all my will to the quest for a solution. For as long as it took.

"I'm going to find another way," I whispered. "There has to be something, medically—some other way to stop the parasite. I'll figure it out. I promise."

Alexa stroked the tense muscles of my back through my shirt. "I believe you, love. If that's what you want to do, then I know you will.

But in the meantime, let me be your sustenance. I'm strong and healthy. I can give you this."

Guilt and desire warred in my brain. I wanted so badly to accept what she was offering. But should I? What if she came to resent me? What if I hurt her, or worse?

I breathed in her scent again, allowing her presence to calm me. The fact was, I needed her. I couldn't escape that. I'd already tried to make one choice for her today, and that hadn't been right or fair. If she didn't believe that the risk was too great, then I had to make my peace with her decision—for now, anyway—and do everything in my power to treat her as well as I could. While searching for the cure.

"Okay," I said softly. "I…I accept. I feel so selfish and so grateful, and—"

She cut off my babbling by pulling my head down and pressing her lips to mine. If I was thirsty for her blood, then I was starving for this—the perfect softness of her mouth, the hot stroking of her tongue, the gentle scrape of her teeth. I lost myself in that kiss. The room and its other occupants melted away as we reaffirmed *us*.

When I finally pulled back to breathe, I cupped Alexa's face in my hands and smoothed my thumbs across her cheeks. "That hour without you was the worst in my life."

Her hands tightened on my hips and she pulled me closer. "Don't you ever do that again," she said, her voice ragged.

I would have gone right back to kissing her if Kyle hadn't spoken up. "Finally," he hissed. When I glared at him, thinking that he was referring to us, I realized that his full attention was still on the wolf, which was blurring around the edges. Just like he had done in his human form.

"Look," I breathed, turning Alexa toward the window. Moments later, a very naked Darren appeared on his hands and knees. Almost immediately, a spasm racked his entire body and he vomited. I watched him cough and spit and gasp for breath, wondering how much agony he was in. I could only imagine what it felt like to endure that kind of transformation—the pain must be crippling. How he even survived it was a medical miracle beyond my wildest dreams. A moment later, the main door opened and that same arm thrust in a set of scrubs. Keeping his back to us, Darren lurched to his feet and reached for the clothes.

When he had pulled on the pants, Helen let us back into the conference room.

Darren glowered at me and Alexa, but his face smoothed when Helen rested a hand on his bulging right biceps. "I apologize," he told her, his tone formal.

"You were provoked," she said, stroking him lightly. "Go and change, then meet us across the hall."

His eyes narrowed; I could tell he didn't like the idea of leaving her alone with us one bit. But he obeyed the order. I gave the pool of vomit and rabbit remains that were scattered on the bloodstained floor a wide berth as we followed Helen out the door and into an identical conference room across the hall.

"If you have decided to feed from her," Helen said to me once we were all seated around the table, "it will be best to do so under supervision the first few times. It will be easy for you to get carried away and take too much."

"I want us to do it now," said Alexa. "Show me."

"Kyle will help." From her purse, Helen extracted a scalpel. It was sterile—I could tell from the packaging.

I checked Alexa's expression to see if she was having misgivings, but she only looked confused. "Can't Val..." A flush crept into her cheeks, and she cleared her throat before continuing. "I mean, why not...bite?"

A stab of arousal jolted through my body, leaving me throbbing. Alexa wanted me to bite her. Fucking hell. I reached for her hand under the table and squeezed hard, my mind's eye overwhelmed by visions of me sinking my teeth into the buttery-smooth skin of her inner thigh while making tiny circles with my thumb against her—

Helen laughed low and rich, and I caught her regarding Alexa appraisingly. My jaw clenched, and I had to fight an urge to growl. "Biting is certainly our most common method of feeding," she said. "But Valentine's teeth are dull, and a bite from her right now would be quite painful for you. If you like," she continued, meeting my gaze effortlessly, "you can elect to have a special kind of dental surgery that will elongate and sharpen your canines. The modifications can either be subtle or more extravagant, as you prefer."

I made a mental note to talk more with Helen later about the surgery. If Alexa wanted me to bite her, then I was going to do my damnedest to make it as pleasurable as possible for her. The idea of biting was much more palatable than using a scalpel anyway. As Helen handed it to Kyle, I watched him warily, hating that he was going to cut into Alexa, even though it was what she wanted.

"Roll up one of your sleeves," he told Alexa, who picked her right arm. "It takes practice to get good at doing this yourself, so I'll do it this time. The trick is not to go so deep that you're bleeding heavily. On the other hand, you don't want only a shallow cut that will barely bleed at all."

Alexa nodded. "Come here, Val," she said, pushing her chair back so that there was space for me to kneel at her right side. I stood, wiping sweaty palms on my jeans. My heart, pounding against my rib cage, felt torn in two: equal parts desire and fear.

Kyle cradled her elbow in one hand, and held the blade poised above her arm in the other. "Just tell me when."

Alexa cupped the back of my neck with her free hand, drawing me closer. "I love you, Valentine Darrow," she whispered. "And I want to be inside you this way."

Tears sprang into my eyes at the depth of emotion in her voice. I blinked furiously to stop them from falling and leaned in to claim her mouth in a gentle kiss. "I love you, Alexa Newland. And I need you—in all ways."

She smiled as she told Kyle that she was ready. She didn't so much as flinch when he drew the scalpel across her skin. I could feel her gaze on me as I watched the blood rise from the open lips of the cut.

"Take it," she whispered.

My hands replaced Kyle's; I held her arm with a feather-light touch as I bent my head. I sealed my lips over the gash and let my tongue trail across her broken skin. The flavor burst across my tongue, bright and hot like the dawning of the sun.

Alexa's hand moved into my hair, her fingers tightening as she urged me even closer. I groaned as I hollowed my lips and drew her blood into my mouth. Its taste was rich and complex, like her scent only far more potent. The world's finest wine, mixed with ambrosia from heaven.

Nothing could have prepared me for this sensation.

Heat and light spiraled down my throat, soothing the ache, filling the dark void of thirst. I had been empty—a well of need, the vacuum of deep space. She was making me whole again, replacing the nothingness with her very essence. My love, my desire, my life. She was my life.

"Oh God, Val," she whispered, not in pain or fear, but in pleasure.

My grasp on her arm became less gentle, more possessive. I drank and drank, desperate to have more of her inside of me, until it was impossible to tell where I ended and she began. She was liquid strength and vitality, mending my broken body, soothing the desperate need for her that burned at the heart of me—that eternal, unquenchable flame.

"Valentine. Stop." The cool voice was distant, and I paid it no mind. I needed more of her. I feathered my tongue along her skin, and was rewarded by a low gasp. She wanted me. Wanted this. Desire thundered in my brain, and I clutched at her thigh with my free hand, wanting my fingers inside her just as my teeth were.

"Convince her to stop, Alexa. If you don't, we'll have to use force."

"Val." Alexa's voice was more distinct. "It's time to stop." I paused, conflicted. Stop? Why was she telling me to stop, when she wanted to give more? I could feel it in the way her body was responding to me, in the enhanced sweetness of her blood. She tasted even better now than she had a few moments ago. I gripped her leg even harder to stop myself from taking her here, in front of an audience: flattening my hand against her stomach, diving down beneath the waistband of her jeans, slipping beneath her—

She tugged gently on my hair. "I love you, Val. I love doing this for you, and it feels so good. But that's enough for now."

Enough? I would never get enough. Stopping was impossible, but she was asking me to. She was everything to me, and I could deny her nothing. I fought against the urge to draw her even deeper inside of me, and instead forced my mouth to move gently against her fragrant skin. Pulling away from her was the hardest thing I had ever done in my life—harder even than speaking the words to push her away, mere hours ago.

I licked my lips, seeking every last drop of her, and blinked hard as my vision snapped into focus. Kyle was fixing a Band-Aid onto her arm. For the first time, she winced.

"I know, the cream stings a bit," he said, smoothing down the adhesive strips. "But it will help you clot faster. I'll give you some to take home."

Alexa nodded but never looked away from me. She cupped my cheek, her thumb dipping into the corner of my mouth. When she held it out to me, I could see a smear of dark red. I curled my tongue around her finger and her breathing stuttered. Never had I glimpsed such desire in her eyes. I wanted the room to empty so that I could give her what she so clearly needed. Even now, a few feet away, I could hear the drum roll of her heart within her chest. Her pupils were dilated, her skin flushed. And when I took a deep breath, I could actually smell her. Now, now I understood what Helen had meant about feeding and sex being a cycle. I wanted to make love to Alexa more urgently than I ever had. But it wasn't safe.

"Are you all right?" I whispered.

"I feel fine." She cocked her head slightly and worried her lower lip with her teeth. "Was that...okay?"

"You couldn't tell?" I wasn't sure that she would want a kiss after I'd been drinking from her, so I contented myself with leaning forward and resting my hands on her knees. "Babe, there aren't words for how good you taste."

She embraced me then, folding me into her arms and lightly massaging the back of my scalp with her nails. It felt incredible.

"I love you," she murmured into my ear, her warm breath bathing my sensitive lobe. "And I want to do that again."

I shuddered, barely resisting the urge to tear into her neck with my dull teeth. "Me, too," I managed to say. Would this craving ever let up? Would I ever not be a danger to her? The cold fear pierced through my euphoria, and I sat back on my heels. "Maybe in a few days?"

She looked as disappointed as I felt. "That long?"

Helen's laugh was knowing. "Valentine is right. Give yourself at least three days to recover, if you're going to let her take that much every time." She turned her attention to me, and for the first time, I met her gaze without flinching. "And how do you feel?"

Only when I pondered her question did I realize that it was the absence of pain and weakness that I was experiencing. I smiled, exhilarated. "Different. Stronger. It's because of the...?" I gestured aimlessly, uncertain of the vocabulary I should use to describe what had just happened. What I'd just done to Alexa.

Helen nodded. "You'll experience these effects for several hours. The easiest analogy I can provide is to performance-enhancing drugs:

drinking blood from a human will make you physically stronger and faster. All of your senses will temporarily improve. Right now, I imagine Alexa's blood must be a relief to you, serving as a panacea for your injuries." Her expression was a mixture of both wistfulness and desire. "It is not only the parasite's thirst that drives us. The stimulation is…heady."

I heard the word she wasn't saying. Addict. Blood wasn't only her sustenance—it was her drug. As it would be mine. I shivered, and Alexa's hand moved immediately to the nape of my neck, rubbing and massaging my tense muscles there.

"It's okay, love," she murmured. "You'll always have what you need. I promise."

I chose not to call her on the lie, knowing that right now, we needed to cultivate hope. When she stood, I watched closely to see whether she was in danger of fainting, but she didn't even waver on her feet. "Come on. Let's go home."

I stood slowly and reached for her hand, kicking myself for what I was about to do. I wanted to go back with her to our apartment, so very badly. But I just couldn't. Not yet—not until I had myself under better control.

"I think I should stay here for a while." When pain flashed across her face, I shook my head, knowing what she was thinking. "I'm not leaving you. I'm just—I'm afraid that I'll hurt you. I'd rather spend a few weeks here, learning to control myself, than…" I trailed off, not wanting to say it.

"I understand," she said after a moment. But displeasure was written plainly across her face. I threaded my arms around her, hating myself for continuing to make her unhappy.

"It's going to be so hard to be apart from you. Will you come and visit, when you can?"

She rested her head against my chest. After a few moments, I realized that she was listening to my heartbeat. "I'll come every day," she finally said.

"You'll eat something, right? To replenish what I took?"

"Mmm-hmm." She pressed even closer, weakening my resolve.

"Maybe you can stay a little longer? To see whatever room they give me, so you know where it is?" I was grasping at straws, but I couldn't bear to watch her walk away. Not yet.

She smiled brilliantly at me. "I'd like that."

"Okay," I whispered, kissing her forehead. In a minute, I'd ask Helen about the room she had offered, and about those records that she said I'd have access to. In a minute.

For now, I needed to hold on to Alexa and savor the hope that just maybe, thanks to her, everything was going to be okay.

CHAPTER EIGHT

B ut that night, I dreamt of my attacker. It was only a jumble of images and sensations: the pungent smell of decay, the smooth metal of the knife handle against my stinging palm, the sickening thud of my head connecting with the pavement. I woke pouring sweat, thigh and shoulder throbbing dully, reaching for Alexa—

I was alone. I took some slow breaths to try to calm my heart rate. The absence of sharp pain from my cracked ribs was a surprise, and I tentatively tried inhaling deeply. Only a faint twinge. My surprise sharpened when I realized that for the first time since I'd woken from the coma, my throat didn't ache. I was thirsty, of course—I would never completely escape thirst again—but the persistent burning pain was gone.

My thirst had abated thanks to Alexa's blood. Did I have the same source to thank for the healing of my bones? Helen's prediction that the salutary effects of my feeding would wear off in a few hours had been true—the familiar aches and fatigue that had disappeared last night were present this morning. But they were noticeably diminished. Was Alexa's blood having an additional, unforeseen effect? It seemed impossible, but since yesterday, my definition of that word had radically changed. Despite the maelstrom that my life had become over the past twenty-four hours, one thing was clear: I needed to find out as much as possible about this parasite and its effects so I'd know what I was up against.

I sat up against the headboard, pulled the blankets to my chin, and stared at the unfamiliar room. It looked for all intents and purposes like a hotel, down to the reading lamps mounted on either side of the bed and the cookie-cutter alarm clock that sat atop a nightstand to my left. I wondered whether, if I opened the small drawer, I'd find a Gideons Bible. Rays of light cascaded through the windows to my right, and I remembered Clavier's passing comment yesterday, about how the parasite made its victims more sensitive to the sun. How did that work? Would it actually burn me, or was that a myth?

So many questions. The prospect of attending my Anatomy class paled in comparison to staying here and beginning to look through the Consortium's medical records, and I decided to skip out on school today. It wasn't a particularly good idea, seeing as I had already missed so much—but I'd be of no use to my professors or classmates with my attention so completely diverted.

Just today, I promised myself. One day to familiarize myself with the Consortium's research so that I wasn't so much in the dark. But after this, no more skipping. I had to make a concerted effort to get caught up with my medical studies. I needed that degree now more than ever, if I was going to make research into the parasite my life's work. A PhD would probably help, too. I rubbed the back of my neck while contemplating how soon to talk to my advisor about that. This mattress was too soft. I missed my own bed, not to mention Alexa's sure and certain hands. She was so very good at kneading out the tension that never failed to pool in my neck and shoulders. Tuesday was her busy day, but I would see her tonight. She had promised.

In the meantime, I was going to focus. I slid out of bed, bracing myself for the pain of my left foot meeting the floor...but the surge of discomfort was far less sharp than it had been yesterday. I went to the chair in front of the small desk over which I'd draped my jeans and fished the card that Helen had given me yesterday out of the back pocket.

"Call me tomorrow, Valentine," she had said, curling her fingers around mine as she handed over the card. "Or the next day. Whenever you are ready to learn more."

Taking a deep breath, I lifted the phone from its cradle and punched in the numbers. Suddenly, I felt disconnected from myself—as though I were hovering above my own body, watching the quick motion of my fingers without feeling the compressions of the keys. The hands of a monster. How had my life become this?

"I'm ready," I whispered as Helen's phone began to ring, hoping that hearing my own voice would ease the eerie sense of separation I was feeling. I was going to fight what had happened to me, and eventually, I was going to win. For myself. For Alexa. For us.

❖

The Consortium had a library on the eleventh floor, complete with a reading room, computers, and a reference librarian who had been born at the turn of the nineteenth century. Helen's secretary had arranged for me to spend the day there, with the promise that Helen herself would join me once night fell. I hadn't left since the morning, unable to pry myself away from the wealth of information that Consortium members had compiled about both the vampire parasite and the Were virus.

While the latter fascinated me intellectually—particularly because the increased regenerative capabilities of Weres had profound implications for modern medicine—I concentrated almost all of my attention on the parasite. I learned that it released toxins when my skin was exposed to the sunlight: that for now, I would be fine so long as I applied sunblock, but that once it gained control of my blood—at which point I would be known as a "full" vampire—I would barely be able to spend two minutes in the sun without a major systemic shutdown. The thought of never again being able to enjoy the heat of the sun pounding down on my scalp as I jogged through Central Park, or spend a beautiful Saturday morning window-shopping in Soho with Alexa, made my stomach hurt. I forced those thoughts out of my head and concentrated on the facts, rather than their consequences.

There were, I learned, some beneficial aspects of becoming a full vampire—though as far as I was concerned, they didn't outweigh the negatives. Because the parasite essentially replaced the host's red blood cells, the effects of its chemical reactions with consumed blood were more pronounced. To use Helen's drug analogy: full vampires got more of a high off human blood than I could. They would be stronger, faster, and have keener senses…until the effects wore off. Or until they drank again.

A cool, gentle caress against my neck startled me. "Didn't your parents tell you not to read in the dark?"

I turned to the sight of Helen leaning over my shoulder. She smiled slightly—the briefest show of teeth—before shifting her attention to the page I'd been reading. Dusk had fallen without my knowledge. The cobalt clouds scudding above the city's twinkling lights matched the shade of Helen's sweater.

"Clearly, I shouldn't worry about my eyesight any longer," I said, nodding toward the screen. When she laughed quietly, I felt emboldened to ask the first question on my mind. "What does it feel like, for you? I mean—the changes that come, when you...drink?"

She settled into an armchair next to me and crossed one slender leg over the other. "Power," she said. "Or perhaps more accurately, potential. Life returns to me when I feed: the world becomes more vivid. My body grows stronger and my mind sharper. I am confident in my abilities—or perhaps, I should say, my capability."

"To do what?"

Her smile lasted longer this time—long enough for me to notice the pointed tips of her canines. As though she knew where my attention was focused, she teased one sharp tooth with her tongue. "Anything."

Anything. I fought back a shiver. Once you experienced that sensation, I imagined, you never wanted to come down. No wonder full vampires needed so much blood. "That sounds like almost a transcendental experience," I said. "But honestly, it seems to me like the Weres get the better deal. No biological imperative to drink blood, no craving to make it even harder to resist, and they shapeshift."

Helen's eyebrows arched, two perfect bows over her eyes. "In other places and times, there have been power struggles between our two factions. Many of the warmongers have made similar arguments over the years—that we should serve them, because they are more powerful."

My mind reeled. "I didn't mean—"

"I know. You are simply speculating, based on what little you know. It is safe to do so with me, but be careful, Valentine, to whom you speculate in the future."

I nodded, feeling like a schoolgirl taken to task for making unwarranted assumptions. I suppose, in Helen's eyes, that's exactly what I was. It should not have been a surprise that the political undercurrents ran just as deep in this community as in any other. Probably, they were deeper, given that the players were practically eternal.

"The necessity of Weres to change once every month is an annoying inconvenience most of the time," Helen explained. "It has the potential, however, to be their greatest weakness. Consider if someone knew the secret and wished to take advantage of them—either individually or as a collective. It could be done easily, on the night of the full moon, when they are all beasts.

"Moreover, they are inherently volatile. You saw Darren yesterday. He has been a Were for just shy of one hundred years, yet a superficial head wound was enough to provoke his change. He fought hard against the impulse, but to no avail. A Were's life is schizophrenic: a constant struggle between the personality of the human and the will of their animal half."

I tried to imagine what that would be like—constantly battling for dominance against an entirely different entity in my head—and grasped Helen's point. The defining attribute of each species was a biological curse. Some measure of power came along with that curse, but for vampires and Weres, long life would always be a struggle.

"I see," I murmured. "That sounds very difficult."

She inclined her head. "Was there anything else you wanted to ask?"

I sat up straighter, remembering the original question that had prompted my call to her this morning. "Yes. I woke up this morning feeling better than I ever have since my attack—like I've healed more in the past twenty-four hours than in the past week. I know you said yesterday that the effects of feeding don't last beyond a few hours, but I can't help but think that my sudden improvement must be related to drinking from Alexa. Do you have any explanation?"

Helen leaned back, crossing her arms beneath her breasts. "Interesting," she murmured. "So she is the one."

I had never had or expressed any doubt that Alexa was my one and only, and Helen's unsought confirmation confused me. "How do you mean?"

"Yesterday, I was speculating that Alexa's blood would be a viable substitute for your parasite. But it is impossible to know whether you are matched in that way until after the fact. If you are indeed experiencing long-term beneficial effects from feeding already, then my guess was correct."

"So this is normal?"

Helen cocked her head slightly. "The arrangement that you have made with Alexa is very rare. Few of us find human mates, and even if we do, those mortals may not be willing to make the sacrifices necessary to feed us. Often, they do not survive long." She shrugged, but behind her calm exterior, a flicker of remembered pain flared in those brilliant eyes. "For as long as you feed exclusively from Alexa, you will not only halt the parasite's progression—you will also attain a more permanent strength."

"I don't know if it's worth it," I blurted. Fear had risen to the forefront again at her oblique mention of the dangers involved in Alexa's and my agreement. "I'm so terrified of hurting her. I hate that I felt so out of control yesterday, and if I ever took too much I'd—I'd— Jesus, why does she even want to be with me still, now that she knows what I am?"

On the verge of breaking down, I locked my jaw and looked away toward the windows. I knew I was visibly trembling, but I forced myself not to give in to the sobs that wanted to rip their way out of my throat. I didn't want to betray any weakness in front of Helen.

A moment later, her cool fingers firmly gripped my chin, turning my head so that I was forced to meet her gaze. "You cannot do this to yourself," she said, her tone sharper than I'd ever heard it. I would have flinched, had she not been holding me. "To live out an eternity crippled by guilt for what you are is nothing but pathetic nihilism. You are a vampire: powerful and untouched by time. You are beautiful now, and the passing of the years will only make you more so. This rash impetuosity of youth will be replaced by wisdom and patience. You will be a force to be reckoned with, Valentine. You must never apologize. And you must never let anyone convince you to be less. If Alexa cannot embrace what you have become, then you must let her go."

She spoke with an intensity that riveted me, even as my chest constricted in fury that she would dare presume to tell me what to do when it came to my lover. "Alexa has always loved me for exactly who I am," I said stiffly. "That should have been at its most apparent yesterday, when she volunteered her blood only minutes after hearing the whole story." Helen couldn't have been more off base by accusing Alexa. She wasn't the so-called "problem"—I was. But how was I supposed to wholeheartedly embrace my newfound vampiric nature when giving up rigorous self-control meant the possibility of killing her?

Helen's fingers loosened. She rose, smoothing her hands over her charcoal slacks as she stood. "Her loyalty and love are remarkable gifts," she said softly. "Don't poison them with your own guilt."

Only when she had gone did I realize that Helen's tirade—if not the words with which she expressed it—was familiar. My father had taken a similar tack during my senior year of college in one of his attempts to persuade me to take up the family mantle rather than pursue a master's in what he had called "psychobabble."

I had told him to fuck off. Maybe I should have told Helen to do the same.

❖

I frowned hard at page 172, trying to bully my brain into focusing on the material. I had an exam next Monday and wasn't remotely prepared, but it was impossible to concentrate. Alexa had left half an hour ago, after bringing over Chinese take-out for dinner. She sat at the desk and I perched on the bed, and we kept the door open lest one of us get carried away. Our conversation had been stilted, even when she had moved to the bed and offered me a shoulder rub. I had allowed that, but my inability to relax had made her attempts fruitless.

I craved her blood. I craved her body. At least tomorrow, I'd be able to have the former. My throat ached sharply, nostalgic for her taste.

A knock at my door yanked me out of my brooding. Maybe Alexa had come back for some reason. The thought both thrilled and frightened me. But when I looked through the keyhole, I saw the Consortium's receptionist. Why hadn't she just called up?

"Hello," I said politely, swinging the door wide open. "What can I—"

She walked right in, kicked the door shut with one of her stilettos, and grabbed the collar of my shirt.

"We haven't been properly introduced," she murmured, mere inches from my mouth. Her breath tasted like cinnamon. "I'm Giselle." And then she kissed me.

I tried not to react, but my body betrayed my mind. Giselle kissed as though she were as starving for passion as I was. Twin flames of need twisted in my gut. To fuck. To drink. Yes.

Only when the backs of my legs hit the bed did I regain enough sense to tear my lips away. I grasped her upper arms firmly but gently and held her as far from me as I could. "No." But my voice was a pant of desire, devoid of any authority.

She relaxed in my grip, and I let go, believing that she was going to honor my request. Instead, she pulled aside her shirt collar and, with one long, pink-tinted fingernail, drew a furrow just below the bone. I had one split second in which to register just how persistent she was being, before the sight and smell of blood assaulted me. The tiny red ribbon beckoned, but I forced my feet to remain where they were. I was struggling so hard against my thirst that I didn't even register her grip on my hand. But when her tongue touched my fingertip, a jolt shot down my spine.

"I see how thirsty you are, Valentine," she said, ending each sentence with a twirl of her warm tongue around my finger. "Every day. You're suffering. Denying yourself. You really shouldn't."

She sucked hard and I moaned. I couldn't help it. I was wet. Blood was dripping down her chest. She wanted me to take her. I needed to take.

But not her. The thought knifed through my instincts, granting me an instant of clarity. An instant in which to realize that her blood didn't smell right, and her body didn't feel right, and good wasn't enough, once you'd had the best. No.

I pulled my hand out of her grasp. "Get out, please. Now."

She pouted. "Valentine…"

"I don't blame you," I said, trying to calm my heartbeat and my breathing. "I know who sent you. But get out, please. And don't come back."

With a huff, she spun on her heel—no doubt to find some vampire who would willingly take advantage of the blood she so freely offered. The door rocked on its hinges behind her. I leaned against it until my pulse had returned to normal, holding an image of Alexa in my brain: smiling broadly as we rode the Carousel at Central Park on our second date. I would have given anything to go back to that moment.

When I felt calm enough, I went to the phone. Helen's secretary picked up and, after a moment of waiting, Helen greeted me directly. What I had to say was very simple.

"I am in love with Alexa. She is the only one I want. I may not be choosing the normal path, or the easy path, but I am doing what's right for me. For us. And I would ask you to respect that. Don't ever send someone to me again."

Her voice was low. Musical—as though she were secretly amused by my vehemence. "Very well. I will never send anyone to you again… unless you ask me to."

My lip curled in a snarl she couldn't see. "That will never happen."

I hung up the phone and retreated to the bed. My entire body ached with unsatisfied need, and I knew that sleep was a hopeless proposition. At least that gave me more time to work. At least tomorrow, I could taste her again.

But I would still be starving.

CHAPTER NINE

Alexa's phone was still off.

I leaned against the wall outside my Physiology lab, combing my fingers through my hair in frustration as I tried to figure out what to do. She had called me early this morning before going into her first class, but now it was almost two in the afternoon, and I was still getting her voicemail. I was starting to feel all panicky inside—my palms were sweating, and my heart was flopping around in my chest like a fish out of water. I hated being this needy. It was my own damn fault, too, for insisting on the separation period. I had done it for her safety, but after three weeks of sleeping alone and seeing her only briefly each day, I was starting to go crazy. I missed her. I didn't want to lie in bed awake, thinking about how much I needed her, so I stayed up far too late every night, studying or reading the Consortium's files. And when I did sleep, I dreamt only of him. I felt his knife pierce my shoulder, his teeth dig into my skin. I saw my blood pooling on the ground, and the flash of color across his knuckles as he backhanded me into oblivion. I heard him taunt me, calling me by name. Every night, he was there in my head, waiting for me. Between the loneliness and the nightmares, I was exhausted. And my body was physically aching for her touch. I was completely off-kilter.

If Helen had intended for Giselle to relax me, her plan had completely backfired. Ever since getting slapped in the face by just how closely linked sex and feeding were, I had insisted that I drink from Alexa under full supervision. While her blood tasted sweeter than ever, our lack of physical intimacy made the act of feeding feel…empty, somehow. I was frustrated, and she was frustrated—though admirably trying not to show it—and yet every time I thought of taking her body as I took her blood, my terror at hurting her eclipsed even my desire.

Clearly, she had just forgotten to turn her phone back on after class. Obviously. And yet, something in my brain wouldn't let me believe it. What if she was angry with me? What if something had happened to her? What if—and this was the thought that really sent me off the deep end—she had finally decided that I wasn't worth the effort?

Because these days, I required a lot of effort.

I could see the physical changes in Alexa's body already. Dark circles lurked beneath her eyes, made all the more distinct by the pallor of her cheeks. A month ago, we had been in the habit of calling a five-mile run a "light" workout, but now, she confessed, she could barely manage three. She had lost more weight, too. Most nights, she brought take-out for both of us to eat while we caught each other up on the latest news and tried to savor what little time we had together. We ate in my room—she sitting at the desk, I perched on the bed. So I knew she wasn't starving herself. Her body just couldn't keep up with my appetite.

Every fourth night, I drank from her under the watchful eye of Consortium staff, but it never grew easier to stop. The knowledge that my control was still in tatters kept me in that featureless, impersonal room, even though I was sleeping horribly there. I chose a new spot on her arms each time because her bruises refused to fade. They started off red, then shifted through each color of the rainbow. But the pale violet ovals endured. I started to hate them.

I started to hate myself.

As she grew weaker, I became stronger. I was making unnaturally fast progress in my physical therapy, and the scars that had been so grisly and prominent before were already beginning to fade. But everything I gained was at her expense. I had become the parasite.

By now, the halls were crowded with other med students leaving their classes, laughing and chatting as they relaxed into the Friday afternoon.

"Hey Val," someone called. "Come out tonight. We're going for sushi."

I managed to smile and make an excuse while hitting speed dial yet again. Still, nothing. Baring my teeth, I pushed off the wall and stalked out of the building. I wasn't going to be able to take a deep breath until I knew she was okay. Her last class of the day started in an hour. If I caught a cab to Washington Square, I'd be able to get to her classroom with plenty of time to spare. I could even bring her a chai latte, and make it look like I was trying to recreate the old days.

Clutching my phone in my pocket so I'd feel the vibration in case its ring failed to penetrate through the sounds of the busy streets, I hurried out to First Avenue and flagged down a taxi. Fifteen minutes later, I was shouldering my way into the Starbucks on the east side of the square. There was a line, of course. Damn it. I tapped my foot as I waited, and absently surveyed the crowd.

And then I saw her. She already had a drink. She was sitting at a small table in the far corner, hands curled around the girth of the cup, and she was laughing at something her companion had said. The other woman turned her head slightly, tucking a strand of wavy black hair behind one ear, and my fingertips bit hard into the palms of my hands.

Olivia Wentworth Lloyd.

I had been running into Olivia at official functions for as long as I could remember. She had always been gorgeous and smart and charming—the clear queen bee in the gaggle of political celebrities' children. I, on the other hand, had been shy until puberty and awkward throughout my tweens. My parents—both before and after their divorce—had often held up Olivia as an example of everything I should be, and was not. I had alternately envied and admired her, both from afar and from up close, when we had ended up overlapping for a year at the same private girls' high school.

She had come out as a lesbian shortly after finishing college, a year before I'd told my family. When, in a fit of snarkiness, I pointed out to them that I was "just trying to be more like Olivia," they were not amused. She was a hotshot district attorney now. Just a few months ago, *Curve* had dubbed her "the female JFK Jr."

As I watched them, she punctuated something she was saying by lightly touching Alexa's arm.

Her hands. On my lover.

Crimson streaks shot through my vision as I stalked mindlessly toward their table. My tongue curled automatically around one of my slightly elongated canines, subtly testing its sharpness. I was going to tear out her fucking throat, and I was going to enjoy it.

Alexa saw me coming, and a stunning smile bloomed across her lips. Even in the throes of my rage, her beauty pierced me. "Hey, love. This is a nice surprise."

Olivia whirled in her seat. "Val, hi, long time no—"

"What the hell is going on here?" I demanded, barely restraining myself from throwing a punch first and asking questions later.

The bridge of Alexa's nose wrinkled. "What do you mean?" She was confused, but I would have bet every penny of my unclaimed fortune that Olivia knew exactly what I was talking about.

"Val," she said again, and now her tone was patronizing. "I was on campus for the law school's career fair, and saw Alexa there. We're just having coffee. Talking. Catching up."

I stood there, literally shaking, my gaze darting between the two of them. Olivia looked annoyed. Alexa looked worried. And pale. Damn it, she looked sick. Maybe I should just turn around and walk away. Olivia had it all: wealth, looks, charisma. She and Alexa shared an interest in law. Who was I kidding—they were fucking perfect for each other. Not to mention the fact that Olivia wouldn't need Alexa's god damn blood to survive. I was making her suffer. It would be so much better if Olivia and I just switched places.

I was turning to go. I really was. And then Alexa caught my hand. "Sweetheart," she said quietly. A dozen different emotions were packed into the intonation of that simple term of endearment.

Olivia stood. "I'm heading out. Nice chatting with you, Alexa. Take care, Val."

I wondered if she meant that as a warning. I took it as such. Sinking into the seat that Olivia had just vacated, I propped my elbows on the table and rested my head in my palms. My righteous anger had been replaced entirely by guilt.

"She wants you," I said, not meeting Alexa's eyes. "She can give you so much more than I can. I think…I think you should take what she's offering."

"What?" Her gentle fingers slipped under my chin, tilting up so that I couldn't escape her. "Val…where is this even coming from? I'm yours! I'm with you. I barely even know Olivia—she's an acquaintance at best. It's just like she said: I saw her at the career fair, recognized her from that party of your father's a few months ago, and we got to talking about my potential career paths." She leaned forward to press a quick kiss to my lips. "You're acting like she proposed marriage."

"She was flirting with you." I was trying to make a factual statement, but it came out sounding mournful.

"Well, yes." Another quick kiss. "You know that I love when you get possessive. But that's just how she is, right? You told me so yourself, before you introduced me to her. Remember?"

I did remember. That didn't help. "My point is still valid. Ever since the attack, all I've been is a drain on you. Pun not intended." I shook my head angrily. "You deserve so much better than to be exhausted and weak all the time." Not to mention frustrated and in danger, I added silently.

Alexa's jaw clenched. She took a deep breath. "I know that you're just trying to do the right thing," she said slowly, "but it drives me nuts to hear you say stuff like this. In case you haven't noticed, I'm pretty smart. And I'm more than capable of making my own choices— something you seem to have forgotten."

I blinked, blindsided by the sharpness in her tone. But she was right. My self-flagellating routine wasn't giving her any agency at all.

Her expression softened. "All this talk of 'deserving' is ridiculous. I want you. I love you. I love feeding you." Her eyes closed briefly. "God, Val, you have no idea what it's like—what an incredible feeling it is, knowing that I can do that, be that for you."

My chest felt tight and tears pricked against my lashes. Beyond words, I reached across the table to cup her cheek. I smoothed my thumb across the corner of her mouth, and gasped when her tongue darted out to taste my skin. Love and desire, need and fear slammed together in my heart. She made me feel so much. I trembled at the force of it.

Alexa rested her hand over mine and squeezed lightly. "This isn't like you. Last time you saw Olivia, it seemed like you actually enjoyed talking to her. Now you take one look at her and halfway convince yourself to walk right out of my life. Which, by the way, is crazy. What's going on?"

I swallowed hard, determined not to break down in a fucking Starbucks of all places. "I miss you," I whispered, knowing that I could be nothing but honest. "It's so hard to fall asleep without you, and when I do, I just have nightmares anyway." And then I hiccupped. Which made me sound even more pathetic.

"Come home," she urged for the hundredth time. "Please, Val. Please. Do you think I'm doing any better?" My stomach clenched as I realized what she was implying—that by keeping us apart, I was making her unhealthy. And she couldn't afford to be unhealthy, not with me drinking from her.

"I want to," I said quickly. "You know I want to, and you know why I…" I shook my head. Not being with her, not touching her the way I wanted to, was slowly making me insane. But I had to keep her safe. "Soon. I promise. I'll talk to the Powers That Be, okay? See what they think."

Alexa nodded. I knew she was disappointed, but she didn't dwell on it. I felt the cloud of self-loathing descending on my shoulders, and physically shrugged it off. No. I would find strength in her patience, and the courage to be with her the way we both needed. I would. I was determined.

She pulled me out of my self-psychologizing with a soft kiss. "So. Walk me to Vanderbilt?"

"Yeah, of course."

She laced our fingers together as we left the Starbucks. "What brought you over here, anyway?"

My earlier concerns felt so silly now, after her declaration. "Your phone's been off all day. I was worried, so I decided to meet you at your last class, chai in hand."

But Alexa didn't roll her eyes at my stalkerish tendencies. "Aww. You're sweet when you're neurotic."

That made me laugh, of course, which had probably been her intent. "I was trying to call you because before I left this morning, Kyle gave us invitations to a party tonight."

Her expression became speculative. "A vampire party?"

"There might be shifters, too. I don't know."

"Where?"

I grinned. Alexa enjoyed going out to clubs, so she was going to squeal when she heard this. "Luna."

"Get out!" She stopped in the middle of the sidewalk, forcing the crowd around us. My smile grew wider. I laced my arm through hers and gave her a tug to keep us moving.

"For real," I said. "Starts at ten. What do you think?"

"Yes. Absolutely. That's perfect—I'll have time for a nap before we have to leave."

I struggled to keep my face smooth at the reminder of how little energy she had these days. We had reached the front door of Vanderbilt Hall, so I pulled her off to one side and wrapped my arms around her. Despite my resolution, a very large part of me wanted to suggest that I follow my gut and take that nap with her, instead of going back to the Consortium's facility.

But what if I hurt her?

The warmth of her lips against my neck sent twin pulses of thirst and desire down my throat. I couldn't risk it—not without talking to Helen first. As much as I needed Alexa, as much as she needed me…I would not see this end in tragedy.

"How about you give me a wake-up call at eight?" she murmured against my skin. "Then I'll come up and hang out with you until it's time to leave."

"Okay," I said into her hair. "Will you bring me something suitable to wear?" The request wouldn't be a hardship for her, I knew; Alexa loved dressing me.

"Sure." Reluctantly, I thought, she stepped away. Her fingertips trailed across my face. I turned my head to kiss them as they passed my mouth, and her eyes immediately grew a shade darker. "See you soon," she said.

I sighed as I watched her go. I would have been completely out of my league in her Torts class, but I wanted to follow her in there anyway.

❖

Above my head, stars. Below my feet, water. For a moment, I thought I knew how God had felt, hovering in chaos on the brink of creation. But then Alexa slipped her arms around my waist and pressed her lips to my jaw, and I remembered that God hadn't been this lucky.

"Unbelievable," she breathed.

I skimmed my hands across her hips and she sighed against my skin. She had pulled out all the stops tonight. Her black dress was both a halter top and backless. Looking at her made me feel dizzy. Hot. Thirsty. I wanted her more than I ever had. For all my talk this afternoon, I'd nearly lost control the second she walked into my room, an hour ago. I probably would have given in to the urge to take her, if she hadn't been so obviously excited to see this club.

It was, as Alexa had said, unbelievable. Luna sported two dance floors, the second directly on top of the first. The club was a tall cylinder built over a large pool of water. A glass circle the precise size of the pool was set into each floor. The circles were ringed by a broad walkway that held high tables and chairs on this floor and private booths—or so Kyle said, anyway—on the floor above.

I glanced down at Alexa again, and again, my head spun. I dared to run my fingers up her naked spine. In response, she bit my chin. A rush of wetness pooled between my legs. Every time I went out in these leather pants with her, I creamed the lining. Throwing caution to the wind, I swirled my fingers across her back in random patterns. I could take a few risks—we were in a public place. I wasn't in danger of losing it here.

Or was I? Not even twenty yards away, a vampire had backed his…date? victim? against the wall, and was sucking hard on her neck. I shivered, mostly at the raw carnality of the act. I had been to my fair share of crazy parties, but this one—where drinking someone else's blood seemed to be as acceptable as bumping and grinding—topped them all.

"You should definitely check out the upstairs at some point," shouted Kyle, who was hovering near my elbow. "It's a totally different perspective." He had turned into a valuable resource over the past few weeks—there were a few questions, particularly about the act of feeding, that Helen couldn't answer for me. But Kyle could. Sometimes, I even thought that we might be becoming friends. But then he would look at me with this undisguised longing on his face, and I'd remember what I was and what he wanted.

Below me, the water—lit from beneath—was a swirling rainbow of colors. Apparently, the pool was open for swimming at times; the glass circle would split in two and withdraw under the walkway, inviting patrons to shed their clothing and dive in. I shivered at the thought of Alexa undoing the simple knot at the back of her neck and letting her dress pool to the floor. Yeah. Good thing this wasn't that kind of party.

"Holy shit," Kyle hissed suddenly, as a tall man wearing a brilliant white suit stepped into my immediate field of vision. Shaggy dark hair fell across his forehead. He smiled lazily, in a way that probably charmed the pants off most women. And maybe even men—my gaydar didn't seem to work on him.

"Valentine Darrow," he said. "The new kid on the block." He extended his hand. "Sebastian Brenner."

Alexa disentangled herself from my embrace and regarded Sebastian with frank curiosity. "You own this place."

I raised my eyebrows. His name hadn't registered with me, but then again, I wasn't up on the club scene the way Alexa was. He looked only a few years older than us, which made owning one of the most exclusive establishments in the City an impressive feat.

He seemed bemused. "I do indeed. And you are?"

"Alexa Newland. And in case it's not obvious, I'm impressed." I loved Alexa's frank and honest approach to conversing with famous people. She didn't simper, flatter, or sugarcoat. Her straightforwardness had utterly confused my Machiavellian family when I'd first introduced her.

"I'm so glad that you're enjoying it," Sebastian replied to Alexa, but he was looking at me. Which was bizarre. Why would any man stare at me when he could be ogling her? Not that I wanted him to.

I curled one arm around Alexa's waist. "Have you met Kyle?" I said, who was practically vibrating next to me, presumably at his proximity to this big shot.

Sebastian glanced at him briefly before zeroing back in on me. "Ah, yes. One of Helen's playthings." He took my free hand. "Allow me to buy you both a drink."

As he ushered us toward a spiral staircase opposite from the bar, I looked over my shoulder at Kyle, trying to figure out whether to dig in my heels and chew out this arrogant bastard for the insult that he'd made. But Kyle didn't look upset. The second we moved away, another woman took my place at his side, and I watched her draw one bright red fingernail from his jaw to his collarbone. Eyes closing, he tipped back his head to give her more room to work with.

Sebastian hadn't been wrong. Kyle was a vampire chew toy.

I surveyed the clientele as the crowds parted for us. The vampires were fairly obvious, with their pale skin and human hangers-on. But then there were other humans who were clearly not food sources. They moved in groups or singly, sometimes interacting with the vampires, though never in a subservient way. More like two species of predators, coexisting in the jungle—separate but equal. And that's when I realized that the others weren't truly "human" at all. They were shifters. My analogy had been apt.

When we reached the top of the stairs, Sebastian bent his head to speak briefly to a woman wearing a floor-length satin gown and a fresh bite mark near one shoulder strap. The dress's deep blue color was identical to the wall paneling. Sebastian noticed me staring at the bite, and leaned in close.

"We vet our servers in more ways than one," he murmured against the shell of my ear. I couldn't hold back a shiver, and he laughed softly. I watched the woman weave her way through the throng of people to the chrome-plated bar, while he led us across the room. It was clever to employ someone who could both bring drinks on a tray and be a drink in and of herself. Clever, and diabolical. I squeezed Alexa's hand, more grateful than ever that she had insisted upon being my one and only. As we crossed onto the glass, I looked down at the crowd below, writhing to the thick electronic beat. Occasionally, the bodies would separate just long enough for me to see a flash of rainbow-tinted water. Surreal.

Sebastian paused at one of several alcoves, separated from the dance floor by a floor-to-ceiling black curtain. He flung the fabric aside, revealing the most luxurious booth I'd ever seen. Sliding gracefully onto one of the dark blue leather benches, he smoothed one hand over the chrome table in a proprietary gesture. Directly opposite the curtain, a window, cut the width of the table, looked down on the busy street below. I gestured for Alexa to precede me so that she could have the best view. No sooner had we settled ourselves than the server returned, bearing a tray full of drinks.

"I took the liberty of ordering one of our specialties for you both," Sebastian said. "It's called a Waltz on the Moon."

I cradled the stem of the cocktail glass and took a small sip. A subtle blend of fruit flavors flowed over my tongue: banana liqueur, a hint of apples…and was that lychee, too? I would have to ask one of the bartenders later. "It's very good."

Alexa had closed her eyes to taste it, and the sight of her savoring the concoction only heightened my need. I let my right hand rest on her thigh, just above her knee. "Mmm," she said. "Yes." I wasn't sure whether she was responding to my comment or my touch, but it didn't really matter.

I took another sip and then leaned toward Sebastian. "Tell me. Why are you giving us the VIP treatment?"

He laughed, throwing back the shot that the server had brought him with one practiced flick of his wrist. "Am I not allowed to be curious about the newest member of our little community?"

"You're no vampire," Alexa said, before I could. She frowned as she tried to figure him out.

But I already had. "What do you become, when you shift?"

He had just enough time to salute me with the empty glass before it was taken from him and replaced with a full one. "How did you guess?"

"You may not be a vampire, but you're not beneath them on the food chain, either."

He flashed his teeth at my assessment. "Technically, it is possible for a vampire to take blood from a shifter. But exceedingly rare." He shrugged. "The act of feeding usually triggers the change."

This was new information to file away. Remembering Darren's reaction to our assault, I could imagine that Weres in general didn't take well to being bitten. I looked him over again, trying to guess his animal half. He carried himself like a crown prince—confident in his superiority yet effortlessly charming. He didn't seem like a loner, so it was unlikely that he was a feline. But neither did he strike me as a dependent person who wouldn't feel whole without a pack.

"So if you were to bite me, Valentine," he said playfully, "it's likely that I would transform into a large black wolf before your very eyes, and tear out your throat."

Very deliberately, I leaned over to kiss Alexa's neck, just behind her ear. "Fortunately, you'll never have to test that theory."

He smirked. It looked good on him. "Never say never."

"How were you bitten?" Alexa asked. I glanced at her, wondering what she thought of this banter. The city lights illuminated her hair, making it glow.

Sebastian threw back his second shot, leaned against the wall, and crossed his arms over his chest. "I wasn't." He seemed pleased by our expressions of shock. "I'm a pureblood. Both of my parents are werewolves."

My brain was tripping over itself at the knowledge that the mutation caused by the lycanthropy virus could be inherited. At least this explained his superior attitude. "Have you been shifting since…the beginning?" I asked awkwardly. It was hard to visualize what would happen to a newborn werewolf on his first full moon.

"No. The transformation is triggered by puberty." He laced his fingers behind his head. "Enough about me. You're an intriguing—"

But we never got to hear exactly what I was that he found so fascinating, because at that moment, a stunning South Asian woman wearing a dark red sari ducked inside our booth and crouched next to Sebastian. She murmured something that I was unable to hear over the music, and Sebastian immediately got to his feet.

"I'm going to have to take my leave," he said as the woman stepped away. "Something has come up, and I need to attend to it immediately. I apologize." On anyone else, that might have sounded like an excuse, but he seemed genuinely regretful. "Please, feel free to stay in the booth. And your drinks are on the house."

"Take care," I said. And then he was gone, the curtain swaying in the aftermath of his departure.

I leaned back against the warm leather and fiddled with one of my cuff links. They were silver buttons—Alexa had given them to me for my birthday, along with the black silk button-up shirt that I had on right now. I ran my fingers along the hem of her dress, glad to finally be alone with her again. Sebastian was interesting, but his proprietary attitude was grating. The way he'd taken my hand downstairs, the way he had ordered our drinks…it almost felt as though he was treating us like escorts. I wanted to bring him down a peg.

"Do you want another round?" Alexa asked.

"Sure. Scotch?"

"My thoughts exactly."

I grinned at her wickedly. If we were on Crown Prince Sebastian's tab, then I was going to go all out. I pulled aside the curtain just enough to flag down a server, and ordered two of the finest scotches she could produce—ice in a glass on the side.

When the drinks arrived, Alexa picked out the most perfect ice cube she could find, dropped it into her glass, and crawled onto my lap. I groaned, my hands automatically going to her waist.

"You feel so damn good," I whispered, leaning in toward her.

"He wants you," she said.

I paused inches from her mouth. That was not the response I'd expected. "He wants me? No way. Men like him are not interested in women like me."

"You're wrong." Alexa bypassed my lips entirely and gently took my earlobe between her teeth. My rational brain was screaming at me to back off, but I couldn't stop my hips from bucking into her.

"Doesn't...matter," I managed. "Just. Want. You."

"Oh?" She pulled back to look at me. "Well, I want my scotch."

I barely managed to stifle a shiver; assertive Alexa made me weak in the knees, every time. I reached for her glass, swirled it once, and then held it to her mouth. She swallowed, licked her lips, and kissed me. I sucked the scotch from her tongue, and when she clutched my hair in both hands, I growled. Need welled up hot and fierce like magma, bursting into my blood. When she broke the kiss, I tried to complain— but she pushed two of her fingers into my mouth and switched her focus to my neck. She sucked hard on my pulse point and my heart tried to beat its way out of my chest. When she dug in her teeth, I groaned her name.

With one last nip at my tender skin, she eased her weight back until our eyes were level. "What do you need, Val?" Her voice was low and smoky, the words slow. Deliberate.

I was going out of my mind. "You. Need you. So bad."

"You're coming home with me tonight." It wasn't a request. The fear, the anxiety—all of it turned to ash beneath the blazing tide of my love for this woman. I looked into her fathomless eyes and found myself.

"Yes."

The cab ride home was a struggle to remain clothed. I pushed Alexa's dress up as high as I could without exposing her, teasing her smooth thighs with my fingertips until the heady aroma of her need was thick on the air. She retaliated by popping open each button of my shirt and pressing hot sucking kisses to the skin she revealed. I was going to have marks everywhere. I couldn't get enough.

We stumbled up the front steps and into the apartment, but Alexa didn't give me any time to reflect on how it felt to finally be home again. She dug her fingers beneath the waistband of my pants and tugged, pulling me into the bedroom.

"Watch," she commanded imperiously, her hands going to the complex knot at the nape of her neck. A moment later, the dress was a black puddle at her feet. Thirst ignited in my throat as I took in the pale lines of her naked body. I wanted her—all of her—with an intensity I'd never felt before. It was hard not to take control from her—not to press her into the wall and slide both my teeth and my fingers inside her body—but I forced myself to comply with her seduction. For now.

She divested me of my shirt and undid the button and zipper of my pants with her teeth. And then she pushed me backward until my hamstrings hit the edge of the bed. I toppled. She followed, crawling up my torso until our breasts were aligned. I squeezed her hips hard at the so-soft sensation. She slid one thigh between my legs and we rocked together—hands stroking and bodies melding—until sweat slicked between us.

"Need you, need you," I gasped, clutching hard at her shoulders in an effort to get closer—to warm all the places inside me that had frozen without this. I had been so foolish. This passion was at the very heart of us, and to deny it, to refuse to feed it, was worse than folly—it was sacrilege.

"I'm right here," she said against my lips before moving back down the length of my body. "I love you, Valentine. And I need you. I need us—like this, always." One hand remained at my breasts, twisting and tugging, connecting twin points of fire. And then she dipped her head and made love to me with her mouth, drinking me in. I the chalice, she the priestess. Helpless, I could do nothing but sob out her name in relief, in ecstasy, in love.

I shouted my triumph, my surrender, as the world turned to molten flame.

When I opened my eyes, she was lying next to me, lightly running her fingers through the sweat-dampened hair at my brow. She smiled brilliantly. "Welcome home, love."

Home. Yes, this was home—not this shabby apartment on the Lower East Side, but Alexa. I was driven by one imperative now: to claim her as my own in all possible ways. To hold nothing back. To come to her as wholly myself and to be embraced, body and soul. Galvanized, I rolled on top of her and bent my head to her breasts. Beyond words, there was this: the salt-cut sweetness of her skin, the low whimper that caught in her mouth, the frantic glide of her heat against my stomach. It was hard, so hard, to make my mouth soft against her when the thirst flared, goading me to sink my teeth in and take. But not yet. Instead, I flattened my hand between us and filled her.

I kissed my name off her lips, cupping her face gently with my other hand. My arm rose and fell in a strong rhythm—I the tide and she the moon. My heart was bursting, seeping gold, shedding its old skin and donning a new. When she was beyond the ability to return my kisses, I pulled away just enough to look into her soul.

You are my home, I told her silently. *Not this place, but you. You— my anchor, my lodestone, my sunrise. My ambrosia.*

Trembling as though she could hear my thoughts, she threw back her head. My gaze dropped to her neck—to the pulse thundering beneath her skin. "Take me," she groaned, driving herself down on my fingers. "Do. It. Val—"

Finally, I gave myself over to instinct, sheathing my teeth in her jugular in one powerful, surging motion. Her scream was staccato, the air suddenly forced from her lungs as her smooth muscles contracted around my hand. I drank without remorse, savoring the aromatic richness of her blood as she leaned her forehead against my shoulder, gasping. Bearing down hard against her thigh, I groaned into her skin as the ecstasy found me a second time.

Finally, her body quieted. As intoxicated as I was by the very essence of her sliding down my throat, I managed to pull away. She shuddered at the sensation of my teeth leaving her, and I tenderly stroked the back of her head with one hand.

"Where's the ointment, baby?" I asked, letting my tongue dart out to catch the blood that was still welling up from each tiny wound. So good. Blindly, she fumbled with the drawer of the nightstand before handing me a fresh tube.

"Prepared, I see," I said as I quickly smeared the oily paste over the bite.

She kissed my temple. "Just hopeful." She stretched, throwing her arms around my neck. "I should have seduced you two weeks ago. That was so much better than you biting me in a sterile room with the world looking on."

I completed the job with a Band-Aid and pulled back just enough to meet her gaze. "Does it bother you that my thirst gets all tangled up with, you know, wanting you?"

She smoothed the hair back from my eyes and gently kissed my lips. "Not in the slightest. And in case you haven't noticed, I react pretty strongly to your teeth in my skin."

I shivered at the promise in her voice and leaned down to press a kiss behind her ear. "You're amazing, you know that? So. Fucking Amazing."

"And you," she said, punctuating each word with a kiss, "are mine."

We yanked back the covers then, and slid beneath them. Alexa cuddled close immediately, and didn't stop moving until she was lying half on top of me. For the first time since I'd come home from the hospital, I felt at peace. There was no trace of the incessant low-grade panic that had been tearing up my stomach like an ulcer. I was complete.

CHAPTER TEN

But even Alexa's embrace couldn't protect me from the nightmare. The next morning, I woke, gasping and sweating, from the memory of my leg crumpling beneath me as I tried to run. Blinking in the warm light that filtered through the blinds, I pressed the heel of my palm over my racing heart until it began to calm. Fortunately, I hadn't woken Alexa. She had turned onto her back during the night and was snoring lightly. Adorable. My fingers itched to brush away the dark smudges under her eyes.

I rolled out of bed cautiously so as not to disturb her and pulled on a pair of sweats and a T-shirt. Somehow, while brushing my teeth, I migrated from the bathroom sink to the doorway so that I could continue watching her sleep. I couldn't stop smiling, which made me drool toothpaste onto the floor.

"You were really stupid for staying away," I admonished my reflection, once I had spat and rinsed.

Finally, I decided that I could tear myself away from her long enough to prepare breakfast ingredients for whenever she woke. I was thinking omelet. A huge, cheesy, ham-and-veggie-laden omelet, chock full of everything that her body so desperately needed to replenish what I was taking. Maybe now that her prodigal chef had returned, she'd put on some weight.

Ten minutes later, I was chopping up a red pepper and humming along to my favorite U2 album when a knock came at the door. I glanced at the clock over the oven and frowned. Who the hell would be visiting us at ten a.m. on a Saturday? Keeping the chain on, I cracked the door. The tall man standing behind it was probably the last person I would have expected.

"Penn?" I undid the chain and let in Jack Pennington, my father's head of security. Dread punched me in the gut as my brain cycled through the potential reasons for him being here. "Is my father—"

"He's fine," Penn said brusquely, and I sighed in relief. Despite my complete disillusionment with everything my father stood for, he was still my dad. A part of me would always care.

"You look like you're making a smooth recovery, Val," Penn said as he took a seat on my couch and set his briefcase on my coffee table. He looked like a former NFL linebacker—strong and huge, but starting to go soft. His thinning salt and pepper hair was cut in a military style. He probably would have seemed intimidating if I hadn't known him since I was six years old.

"Alexa's taking good care of me." I could never resist flaunting my queerness in front of my father and his cronies, despite the fact that it was a juvenile move—like poking your older siblings repeatedly until they blew up in your face.

Penn didn't answer. Instead, he flicked open the briefcase to reveal a gun. The weapon was sleek and black. My first thought was that he had come to kill me, and I was a fucking idiot for being so trusting. Adrenaline blazed down my spine, and I took a step backward, hoping that he wouldn't realize Alexa was home. I couldn't fight—the enhancing effects of her blood had worn off by now. In the wake of my attack, why hadn't I decided to learn a martial art? Why was I still so helpless?

But then he gestured toward the weapon, palms up, and I realized that something else entirely was going on, here. "Fucking hell, Penn," I muttered breathlessly. "You should warn a mugging victim before busting out a gun."

Naturally, he found this funny. "After what has happened, it's good that you're paranoid." He ran one thick finger along the barrel in a loving gesture that really creeped me out. "The Colt M1911A1—single-action and semiautomatic. The gun of the Armed Forces for decades, until it was replaced in the nineties by the Italian piece of shit Beretta." Penn looked like he wanted to spit on my carpeting. Thankfully, he refrained. "Compliments of your father, who wants you to be able to defend yourself."

I didn't feel like admitting that I'd just been thinking along those same lines a split second ago. "Wow, you know, thanks ever so much for this. Daddy dearest sure knows how to make a girl feel loved and cherished. What says 'get well soon' better than a fucking gun, one whole month after the incident?"

"Your father is a busy man, Val," Penn said, unsmiling. "He's doing what he believes necessary to keep you safe." From a folder in the top pocket of the briefcase, he extracted a manila envelope. "Fifteen lessons at the firing range on Twentieth, between Fifth and Sixth. And the certification necessary to own any weapon you want."

Any weapon? That seemed extreme. I'd never touched a gun in my life, and before thirty seconds ago, I had never wanted to. But as I continued to stare at it, I felt myself becoming more and more curious. The damn thing attracted me on some level. Unlike a Were, I was inherently defenseless—unless I was hyped up on blood. Sure, I could sink my teeth in if a person got close enough, but it wouldn't be hard for them to wrestle me off. By now, thanks to Alexa, I was probably slightly stronger than the average woman, but that certainly didn't mean anything against someone like the rogue vampire who had attacked me. I had the potential to be one hell of a sprinter, though that was meaningless if I were injured the way I had been in that alley.

But a gun—a gun would even the odds. It was a no-frills weapon— sleek, mean, deadly. I wondered if it was heavy. My fingers twitched, but fortunately, I managed to rein in the impulse before my hand moved. Most of me didn't want to accept this gift. Damn it, I deserved better from my father than a visit from his lackey.

Or did I? If I were being honest, I had pushed him away just as much as he'd pushed me. I looked at the Colt logo embossed on the gun, then over at Penn. "Ooh," I said, trying to be flippant. "A picture of a horsie. That's my favorite part." But he didn't roll his eyes. He smiled, as though he knew what I was actually thinking.

"Try it once," he said as he rose from the couch.

I shrugged, not wanting to commit. But I knew I would.

"I'll tell him that you're doing okay," he said, his hand on the doorknob. I knew he would do exactly that: Valentine's doing fine, sir, he would say. But in this moment, it didn't feel right.

"Tell him thanks."

Penn, halfway out the door, nodded once. When he was gone, I turned back to the pistol. I really did want to hold it, so I crossed over to the table and lifted it into my left palm. It was heavy—heavier than I'd expected, anyway. The checkered texture of the grip was rough against my palm. I just stood there, cradling it in my hand, afraid to do anything else. While I doubted that it was loaded, I didn't want to find out the hard way.

And that's when Alexa walked into the room in nothing but my ·Bon Jovi T-shirt, rubbing her eyes. God, she had nice legs. Just looking at her made me want to—

She suddenly came to a halt, and her mouth rounded into an "O." "Valentine," she said in that quiet voice that meant she was on either the edge of panic or a blow-out. "Why are you holding a gun?"

I lowered it back into the briefcase and snapped the lid shut. "You just missed Penn," I said, taking a seat on the couch and holding out my arms.

She still looked suspicious, but perched next to me nonetheless. "Your father's security guy?"

"Yeah. He was passing along a present from Dad." I pointed to the briefcase.

"How thoughtful," she muttered, calming down enough to shift her weight so that she could recline against one armrest and rest her legs in my lap. I immediately began to massage her calf muscles. She closed her eyes and let out a tiny moan, and I sighed happily.

"Good morning," I whispered.

"Mmm." She opened one eye, and the opposite corner of her mouth curved slightly. "You're hot."

I laughed. "You just noticed?"

"What are you going to do with it?"

I frowned at the non sequitur before realizing that her brain had ping-ponged back to the damn gun. She was tough to keep up with, sometimes. "Do you know how to shoot one?" I countered.

"Harder," she said, and I dug my fingertips more firmly into her muscle. The moan reemerged, but louder this time. "And yes. Wisconsin farm girl, remember? Good with shotgun. Older brothers."

"Not so good with complete sentences, though," I teased. When she stuck out her tongue, I started throbbing.

"Answer my question, vampire."

"He paid for fifteen lessons at some firing range here in Manhattan," I said. "I guess I'll take them."

"Mmm." Alexa bent one knee so that her heel was pressing firmly against the crotch of my sweats. I tried not to make a noise, but failed. "You need to take me. Now."

"O-okay." It was hard to maintain any kind of coherent idea when she was swiveling her foot against me, but... "But I was going to make you an omelet. You need to, oh God, to eat more, and—"

She shifted her legs off me, and I groaned in disappointment. And then she was straddling me, anchoring my head to the back of the couch with the strong grip of her fingers in my hair. Slowly, she licked her lips.

"Fucking now," she whispered, bending toward me. When I skimmed my hands up her sides, she shivered beneath my touch. That was the only signal I needed; in another second, she was lying on her back and I was looming over her, my thigh pressed hard between her legs. Flipping her was such a rush.

I leaned in close to trail my tongue from her clavicle up her neck to swirl around her earlobe. "Omelets later," I agreed.

We didn't leave the apartment that day. Or the next. Mostly, we slept, made love, and half watched movies. Neither of us turned on our computers the whole weekend. The outside world was irrelevant. But all too soon, Monday intruded.

I was in a cab, heading to the Consortium's facility to pick up a few changes of clothes that I'd been keeping in "my" room—which, thankfully, I didn't need anymore, when my phone rang. Alexa.

"Hey, baby," I said, saturating my voice with all the warmth that I could manage, remembering how incredible it had felt to wake up that morning to the sensation of her arm curled around my waist. I hadn't taken her for granted before, but I really wasn't going to now.

"Val." Her voice was tight and urgent. "It's...it's Olivia. She's been attacked—I just saw it on the news."

"What?" Instantly, my brain made the link to my own mugging. A dozen questions flew through my head, from how badly she was injured, to how in the hell I was going to be able to put up with her drooling over Alexa for all eternity. That last one wasn't charitable at all, but my neurons were indiscriminate.

"She was mugged," Alexa continued, corroborating what I had already guessed. "And she lost a lot of blood."

"Fuck. Where is she?"

"Tisch."

"Okay. Thanks. I'll go see her right now, before class."

"Val…" Alexa's voice quavered on the single syllable, and my heart contracted furiously. She was scared. "Do you—do you think it's all connected somehow? You and Olivia being in the same social circle…"

"My God. Like a terrorist attack?" It was certainly possible, given her father's status as the Senate majority leader and my father's role as the head of the Treasury. But when Alexa's breathing sped up, I abandoned my speculation. "Hey. It's going to be okay. I'm going to talk to Detective Foster as soon as I can, all right? In case she hasn't made the connection between me and Olivia. And who knows, maybe this is a coincidence."

"Yeah. Yeah. Okay." She paused for a moment. "I didn't want to let you out of my sight this morning, but it's much worse now."

"For me, too," I said fervently. "Be careful. I love you. I love you."

"I love you, too. So much."

When she ended the call, I felt bereft. I stared at my phone for a moment before thumbing through its menu to launch the Web browser. While it connected to the Net, I gave the cab driver new instructions: NYU's Tisch Medical Center. I would get my stuff from the Consortium facility later, after my classes—which, conveniently for me, were located in the building adjacent to where Olivia was at this moment presumably battling for her life. Damn it.

The article was prominent on the front page of the *Times* online. Olivia had been the victim of a "brutal mugging" on Friday night; having been "savagely beaten," she was in stable but critical condition. Friday night. That meant I'd seen her a scant few hours before she had been attacked. God.

I leaned my head back against the faux leather of the back seat and tried to figure out why a terrorist organization might arrange for someone to turn the children of prominent politicians into vampires, but was no closer to coming up with a viable explanation by the time the cab pulled into the circle in front of the hospital. I was probably barking up the wrong tree, anyway. I paid the driver and dug my ID from my coat pocket as the automatic doors parted for me. Wearing this, I could probably get access to Olivia even if she wasn't taking visitors.

A nurse told me that she was on the ninth floor, so I rode the elevator up. When I neared her room, I slowed down to scope out who was inside. Sure enough, both her mother and father were sleeping in two chairs near the head of the hospital bed. Olivia was covered in a mountain of blankets, and had needles in both of her arms. She looked pale and fragile. I shivered, seeing an echo of my past self.

And then I got angry. Whoever was doing this was a monster, and I wanted to see him thwarted at every turn. Why the hell hadn't the Consortium stopped him, yet? How hard could it be? Did they just not care? Wasn't he, every time he tried to turn someone, threatening to expose them…us? I hadn't been able to feel this kind of rage when it had been me lying in that bed; coping, surviving, had taken every last ounce of energy at my disposal. But watching Olivia take shallow, raspy breaths made me grind my teeth. Was the parasite systematically devouring her red blood cells, even now?

"Valentine?"

I turned, unsurprised to hear that familiar accent. "Dr. Clavier. I should have known you'd be here." Without waiting for him to comment, I gestured toward Olivia. "Did he turn her?"

Clavier shook his head once. "He appears to have failed. The police reports indicate that he was interrupted in the act. She didn't lose as much blood as you did."

Relief eased my jaw muscles. No one deserved this curse. With Clavier at my heels, I stepped into the room and quietly approached the foot of the bed. Olivia opened her eyes, one of which was badly swollen and bruised. Even so, she managed to look surprised.

"That's a nice shiner you've got there," I told her, deciding to take the liberty of inspecting her chart.

She blinked and winced. "Val?" she croaked. "You're…but I thought I was your…arch-nemesis or something."

Maybe it was because Olivia was badly injured and I felt a kind of empathy with her now. Or maybe it was because I had spent the weekend in Alexa's arms. Regardless of the cause, I felt pretty awful for the way I'd treated her on Friday.

"Not unless you want to be," I said quietly. "I'm sorry for being such a jackass on Friday—I was having a monumentally bad day." I looked down and continued scanning her chart. "You know, I would have given you a tour of the med school if you'd asked—you didn't have to go to such lengths."

"You're…a laugh riot."

I could tell that speaking took a significant amount of effort; unsurprising in someone who had sustained head trauma similar to mine, and was also having trouble taking a deep breath on account of three badly bruised ribs. That fucking bastard.

"You need anything? Ice chips?" Clavier could run all the tests he wanted; this was my version.

"Pain meds?" she whispered hopefully. In that moment, I was completely convinced that she was not a vampire. The pain all over my body had never ranked over the thirst in my throat.

Clavier stepped out from behind me. "I'll ring for the nurse," he said. Olivia immediately looked relieved. In the chair nearest me, her mother stirred.

"I'm going to go," I said. "Class, you know. But uh…feel better, okay?"

"Yeah. Thanks, Val."

I checked my watch as I walked back down the hallway toward the bank of elevators—twenty minutes until class, an hour in class, and then I'd finally have the rest of the day to myself. That was good, because I needed to do some major research over at the Consortium. I didn't care how good an investigator Devon Foster was—she couldn't help but fumble in the dark over this case. I rounded the corner, preoccupied by my planning, and literally slammed into the detective herself. She winced and took a quick step back, then frowned in suspicion as she recognized me.

"Valentine? What are you doing here?"

"I know Olivia," I said bluntly, dispensing with a hello. I still wasn't over the way she'd looked at Alexa. Drinking from her hadn't quelled the increased possessiveness I'd been feeling ever since my attack. Maybe intense jealousy was another vampiric attribute. I'd have to ask Helen. "She and I have run in the same social circles since we were young. I was going to call you, to tell—"

"We're well aware," Foster snapped.

I arched my eyebrows. "All right then." I turned back toward the elevators, but she stopped me with a hand on my forearm.

"Look, I'm sorry," she said. "It's been a rough weekend. As you can imagine, there's even more pressure now to get this case squared away."

I turned back to her and nodded. My temper worked the same way, after all, flaring up over nothing when I was under stress. "What can I do to help?" As if I didn't know better than she did.

Foster spread her hands out in front of her, palms up. They were callused, probably from weights at a gym. "If you remember anything else..."

"You're always the first to know."

"Thank you. Really." She smiled halfheartedly and then turned toward Olivia's room. I found myself eyeing her gun, cradled in a hip holster today, as she walked away. I wondered if there was some part of her that hoped she got to kill this guy herself—to take him out, instead of bringing him in.

And then I wondered if deep down, that's what I wanted as well.

❖

The Consortium had a lounge on the facility's top floor, sporting a 360-degree view of midtown. Comfortable chairs were arranged in clusters near the windows, and a bar took up the center of the room. The bartender had been serving drinks since 1881. During my self-imposed separation from Alexa, I had often come up here at night to drink a scotch and brood over the city lights. It was a good place to think.

As soon as my Neuroanatomy class finished, I called Kyle to ask him to meet me there. When I arrived, I found him catnapping in one of the chairs. His face was ashen, and an ugly bruise peeked out from under the collar of his button-down shirt.

"Hey," I said, crouching next to him and placing a gentle hand on his arm. "Are you all right?"

He opened bleary eyes and blinked several times before he was able to focus enough to recognize me. "Hey, Val. Yeah. I'm okay." He gripped the edge of his chair and pulled himself out of his slumped position. "Helen was thirsty last night."

"Jesus," I breathed, feeling the skin on the back of my neck start to crawl. Right then and there, I made a vow never to do that to Alexa—to take so much that she could barely sit up. Never. "I'm sorry, Kyle. I didn't realize. You should sleep, and—"

"No," he insisted. "I'm good. Really. What's going on?"

I was worried that the only reason Kyle had agreed to meet me in his current state was that he hoped to get in my good graces so that I'd deign to suck on his neck someday. Something else that was never going to happen.

"I need to know everything I can possibly know about this rogue vampire," I said, taking the chair next to his.

Kyle looked dubious. "That's all anybody's been talking about since Saturday morning. Helen deployed a team to hunt him down almost two months ago, but they haven't come up with anything. I don't think there's much to know—he seems really good at giving everyone the slip." He looked at me sideways. "You still don't…remember?"

I sighed in frustration. "Just flashes. Not nearly enough to be helpful." I stretched my feet out in front of me and watched the afternoon sunlight glint off the Chrysler Building. "I know the woman he attacked this weekend, and seeing her lying there like that, like I was…I just want to do something."

Kyle was staring off into space. I wondered if he had fallen asleep with his eyes open. "You could always try the Red Circuit," he said suddenly.

"The what?"

On top of looking like death warmed over, Kyle now seemed ill at ease. "I don't know if you're aware of this, but that party at Luna was very upscale. Classy and relatively tame. The Red Circuit is completely different. I've never been myself, but everyone says that those parties are savage. Brutal." He turned to look me in the eye. "Someone like this rogue vamp, though—that might be his thing."

I nodded, afraid that he was right on the money. While the idea of this Red Circuit might be morbidly fascinating, it also frightened me. I didn't want to acknowledge my own inner monster, not to mention someone else's. "Surely Helen would send people there to investigate."

He shrugged again. "I don't think that would do much good, unless he's bragging about the people he's killed—or turned."

"And if they haven't caught him by now, then he's not that stupid," I finished for him. I didn't say the other thing that had suddenly popped into my head: the notion that if I could be in the same room with the rogue vampire—if I could see him—then maybe I'd be able to recognize him.

Kyle rested one hand lightly on mine. I blinked at him, surprised; he rarely touched anyone unless they touched him first. "I'm pretty sure Helen knows where they are each week, but she won't tell me. I met someone the other night at Luna who might be able to get me in, though."

"Is there enough room for me to tag along?"

Kyle leaned back in his chair. "I'll work on it."

I rested a hand on his shoulder as I stood. "Thank you."

"Say hi to Alexa for me," he called softly as I turned to leave.

I closed my eyes during the cab ride home in an effort to sort through the jumble of thoughts in my brain. I had no doubt that the Red Circuit would be profoundly disturbing, but it also sounded promising. Whatever the rogue vampire's motivation, he was clearly a sadist, and a party where even the veneer of civility was discarded seemed like exactly the kind of entertainment he'd look for.

"Hey, lov—mmph!" No sooner had I stepped into the apartment than Alexa's arms were around my neck, her lithe body pressing me up against the wall next to the door. She kissed me fiercely and I met her with all the love and passion in me, wrapping the thick strands of her hair around my fingers and urging her even closer than she already was.

When she finally pulled away, licking her lips, I was gasping for air. I watched as she closed the door and set the bolt and chain. She kept one hand on my stomach the entire time, stroking my abs through the fabric of my sweater.

"You okay, baby?" I asked, once I had my breath back.

She led me to the couch; I lay down and she snuggled in on top of me. "It was so hard being away from you today."

"Yeah. For me, too." I ran my palms firmly down her back and she hummed deep in her throat.

"How's Olivia?"

I settled in on her lower back, massaging in small, tight circles. It felt so good to touch her. "She's okay. Awake. And not a vampire."

"Oh?"

"Apparently he got interrupted. Didn't have time to do enough... damage." She felt my wince and kissed my chin.

We lay there for a good half hour—me gently working out the tension in her muscles and telling her about everything I'd learned, and her punctuating my narrative with the occasional question. While she listened, she rested her head over my heart. When I got to the part about the Red Circuit, her grip on me tightened.

"That sounds awful," she whispered. And then she raised her head to glare at me. "You're not going. You're not even contemplating going. Right?"

Her insistence didn't faze me—I knew I'd feel exactly the same way if our roles were reversed. "I might be able to recognize him if I did," I said quietly.

"Hell no. Hell no." Alexa grasped my head in both hands. "Because he'll definitely recognize you, Val, and what do you suppose he'll do then?"

That was true. She was right. He would know that I'd want vengeance. "I hadn't thought of that," I admitted.

"You really won't, right?" she pressed. "Maybe there's a way to tell Detective Foster?"

My jaw clenched as I had a sickening epiphany. "They wouldn't let her live," I realized out loud. "Not whoever's in charge of that party… and I bet not the Consortium, either."

"Shit," Alexa whispered.

I sat up then, rearranging us so that my back was to the couch and she was straddling my lap. "Kyle might have a way in for me," I said softly. "He's looking into it."

Her eyes narrowed. I met them without flinching. "If you go, I go," she said finally.

"That's craz—"

She pushed one finger against my lips, halting my protests. "You listen to me. We are a team—so much stronger together than apart. Have you really not learned your lesson by now, after everything that's happened? Really?"

I shook my head, even as I realized that trying to convince her to stay would be useless. "Weren't you listening? From everything Kyle's heard, this place is going to be chaos!"

But she showed no sign of backing down. "Either I go, or you don't."

"Okay," I finally conceded, both frightened for her safety and relieved that we could watch each other's backs. "Thank you."

Fortunately, my stomach growled at that moment, lightening

the mood. She leaned in and grazed my jawline with her teeth before whispering, "Hungry?" into my ear.

I shivered, but didn't surrender. "Mmm," I whispered back, letting my hands drift down to her hips. "What if I'm thirsty?"

Alexa yanked the neck of her sweatshirt down over one shoulder. "Have a drink, then."

Arousal and need slammed into me. At the jolt that ran through my body, Alexa smiled. She caressed the back of my neck, then pulled me forward until my mouth rested against the soft skin at the juncture of her shoulder and torso. Saliva flooded my mouth as I traced her warm skin with my tongue.

And then I bit down. The rush was instantaneous—hot, thick, rich—and I swallowed to the sound of her low moan. Fuck, this was hot. So. Damn. Hot. So—

The images flooded my brain, a kaleidoscope of agony: *rain in my eyes and vomit coating my tongue and his laugh ringing in my ears. The burn of the knife pinning my arm to the earth. I knew I was going to die. Olivia, pale and bruised, covered by a mound of white blankets. "Please," I tried to whisper, but gagged on the blood trickling into the back of my throat.*

I snarled as the vision unfolded, barely registering Alexa's flinching movement.

"Easy, love, easy," she said, her voice strained in a way I'd never quite heard before. But it was only when her fingertips brushed against my cheek that I finally had the sense to pull away. I came back to myself, rather than the dark alley: to the sight of Alexa, left hand pressing into her right shoulder in an attempt to slow the blood, her teeth clenched in pain.

"What the hell," I muttered, horrified at myself. Jumping up and going to the kitchen, I moistened a fresh washrag and hurried back to clean the blood both from her arm and palm. She watched me silently, and I felt the panic return to my gut.

"What just happened?" she asked, once I had fixed her newest Band-Aid in place.

I leaned back against the couch and grabbed a fistful of cloth in each hand. "I saw him, in my head. It was like I was back there, feeling it all over again for the first time." When I shuddered, Alexa moved back into her original position and wrapped her arms around my neck.

"Why, do you think?"

I rubbed my cheek lightly against her hair, struggling to hold myself together against the riptide of despair that was threatening to engulf me. How had I lost control? How had I been so absorbed that I'd hurt her? What did this mean? I had finally dared to hope that we could make this work, that we'd be okay. Was I doomed to be bad for her forever, no matter what we tried?

"Don't know," I said hoarsely. I thought back to what had flashed before my mind's eye: the attack, and Olivia. "Maybe…maybe it was seeing Olivia, in the hospital?"

She kissed me lightly. "Oh, love. I wish I could have been there with you. I can't imagine how hard it must have been, to see her like that. To remember."

I shook my head. Why was Alexa trying to comfort me, when I had just practically attacked her? It made no sense. I felt like I was going to be sick. "I hurt you," I whispered, feeling the heat rise behind my eyes as I fought the urge to cry.

"It's fine. It really is. Look at me."

One tear spilled out when I did. She caught it on her forefinger. "You've had that bastard in your thoughts all day, love," she pointed out. "It's no wonder that he popped into your mind." She cradled my head against her neck and I took a few deep breaths. She smelled so good, so warm. So vibrant. So alive. I could have—

Like clockwork, her grip on me tightened. "If you're thinking about leaving me again, then you'd better quit it. Right now."

I pulled back, not even bothering to wipe the moisture from my face. "I can't leave you again," I said, hoping that my voice conveyed the deadly seriousness that I felt. "It was a mistake the first time. I don't think I'd survive a second."

Suddenly restless, I got to my feet. Usually, I was a fan of talking through whatever problems were confronting us, but I suddenly wanted nothing more than to forget this had ever happened. "Are you getting hungry? How 'bout I cook us some dinner?"

"Okay," she said, but didn't let me escape to the kitchen. Or rather, she escaped there, too. Within a few minutes, she was bumping my hip with hers as she chopped vegetables and shared the latest gossip from her peers.

She seemed perfectly fine. And she was probably right about the source of my disconcerting flashback; all day, I'd been obsessing about how to bring the rogue vampire to justice. So I kept up the best happy façade that I could muster, for both our sakes.

Deep down, though, I couldn't help but continue to worry over the fragile equilibrium we had just managed to find.

CHAPTER ELEVEN

The car picked us up promptly at 10:30 outside of our apartment. It was a nondescript black Honda. When Alexa and I slid into the back, Kyle turned around from the driver's seat.

"Valentine, Alexa, meet Monique."

I reached across the gap to take the cool hand of the beautiful vampire who had homed in on Kyle at Luna, after Sebastian dragged Alexa and me away. Her honey-colored curls hung in tiny corkscrews down to her shoulders, and her long, dark fingernails matched the shade of her fur coat.

"Pleasure," I said, even though she creeped me out—particularly the way her predatory gaze lingered on Alexa. I wrapped my free arm around Alexa's shoulders, pulling her close. Mine.

"Hello." Monique seemed uninterested in me, withdrawing her hand quickly from my grip and stroking her fingers through the close-cropped hair on the back of Kyle's neck. "Take the Williamsburg Bridge."

"Looks like we're going to Brooklyn," Alexa whispered as Kyle headed out on Avenue C toward Delancey. I nodded, settling in for the drive with my hand on Alexa's knee. Apparently, the location of the Red Circuit shifted each week. Information about its whereabouts was top secret. I wondered about the distribution channels: did news of a party spread by word of mouth? Or was there some other mechanism?

We didn't speak much as Monique guided Kyle along the Brooklyn waterfront. I tried to steel myself for what I might see tonight, but the uncertainty was far more anxiety-producing than any facts would have been. "Brutal," Kyle had heard. What was the definition of "brutality" for those who lived by drinking the blood of others? The rogue vampire had called his bloody assault on me "beautiful." I nervously picked at a thread on my down jacket, suddenly wishing that I'd thought to bring my gun. But that would have been fruitless—I hadn't gone to the firing range yet and had no idea how to use it well. If I saw him, I would call Helen. She would know how to bring him in.

"The Steiner Studios?" Alexa was leaning forward, her face almost pressed against the glass. She turned toward me, one perfectly manicured eyebrow arched in a mixture of surprise and amusement. "There's a clandestine vampire party at the Steiner Studios?"

I glanced over at Monique, wondering if the question would offend her, but she didn't even acknowledge it. Instead, she directed Kyle to a parking spot. When we got out, she didn't so much as pause to appreciate the sparkling beauty of the Manhattan skyline—a metropolitan Narcissus admiring its own reflection in the East River. Monique headed straight for Sound Stage Four, and we followed in her wake.

There were no guards posted at the outer door. The inner door was attended only by one woman, who immediately stepped forward and tried to offer Monique some sort of ticket. She waved it away. "We're here for the fights," she said. "Out back, I presume?"

"The fights?" Alexa whispered, but I shook my head. I didn't know what was going on here any more than she did.

"Yes. Go straight through—you'll see the signs." The woman threw open the door, revealing a sprawling space, crisscrossed above by catwalks. At the far end, a massive stage was overshadowed by a dramatic urban backdrop—New York as it must have looked during the Great Depression. In striking counterpoint to the period feel of the scenery, a DJ and several nearly naked dancers commanded the stage. But I barely spared them a glance. Monique was on the move. She strode purposefully through the crowd that had gathered in the staging area and we crowded behind her like sheep. When she drew even with the bar—clearly constructed just a few hours ago from spare plywood—she paused and turned to Kyle.

"Get me a drink, then meet me outside." She pointed to an exit sign. "That way." And then she turned to me. "See to it that no one else touches him."

Kyle willingly obliged, shouldering his way through to the bartender, but I stared after Monique, disturbed that she thought she could order me around that way. Then again, we were in her debt. And she was older than I was. The ageless, I had noticed, were somewhat obsessed with their own longevity. Lived time had a lot of cachet.

"'See to it that no one touches him?'" Alexa repeated, pressing close to me. I wrapped my arms around her and took comfort from her familiar scent. "How are you supposed to do that?"

"I have no idea," I said, watching as Kyle returned with an elaborate cocktail and three beers. He passed two of them to us.

"This place is sweet!" he said eagerly, gaze darting around the room. "I wonder what film they just made in here. And check out that stage—think they only let the pros dance up there, or will we get a chance, too?"

"No idea," I said, catching several vampires in the act of looking Kyle up and down, as though he were a gourmet snack. Which, given the fact that he basically belonged to the Master of New York, wasn't far from the truth. "But we should get outside, huh? Give Monique her drink?"

"Yeah. We can always come back in here later."

Thankfully, we hustled toward the exit sign and didn't meet with any opposition along the way. As we stepped into the night, a chill breeze rose off the water, and I felt glad of my winter coat. The area we had just entered must, I imagined, normally serve as an assembly point for materials that would later make it onto the stage itself. For tonight, though, the outdoor space, bordered by a tall fence, had been converted into an arena. A sense of dread opened in my chest as I realized that this must be the site of Monique's "fights."

The women stuck out in the mostly male crowd, and I spotted Monique with little effort. She was standing by a crude plywood stall that had been labeled "Bookie." Now, the disinterest she'd shown the club portion of the Circuit made sense. For Monique, this event was all about betting. But on what, exactly?

We joined Kyle as he jostled through the crowd toward Monique. I scanned the faces before me warily, afraid of my own reaction if I recognized my attacker. Alexa's warm presence at my back was simultaneously a comfort and an anxiety. At least there were more shifters than vampires out here—I didn't have to worry about Weres lusting after Alexa's blood. Not while they were in human form, anyway.

When we reached Monique, she accepted her drink without a word of thanks. "Go find me a place close to the action," she said, pointing to where the crowd was thickest. "On that side."

Ever obliging, Kyle persistently worked his way toward the spot Monique had indicated. As we drew closer, it became possible to see the arena itself—just a circle of concrete formed by a thin line of chalk and the throng of not-so-human bodies. Within, two men, each wearing only a pair of shorts, were stretching. One looked middle-aged—silver-haired and distinguished. The other was younger, with a thick dark mane that flowed down to his shoulders. Both of them were strong, fit, and apparently unfazed by the cold.

Epiphany struck. "Those aren't humans, are they?"

Kyle shook his head slowly. "I've heard of this, but never seen it. Dogfighting."

Alexa pressed closer, and I drew her in front of me so that I could hold her. "What does that entail?" she asked.

At that moment, a sharp whistle pierced the air. "I think we're about to find out."

Monique joined us as the referee—a tall, thin woman wearing a bomber jacket with a rifle strapped across her shoulders—held up the hand of each man in turn. It was just like a boxing match: she shouted their names and the crowd applauded. But unlike a boxing match, when she finally blew the whistle, each man dropped to his knees.

Their outlines began to blur. A hush fell, so profound that it was possible to hear a choked-off groan from the silver-haired man, and the harsh, panting breaths of his opponent. This part of the fight, I realized, was in many ways a race: to see who could transform first. The process was happening faster than it had with Darren, and I wondered whether that was because these men were actively encouraging their beasts to come forth.

I cringed as the younger man's spine arched at an impossible angle…and suddenly, he was no longer a man. But his opponent was only a second behind. Clutching Alexa's waist tightly, I watched in awe as both contenders met in the center of the ring.

The wolves were gray and black. They circled each other, lips pulled back over razor teeth as they snapped and growled. The breathless pause of the crowd was broken by dozens of voices at once, each shouting the name of their champion—inciting him on, driving him mad. When Monique put her fingers to her lips and issued a piercing whistle, the wolves' ears flickered. The gray wolf lunged first, trying to get hold of his rival's throat, but the black wolf was agile and dodged the attack. A well-aimed swipe at the older wolf's haunches drew first blood, and the crowd howled in pleasure.

My breaths were shallow and fast, and I could feel the adrenaline soaking into my infected blood. There was something compelling about this raw violence—something viscerally satisfying about the shifters' ability to shed their human forms and fully embrace the Other that lurked in their cells. Thirst flared in my throat, and I had to stop myself from immediately gratifying the impulse. I focused on Alexa instead, willing myself to remember my humanity through her reactions. Horror dawned in her expression as the wolves grappled, shedding fur and blood. She cringed when a pair of snapping jaws bit through the gray wolf's right ear.

And when, at the last, he stumbled, opening himself to his adversary, she cried out as his life was extinguished by those sharp yellow teeth. I held her trembling body tightly as we both watched, unable to turn away, as the black wolf chewed into the belly of his enemy, seized the still-beating heart between his powerful jaws, and ate it.

I wanted to be disgusted. I wanted to be outraged. But part of me felt an ecstatic, empathetic triumph with the victor, and joy in having witnessed the beautiful brutality of his conquest.

Thankfully, Alexa kept me human.

"Val!" she said, spinning in my arms, her eyes swimming with angry tears that she would not allow to fall. "But…but how can they—" She drew herself up to her full height. "This is murder for sport! It has to be stopped!"

I cupped her face in my palms before she could say anything else. If the right person—or the wrong one—heard her talking like this, they'd want to ensure that she didn't make trouble. I would not allow that to happen.

"Babe, listen to me. I know. And I agree with you. But we have to play it cool here. Everybody's drinking the Kool-Aid, okay? Look around you."

She took in the boisterousness of the nearby observers—belly laughs and toothy grins if they collected their money, clenched fists and liberal obscenities if they had to pay. This wasn't the time or the place to demonstrate displeasure.

"You want to get out of here?" I asked. "We can catch a cab home."

She shook her head, eyes still shining with fury. I could tell that she was too choked up to say anything. I tamped down the part of me that wanted to make a bet on the next fight—the part that wanted to push even closer to the front for a better view. I would not devolve. It was just the parasite, dredging up my id. And I had sworn to fight it.

"Come on," I urged. "Let's go, before the next one starts."

"But you haven't had time to look. For...him."

"I'll keep an eye out on our way back," I promised, slowly drawing her toward the periphery. "I don't like what this place does to me."

She nodded as if she understood, but there wasn't any way she could. I was just as dangerous as those wolves. Only far more subtle.

Chapter Twelve

I stood with my feet shoulder-width apart, my right slightly in front of my left, and focused on squeezing the trigger slowly. It was important to keep the pressure constant; whenever I squeezed suddenly in anticipation of the gun's kickback, my hand jerked and threw off my aim. Greg, my instructor, was trying to break me of that bad habit today. I shut my right eye, lined up the front sight with the rear notch, and squeezed off eight rounds in rapid succession.

"Much steadier that time," said Greg, who was hovering behind me. I put down the gun and pulled off my goggles and earmuffs as he flipped the switch on the target's conveyer belt. As it grew closer, I nodded in satisfaction. No bull's-eyes, but three of my shots had penetrated the second innermost ring.

"You're catching on quickly."

"Thanks."

The day after the Red Circuit party—almost two weeks ago, now—I had called up the firing range and scheduled my first lesson. My fragility was unsettling. To play it safe, I would have to resort to the brutal violence of a gun to defend myself. It simply wasn't fair: if I had to drink blood for the rest of my existence, it seemed that at the very least, Fate could give me a permanent paranormal ability. When I had made my complaint to Alexa a few days ago, she had pointed out that I was going to live forever. But I didn't see that as a benefit—more like a curse. We hadn't talked yet about what we were going to do when it became obvious that she was aging and I wasn't. I didn't want to think about it. Not now. Not yet. Not ever.

I exhaled quickly in an effort to dispel the surge of panic. "So," I said, turning to Greg. "Same time on Tuesday?"

"Will do." We shook hands, and then I was alone with my equipment. I carefully packed my gun back in the briefcase that Penn had used; almost two weeks later, I hadn't yet gotten a holster for it. The thought of actually carrying it on my person still seemed more than a little creepy, Second Amendment notwithstanding.

I had decided to come to the Westside Pistol and Rifle Range every Tuesday and Thursday in the late afternoon until my lessons were up. This was my third session, and now that I was feeling fairly confident about my ability to handle the gun safely, I could think about things like my technique. I hadn't expected to enjoy shooting, but it really was a sport, and I was finding it a welcome challenge that wasn't nearly as physically taxing as my efforts to regain my strength and stamina. Now that my leg was mostly healed, I had started running again. Getting back into shape was painful. Add to that the fact that I put my shoulder through hell five days a week with a free weight rotation, and I was constantly sore. Everywhere.

The disconcerting thing was that I was capable of less this week than I had been the week before. I knew exactly why that was the case: I hadn't fed from Alexa since…well, it felt like forever. She had tried cajoling, threatening, and even begging, but I hadn't given in since losing control that Monday night. It frightened me that I had hurt her without even realizing it, and I hated that my drinking from her—which we had tentatively established as an act associated with intimacy and love—had been sullied by my memories of the attack. I wasn't going to be able to hold back for much longer, though; my thirst was becoming overwhelming. She knew it, and was worried. How messed up was it that she was fretting about how I wasn't drinking her blood?

When I realized that I was descending into my brooding "she doesn't deserve this" routine, I tried to snap myself out of it by reminding myself of everything that I had to get done over the weekend. I had finals next week, and they were going to be difficult. My professors had been incredibly understanding and tolerant of how much work I'd had to make up, given the mugging, but I wanted to show them that I could be an academic superstar despite my setbacks earlier in the semester.

It was just after six now, and I hurried to the nearest subway station. Alexa had said that she would take care of dinner tonight, but I wanted to try to beat her home. Next week was busy for her, too, especially because she was taking one class more than the rest of her cohort. Talk about a superstar.

As the subway hurtled across town, I let myself dream about our future—not our distant future, because that scared me—but about the next few years. Once Alexa graduated, she would find a job here in the City, which shouldn't be too hard for someone fascinated by corporate law. I would finish my four years of study, and then we'd either stay here in New York for my residency, or go elsewhere, depending on how she liked her job. I was determined to make myself as appealing a candidate as possible, so that I could go anywhere Alexa wanted to be.

And then…in the past, I had rarely thought that far ahead, mostly because I had figured that my clinical rotations would show me the path I'd like most to take in the medical field. But now, I knew that I was destined to be a microbiologist. I wondered if the Consortium would hire me in that capacity, to do research on the parasite. Or maybe it would be best to get experience in another lab working with related organisms before turning my focus back to the one that was hell-bent on consuming my blood.

While that particular part of my future path was blurry, I could see Alexa so clearly. She was always there at my side, holding my hand. My hopeful mind's eye saw her healthy, radiant, full of life and energy. Not pale and weak. That result was what I was working for now: To find a way to help vampires exist without having to drink from humans. To improve Alexa's quality of life. The reminder made me wish that I'd brought one of my textbooks along on the ride to study during the commute.

But when I glanced down at the briefcase that rested on my knees, I was reminded of one of my short-term goals. Justice. The trail had apparently dried up for Detective Foster and the NYPD; Olivia hadn't been in the news for a week now. She and I were probably the only people in New York who could make a positive ID of the rogue vampire, and I was the only one who could get into the Circuit. I wanted to go back. I needed to. The bastard continued to haunt my dreams, as though he was tormenting me at my failure to obtain closure. But as much as I wanted to rush into this, I knew that it was a dangerous proposition.

I wasn't yet good enough with my gun, if things went south—and I wasn't going back there unprepared.

Stepping out of the sliding doors, I jogged up the stairs and walked briskly down Seventh Street toward our apartment. Maybe I really should look into taking up a martial art, too; the gun would only help me at a distance. I'd heard good things about jujitsu from one of my bartender friends, a petite woman who had taken down a knife-wielding assailant with a throw when he had tried to steal her cash. I bared my teeth as I imagined pinning the rogue vampire to the ground. When I got home, I would give Cindy a call to find out the name of her dojo. Maybe Alexa and I could even take lessons together. We could spar with each other. That would be—

The hot, spicy smell of fajitas yanked me out of my daydream as I took the indoor stairs two at a time. No matter how worried I was about the potential that I might seriously hurt her, seeing her again after a full day apart was a relief. And exhilarating. I was head over heels, and it felt so good.

"Baby, that smells delici—oh my God." My keys and briefcase fell to the hardwood floor as my hands went limp in shock and desire. Alexa was wearing nothing but a pair of tight dark jeans. She had pulled back her hair, and the end of the ponytail swished lightly against her bare shoulder blades. Her breasts were swaying tantalizingly as she stirred the steak and vegetable mixture with a spatula. I couldn't get across the room fast enough, shedding my jacket as I went, until I finally stood behind her. There was no way that I could resist threading my arms around her chest to cup her breasts. Immediately, her nipples tightened.

"Where do I apply to be your human bra?" I whispered into one ear. When she shivered instead of giggling, I realized that she was already very aroused. And who could blame her? We hadn't made love since last Monday either, since I was afraid that sex would trigger my impulse to feed.

"How about right here, right now?" she said breathily.

I laughed. And then I smoothed my thumbs over her nipples. Her knees buckled, and she had to grab the counter with her free hand for support. "Someone's sensitive today," I murmured, unable to stop myself from sucking on a scar that I'd made a few weeks ago between her neck and shoulder.

"Oh, Val," she muttered, true surprise coloring her voice. "That feels…oh, that feels so good."

"You feel so good." My mouth blazed a trail to her earlobe. "You're trying to seduce me, aren't you?" It was obvious, and it was working. Just like that night in the club, I could feel my fears dissipating in the face of how much she wanted me—and how much I needed her right back.

"If I say yes, will you stop?"

"No."

"Yes."

I spun her around, sandwiching her body between me and the counter, careful to slide her away from the hot stove. I leaned in to press a line of kisses along her jaw. When she turned her head to capture my mouth, I pulled away. "Knock it off," I said, grinning. "I'm teasing you."

"Are not." She made a grab for my hair, clearly hoping to pull me closer, but I caught both her hands and held them above her head against one of the cupboards. She pouted. "You big meanie. This is my seduction."

I shook my head before letting my tongue trace her protruding bottom lip. "Nope. Not anymore." I reached over to turn off the burner and the oven with my free hand. "If I let you go, will you keep these to yourself?"

"I can't touch you?" Her pout grew even more pronounced. I knew she was playing with me—teasing me in her own way—but submissive Alexa was even hotter than her assertive counterpart. I let go of her wrists and almost gave in to the impulse to take off my sweater. But there was something so damn sexy about staying clothed while she got naked.

"Put your arms around my neck." Her pupils dilated at the imperative. I had to hold back a shiver of my own as her palms gently brushed the short hairs along my nape. When I pressed our breasts together, she groaned at the soft friction of cashmere against her nipples. My mouth hovered barely an inch from hers, but still, I refused to give in. I wanted to savor this moment: her quick, warm breaths puffing against my face, her fingers massaging my scalp, her dark, hungry eyes conveying the magnitude of her need.

"Please, Val," she whispered. "Please kiss me."

Her appeal undid me, and I kissed her like the starving woman I was. Our tongues tangled together, not in a battle but a dance. My need for her was an all-consuming force; without even second-guessing the impulse, I lifted her off the ground. Automatically, she wrapped her legs around my waist. She was hot against my stomach. My head was swimming. All I could think about was being inside her.

Lurching backward, I staggered toward the bedroom. Our lips never separated. We didn't quite make it to the bed. I got as far as the rug in the living room and then decided that was as good a place as anywhere to take her. I lowered her onto it and followed her down, planting my hands on either side of her head. She barely had time to take a deep breath before I was kissing her again. Her legs parted beneath mine and I ground into her before shifting slightly so that my right thigh was rocking against her. There was no room for doubt or uncertainty, not with this much love and want and need crowding my heart.

Alexa tore her mouth from mine long enough to gasp, "Touch me."

I reared up into a kneeling position, grabbed her jeans, and yanked them down her legs until they caught around her ankles. She wasn't wearing any underwear, and the sight of her, fully unveiled before me, made my heart contract in awe. I needed to taste her in every way possible.

Now.

I forced my lips to take their time, to explore the landscape of her body—to linger in the dips and crest the swells until her pleas were incoherent. When my head was finally even with her navel, I touched her the way she wanted me to, glorying in the wetness that coated her softest skin. She surrounded me, hot and pulsing, and I held nothing back.

"Val, Val, Val," she chanted as I watched her body take me in, over and over and over. I allowed my lips to linger on her inner thigh, feeling the pulse that hammered wildly just below her skin. Mine. Every inch, every drop of her, mine.

I bared my teeth, curled my fingers, and claimed her.

She screamed as her release flooded my hand and her blood poured into my mouth. Triumphant, I greedily drank her in. The hot rich taste of paradise cascading over my tongue, the liquid strength essence of her life given in love flowing between us. More I needed more needed so much blood.

So much blood. I was going to die. Helpless rage slipping out of my grasp, Olivia cold and weak, face as ashen as the white sheets of her hospital bed. White like the exploding pain behind my eyes, skull crashing hard into the asphalt...oh God, so much blood.

"Sweetheart, it's time to stop."

Impossible. It would never be time to stop. We would never be separated. No mine, no yours, just ours till death do us part. So beautiful, the current joining us. Someday, Valentine. Someday you'll appreciate the beauty in this. His teeth in me my teeth in her full circle, full circle, full—

"Val, love...stop. Stop—you're taking too much. Stop!"

Stop you bastard you fucking bastard what did I ever do to you why me why now get up Valentine get up you have to get up. Someone groaned in the distance, low and tortured. The wheeling stars and his slithering fist and the stench of rot and the knife handle under my palm and the blood, the blood, the blood.

"Val...stop..."

Hands in my hair, hands under my shirt, pushing, pushing me, no, no, hers not yours. *I belong to Alexa. Alexa.* I needed to apologize to Alexa. To beg her forgiveness. *Alexa, I'm sorry, I'm—*

Her hand slid off my scalp as though it were boneless. I raised my head in confusion. Blood trickled down my chin, but I made no move to wipe it away. What the hell had just happened? I could sense the strength flowing into my muscles, but instead of the sparkling clarity that normally came with drinking from Alexa, I felt groggy. And... full.

"Alexa?" As gently as possible, I touched my hand to the wound in her leg. It wasn't bleeding at all. That was a bad sign. She didn't so much as twitch. If her wound had been gushing with blood, that would mean her heart was still pounding. I looked down again, the wound was clean. No blood. Panic slammed into my gut, forcing the breath from my lungs. *Oh God. Oh God oh God oh God oh no what the hell have I done—*

"Baby, please please, baby, please!" I was shaking and tears were mingling with Alexa's blood on my face, and I pressed two fingers hard against her jugular but there was nothing to feel, nothing. I had taken it all. She had tried to stop me—I could remember her feeble attempt to push me away—but I had let the memories and the thirst consume me. I had lost the fight for control, and now, she was…she was…

She was dead. I had killed her. My nightmare, come to life.

So still. She was so still. Glorious, vibrant Alexa, turned to stone. The future disappeared.

I could hear myself sobbing but the core of me, the very heart of me, was frozen just like her. There was only one course of action left to me: to kill the monster that had taken her life. Tears blinded me as I half staggered, half ran for the door. I wrenched at the handle and didn't so much as flinch when the entire door came off its hinges. Shoving it to the side, I considered my choices. Not down, but up—up, to the roof. My hands were covered in her blood. It had been hubris to think that I could fight against the monster that was eating me alive. Why hadn't I forced myself to stay away from her? Why had I given in? Selfish, so selfish, and she had paid the ultimate price.

I hoped that hell was real. Just an hour ago, I had wished for lasting superpowers, but now I was obscenely grateful for my own fragility. I threw open the heavy door to the terrace. The cold December wind swirled around me, beckoning me to the parapet. I would follow it. The voice screaming shrilly in my head urged me on.

I'll follow you, Alexa. I'll spend the afterlife in fire begging your forgiveness across the abyss between us. I'm sorry, baby. I'm sorry I wasn't strong enough to let you go. I swear I wanted forever with you, but not like this. Why couldn't you have loved me less why why why—

Mercifully, it went silent as I climbed onto the wall.

alexa

CHAPTER THIRTEEN

Valentine looked pissed.

I could see her reflection pacing back and forth across the living room from the small vanity mirror in our bathroom. Or rather, I could catch an occasional glimpse of her tall, tuxedoed form as she passed by the doorway and then I had to follow her trailing voice when she moved out of my line of sight. This was the second time I had ever seen Val in a tux and only the first where I'd be going as her date. The other time around had been a party celebrating her father's second term as Secretary of the Treasury. That time, I'd explicitly not been invited. Today we were going to her cousin's wedding. Despite her mother's vehement protestations many months before, Val insisted that I go as her "plus one."

"So you're saying that the vice president is more important than family?" Val's reflection tugged at the loose end of her bowtie, undoing the half-formed knot. "Don't tell me you can't squeeze one extra seat in at the table when you really mean you don't want to."

Val's voice rose and she stopped pacing just outside the bathroom. I paused, mascara brush poised above my right eye. "Oh please. Pritchard won his election because he's a Darrow and because the second congressional district has voted red for the last forty years. There are more gun stores than bookstores in that hillbilly town. I'm sure the vice president's form-letter endorsement had nothing to do with it."

Val continued her angry striding across the room. I put down the mascara and moved to the doorway so I could keep her in sight. Val and her father brought out the worst in each other and I wanted to be near in case she decided to make target practice out of our brand-new TV.

"I don't buy it. You put that closeted little prick on the phone so he can tell me himself. Hello? Hello?" Val stared down at her phone for an angry moment before throwing it at the couch. "The fucker hung up on me."

A kaleidoscope of emotions cascaded across Val's face before she finally settled back on pissed. She stomped over to the couch and dug her phone out of the cushions. She glanced at me then, love softening the clench in her jaw. "I'm sick of being bullied by my family. If he wants to insult me, he'll have to do it to my face." With a parting snarl, she turned and stormed out the door.

"Don't let her go alone." The voice was insistent. "Get up. Get up. She needs your support."

"Val is a big girl." I reasoned with the voice. "If she needed my help, she would ask for it." But even as I argued, my body flickered to life. I opened my eyes; the pale blur of the ceiling slowly coalesced into a light bulb, a water stain, an intricate web of cracks. Was I on the floor? What was I doing there? My limbs felt cold and heavy as I fought to get upright.

My legs twisted awkwardly beneath me, impeded somehow. I looked down to find my jeans pooled down around my ankles, binding my legs together. Clumsily, I pulled them up. The inside of my left thigh stung sharply as rough denim chafed over the punctured skin. Valentine? I had the haziest recollection of Val's mouth moving over me as her tongue teased the sensitive juncture of my inner thigh. But instead of warming me, the memory sent me into a paroxysm of shivering.

"Val?" Goose bumps prickled over my icy skin. I grabbed my sweatshirt from the couch and pulled it awkwardly over my head. The apartment door was hanging off its hinges and a sickly wedge of fluorescent light spilled into the foyer. Slowly, painfully, I got to my feet and stumbled out the door. The voice was gone, but the imperative was still there.

Find Valentine.

I started down the stairs toward the front door. It was an effort just to put one foot in front of the other, as though the cold had frozen the synaptic messages from my brain to my legs. I had barely managed a few steps when a banging from above caught my attention. I squinted up the stairwell, trying to determine where the sound was coming from. That was when I saw the blood. It was on the banister and the steps, still fresh. I began to pull myself upward, hauling my clumsy, recalcitrant body up the flights of stairs with hands and elbows and knees until I reached the roof. The door was ajar and I nearly fell in my haste to get through it. I squinted into the night. A sudden cold breeze blinded me, and I had to blink back tears. I caught a glimpse of a shadow at the far end of the roof, an unmistakable silhouette against the bright, blinking lights of the cityscape beyond.

"Val!" I shouted, willing my voice to carry over the gusting wind and the traffic below.

The shadow lengthened and grew impossibly tall. Val had climbed onto the wall that encircled the roof space. I broke into a run, panic filling my heavy limbs with strength. "Oh my God, Val. Get down from there!"

She turned, but didn't seem to recognize me. "Don't come any closer!"

I pulled up short about six feet away from her, close enough to see the blood—my blood, I realized—trailing from the corners of her mouth and soaking the front of her sweater. I had never seen so much of it before. No wonder I had passed out downstairs. "Val, it's me. Alexa. I fainted, that's all. I'm okay."

"Alexa?" For a split second, recognition sparked behind her eyes and I was hopeful. But just as quickly, something dark and tortured extinguished it.

"Val, love, please come down from that wall. Please?"

"Go away." Like her eyes, her voice was flat and distant.

Desperation made my voice shrill. "I need you to get down from there."

"I—I can't. It's not working. I can't do this anymore." The wind gusted around her, ruffling her hair and whipping at the shirttails peeking out from under her sweater. She swayed precariously, rising to the balls of her bare feet and then rocking dangerously back on her heels.

"We can, Val! We can. We can do anything if we do it together." I couldn't help inching closer to her. There was a wildness in her expression that I didn't trust.

"Stop! Stop it! I told you to get away from me!" She backed up toward the edge of the wall and I immediately froze.

My hands rose, an instinctive gesture of surrender. "Okay. Okay. I won't move." My heart was hammering in my chest, pushing adrenaline in waves through my body. I felt nauseous but I clamped my jaw down and swallowed the dry heaves that snaked their way up my esophagus.

"It's getting worse. The need, the thirst. I can't control it."

The wind, the traffic, the other sounds of night retreated as I focused my attention on her tense stance. I willed her to believe with my words, my heart, my soul. "We'll figure something out. It'll be okay."

"I thought I killed you!" The rawness of her pain tore through the darkness and stabbed at my heart. Self-loathing crept behind her eyes like a predator and it dared me to try to wrench her back from the abyss.

"You didn't, sweetheart. I'm right here. Touch me and see for yourself. I'm right here." Slowly, carefully, I reached my hand out to her.

I watched anxiously as a series of emotions rifled through her system. Her misery was electric and her despair suffocating. Even the need that showed so starkly on her face metamorphosed between hunger and desire and love. It felt like Russian roulette.

When she spoke again, her voice was low and sad. "This is no way to live."

"Neither is death, Valentine."

She stared at me for a full minute as I held my breath. The words had just tumbled out. Dumb, dumb, dumb, I berated myself. I wanted to take it back and apologize. This was far too important a moment to make light of. How could I be so callous?

I saw her tense and then a fine tremor passed through her body. She began shaking. Impulsively, I took a step toward her. I couldn't reach her in time from where I was standing but by God, if she jumped, I was going over that wall with her.

I was so caught up in the surety of my intended self-annihilation that it took me an extra moment to register the low rumbling sound emanating from Val. I glanced up, cautious and confused.

She was laughing.

Tears streamed down her cheeks and mingled with the blood at her lips. Shaking her head, she lowered herself carefully from the wall.

Her bare feet hit the roof with a muffled crunch of gravel. Somehow, in the short time it took to get down from the edge, I had closed the distance between us. I collided against her long, slender frame and her arms wrapped around me instinctively, protectively. She was solid and alive.

"Oh Val." My body shook with violent, wrenching sobs. Tears flowed freely down my face. I couldn't breathe or think or move.

She held me. "I'm sorry, baby. I'm so, so sorry." Strong, comforting hands stroked my back and arms. She pressed a kiss into my hair. Carefully, she led me away from the wall toward the door.

We stumbled back into the apartment, my arms wrapped possessively around her waist and her body pressed tightly against mine. Dazedly, I watched her pick up the entire door as though it were made of corkboard instead of solid wood and fit it back into place. A sense of pride filled me: I had done that. I had made it possible for her to be strong.

But even as I opened my mouth to comment on how impressive her increased strength truly was, Val began to gently hustle me toward the couch. She sat me down and hurried into the kitchen. I felt the separation from her keenly and wanted to follow her, to keep her in my sight, but my head was a throbbing mess. The adrenaline kick that had propelled me up the stairs was finally wearing off and in its wake, a heavy, dull ache flared in my skull and reverberated painfully down my spine and limbs. I sat and waited for Val to come back, measuring the passing of time with the beat of pain that coursed through my body.

A few minutes later, she returned with a large glass of orange juice and a handful of painkillers and vitamins. She had removed the bloodstained sweater and washed her face. I could see no trace of her feeding on the oxford shirt she wore underneath. If it weren't for the ghostly look on her face and my splitting headache, this could have passed for domesticity on any other weekday night.

She sat on the opposite end of the couch, fear furrowing her brow and regret glinting nakedly in her eyes. I scooted closer to her and put my hand on her thigh. I could feel her quivering as if she was fighting the urge to flee.

"It's okay, love." I stroked her leg reassuringly. I took a sip of orange juice and forced myself to swallow around the gag reflex that spasmed in my throat as the sudden acidity washed over my tongue. I forced myself to take another sip. "I'm okay. I'm feeling much better already."

I swallowed the handful of pills and washed them down with a gulp of juice. Val watched me silently, her worried eyes never leaving my face. I tilted the glass back and drained the rest of its contents. She immediately jumped up to refill it. I recognized the action for what it was, a guilt impulse compelling her to excessive solicitousness, and I allowed her the comfort of pandering to my needs. When Val returned again with a second glass of juice, I patted the cushion next to me and beckoned her close. She hesitated only a moment before sitting carefully by my side. Her thigh pressed against mine and my cold body hungrily drank in the warmth that radiated from her. I leaned against her, nestling my head against her shoulder.

"I don't know what to do." She buried her face in my hair. "I—I just lost control for a minute and when I came to, you weren't moving. There was so much blood. I thought…" A fresh wave of terror suddenly broke across her face. "Oh my God. What if I turned you?"

My heart felt like a moth fluttering against a window, but I took a deep breath against the sharp surge of unwarranted panic. "I'm fine, and you know it. You didn't take nearly enough. And your blood didn't mingle with mine. All I did was have a fainting spell. Just like someone at a blood drive."

Val's breathing was ragged. "I put you in danger. Not just today—every day." Her voice hitched in her throat and I wrapped my arms around her torso to keep her from pulling away.

"Shh. Val, sweetheart, we'll make it work. I've been running myself ragged with extra courses and other stuff. If I drop Law Review and the women's studies course I've been auditing, I'll be in a much better place to take care of myself physically. It won't happen again."

Val pulled away and stared at me with naked anguish. "You can't quit Law Review! You worked so fucking hard for it! And you were going to ask that women's studies professor to write you a recommendation for your summer clerkship. I can't let you throw away your future for me. I won't!"

"It's not just my future, it's ours. Besides, it won't hurt me at all. Dropping a couple things from my schedule will put me at the exact same level as most of my classmates. I'll just be trimming off some extracurriculars."

"But you are not like most of your classmates! You are Alexa Newland. You are extraordinary. I want you to be able to be fucking extraordinary!" New tears overflowed and streamed down her cheeks.

I leaned in and kissed them away, one by one. "My life is extraordinary because you're in it. I will never give you up. Everything else is just going to have to bend." Val started to protest and I stopped her with a finger on her lips. "No, Val. This is not negotiable."

She nodded once, reluctantly, and I kissed her softly on the mouth. "Come on. Let's go to bed."

Tenderly, lovingly, Val helped me up from the couch. The dizziness was gone but I leaned against her anyway for the comfort. We stripped silently and took turns brushing our teeth and washing up in the bathroom.

When we crawled under the sheets, I immediately curled into her warm embrace. I let the strong, steady beat of her heart lull me toward sleep. Just as I skirted the edge of unconsciousness Valentine spoke, so softly I could have dreamed it. "What if I need more?"

I continued to breathe deeply and evenly, feigning oblivion. Eventually, she relaxed against me, surrendering to her own exhaustion.

But sleep did not come to me that night.

CHAPTER FOURTEEN

I stayed in bed listening to the even rumble of Valentine's slumber. Even though sleep eluded me, it was calming just to feel her breath against my neck and her warmth along my back. But as the hours ticked by, I couldn't stop my mind from racing and my muscles were starting to cramp from holding still for so long. The glaring red LED lights of my alarm clock told me that it was half past three in the morning. Carefully, I extracted myself from Val's embrace. It wasn't easy. Even unconscious, she tightened her arms around me as I started to pull away. Slowly and gently, I inched my way out from under her and when I was finally free, I slipped my pillow into her arms as a placeholder until I came back.

Something Val had mentioned earlier was weighing heavily on my mind. She said that the thirst was getting harder to control. I knew that today's incident was partly my fault for wearing myself so thin over the last few weeks. I felt no guilt for offering that to Val as an excuse for my fainting spell. But I also knew that she had taken quite a bit of blood. I wasn't sure if I could have held up through that, even had I been fully rested and healthy. The fact was that Val's control over her thirst would always be tenuous. I knew that she would fight it as hard as she could, but that didn't have to be the only solution.

I pulled my laptop out of my bag and plugged it into the outlet by the sofa. I rearranged the cushions into a comfortable nest as it booted up. My first inclination had been to flip through Val's medical texts for some kind of inspiration, but the last time I had tried reading over her shoulder, I think I'd understood maybe two out of every five words I saw. I was hoping the Internet could dumb it all down for me. I spared a glance toward the bedroom. My heart stuttered painfully in my chest as I remembered just how close I had come to losing her. If there was an answer out there, I would find it.

I shook the morbid thoughts from my head and focused on the matter at hand. How did one research becoming an unending blood bag for one's lover? I typed "blood production" into the search engine and called up a page of mostly technical-looking Web sites. I clicked on the Wikipedia entry for red blood cells at the top of the list.

About halfway down the page I sat up and grabbed a pad and pen. Excitement seared through me like wild electricity. I had to force myself to calm down. I'd only been at this for five minutes; I couldn't let my anxiety cloud my objectivity or else I'd be tilting at windmills all day. I wrote down the word "erythropoietin" and circled it emphatically. Erythropoietin, I learned, was a hormone synthesized by the kidneys that stimulated red blood cell production and was most often connected with doping in sports. While plasma replaced itself within a day or two after blood loss, red blood cells took up to five weeks to be completely replenished. The low levels of hemoglobin in my blood could explain the exhaustion and fainting. If the Web site was correct, use of erythropoietin could decrease my recuperation downtime between feedings. If Val fed more often, she should be able to control her thirst better.

I followed the link for erythropoietin and read about its use by people suffering from anemia and by patients recuperating from chemotherapy. With trepidation, I clicked a link for more information about adverse effects. My heart sank a bit as I read about the constriction of small arteries, blood clots, and increased risk of stroke, heart attack, and congestive heart failure. I sighed. It wasn't ideal, but it was something.

By the time the sun came pouring through our living room windows, I had compiled a short but hopeful list of solutions, adding homologous and autologous transfusions to the tally. Nothing was perfect, but I felt better knowing that there were medical possibilities out there. I bookmarked the relevant Web sites and made a note to myself to talk with Dr. Clavier. Surely he would help me arrive at a definitive answer.

I was about to close down the Web browser and the computer when a three-dimensional image of a red blood cell caught my eye. I had been staring at these concave little almost-donuts all morning and had never taken the time to really appreciate their simplistic beauty. Val once told me that the vampire parasite infiltrated the red blood cells and exploded their way out. Somehow, it was my blood that was barring the path of these parasites from consuming my lover's soul. On a whim, I typed in "vampire" and hit Search.

As I scrolled through pages and pages of folklore, fantasy, and gothic culture, it occurred to me that vampires and their like had managed to live in plain sight by hiding behind a mythology that stayed just a few steps ahead of what could be explained by science. As long as there was even a hint of doubt, they could shroud themselves in denial. The struggle must have become easier in modern times as science became a litmus test for truth. It was a miracle they survived the Middle Ages, when speculation and superstition alone could have blown their carefully constructed cover. I was grateful that Val could exist in relative safety in our world. My heart twinged briefly but painfully at the realization that I wouldn't always be there to watch over her. Immediately, I pushed that thought aside. Val would always be taken care of. I had to believe that. I wondered, as I clicked through page after page of bogus vampire material on the Internet, if perhaps Helen or those of her Consortium had orchestrated this informational web of deceit. If it kept Val safe, I was glad for it.

The most brilliant element of it all was that fragments of truth lay scattered in the piles of fiction. If you knew what to look for, the secret of the vampires was sitting just a keystroke and mouse click away. Infection, agelessness, blood drinking. Even information about the parasite that caused vampirism could be found if someone looked in the right place and believed the right things. As an insider privy to their secret, I was shocked that the rest of the world remained oblivious when the clues were all out in the open. Skepticism, I reminded myself, was a powerful thing. After all, how could one take vampires seriously if they could bewitch with a gaze, burst into flames when touched by the sun, or transform into a bat at will?

Shaking my head, I closed the page on vampiric animorphism. Popular myth had almost gotten that part right. Wereshifters were alive and well in New York City. I shuddered as I remembered that night at the Consortium's facility when Valentine's secret was revealed to me. I hadn't wanted to believe. How could I, when I had been programmed by a lifetime of skepticism? If that guard hadn't transformed into a wolf right before my eyes, I'd probably still be a disbeliever. It defied logic. It defied science. When he shifted back to human form, the cut on his forehead had already completely healed. Incredible.

I stopped myself mid-click. My cursor hovered over the shutdown button. He healed. In the twenty minutes from when he sustained the injury until he settled back into human form, the cut had completely healed without even leaving a scar. He had even walked out of the room on his own two feet, with no evidence of any kind of trauma.

Heart pounding, I reopened my Web browser and typed "werewolf" into the search bar. As expected, the page filled with entries on film, fiction, and the occult. Just like vampires, there were examples of werewolf myths in almost every culture. And just like vampires, most of the information was useless. I sifted through sites and blogs and message boards. I didn't know nearly as much about shifters as I did about vampires, and I could kick myself for not asking more questions when we were at the Consortium facility. It was a lot harder to glean fact from fiction without having that base of knowledge to build from.

All I really knew was what Helen had told us while we'd been trapped in the copy room: that shifters came in all sorts of animal flavors and that the condition was caused by a virus. I started stringing together all of the keywords that I could think of that I knew to be true. This produced a reasonable search result of twenty pages. Starting at the top of the list, I followed a link to a graduate student's no-frills, academic-looking Web site. Interestingly enough, the site didn't mention werewolves or shifters or lycanthropy directly. The more I read, the more I realized that the site's author was either a shifter herself or knew one intimately. The fact that the page had popped to the top of my list even though it lacked some of the keywords I had supplied meant that lots of other searchers, looking for the same information I was after, gravitated to this page as well. That lent it an authenticity in my book.

Unlike Wikipedia, the site was short on folklore and mythology but heavy on chemistry, biology, and physiology. The first section of the site covered the virus that caused the wereshifter condition. Colloquially referred to as the lycanthropy virus, I learned that it came from the genus *Morphoviridae* and that the different species names determined the animal form of the transformation. Werewolves were the product of *Morphoviridae lupus.*

I skipped ahead to the section on shifter physiology. Scrolling through pages of information about human and animal anatomy, I finally found a mention of metamorphosis and regeneration. Eagerly, I scanned the text and clicked through the affiliated links. According to the site, frenzied regeneration was the beneficial side effect of the transformation process. The act of changing back and forth from human to animal form was so violent on the system that an elevated healing ability was necessary to undo the damage from shifting: muscles, bones, and tissue stretching and pulling as the body poured between the vessels of its two forms.

There it was in black and white pixels right before my eyes.

Every time a Were shifted, it healed. Completely. If I became a shifter, I could produce all the blood Val needed and gain it all back when I transformed. And best of all, I could sustain this indefinitely. Shifters, like vampires, didn't age.

Roughly an hour later, I was standing in the doorway to our bedroom, looking down on Val's sleeping form, debating whether to wake her. My body was vibrating with excitement. I had filled several pages of my notepad with my findings. I had even identified the author of the Web site—Karma Rao, a post-doctoral fellow in ancient art history at the Metropolitan Museum of Art right here in Manhattan.

I had come into the bedroom with the intention of telling Val the great news. But seeing her sleeping so peacefully made me hesitate. A full and restful night of sleep had been hard to come by for both of us lately. While Val had been reluctant to share the details of her nightmares, I knew that her assault still haunted her. Even dreamless, she whimpered at the slightest touch and her body flinched and spasmed defensively throughout the night.

Outside, a car horn blared and Val stirred. Slowly, two sleepy blue eyes blinked awake and stared first in confusion and then in panic at the pillow nestled in her arms. "Alexa?"

I crossed the room and slipped into bed. She tossed the pillow aside and immediately took me into her embrace. I kissed her lightly on the neck. "Good morning, sweetheart. I'm right here."

"Where did you go? Is everything okay?" I heard the fear in Val's voice and kissed her softly on the lips to quell it.

I propped myself up on one elbow so I could see her reaction as I told her. "I found an answer. The answer. To how I can feed you indefinitely."

Waves of sorrow washed over her face and settled in a grinding clench of her jaw. She started to pull away, but I wrapped my free arm around her waist and held her to me tightly. "No, Val. I'm not blaming you for last night. That's my fault, too. But I've figured out a way so last night never happens again."

"How?"

"I become a shifter. A werewolf…or a were-anything, actually."

It took several seconds for my words to sink in, but when they finally did, Val reacted explosively. She twisted backward out of my grip and stumbled to the floor, backing up until she hit the far wall. "God, no."

"It solves everything! I'll be able to regenerate all the blood you need—"

"No! I can't let you!"

"—and we can be together, forever."

Val slumped to the floor and buried her head in her hands. I crossed the room and sat next to her. Our shoulders touched, but she didn't react. She didn't run away either, which I took to be a good thing.

"You don't know what you are asking for." There was a sadness in her voice that I didn't expect. It tore right through my layers of stubborn insistence and wrenched at my heart.

"Sweetheart, it makes so much sense. I'd be stronger. You wouldn't have to be so careful around me. And I'd be immortal, too. You could keep your soul forever." I wrapped my arm around her shoulder and leaned into her.

"You wouldn't be human."

"I'd be better."

Val looked up and I saw that she was crying. I reached to brush away the tears but she intercepted my hand and held it tenderly in her own. "I would give anything to be human again. For our lives to go back to normal."

"Val, what happened to you wasn't your fault. You were a victim. I'm not a victim here. I am choosing this. For us. For me. I don't care what you believe. You are still human. And I will be, too, after the procedure."

"It's not the same! There has to be another way. I could learn to live on less. You won't need regeneration."

"Drugs and transfusions may help me keep up my blood levels, but they won't change the fact that someday my body will stop being able to sustain you." I reached for her face and tilted it until she met my gaze. "All couples go through changes and hardships in their relationships. So you have a funny diet and I'll get a little hairy sometimes—we'll be together, and that is the only thing that matters to me."

"Alexa, I—"

I leaned in and kissed her softly on the lips. "Valentine Darrow, you are my always and forever."

She kissed me back, the last of her resistance scattering in the wake of our commitment. "I love you, Alexa."

"I love you back."

We spent the next hour going through the notes I had taken in the morning. I wanted to call Helen to ask some additional questions, but Val immediately dismissed that idea. She didn't trust Helen when it came to my welfare. "Helen's the one who encouraged me to feed off you in the first place." She shuddered.

"She did point out the risks. We knew this could happen." I squeezed her hand to stave off the rush of guilt I knew was coming. She winced, but left it at that.

"Let's just talk to someone else first, okay? How about Kyle?"

I shook my head. "He's a sweet kid, but I don't think he'd know enough to answer all of our questions."

Her eyes slid over the pages of my notepad, now scattered all over the floor. She picked up the top sheet. "How about this Karma Rao? She knows a lot and seems to want to help."

"I'm not sure." I frowned. "I mean, it occurred to me before, but we don't know anything about her. How do we know if we can trust her or not?"

Val pulled me toward her and placed a kiss on the furrow in my brow. "We're smart girls. I'm sure between the two of us, we'll be able to tell if she's genuine."

"Yeah." I smiled, feeling the possibilities coalesce. "I'll e-mail her and set something up as soon as possible."

After another kiss, Val left me to it, and I took my time typing out a cautious inquiry to Karma. By the time I sent the message, I could smell waffles. Belgian waffles. I stood and went to the threshold of the kitchen, pausing to watch as she deftly sliced the strawberries that would crown my favorite breakfast. From her careful, elegant hands to her short, tousled hair, to the way her bottom lip jutted out slightly while she was concentrating…I loved her. And if this plan worked, there would never have to be an end to this warm, wonderful intimacy that we shared on so many levels. We'd have it all.

Every day of forever.

Chapter Fifteen

Val and I met Karma on the steps of the Temple of Dendur. In 1963, the temple was gifted to the United States government and shipped, stone by stone, to be recreated in the Sackler Wing of the New York Metropolitan Museum of Art where we were now standing. It was Sunday morning, minutes after the doors opened to patrons, and we were alone in the sun-filled atrium that housed the temple.

Karma was slender and petite. When she approached to greet us, she stood a full foot shorter than Valentine. She had thick black hair that fell in waves to her shoulders and curled softly against the high arches of her cheekbones. Her large, almond-shaped eyes were wide-set and a striking golden brown in color. The morning light that streamed in through the large wall of windows reflected softly off her light caramel complexion, giving her skin an ethereal glow that far eclipsed the beauty and majesty of the temple behind her.

She led us toward the windowed side of the room and we sat on the low wall that separated the temple from a shallow reflecting pool.

"I'm Alexa Newland, and this is my partner, Valentine. Thank you for meeting with us on such short notice."

"Your e-mail was intriguing." Karma's handshake was firm and sure. "It's not often that I get requests for meetings from a human who is so aware of and curious about our existence."

"You could tell I was human from my e-mail?"

Karma smiled. "The newly transformed tend to have a desperation in their requests that I didn't sense in yours. And I know all of the Weres in New York who want to be identified, so…"

I tried to read Karma's face for any sign of concern, but she just continued to smile in her relaxed and curious way. "Is it a problem that I'm human? Will you get into trouble because you are talking to me?"

"Well, you may be human but you aren't exactly an outsider, are you?" Karma's eyes flicked to Val before settling back on me.

I felt a flutter of apprehension in my chest. "How did you know?"

"The circumstances surrounding Valentine's…initiation…into our community have been much gossiped about. And we've met once before."

"That night at Luna." Valentine, who had been quietly holding my hand up to this point, spoke a split second before I could ask for clarification. "You were the one who came and got Sebastian."

Karma nodded. "I apologize for not introducing myself formally at that time, but there was an urgent business matter that required our attention."

"You work for Sebastian?" From the way Sebastian had been ogling Val, I had a hard time believing that he could employ attractive women and still be productive.

Karma smiled wryly. "With him. No self-respecting woman would ever work for Sebastian Brenner."

I stroked Val's hand idly with my thumb. The tension that had been coursing through her since we arrived at the Met seemed to have dissipated a little. Unlike the other vampires and Weres we had met so far, Karma radiated warmth and openness. I had hoped, from studying her site, that she would be helpful. Friendliness was an unexpected plus. I had spent all morning practicing the request I was about to make, but something in Karma Rao's golden eyes told me that she could be trusted with the unadorned truth.

"You mentioned that you had some questions," she said into the pause.

I took a deep breath, hoping that I wasn't making a mistake. "I want to know more about the regenerative powers of Weres. Is it true that transformation can repair almost all corporeal damage?"

She nodded once. "If the physical damage done to you in human form doesn't kill you, a Were's regenerative abilities can mend any wound instantaneously at the point of transformation. It is the only way we can survive the shifting process."

"How about in human form? Do Weres have heightened healing while human?"

"Yes, depending on how old the Were is, I'd estimate that healing happens three to ten times faster than the average human."

"Everything heals? The skin, bones, tendons, muscles…"

"And blood." She finished for me, a flicker of comprehension sparking in her eyes. "Yes, everything regenerates to its original state before the trauma."

I smiled at Val. This was exactly what I had hoped. "I want to know if you think it would be possible to be deliberately infected with the lycanthropy virus. If it's planned, can we insure that the transformation will take?"

Karma leaned back and gazed at us speculatively. "It has been done before—family members or spouses becoming infected in order to stay close to their loved ones. With the proper facilities, the virus can be introduced through blood transfusions or tissue grafts."

"What's the success rate?"

"There are a few documented cases of humans being immune to the virus. I would say that is less than two percent of the population. But in a controlled medical environment, the virus can be continuously applied until it takes."

Val shifted uneasily next to me. "What's the mortality rate?"

Karma hesitated. "It's much better now. We've managed to control the viral introduction better than we used to. It's certainly safer than how it's done in the wild."

"What is it?" Val's voice was barely a whisper.

"Six to seven percent." Karma admitted reluctantly. "Alexa is young and healthy; that should lower it to about five percent."

"One in twenty." Val looked like she was going to be sick.

I took Valentine's face in my hands and gently kissed each cheek and then her lips. I lifted her chin so that she had to look into my eyes. "Val, you can't focus on that. I refuse to live my life in fear of what could be. I also refuse to live with regrets of what might have been."

Although I was sure Karma had figured it out, it was important for me to come clean to her. She was being very helpful and generous with her time and information. "I want to be infected." I looked at Val before turning back to Karma. "My blood is the only thing preventing the vampire parasite from consuming Val's soul, and right now, I just don't have enough of it to sustain her."

I kissed Val one more time on the lips for emphasis and turned my attention back to Karma. Karma had politely turned away from the intimacy and was staring at the temple. She was quiet for so long, I thought perhaps we had miscalculated in trusting her or we had managed to offend her.

When she spoke again, she was still staring into the distance. "Petronius built this temple in fifteen BC and dedicated it to Isis and Osiris. Are you familiar with their story?" Val and I shook our heads.

"Isis was the Egyptian goddess of motherhood, life, and fertility. Initially, she was quite obscure and had no temples or followers of her own. Eventually, she was adopted by the Greeks and Romans into their pantheons and worship of Isis would spread across the world.

"In the most popular story about Isis, she was instrumental in resurrecting her husband Osiris after he was slain and dismembered by Set. She traveled the world gathering up the pieces of his body and revived him with her magic." She looked at Val. "Morbidly romantic, don't you think?"

Val nodded solemnly, but indignation bubbled up inside me like angry lava. There was nothing morbid about this at all. It was a clever and elegant solution to so many of our problems, and I didn't want Valentine to back out of our decision based on the ignorant opinion of a stranger. I opened my mouth to protest when Karma cut me off.

"I'll help you." She smiled at me. "I'll probably be ostracized when the Were community finds out, but you seem like good people. I'll do what I can to assist you."

"I don't see how the Were community has anything to do with this," I interjected. "This is a personal matter."

Karma shook her head. "What you are proposing would look like slavery to a shifter." She raised her hand to curtail my indignation. "Try to see it from our perspective; you are deliberately infecting yourself so you can sustain your vampire lover. You are purposefully subjugating yourself to her well-being. There is enough tension between our two species without introducing the idea of breeding us like cattle."

"Ah, politics," Val murmured. She and Karma stared at one another for a long, silent moment. They looked like they were evaluating each other, but I couldn't be sure. Being able to feed Val and share eternity with her weren't the only reasons that I wanted to become a Were—it would be a relief to finally be a member of this club, instead of an outsider.

"I'm not subjugating myself," I said. "This was my idea from the beginning and servitude has nothing to do with it."

"I know." Karma's tone softened. "That's why I am willing to help. But if the nature and circumstances of your rebirth become public knowledge, there is no saying how the masses will react to it. There are many in our community who would seek to use that information to rally the Weres and consolidate power."

"We'll be discreet."

"This is not going to be easy. First of all, you are going to have to go outside of the Were system. Secondly, it may not work. As you know, any kind of trauma causes a Were to shift." Karma turned to Valentine. "The simple act of feeding would most likely trigger the transformation. It could be very dangerous for you."

"It's not me I'm worried about," Val said, stubbornness coloring her voice.

Karma smiled at us both sympathetically. "When it is done, I can teach you how to be a Were. But until then, it's best that we have very limited contact."

I nodded. "I understand."

The first of the morning museum visitors finally began drifting into the room. Karma glanced at her watch and then slowly rose to her feet. She shook my hand and then Valentine's one last time. "Good luck to you both."

❖

Helen's secretary was testy when we showed up unannounced. She tried to give us the runaround by telling us that Helen was out of the office, but even my ordinary human hearing could pick up her voice through the closed door. Time, I felt, was of the essence, so Val and I settled into the plush leather sofa outside Helen's office to wait it out. She had to come out eventually and we would be there to corner her.

About twenty minutes later, the door finally opened and Helen stepped out wearing a brown crepe silk skirt suit and holding a stack of files. If she was surprised to see us there, she didn't show it. She just placed the folders on her secretary's desk and instructed her to file them. Then with a quirk of her lips, she asked us to step into her office. I took Val's hand in mine and we followed her in.

"Would you like something to drink?" She gestured for us to sit in the armchairs facing her desk.

Val and I both declined the offer. The windows of her office were shaded with a special filter that significantly blocked the sunlight entering the room. Looking through the windows at the city beyond felt like looking through a pair of dark sunglasses. To compensate for the darkness, small inset iridescent bulbs studded the ceiling and bathed the large office in light. Helen leaned back against the black leather of her office chair and regarded us curiously.

"I have an idea for how I can sustain Valentine better, but I'll need your help." I hated starting the conversation with a request, especially of Helen, but under the circumstances, I thought she might appreciate the candor. Below Helen's field of vision, Val rested her hand lightly on my thigh. The warmth was reassuring. "I've done some research and I think I can feed Val indefinitely if I become a Were."

If Helen was surprised, she didn't show it. She leaned forward over her desk and locked gazes with me. I could almost feel her peering into my soul, sorting through all my emotions and motivations, judging and calculating the merit of my suggestion. I swallowed uncomfortably at the sudden dryness in my throat but returned her gaze openly and boldly. Val was mine and I was going to do everything under my power to keep her soul intact. To prevent her from becoming like the vampire staring at me from across the desk.

After what felt like an eternity, Helen leaned back into her chair. "It won't work." There was a hint of regret in her voice. "Vampires have tried feeding off of Weres for generations and all we have to show for it is righteous indignation from the Weres and a bevy of dead vampires."

"I would never hurt Valentine."

"You may not want to, but your animal half will have very different opinions." The initial spark of interest was fading and I could tell that Helen was preparing to dismiss us. "Besides, the Were community would never stand for it. This could spark a civil war. I appreciate—"

"You don't understand." I slammed my hand down on her desk for emphasis. Helen flinched in surprise. "I love her. I will not let her lose her soul. Not if I can save her. It will work because we will make it work. It will work because it has to."

Helen lifted her chin slightly and stared at me unblinking. "Noble proclamations with absolutely no basis in reality."

I leaned forward, closing the distance between us. There was an icy sharpness to her aura that palpably hurt me as I got closer, but I needed to make my point clear. I was in her personal space now and I could tell it made her uncomfortable. She held her ground and I looked her straight in the eyes. "Tell me, in all the history of vampires feeding on Weres, how many of those stories involved a love like ours?"

"Baby—" Val took my hand and chafed it between hers. I could still feel the sting from slapping Helen's desk. I sat back down and brought her hands to my lips and kissed them softly. Tears burned behind my eyes but pride held them at bay. I would not show weakness in front of Helen.

Her gaze flicked from our joined hands to Val, finally settling on me. "I need you both to leave my office now."

"Wait a minute, I—"

Helen raised a perfectly manicured hand and cut me off. "I need to make a private call. You can wait outside until I'm done."

I wanted to protest some more and make my case stronger but Val tugged me gently to my feet. "Come on, babe. We'll be right outside." Reluctantly, I followed her to the waiting room and settled back into the couch. Val sat closer this time and wrapped her arm around my shoulders. I leaned into her, decorum be damned. I needed this connection and I didn't care who saw it.

While we waited, my mind wandered. It was possible to do this even without Helen's assistance. Karma was reluctant on this matter, but she had still offered to help. If pushed, she could probably do something. In for a penny, in for a pound. And Sebastian Brenner seemed unscrupulous enough. I was sure there was something we could offer him—well, something short of Val herself—that would persuade him to either turn me himself or find someone who could. Barring that, there was always the Red Circuit. Despite Valentine's recent preoccupation with my well being, I knew that vengeance was still on her mind. If the Circuit could house sociopaths like Val's attacker, surely there would be a handful of Weres willing to turn a girl for sport. I shivered at the implications, flashing back to the memory of the black wolf's muzzle, glistening with the blood of his opponent. That would have to be a last resort. There were other options and we could explore each one until we found the one that worked.

The phone on the secretary's desk buzzed once. "Ms. Lambros is ready to see you again." She escorted us back inside where we found Helen standing by the window, gazing out at the city skyline. Even though the brightness outside was muted by the tinted shade, I could see Helen wincing in discomfort. I wondered if it was the feeble rays coming through, or the memory of sunlight on her skin that made her ache so.

"What you are asking for is expensive."

This was not the response I expected but it seemed like a minor inconvenience. I glanced at Val, who wore a furrow of confusion in her brow. "Money is not an object. I'll make it happen."

"Oh, it's not money that this will cost." Helen turned to us, her face pinched in shrewd calculation. As she stepped away from the window, her hand rubbed absently at the arm that had been closest to the light. "I will be calling in a huge favor. A mark that I have held for over a hundred years. Do you have any idea how much that is worth?"

My spine began to tingle. The way that Helen spoke of favors reminded me of Faust. We were bargaining for Valentine's soul and I was offering mine in return. I didn't hesitate. "Name your price. It's yours."

Helen laughed coldly. "We'll see if you ever amount to anything I want. In the meanwhile, Valentine is important to me. All vampires are important to me. If you promise to do everything in your power to keep her satisfied, I'll do this. For her."

Fury rose in me. "Yes," I said, leaning forward again, using the force of my anger as a shield. "For her. I don't want any part of your politics."

Helen held her ground, baring her teeth in an expression that bore only superficial resemblance to a smile. Val took my hand and squeezed in sympathy and caution. "Baby, are you sure?" she murmured. "We can find another way."

I unclenched my jaw and exhaled my anger, never taking my gaze from Helen. "When do we start?"

"Right away. The next full moon is in twenty-six days. The

Were sample will arrive in two days and we can introduce the virus immediately. That will give us ample time to prepare you before your first lunar transformation."

"Were sample?" Val's tone was suspicious.

"The donor would prefer to remain anonymous at this time, so we will use his blood to treat Alexa. But rest assured, I have known him for a very long time and he will be a remarkable sire. Weres are very serious about lineage and you, Alexa, will be descended from the finest."

"Her animal half, what will that be?"

Helen turned to Val and regarded her intensely."Does that matter to you, dear Valentine?"

Val swallowed audibly and looked away. "No," she murmured, "just curious."

"Panther. Alexa will become a Werepanther. An exceedingly rare and noble incarnation. She will be the only one in the northeast, as a matter of fact." Helen didn't look at me as she said this. I could feel her condescension like a beast as it clawed down my throat and seized my stomach. She wanted me to be grateful, and I was, but not for her reasons, and certainly not in any way that I would be willing to prostrate myself in front of this vile woman. "Come by the West Side facility tomorrow night. Darren will be there to give you your first lessons as a Were."

"Thank you." My voice was measured and cold.

"My pleasure." Her gaze never left Valentine.

CHAPTER SIXTEEN

On the cab ride back from Helen's office, I called Karma and told her what had transpired. She immediately offered to come over and start with my education. I was grateful that she was so willing to help; it was a pleasant contrast to Helen's pound-of-flesh approach. By the time Karma arrived at our apartment, I had mostly shaken off my simmering anger. I'd have a preturnaturally long life ahead of me to prove to Helen that I ought not to be underestimated. And it shouldn't matter what she thought, anyway. Except, of course, that it did—as Val's mentor, and as one of the most powerful people in the City. Maybe after I'd been infected, I'd feel more capable of mustering up some indifference to her and her machinations.

As Karma took a seat in our living room, I realized that this was the first time we had ever had a guest at our dining table. Val and I had just picked out the secondhand table days before she was attacked. And since then we had no time for entertaining. We had originally chosen the large, unfinished wooden table with lavish dinner parties in mind. I pushed away the wave of sadness that momentarily threatened to overwhelm me.

Karma was dressed casually in dark jeans and a black turtleneck sweater. She carried a large brief bag that now lay open on the table displaying multicolored files and folders, all labeled meticulously in tidy block letters.

Val entered with a pitcher of water and three tall glasses on a plate. After setting them down carefully away from the papers, she took the chair next to mine and scooted closer so that her thigh could press against me. "So, this is what Shifter 101 looks like?" She smiled but it didn't quite reach her eyes.

"It's all the notes I compiled while researching for the Web site. There are even things in here that I didn't put online." Karma pulled out a light blue folder thick with papers and handed it to me. "Here is some research that has been conducted secretly over the past few decades. There is information about healing, feeding, mating, and other behaviors in human and animal forms."

I flipped through the file and marveled at the breadth and depth of information. "I really appreciate this. You didn't have to come all the way here just to drop off files. I would have been more than happy to pick them up from the museum."

"I know. I came here to talk about how you feel." Karma held my gaze steadily.

Apprehension prickled across my skin. "I feel fine."

"Now maybe, but you need to know that becoming a Wereshifter is more than a physical change. It is an emotional, psychological, and spiritual transformation. Inviting an animal into your consciousness is unlike any experience you have ever imagined."

"Is it dangerous?" Val asked. I could hear the careful modulation of her voice—she was anxious, but putting on a brave front. I reached for her hand and our fingers interwove automatically.

"It can be. That's why I'm here. If you know what's coming, it may help you adjust a little better." Karma's eyes crinkled in remembered pain. "I wish someone had been around to explain things before my first full moon."

"What is it like?" I leaned forward, thirsty for more details.

"It has been described many ways by many people: 'out of sorts,' 'not myself,' 'like being watched all the time.'" Karma tapped a pink folder in the pile. "Testimonials. For me, it feels like dreaming when you are awake. It's like being aware of two realities at the same time. It is very disconcerting and distracting until you get used to it."

"How long does that take?"

"It will be practically unbearable for the first lunar cycle, and probably longer. You may need to get medication for it. Valium and Klonopin work well to quell your anxiety. But you need to remember that it will get better. You just have to wait it out a few months, possibly a year."

Val nodded. "Whatever medication you need, you'll have. That much, I can do."

"And," I mused, "doing this now means that I'll have the rest of winter break to adjust." School didn't start up again until mid January, which gave me almost three weeks to assimilate to the virus. It wouldn't be easy, but I'd find a way.

"While in human form, your animal self will be subordinate," Karma continued, "but she'll still be there lurking. You will be in control but will have access to her instincts. You'll begin to see things like animals do, sensing social power structures and reading minute body language. If you listen to your panther, Alexa, she can teach you marvelous things you never noticed before." Karma's last sentence was whispered in reverence.

"And in animal form?" Part of me was scared to hear her answer, but the academic in me thrilled to the unknown.

"At first you will feel imprisoned. You will feel trapped and incapable of anything except observation. Paralysis in and of itself is frightening, but now imagine someone else moving you, controlling all of your actions." Val tensed at Karma's words and I wondered if that was what her thirst felt like. "You will begin to despair that you will ever regain control. Do not lose hope. Treat it like you would watching a movie. That helps, sometimes."

"A movie. That doesn't sound too bad." I smiled weakly when Val squeezed my hand in encouragement. "I'll just do that until it feels more familiar."

Karma nodded but didn't smile back. "That's when it gets hard. As you adjust to the panther's presence in your life, she will be adjusting to your presence in hers. Eventually, she's going to try to insert herself and her needs while you are in human form. For many young Weres, this phase is make or break. Animals are hierarchical. By nature, they jockey for domination. If your beast gets the best of you, you may lose yourself forever."

"What does that mean?"

"On a minor scale, it usually involves personality changes. A shortness of temper or a tendency to gluttony." Karma caught my gaze and held it, unwavering. "In the worst cases, the animal takes over and the Shifter goes feral, unable to change back into human form again."

I sat back in surprise, my mind whirling as it tried to process what that would feel like. Feral. God. Val squeezed my hand again, and when she spoke, her voice was steady. She was being my rock, just as I had been hers after the mugging.

"How do we prevent that from happening?"

"You must fight it," Karma told me. "Through the fear, through the confusion, through the hopelessness, you fight it. You master your beast by not backing down and by waiting for her to flinch. And when she does, you subjugate her to your will."

I nodded in understanding. It seemed so logical when she laid it out like that. Practice was destined to be more difficult than theory, I knew that. But months ago, I hadn't even known that this world existed, and now I was in love with a vampire and sitting across my dinner table from a Wereshifter. "Your animal, what is it?"

"A jackal. I was bitten over three years ago while on an archeological dig in Egypt." Karma's lips quirked into a sarcastic grin. "We were unearthing a tomb, but it would have been poetic justice if I'd been at a temple to Anubis instead."

I remembered Val asking Helen about my bestial half. Did it matter? Did the woman choose the beast or did the beast choose the woman? I would never know the natural order of things because my transformation would be planned. I wondered if the panther would suit me.

"Three years," I mused. "It seems like a long time from where I stand, but that's probably not true for you, is it?"

Karma closed her eyes as a shudder passed through her body. Moments passed before she opened them again. "It's still a struggle for me, I won't sugarcoat it. Every Were's battle is unique. And each one is epic."

She pushed her chair back and stood. We rose with her, Val wrapping one arm around my waist as we walked Karma to the door. "You have my number if you think of any more questions. Darren will be a good teacher to you. I know he has helped several others through their first transformations."

"Thank you." I shook Karma's hand gratefully.

Her golden eyes flicked to Val and then me. "Good luck."

❖

Friday night at the Consortium's hunting facility on the West Side was a dead zone. Darren was waiting for us in the lobby and waved us in past the armed guard sitting at the check-in desk. He maneuvered us to the freight elevator and after a hand scan and key code entry, we were on our way to the sub-basement. The elevator doors opened to a large, cavernous space that resembled the inside of an airplane hangar decked out like a zoo habitat. A narrow bubbling stream ran through the center of the room and dense vegetation and small trees filled out the space. On the far wall opposite the elevator, a heavy metal door swung open and Helen emerged, prim, proper, and slightly dangerous in her tailored black silk pantsuit. She beckoned for us to follow her.

Behind the metal door lay a sterile white hallway that led to a set of stairs. We walked up four flights to a catwalk that ended in a small room. The room featured a full wall of windows that overlooked the hangar area we had just been in. There were some chairs and a phone in the room but little else. An observation room, I realized.

"Make yourself comfortable." Helen picked up the phone and punched in a few numbers. "We are ready when you are." She hung up the phone without waiting for acknowledgment.

Val and I pushed two chairs close together and sat. She immediately engulfed my left hand into both of hers. We peered into the hangar below and watched as Darren carefully stripped off all his clothes and set them aside. He was palming something in his right hand when he finally stood, naked. He tilted his head to the right and left, stretching the thick muscles of his neck before jumping up and down a few times like a sprinter preparing to take to his blocks. Then he flicked his right hand out, revealing a four-inch long switchblade. Before we could register what was happening, he jammed the blade into his thigh all the way to the hilt and roared out with a primal scream.

"Shit!" I jumped up and pressed both palms against the viewing window, staring in horror as blood began to flow copiously down Darren's right leg. Gently, Val drew me back down into my chair. Her gaze was full of concern, but thirst lurked in the tense set of her mouth. Even as she turned her attention back to the spectacle below, her tongue flickered over the sharp tip of each canine.

I turned back to the violent spectacle below as Darren fell to his side, pulled the blade from his leg, and flung it across the room. Then a series of seizures racked his large frame, sending him skittering sideways across the hangar floor. Like the time in the conference room all those months ago, his body began to shake faster and faster until it appeared to blur at the edges, like a science fiction hologram flickering into transmission. He vibrated like this for a few minutes until suddenly, he was no longer a man but a wolf rolling over and onto his paws.

"Unbelievable," I whispered. Despite having seen Darren do this before, it still defied all logic. The wolf had circled back and was now sniffing the pool of Darren's blood on the ground. With a harsh grating sound, a small set of double doors in the back of the room swung open and a flash of tan and white streaked across the room. The wolf was on the chase immediately, loping effortlessly through the brush and foliage of the room. Everything was happening at such a frenetic pace that it took me a couple minutes before I realized they had released a small deer into the room as Darren's prey. The wolf would stop every once in a while, reassess the deer's location, and then adjust his angle of approach. Each time he did this, he drove his target closer to one of the corners of the room. It wouldn't be long before the deer either ran out of steam or got itself trapped. I leaned forward to catch as much of the action as I could.

"It's beautiful, isn't it? This dance of death." I couldn't tell whom Helen was speaking to; her attention was riveted on the scene below. "It's a delicate game: studying your target, predicting their next move, then goading them into your trap. It takes time to set up and patience to execute."

Below, the wolf had finally cornered his prey and cut off all escape routes. The deer, wild-eyed and foaming with fear, stumbled over its own legs trying to back away. In an instant, the wolf was on its neck, and with a sickening snap that we could hear all the way up in the viewing room, the deer went down in a boneless heap. I forced myself to watch as the wolf triumphantly gorged himself on his kill.

Helen turned to me then with a shrewd and calculating glance. "Are you sure, Alexa, that this is the life for you?"

I looked over at Val. She was more relaxed now, her thirst having eased, I supposed, once Darren had shifted. Her head was cocked slightly, and she squinted at the scene before her with the same concentration that she gave her medical textbooks. She was the love of my life, and we could have forever. I wasn't going to let Helen's doubts, or even

Karma's much more benevolent admonitions, stand in my way. I would find control, even if the fight was bitter and long.

"Yes. Yes, it is."

❖

The cab ride back to our apartment was quiet. I spent the whole ride absorbed in my own thoughts, replaying every aspect of the hunt in my mind. The exhilaration of the chase warred with the violence and brutality of it. I was glad that in animal form, my panther's instincts would take over because I surely did not have it in me to go for the kill. Val didn't speak either—her thumb made rhythmic circles against the back of my hand, but she seemed distracted. Almost as though she were having an internal debate with herself.

We crossed the threshold of our apartment together, and I immediately headed for the bedroom. I didn't want to think anymore—I just wanted to find reassurance in Val's embrace. When I had stripped myself bare, I turned to find that she was still standing in the doorway, fully clothed. I made my way to her. "Here, sweetheart, let me help."

She pushed my hands away from her gently. "Wait. There's something…something I…" She dropped on one knee and looked up at me, her eyes bright but her jaw set in determination. "Alexa, my love, I know this doesn't feel like the right time and Lord, I imagined this moment happening so differently…"

"Val—"

She held up one hand, cutting me off. "I know I was against you becoming a Were at first. But I can see that it's what you want, and I'd be lying if I said I wasn't relieved. And grateful."

She looked down briefly and cleared her throat, and I could see the moisture rising on her palms. "Alexa, I want to marry you. I want you to be mine and me to be yours. Forever. I promise that I will love, honor, and follow you wherever our lives take us. I want our time together to be full of love, laughter, and happily ever after. I am asking you to be my wife."

My heart melted open in my chest. Blood pulsed through my arteries and veins like magma, setting fire to all my nerve endings. I blinked and found my sight blurred with tears. I looked at Valentine, her beautiful, fragile soul bared before me in all its loving glory. And when my heart relinquished its hold on my tongue, I uttered the only response that I could.

"I can't."

❖

The treatment room in the Consortium medical facility was reminiscent of the sterile guest room that Val had stayed in during her recuperation. There was an adjustable bed, an IV stand, some monitoring equipment, and little else. I sat in the bed wearing a thin hospital-issue cotton gown. I didn't know where Val was; they wouldn't allow her in the room for fear of contamination. I was exhausted. Val and I had stayed up all night talking after I had turned down her proposal. She had been understandably confused and hurt, too, though she'd tried not to show it. I tried my best to explain to her that the timing wasn't right: she had just undergone a life-altering change and I was about to undertake my own.

"When we do get married," I told her, "it will be because we both have all of us to give to the relationship. Right now, everything is just too uncertain. I can't let your fear of losing me be the foundation of our future." We'd reached an understanding by the time we finally fell asleep at 5:30 in the morning, but as I sat alone in the treatment room, I questioned whether I had done the right thing by spurning Val's offer. I could see myself with her forever. Was that enough? Had I been foolish to question her timing, or wise to hold out until both her proposal and my acceptance could be offered out of strength, rather than desperation?

A sterile-garbed technician came in and informed me that they would be slowly dripping the virus—separated from the donor's blood by centrifuge and introduced into a bag of my own blood type—into my bloodstream via the IV. The bag of blood would be slowly transfused into my system over the course of twenty-four hours to minimize the trauma typically associated with rapid infection. I was warned that the process would be very painful, but that they couldn't sedate or anesthetize me for fear of upsetting the virus before it took. I was glad that Val had been out of the room when I heard that bit of news.

The technician hung the bag of blood on the stand and slid the tube over the rails of my bed and attached it to the IV port in the crook of my left elbow. He fidgeted with a few of the monitoring machines by my bed and then turned to face me fully. "Are you ready, Ms. Newland?"

"Yes. Please proceed."

He adjusted a valve at the base of the bag and blood snaked its way through the tube and disappeared into my arm. When he had gotten the flow rate just right, he jotted a note in the chart at the foot of my bed. "If the discomfort becomes too great, just push that red button by your head."

I nodded and he turned to go. He was almost out the door when I thought of one last request. "Can you please tell Valentine that I love her?"

He grunted his assent and the door clicked closed behind him.

❖

Light, hot and sharp. Everywhere. I was trying to hide but couldn't move. The light held me, pinning me in place, stabbing me everywhere it touched my skin. I cried out but the scream ripped a burning gash in my throat and I tasted blood. A ripple in the air, the waft of a familiar scent. Food? I strained my body toward the source and the pain engulfed me like a tornado, shredding my skin and pulling me apart. A groan wrenched itself free from the bottom of my vivisected bowels, rising like bile through my esophagus and exploding in fire across my lips.

My eyes began to adjust. The light was still everywhere but I slowly realized that it wasn't binding me at all. I looked down at myself: arms, legs, breasts, abdomen, all familiar and yet strangely heavy. A tremor and my skin started to crawl, stretching impossibly tight across my flesh and bones while threatening to burst open and spill my guts all over the light.

The scent came stronger—smoky and smooth, like an Islay malt. Spicy and sweet like chai on an early autumn morning. Valentine. *Another tremor and I was flayed open, burning wetness seeping from me like acid tears.* Valentine. *The memory of fingers moving inside me as warmth pulsed from my neck in time to a secret symphony that only we could hear.* Valentine. *I threw myself in her direction, only to break into a thousand screaming pieces.*

I woke up screaming and Val was there. She was lying next to me on the bed, back pressed uncomfortably against the rail, trying her best to give me space. My scream sparked her to action, faster than reason could override, and then she was holding me, soothing me, crooning her love into my ear. It hurt everywhere—everywhere except where Valentine was touching me. I leaned into her and soaked in the comfort that she provided, letting her soft, loving murmurs lull me into the sleep I so desperately needed.

The next time I woke, it felt like surfacing from a dark pool. The pain was still there, but oddly muted—fire flickering around the corners of my consciousness. The acrid smell of disinfectant prickled my nose, but beneath the sharpness, I caught a tantalizing scent that flooded my stomach with warmth. I could hear low-pitched voices conversing nearby, and somehow I knew that there were precisely three people besides myself in the room. The steady beeps of a monitor punctuated their dialogue like a metronome.

"There haven't been any leads on the rogue vamp for weeks. The Circuit is the only possible lead I have." My heart beat faster as I recognized Valentine's distinctive alto. I wanted to soothe away her frustration.

"I want to help you," Kyle said. "But it infuriated Helen that I went on the Circuit without her permission." I could hear the fear that stained his voice.

"So there's no way you—or Monique—can get me back in there." Now she just sounded resigned. And exhausted. My fingers twitched. I needed to hold her. Everything would be all right if I could just be touching her.

"I can't. I'm sorry. And Monique isn't even in—"

"Wait a moment." Karma's accent was more pronounced than I remembered. "She's waking up."

"Alexa!" Currents in the air to my left shifted, and I turned my head in that direction, finally daring to open my eyes. The brightness made my head pound, but I forced myself to keep them open until the dazzle resolved into Val's beautiful face.

"Hi, baby," she said, and now her voice was thick with emotion. Crouching so that our heads were level, she stroked my hair with a feather-light touch. "Kyle and Karma stopped by to see how you were doing."

They entered into my field of vision then, framing Valentine and wearing hopeful smiles.

"Hey," Kyle said. "Welcome to the club."

My muscles felt so strange—as though they had all been unhinged and put together just slightly out of place—but I did my best to smile at him.

Karma stepped forward and briefly rested a gentle hand on my shoulder. "Well fought, Alexa." I heard what she wasn't saying too, though—that the harder battle was still to come.

I swallowed once, wincing at the dryness of my throat, and tried to speak. "Thank you." The words came out in a rasp, but they were intelligible. "For being so supportive."

Karma took her hand away and turned toward the door. "I'm glad you're awake. We'll leave you in peace."

As soon as they had gone, Val climbed into the bed. Her movements were cautious, but I could sense the urgency behind them. "Oh, baby, it was so hard. So hard to watch you in pain like that and not be able to do anything." She cradled me close and pressed soft kisses wherever her lips could reach.

"S'not so bad now." My tongue felt large and swollen in my mouth.

"Good, good." She smoothed the hair back from my sweaty brow, and I sighed in relief at the coolness of her touch. "They said they think it took. You won't have to go through that again, thank God."

"So tired."

She rolled away slightly and I shifted toward her, retaining the contact. She gave me a lopsided smile and wrapped her arms around me carefully. "Go to sleep, babe. I love you. I got you. Always."

CHAPTER SEVENTEEN

The ground was close, caressing my belly like a languid lover. The grass and brush around me tugged at my skin, barely slowing my progress but reminding me that I was prowling ever forward. The air around me was stale and hollow, devoid of sensation. I could feel it slowly lulling me into apathy. I let my head sway back and forth, in time to my gait. Waiting.

Suddenly, from the left, a flash of white and the swish of parted leaves. My skin prickled to life. My muscles screamed electric. Gone was the veil of emptiness—this was the hunt and my blood surged to it. I circled around, carefully testing the air. The initial surge of exhilaration was replaced by an unfamiliar caution. Tension stiffened my muscles and I growled in frustration. I wrenched myself forward and padded slowly to where I had first caught sight of my prey.

A fluttering in the bush just ahead and I was off. The air whistled around me in a breeze manufactured by the pushing and pulling of my claws against the earth. Deep inside, the unease tangled my guts into a knot. The scent reached me then, warm and rich like soil after the rain. I relaxed into my instinct, following the sight and sound and smell of my prey. There was a barrier before me, large and imposing, I shifted to drive the rabbit toward it. She dodged and broke toward my left. The move caught me mid-stride and by the time I adjusted, she was already several lengths away. There was another barrier further ahead. I angled myself to the outside and concentrated on driving her toward it. This time, she didn't dodge and I flushed her right into a corner.

Trapped.

Triumphantly, I edged toward her slowly, cutting off her avenues of escape. The fear that radiated off her quivering body smelled like ambrosia to me. I gathered myself to pounce and then—

A blurring. The rabbit vibrated, fading in and out of visibility. Unconsciously, I backed away a step. I blinked and the rabbit was gone, replaced by a larger form, pale and smooth. The body uncurled and I took two more steps back. A head swiveled in my direction and I stared into a pair of eyes—clear blue and deep like an artesian spring.

Valentine.

A voice in my head. Familiar, yet unwanted. I tried to inch forward but my legs wouldn't respond. The hunger gnawed ferociously in my belly and I tapped into it to force a step. Pain ripped through my body as my muscles attempted to rebel. Valentine. Valentine. Valentine. The thought pounded in my head like a heavy spike. I recoiled from the voice, from the pain, and relinquished my control to the Other inside me. She forced me to run—away from the prey, away from my instincts. Rage clawed through me and unleashed itself in a furious howl.

I woke just in time to stifle the scream that threatened to tear its way up my throat. Val was sleeping to my right, her arm thrown protectively across my waist. She was breathing deeply and evenly, oblivious to my sudden wakefulness. Outside, the night still reigned, but on the edge of the horizon, the barest glimmer of dawn was emerging. I carefully slithered out of the bed and rearranged the blankets to cover her fully.

Helen had arranged for us to stay in the same room that Val had kept during her adjustment period. The familiarity of the room was comforting even if its amenities were not. I tiptoed my way to the bathroom and grimaced when the harsh fluorescent lights buzzed to life as the motion sensor detected my presence. Carefully, I closed the door behind me and leaned heavily against the counter. Staring back at me from the mirror above the sink was a hollow face with unfamiliar sharp lines and dark shadows. I turned the tap to cold and splashed water on my cheeks. I welcomed its icy sharp sting.

I'd been having the dreams for three weeks now. In the early days, I couldn't sleep at all. Dr. Clavier prescribed some Klonopin that helped to quell the anxiety that threatened to beat my heart right out of my chest. I took the pills religiously for the first week and managed a few good hours of rest each night. At that point, I capitulated to Valentine's insistent urging that I let her stay with me. At first I had dug in my heels, fearing for her safety if I suddenly shifted in the middle of the night. She countered by arranging an alarm system: number one on the room's speed dial connected to the Consortium's security force. When I took a different tack, pointing out that her commute to classes would be doubled, she waved me off saying that if she managed it for the weeks of her transition, she could easily do it again for mine.

Finally, I gave in to what, at the core, we both wanted. Val was better at calming me down than any neuroinhibitor. With her to curl up to sleep with every night, I weaned myself off the medication. I could manage about four to five hours of sleep in a row now before the hunting dream would inevitably wake me with the beast's sleep-ending howl.

I eased myself into a cross-legged sitting position on the cold tile floor. In the days immediately after the introduction of the virus, I had demonstrated some of the characteristics of a woman going through chemotherapy. I vomited all the time and lost a tremendous amount of weight. I ached as though in the throes of a severe flu and would frequently be seized by debilitating leg cramps. Valentine had put up a strong façade during that process, but I'd seen the pain in her eyes just as clearly as I could feel it in every movement of my body. I welcomed the suffering, then and now, as proof that the virus had taken hold. And fortunately, by the time the semester had started up again, the worst was behind me and I felt strong enough to go to class.

Val was omnipresent. She had even changed her course schedule to match mine as closely as possible. She waited on me hand and foot, fretted when I didn't finish a sandwich, and threatened to bolt for Clavier every time I had so much as a headache. As a result, I had started to withhold facts from her. It made me infinitely guilty to have to lie to her, but my pain was much easier to bear with just my knowing it. She had fed from me only sparingly, not wanting to stress my body any more than the virus already was.

Tonight would be the first full moon since my infection. All week I had been feeling the panther coming into wakefulness, like a beast slowly emerging from hibernation. The panther's consciousness wasn't fully alert yet but her presence was there. I could be in the middle of a conversation and get hit by a distraction so severe I would lose my train of thought. Karma assured me that this was normal. She recommended that I take the time to study the sensations and get used to them, since they would only get more intense after the first transformation.

The knob of the bathroom door turned and shook me from my

thoughts. Val stepped into the room, blinking adorably. She saw me on the floor and frowned. "Are you okay, baby?"

I stood and wrapped my arms around her waist. I tilted my head up and was rewarded with a kiss. "I'm fine. Did I wake you?"

"No. No, I did that on my own. You should try to get some more rest. For tonight." Worry creased the corners of her eyes.

"Actually, I need to start getting ready if I'm going to make it to class today. There's a special speaker coming in for my Antitrust class and I don't want to have to rely on someone else's notes." I turned toward the sink to grab my toothbrush just as the spark of protest flickered to life in Val's gaze.

"Class?" I could tell from the slight waver in her voice that she was trying to contain the objection and sound reasonable. "I don't know if class today is the best idea."

I spoke around the toothbrush in my mouth. "I feel fine. If I have to stay here for one more day, especially today, I swear I'm going to claw my way out of the building, kitty or no."

"Baby, I just think—"

I spat toothpaste into the sink emphatically. "Val, this is not negotiable. I'm going to be transforming once a month for the rest of… ever. What's the sense in making this a huge deal when it needs to become a part of my routine? Besides—" I could hear the testiness in my own voice and my heart despaired that I was taking my aggressions out on Val. But I was too tired from dealing with the new emotions to sugarcoat. I paused to rinse my mouth and toothbrush in order to rein in my temper. "The panther…I think she needs to be outside. Especially today."

Val's eyes widened. "You can feel…her…already?"

"Yes. It's like she's sleeping. But I can feel her there."

"Wow." I turned around and wrapped my arms around Val's waist and pressed the side of my face against her chest. She hugged me automatically but there was tension in her back and arms. "You'll be careful, right? Do you want me to come with you?"

"I'll be fine." I gave her one last squeeze before stepping back. "But you can call me between every class if that will make you feel better."

Val looked skeptical but she nodded and kissed the top of my head. "I'll do just that."

❖

They moved my Antitrust class from the law building to a small theater in the nearby film school complex. I arrived early only to find that half the seats were already taken. The guest speaker, Christopher Blaine, was a senator from Ohio who co-sponsored the Blaine-Hutchinson Act, a milestone in antitrust law, specially targeted to prevent financial institutions from building up monopolies in the wake of the mortgage crisis. The reason Blaine's lecture was so well attended was not of his legislative accomplishments, but because he was widely considered to be the top nominee for the Democratic presidential ticket. Most of the people already staked out in the best seats weren't even law students, but curious citizens hoping to catch a glimpse of future greatness.

I found a seat in the middle, about two-thirds of the way up. Within minutes, the room started filling up. By the time Blaine stepped to the podium, there were bodies in every seat and even some lounging against the back wall and sitting in the aisles. I flipped open my notebook to a new page and settled in for some furious note taking.

My professor introduced his special guest to a thunderous round of applause and a smattering of boos. The second Blaine took to the podium I felt a prickling in my skin that made the hair on my head feel like it was standing on end. My throat was suddenly dry and I had a hard time sitting still in my seat. I shifted uncomfortably, trying not to create too much of a disturbance. I found that when I concentrated on Blaine's voice, the discomfort grew, so I tried to distract myself by scanning the crowd.

Two rows down, a shaggy-haired man had his arm thrown possessively around a petite redhead. She was leaning away from him, trying to take notes on the lecture. I could tell by looking that she didn't like his public display of affection but what was really interesting was that I could smell it. The disgust rolled off her like a musty rot and it only seemed to intensify in the face of his obliviousness.

I shifted my observation farther down and to the right. A baby-faced guy in a navy blazer and khakis in the front row was leaning eagerly toward Blaine, totally enthralled. His scent, when I was able to isolate it from the bouquet of the room, was sharp and pungent. *Desire,* a little voice in my head informed me. *He wants Blaine.* I shivered against the strength of it.

Finally I focused my attention on Christopher Blaine himself. The electric intensity was still there, but I forced myself to analyze its components. It was a powerful feeling and slightly uncomfortable. It was like fighting the urge to flee. Part of me wanted to attack him, but the rest of me was trying to steer clear. *He's an alpha*, instinct told me. *You need to fight him for dominance.* An image of Blaine lying bloodied and bowed before me flashed through my mind. I gasped out loud and drew the annoyed glances of those sitting around me. I swallowed down the nausea that roiled in the pit of my stomach.

When the lecture ended, I quickly gathered my things and hurried out of the hall. Many of the other students were hanging around to ask questions but I needed to get out of there as fast as I could. I held my breath until I got outside and then sucked in a long, cold drink of winter city air. It made my eyes sting and I closed them, feeling warm tears slide down my cheeks. When I opened my eyes again, Val was standing in front of me with a frantic look on her face.

"Babe! What is it?" She had a large duffel bag thrown over her shoulder. It looked heavy but she didn't seem to remember that it was there. "What happened? Are you hurt?"

I rubbed a hand across my face and brushed the tears away. "I'm fine, sweetheart. I'm sorry I scared you. I had a moment in the lecture, but it's over now. I just got seized by an unfamiliar sensation. That's all. I've got it under control now."

Valentine looked like she wanted to push the issue but I took her hand and led her away toward Washington Square Park. We walked a few blocks and flagged down a cab. I held Val's hand as the cab sped north toward the Consortium hunting facility. She was vibrating tension—I didn't need the panther's awareness to know that. I placed a kiss on her shoulder and snuggled into her arm. Tonight would be my first full moon. I would be ready.

I had to be.

❖

Val walked with me into the vast hunting room. The whole trip to the facility, she kept glancing over at me as if I were going to change right then and there. Karma met us on the way in, but as soon as she saw the looks that Val was giving me, she offered to wait outside. If Helen was in the facility somewhere, she didn't make it known right away. I wasn't offended. I figured she would make her appearance at the most dramatic and emotionally inappropriate time. I couldn't shake the strange, new feeling that she was just waiting for an opportune moment to claim Val for her own.

We walked to the same spot where Darren had shifted for me almost a month before. I turned to Val and stepped into her embrace. She buried her face in my hair.

I didn't know what to do or say, so I took refuge in the pragmatic. "I should probably take my clothes off. No sense in ruining a perfectly good pair of jeans." Val smelled so good, like Belgian waffles and crossword puzzles on a Sunday morning. I backed away from her reluctantly.

"Here, let me help." Her fingers were sure as she gently unbuttoned my pink oxford shirt. I reached back and unfastened my bra and when Val was done, I slipped both the bra and my shirt off in one motion. Val sucked in an involuntary breath and I could see her pupils dilating in desire. I unbuttoned my jeans and slipped them off with my panties. I handed the whole pile of clothes to Valentine, who was gazing at me with equal parts devotion and need. "You are so beautiful."

I stepped in close again and took her face in my hands, then tenderly pressed my lips into hers. I'd wanted it to be a soft comforting kiss but the moment we touched, her desire poured into me like a flood unleashed. I groaned into her mouth and slid my fingers back so I could grasp her hair and pull her closer. My nipples tightened and chafed against the wool of her sweater. When I forced myself to pull away, she cried out softly.

"Wow, that was…wow." I was breathing faster now and warmth suffused my entire body. "I wish we could…I mean…it's getting kind of late." I finished lamely.

Val sighed and nodded her head. "I'll be upstairs. And I'll be right here when you come back. I love you." We kissed one more time and then she took my clothes and exited from the doorway that led to the observation room upstairs. I heard the metal doors clang shut behind her with a brutal kind of finality.

With Val gone, the room felt bigger. I wasn't quite sure what to do with myself. I was suddenly keenly aware of my nakedness and overwhelmed with the urge to cover myself. Perhaps a pair of jeans was worth sacrificing. I sat on the cold concrete floor and hugged my knees to myself. Soon. It would all happen very soon and then things like nakedness and modesty would hardly matter.

I could feel the panther stirring inside me. My own thoughts were becoming increasingly punctuated with primal urges like hunger and fear. The panther didn't like sitting out in the open; she wanted to be in the brush. There were times when I practically shook from repressing the intense urges that bubbled up inside me like random compulsions. Run. Hide. Hunt.

I don't know how long I sat there but eventually, the urges stopped. Or rather, they were replaced by stronger and more compelling physical sensations. My skin tingled and I radiated heat. I untucked my legs and felt an unfamiliar soreness in my limbs. Then, the full-body convulsions seized me. It felt like cramps in every muscle at the same time. Distantly, I heard a cry. Mine?

The nausea hit me faster than I could clamp down and then, I was vomiting my dinner into my lap. I didn't have a chance to clean myself before another round of cramps lifted me from my sitting position and flipped me onto my side. I vomited again and this time there was blood. I wrenched myself back into a sitting position and looked toward the observation room. My vision was filmy, as if something thick and viscous was covering my eyes. I squinted and could barely make out Valentine's shape. It looked like she was pounding on the window and someone was holding her back. My stomach contracted and I rolled into a fetal position. I felt fire within and without. My mind didn't know how to process the assault of sensation. I felt numb, frozen not in oblivion, but in a haze of agonizing pain.

I began to retreat, psychologically and physically. My mind, in a last ditch effort for self-preservation, began to shut itself off from my body, absolving itself from physical responsibility. I let it. It hurt so much. I let myself detach from the nerve endings and the synaptic passages. I let myself fold my consciousness into a box tucked in the recesses of my awareness.

That's when she came alive—the panther. She flowed into all the places I vacated and filled them willingly, eagerly. I felt her muscles stir and her senses prickle, but I wasn't in control anymore. Karma had been right: the sensation was much like watching a movie, but from a distorted, alien perspective while being held immovable in a straitjacket.

The detachment was disconcerting—I had no body, and experienced the sensations of hers only as distant echoes reverberating across the protective shell I'd gathered around my precious consciousness.

I didn't know precisely when the transformation completed, but I was aware of her first steps. Her body elevated, she lurched forward, and then she fell to the ground. She was like a newborn foal learning to walk, and I felt her movements as though I'd sprouted phantom limbs. Her claws scrambled for purchase on the smooth concrete. Again and again, she found herself on the ground. Finally, I tried to help, tentatively daring to reach across the barrier that I had erected between us. I tried to manipulate her muscles like a novice puppeteer, willing her legs to move more slowly, only to find that command dismissed and replaced with a stronger imperative to push harder and faster. It felt like a rebuke, like a mental slap on the wrist, and I withdrew even further into my cocoon. I clearly wasn't in control anymore and the panther intended to keep it that way.

Eventually, she was able to move in a stuttered and uneven gait. The pitching and rolling of her new stride was dizzying and awkward. I would have found it nauseating had my body been my own, but the panther never stopped moving. Her drive to explore the room was instinctual and irresistible. She was halfway around her second circuit when a grinding sound stopped her mid-step. The air pressure in the room shifted and she whipped her body around in a tight circle, seeking the source of the change. For a moment, as the echo of her movements reached me, I couldn't help but be impressed by her strength and agility.

And then, several dozen yards away, a small brown rabbit hopped warily into the room. The metal doors snapped shut behind it, and it skittered forward in alarm before freezing, poised for flight. Even huddled on the edge of desperation, it was cute. It reminded me of a stuffed animal I'd owned as a child.

Every molecule of the panther fixated on the rabbit. Dormant instincts flickered into life from deep within. My logical brain rebelled against the delicious scent echo, but I had no agency. She wanted to sink her teeth into the neck of that rabbit, and I couldn't stop her. Most of me didn't even want to, really—not because her appetite was rubbing off on me, but because feeding was the only way I'd be able to regain my own body.

She prowled, slinking into the foliage around her, willing herself into invisibility. She got very close to the rabbit, close enough that I could make out the pungent odors of urine and cedar shavings under its distinct meat-smell. And then a stray branch caught against the panther's flank, leaves rustling. The rabbit perked up like it had been electrocuted, and faster than my human mind could process, it skittered out of sight.

The panther took off in a bolt. Her legs bunched and stretched like pistons. Between strides, I caught glimpses of the rabbit through the grass and bushes. The panther would get close, and then her prey would veer off at an impossibly sharp angle, making her scramble to readjust. Despite its ultimate purpose, the run energized me; I allowed myself a moment of exhilaration as the ground blurred beneath the panther's feet, but all too soon, she skidded to a stop. While I had been reveling in the power of her movement, the panther had managed to corner the rabbit.

Horror and revulsion at what she was about to do seized my consciousness. I attempted to wrest control back, and when that didn't have an effect, I tried to shut out the scene before me. Neither worked. I couldn't turn off the movie—I would be bombarded by echoes, apparently, until I changed back.

The panther edged forward unfettered, and with a sharp contracting of her haunch muscles, she launched her body at the rabbit, snatched it with her teeth and crushed its neck with a powerful clenching of her jaw. Somewhere inside her I tried to scream at the almost-sensation of my phantom teeth crushing bone, but the panther continued unaware, pinning the bloodied rabbit against the ground with her claws and tearing at the flesh with vicious abandon.

It was over quickly, the rabbit reduced to a scrap of fur and a pool of blood on the ground. Satisfied, the panther backed away and began cleaning herself. As much as I wanted to remain horrified by the brutality of her hunt, I could feel her satiation bleeding over into my mind. The steady, measured motions of licking and smoothing eventually calmed both of us, and lethargy beckoned us toward sleep. The panther shut her eyes and I was grateful. The last thought I had before oblivion claimed us was a prayer that I would wake up as me.

CHAPTER EIGHTEEN

The sound of the door closing behind Val jerked me awake. As usual, the panther reached for control, and I had to focus hard on subduing her. By the time Val had crossed the room, my heart was pounding wildly. I knew she could hear it.

"I startled you," she said quietly as she began to remove her clothes. "I'm sorry."

It had been almost three weeks since the full moon, and while I had made some progress at integrating the two halves of myself, I still had to actively fight the panther's urges far more frequently than I would have liked. During the first few days, I had transformed at the slighest provocation: a slamming door, the wail of an ambulance siren, a paper cut. I'd been afraid that I would have to withdraw from school, but gradually, I had gained the upper hand. I had only missed a week, but the constant internal struggle was draining, and I was exhausted all the time. Like a cat, I slept for much of the day, leaving only to go to class and then come directly back. Every trip that I made out into the city felt like an epic journey and ended with me fighting a massive headache. Between the horns, the sirens, and the crowds, I had my metaphorical hands full trying to hold my excitable feline half in check. Every time I was jostled by a random passerby, I feared that the panther would gain the upper hand. It was a vicious cycle—my anxiety only fed hers.

When Val slid between the sheets, I immediately curled into her body, sighing in relief at the sensation of her skin against mine—warm velvet gliding across smooth silk. She threw one arm around my waist and pressed a gentle kiss to my lips. But her mouth didn't linger, and her relaxed pose betrayed the tautness of her muscles. The thirst was riding her hard, as it had been since my infection.

"How did things go today?"

I didn't answer right away. Instead, I put aside my guilt long enough to bury my face in her neck and breathe in deeply, filling my nose and lungs with her sweet scent. It calmed me. "Today was okay," I murmured. "No accidents. I still slept way too much, though. My grades are going to be in the basement this semester."

Val shifted her hand so that she could massage my scalp, sliding her fingers through my hair as she worked. She took any chance she could get to touch my hair now—the novelty of its dramatic turn from red to pitch black hadn't yet worn off. Somewhere in Karma's files, I had read about the possibility of permanent physical changes as a side effect of the Were infection—hair color, eye color, sometimes even a subtle shift in body type—but I had never imagined that the impact on my appearance would be so obvious. I could still remember the shock I'd felt upon looking into a mirror, the morning after my first full moon, to discover that the roots of my hair were the precise shade of the panther's ebony fur. And it was growing much more quickly than normal, too. During the transitional period, I decided to dye the rest of it dark to match.

"Don't be discouraged, babe," Val whispered. "I wish you could see yourself through my eyes. You've made so much progress in such a short time. Don't you remember what Karma said a few days ago—that it took her months to reach where you are after only weeks?"

I smiled against her skin. "How could I forget? You remind me all the time."

She pulled me a little closer. "Yeah, well, you need the reminders. You're too hard on yourself."

I could have said the same to her. The discouraging fact was that we were at an impasse. I might have gotten much better at retaining control of my other half, but she still emerged every time Valentine began to feed. Which meant that Val was hungry, I was tired, and we both were frustrated. I had tried everything I could think of to keep her in control when Val sank her teeth: meditating, a higher dose of Klonopin, even some herbal teas that Karma swore by. But nothing seemed adequate to the task of convincing the panther that Val's fangs were not a threat.

When I felt the familiar despair begin to engulf me, I rebelled, shifting so that I could kiss Val properly. We had to keep trying. Her soul and our relationship depended on my ability to control the beast within. I would fight the panther on this until I had no more strength to give.

Val's tension increased as soon as my lips met hers. I made the kiss gentle at first, even chaste, until I felt the tightness in her muscles ease slightly. "I love you," I whispered against her mouth. "I want you."

The words were water on boiling oil; I could feel the precise moment when she released the iron hold she'd been maintaining on her desire. The kiss quickly flared into so much more, until our tongues were slip-sliding and our occasional gasps for breath echoed loudly in the empty room. I rolled on top of her, my hips undulating of their own accord, and thrilled to the firm pressure of her hands at the small of my back, clutching me tightly. After a day spent alternately trying to keep my eyes open and working to hold the panther at bay, I felt wholly alive, wholly myself. When I caught her lower lip between my teeth, her body jerked, driving one of her thighs between my legs. The pressure was exquisite, and I cried out.

Val's answering groan sent twin waves of lust and anxiety surging beneath my skin. I tamped down the latter, focusing on how badly I needed to feel her touch on me and inside of me. I sat back on her thighs and shed my pajama top. Her hands immediately found my breasts, and my vision blurred. I wanted her everywhere at once.

But Val had other ideas. The movements of her elegant fingers across my skin became slower, more gentle. No less purposeful, but much less frenzied. She was trying to calm me, so as not to wake the sleeping cat within. I didn't want slow and gentle—I wanted us to fuse like atoms in a star, coming together as the equals we now were. I rocked against her, telegraphing the magnitude of my desire.

She shook her head and rolled me beneath her in one fluid motion. "Shh," she said, pressing a kiss to each corner of my mouth. "There's no rush."

I wanted to disagree—to tell her that this urgency would always be present, even if we lived out every second of forever. That the fire that burned between us was eternal and insatiable in its hunger. But her mouth covered mine again, and her hands were tenderly caressing the sensitive skin beneath my breasts, and my head was spinning at the sensation of her body pressing me into the mattress. I did not protest.

She took her time, kissing every square inch of my torso, it seemed, until I could do nothing but beg breathlessly for her skin against mine. When she finally relented, pulling back just enough to remove her sweater and jeans, I reached for the latest pair of leather restraints furnished by the Consortium. Val paused.

"Can't we try without them, this time?" Her voice was soft and tinged with regret. "You'll feel more…free. Maybe it will help."

I was breaking the mood. The wistfulness in her voice made my heart ache, but I shook my head. "I can't risk hurting you," I said, deftly fastening one of the loops around a bedpost. Once the bonds were in place, Val returned to the middle of the bed and slowly began to work my pajama pants down my thighs. She pressed sucking kisses to the skin that she revealed, even biting gently with just her front teeth sometimes. The panther no longer reacted to those little love nips— another sign that we had made some progress. But I wanted so much more than that. I craved the sense of completion—not to mention the physical ecstasy that we could only find together when she fed from me.

Her mouth moved all the way down my legs. She paused for a long time on my calves while attaching the ankle restraints, and then she ran her hands firmly up the entire length of my body to pay the same attention to my wrists. When she finally sat back and surveyed me, spread-eagled beneath her, her pupils expanded dramatically.

"So beautiful," she whispered, just before taking my mouth in a tender kiss. And then her free hand was trailing down my body to cup my hip and pull me even closer, and her tongue was parting my lips as her fingers caressed the dip between my thigh and abdomen, and I was surging against her as she stroked me with feather-light touches. She moved down my body just enough to ease her fingers inside. Her tongue was a swirl of heat against my aching breasts, and I surged against her as much as the bonds would allow.

She raised her head, and I saw thirst in the tightness of her jaw, the trembling of her lips, the darkness of her eyes. The panther's consciousness shifted, growing more alert as I sensed Valentine's need. The feline presence in my mind was decidedly wary. I didn't know how to calm her, how to convince her that what she perceived as a threat was anything but.

In that fraught moment, Val twisted her fingers inside me, hard. The slight twinge of pain only sharpened my pleasure, but it also compelled the panther to unsheathe her claws. I sucked in a deep breath, trying to send her some kind of signal that she would understand.

"Gently, love," I whispered to Val, wishing that I didn't have to.

"Sorry, I'm sorry," she gasped. When she paused to tenderly kiss my stomach, a drop of sweat fell from her brow to my skin. She was starting to lose control. The panther growled.

In an effort to calm both herself and me, Val rested her cheek on my abdomen. "Should I stop?"

"No. Please." I would have run my fingers through her thick gold hair, had my arms been free. "Just…you were right. About the tone of this."

Feeling her nod, I let my head fall back to the pillow. Relax, I told the panther. Just relax. Val stayed just like that for a few minutes, listening to my heartbeat. Once my pulse was back to normal, her lips began to ghost once more over my skin. And then, so lightly that I almost didn't feel it, she fluttered fingers that were still deep inside my body.

"Val," I breathed reverently. "So good."

"Love you," she said, and the air behind the words tickled my most sensitive skin. My pulse spiked again. Oh, God, she was going to—

When her tongue touched me, I arched into the air and bit down hard on my lower lip to keep from screaming. Nothing could ever prepare me for Val's mouth—for the heat and softness and exquisite, relentless stroking.

As the pleasure built, I thrashed against the restraints. The vibration of Val's answering moan catapulted me right to the edge. Dimly, I could feel the panther respond to the tension that gripped every muscle, but I had no focus, no energy to spare her. Every molecule in my body craved union with Valentine.

As if she could read my mind, Val raised her head. "Babe…" Her voice was low, husky, pleading. The absence of her mouth on me was torture. My head spun.

"Need you," I gasped. Immediately, the pad of her thumb replaced her tongue and she bent her head to kiss my inner thigh.

And then she struck.

The pain of her teeth sinking into my skin merged with the perfect pressure of her fingers against me, inside me. But as I surrendered to that glorious ecstasy, the panther enraged, rebelling against the clench of the parasite's jaws and the sucking pull of its lips. She demanded the use of her own lethal body—of those sharp claws and viciously curved teeth that could protect us so much better than could this frail human shell. Tied down and now apparently injured, she was beyond all attempts at consolation. Appeals to reason—even the kind of animal logic that she appeared to understand sometimes—were futile. Val was a predator. The panther would not allow herself to become prey.

And so we fought. I thrashed against the bonds, not out of passion now, but as a physical manifestation of our internal struggle. My mind was a battleground between her instincts and my will. She pushed at me with the weight of millions of years of evolution, and I pushed back with determination fueled by my love and need for Valentine. The contest was like a tug of war, and I dug in my metaphorical heels, hard. But all I could do was hope to slow her progress. Inexorably, she crowded me out of my own head.

"Val!" I gasped, feeling my control slip dramatically.

The stinging emptiness of her teeth leaving me was the last thing I felt before the seizures began, pain flaying me open for the panther's rebirth. Dimly, I registered Val leaning over the nightstand, plucking the tranquilizer gun from its place in the drawer.

"It's okay, baby," she said, her words coming to me slowly through the agonizing haze. "Don't fight anymore. Just let it happen."

She was right. At a certain point, continuing the battle for dominance only made the transformation process more painful. Bitterly, I capitulated my last mental toehold, giving in to the eerie sense of vertigo that always accompanied the change. Triumphant, the panther shoved me aside, forcing my consciousness into that narrow slice of her primitive brain that I had come to call my prison.

The world shifted sideways. Scent of sex and sweat. Hunger, pain, anger.

Trapped.

I screamed at her as she ripped at the one restraint that had held through the transformation process, but she would not hear. And then she was free, balancing fluidly on the mattress, tail lashing and ears pressed close to her skull. Through her eyes, I watched Valentine point the gun at my face. She was waiting as long as she possibly could, to see whether I could somehow regain control after all. But that battle was hopelessly lost.

The panther growled, lips drawing back from her teeth. Val's chest rose and fell in a sigh. "I'm sorry," Val said, her finger tightening on the trigger.

But the panther was one step ahead. Her haunches coiled, then released as she sprang forward, fixated on the pulse in Valentine's throat. The horror was paralyzing—time dilated as the panther's powerful leap carried her ever closer to Val. In that endless moment, Val's intent to throw herself from the roof made perfect sense. I knew what I would become—one of the lost, feral, my psyche given over to that of the beast. I refused to wake into a world where I had killed my lover.

And then suddenly, her ears throbbed with the sharp report of a gunshot. A sting, high on her flank. I watched in wonder as Val fired into the panther's belly and whirled away, less than a second before razor-sharp claws would have shredded muscle from bone. The panther hissed furiously at her missed opportunity, but the shadow creeping across her vision made it impossible for her to try a second time. The lassitude was stronger than the hunger, the rage.

Her legs gave out beneath her and the darkness spread inward. For those last few moments, I let myself feel despair at failing yet again. And then, I welcomed the oblivion.

❖

The breeze was cool and the sun was warm and the earth gave slightly under her paws as she ran. Hunger temporarily satiated, she ran simply because it felt right. She was free. Exhilarating in the speed of her unfettered muscles, she went faster, bounding over the sweet-smelling grass. For once, I didn't feel confined, either. There was such joy in this—in the wind and the openness, in the heat rising up from the earth and beating down from above.

She crested a small rise and began to run down the opposite hill. To the left, a narrow path had materialized over the plain, leading to the metallic towers of a distant city, sparkling under the brilliant sun. It called to me. Home.

The panther slowed her pace. Surprised, I reiterated the command. Home. *She listed a little to the left and slowed all the way to a walk. I sensed confusion from her as she looked between the shining city and the open field. She took a few steps to the right before balking again under my insistence.*

Home. *Compelled, she padded forward. It was a strange sensation, like handling her by the scruff of the neck from inside her own head. But even as I marveled at having the upper hand, my control slipped. Instead of forging ahead, she began to back away. And then, whirling swiftly, she pricked her ears forward and resumed her bounding run across the plain. I sensed in her a kind of contentment with her choice—an alien certainty that all was as it should be. But she had not risen up against me during our brief disagreement. We had been communicating. And technically, she was right—while in this form, the wilderness was our domain.*

Our. For just a moment, we had been working together. I wondered if perhaps someday we could move beyond the fundamental divide that defined each of us now—beyond a her and a me to an us.

I woke feeling hopeful for the first time since the Were virus had ravaged my DNA. Val was sitting at the room's single desk, reading something. I glanced at the clock: almost noon. The events of the night returned: our lovemaking, my transformation, the close call that would certainly have been fatal if not for Val's heightened reflexes. Waking, groggy and ravenous, in one of the hunting facilities. Finally transforming back in the early hours of the morning, utterly exhausted. I had a dim recollection of my head lolling against Darren's chest as he carried me back to this room.

Disappointment jumped into sharp relief, but still the dream lingered, tempering my despair. What did it mean? Karma might have an idea. Maybe I could treat her to lunch. Somewhere quiet.

Hearing me stir, Val turned in the chair. Her smile was tentative and tired. I ached to be the one who could make her happy, rather than the cause of her stress. She pushed back from the desk and crossed the room to sit next to me on the bed. I slid over so I could lay my head in her lap. She stroked my dark tresses lovingly.

"Saturday's the seventh," she whispered.

It took me a second to comprehend what she was saying. "My God, our anniversary." Tears welled in my eyes and I tried to blink them back, only to feel them tumble and slide down my cheeks. Val's fingers were there instantly, brushing them away.

"I rented us a cabin in the Catskills for the weekend, longer if it works out. We always talked about doing that someday, remember? I want us to get out of here." Her fingers traced the shell of my ear and I shivered in pleasure. "We can get away from all of this complication. Just pack up and go to a place where it's just you and me."

My heart thrilled briefly at the idea. A vacation. That sounded so nice. So normal. But just as quickly, despair clamped down and snuffed the flame before it could grow. "It's not safe. My control is still so tenuous, and you won't be able to feed at all."

"Just for the weekend. I can skip a meal. I really think we need this, especially now."

I heard the sadness she was trying to hide in her voice and it tugged at my self-control. "I don't know, love. It seems so soon. I don't think it's a good idea to be away from the Consortium facilities just yet."

Val's fingers tensed against my face. "I think this is exactly what we need. We were just fine before either of us knew anything about the Consortium." Her voice was rough. "It doesn't feel right here. I don't like having people hovering over us all the time, machines measuring our every move and emotion. I hate knowing that every time we make love, there are three orderlies waiting in the hallway to pump you full of tranquilizers in case I don't get you in time."

Shivering with the memory of how close we'd come to that very scenario last night, I leaned even closer to Val and allowed myself to imagine what it would be like to get away—just the two of us, out in the wilderness, miles from civilization and even farther from the Consortium. I shivered in anxiety but there was more behind it. I wanted it, too. I wanted it so badly that I could feel the panther thrashing inside me, fueled by the power of my need. I took a deep breath, calming the beast within. Val gazed down upon me, hopeful and vulnerable all at once.

"Maybe, but I want to talk to Karma first."

❖

Karma arranged to meet me the next day. I practically had to push Val out the door so she wouldn't miss her exam. I loved her for wanting to prioritize me above everything else, but it wouldn't do either of us any good to fail out of school now. Besides, I told her, I needed to hear

Karma's unbiased opinion on whether the Catskills was a good idea. That seemed to get through, and she left me with a long kiss and a fierce hug.

Like every other floor we had seen so far in the Consortium, the thirty-eighth had its own unique design. The walls were a mosaic of glass and steel, giving the entire floor an open, airy feel. From one end of the hall, it was possible to gaze all the way through the building and see the city beyond. The panther was instantly at ease, more so than she had been in the vampire or medical wings of the facility. I understood instantly that we had arrived in the purview of the Weres.

I stepped into Karma's office and slid the door closed behind me. She was sitting behind a tinted glass desk, typing expertly on a slim laptop. Behind her, a wall of windows afforded a partially obstructed view of Central Park in the distance. My heart lurched at the sight of trees. Perhaps Val's idea of getting away was the right one after all. Karma gestured for me to take a seat in the ivory armchair facing her. I sank into the richness of Italian leather and she snapped the laptop closed to give me her full attention.

"I'm sorry for being so needy. I feel like I've leaned on you a lot over the last few weeks and I really appreciate it." I hadn't planned on apologizing, but when Karma gazed at me with her golden eyes full of friendliness and sympathy, it was hard not to feel overwhelmingly grateful.

"Alexa, I consider you a friend. Even if circumstances were different, I think you and Valentine are people that I would have wanted to know. And now?" She smiled and I could feel some of my tension slipping away. "Now you're family. Tell me how I can help and I will do what I can."

I swallowed around the lump that suddenly formed in my throat. "Saturday is my one-year anniversary with Valentine. She's reserved a cabin in the Catskills and she wants us to spend the weekend there. Alone."

"And you're afraid you aren't ready?"

"I don't know." The note of sadness was back in my voice. I hated it.

Karma reached across the desk and patted my hand reassuringly. "Alexa, the progress you have made in such a short time is phenomenal.

It took me months before I was able to keep myself from shifting every time the heater kicked on or the lights went out."

"But I still can't stop myself whenever Val feeds!"

"That's totally normal. You know that. You told me yourself that the first time you witnessed a transformation was when Darren hit his head." She paused until I had to meet her gaze. "Darren has been a Were for almost one hundred years. Physical pain is the most difficult trigger to control."

"Maybe this weekend isn't a good idea after all."

Karma shrugged. "Only you know if you're ready."

I sighed. This talk was a waste of both of our times; just like every other occasion I bothered her with trivialities. Of course I had to make up my own mind. Why was it that I expected somebody else to have the answers for me? I used to trust my own instincts but somehow, this virus had stripped away my self-control and my self-sufficiency. Every emotion was closer, now, and my patience was in tatters. I probably shouldn't have been surprised, seeing that I had welcomed an animal into my psyche.

I started to push back my chair to leave when the image of the panther running toward the shining city surfaced in my memory. "One more thing. I don't know if it means anything, but I had a dream last night after transforming back." I closed my eyes to pull the images more forcefully to the forefront. "I was the panther and we were running free. In the distance, I could see a city—this city. The human part of me thought *home*. And somehow, I made the panther stop."

"Oh." Karma sat back in her seat and I saw a torrent of emotions wash over her face. In all the time I had known Karma Rao, her interactions with me had always been empathetic and understanding. She had an explanation or an appeasement for every little issue I ran to her with. For the first time, I thought I caught tendrils of alarm and unease.

"Is something wrong with me?"

"No, it's not that." She took a deep breath and I watched her rein her calm back in. "It's unusual, but nothing to be alarmed over. There's somebody I want you to meet. I was planning on waiting for you to settle in more before I made this introduction, but given what you just told me…I think he'll want to meet you now."

I caught the implication in her last statement. "He didn't want to meet me before?"

"It's complicated." Karma reached for her phone and punched in a few numbers. With my heightened senses I could hear the phone ringing both through the handset and down the hall. Then a man's voice, deep and gruff, answered. "Sir, I'm sorry to call your private line but I think it's time for you to meet Alexa Newland." The response on the other end was so low I couldn't make out any words but Karma frowned and I knew the response had to have been negative. "Please, sir, I'm really going to have to insist on this one."

After another unintelligible exchange, Karma hung up the phone. She nodded once and gestured for me to stand. "I'm going to take you to see Malcolm Blakeslee, the Weremaster of New York City."

Malcolm Blakeslee's office anchored the north end of the hallway. It was the only room that featured frosted glass windows so you couldn't see what was going on inside. As we approached, the thick glass doors slid open with a barely perceptible hydraulic swish. Malcolm's office, like Helen's, was decorated expensively but tastefully. Unlike the other all-glass offices on the floor, he opted for pale blond wood furniture and natural cowhide upholstered seating. I sat in one of the armchairs and shifted uncomfortably as the bristles of the hide pricked through my cotton khakis.

Malcolm Blakeslee was a mountain of a man. His age was impossible to place. Tall and broad-shouldered, his most distinguishing feature was a thick wavy coif of golden brown hair streaked with white that brushed back majestically from his broad, unlined forehead. He had a high, aquiline nose separating a pair of dark obsidian eyes. A meticulously close-cropped beard framed a thin mouth that was curled in an open snarl of disdain. It was like being in the presence of Val's family, except even more personal, somehow. I wanted to shrink into my shoes.

"Alexa Newland." He uttered my name like a judge issuing a life sentence. "I had no intention of ever making your acquaintance. But Karma insisted." The disdain in his voice stung.

"To be honest, sir, I don't even know why I'm here." Somewhere inside me, the panther stirred, rising to the challenge of the alpha before me. I felt an answering surge of resentment. *How dare he pass judgment on me, just because the choice I made didn't line up with his world view?*

Karma spoke then, her voice soft and deferential. "Alexa, tell Mr. Blakeslee about your dream."

Malcolm raised one eyebrow expectantly and I launched into my story. I didn't see why Karma thought it was such a big deal. It was just a dream, after all. But when I got to the part about the city, even Malcolm's mood changed. The animosity was replaced with speculation. "How long have you been Were?"

"Six weeks."

Malcolm and Karma exchanged a glance. "And Helen orchestrated your transformation? I don't think your donor was present or I would have been made aware of a Werepanther in my territory. What method of infection did she use?"

I still hadn't figured out where this line of questioning was going, but I didn't think any of the information he sought was privileged. I may have owed Helen a favor, but she hadn't asked me specifically to be discreet about my circumstances. "Blood. The donor's blood was introduced into my system slowly over a twenty-four-hour period."

Malcolm frowned. I got the sense that he hoped whatever was special about me was due to some kind of scientific process. From everything Helen told me, my operation was standard procedure through and through.

"Can I ask what this is all about?"

Karma looked first to Malcolm for guidance and when he gave her the nod, she proceeded with her explanation. "In your dream, you were able to express a desire to your panther and she listened. Moreover, you were able to influence her behavior based on your thoughts."

"It was just a dream." I still didn't get why this was such a big deal and I was starting to get frustrated by the lack of communication. "Can somebody please just tell me what's going on?"

Karma started to answer but Malcolm cut her off. "What is your game, Ms. Newland?" His voice was a snarl, a barely contained threat.

"I have no idea what you are talking about."

Malcolm got up from his chair and began to pace the room. I knew then and there that a lion waited on the other side of his full moon.

"What did Helen Lambros promise you in exchange for feeding her latest bauble?"

The panther roared inside me at the rush of anger that escaped my control. I took a few deep breaths and willed myself to composure. "She didn't have to offer anything. It was my idea in the first place. Valentine Darrow is the love of my life and I have no intention of letting her soul slip away from her because of some random act of violence."

Malcolm stopped in front of the wall of windows on the far side of his office. He looked down on the tree-lined avenue studded with steel pavilions that made up Dag Hammarskjold Park. "Do you really believe it to have been a random act of violence?"

My heart stuttered in my chest. Malcolm's tone was so matter-of-fact. He might have been trying to goad me into a reaction, but there was also a kernel of truth in his hypothetical. "You think Val's attack was planned?" I shuddered and the panther clawed back to the surface of my consciousness. I clenched my fists and forced her back. This was no time to let loose my beast. I had to think.

Malcolm shrugged noncommittally. "I am ignorant on this matter. The vampires rarely fill me in on their plans, and more often than not, it becomes my job to fix the damage they wreak." His glare bore into me as punctuation.

"So am I damaged in some way?"

Malcolm went back to contemplating the view. He was quiet so long, I thought he was dismissing me. I was just about to get up and excuse myself when he spoke again. "There are barely a handful of Weres who are able to control their beasts during the transformation. All of us are Weremasters and centuries old. As you've been advised, I'm sure, most Weres have a hard enough time staying in control while in human form. Retaining control in animal form is a rare gift."

"But it was only a dream. It doesn't mean anything. I still shift every time Valentine bites me." My voice broke as I uttered Val's name.

"The panther is part of your psyche. She doesn't distinguish between sleeping and waking. If you are a panther in your dreams then she is in control. You are, effectively, a bystander in her dream." Malcolm turned to me, dark eyes blazing. "You have to stop basing your progress as a Were on your ability to feed your lover. I find that absolutely revolting. I intended all along to have nothing to do with you, but somehow, you have managed to stumble upon a gift that so few of us possess."

"Valentine is mine." I insisted stubbornly. "And I am hers. There is nothing revolting about that."

"There will come a time when you will have to choose sides, Alexa Newland. Will you choose what is within or will you choose that which is without?"

"I will always choose Valentine."

Malcolm smiled then, though without mirth. "We will see. In the meanwhile, I will help you master your panther. Your awarenesses are opening up to each other far more rapidly than is the norm. The struggle for dominance has begun. You need to assert your will at every opportunity, especially when she's fighting to take control of the transformation."

I ran my hand through my hair in frustration and shook my head. "What do you think I've been trying to do for the past three weeks?"

"You can fight her on your turf, but not on hers. Instead, you need to speak to her in a language that she understands. Tap into your instincts. Impose your will onto her by showing her how you feel in her terms." Malcolm's demeanor gentled then. "When you achieve harmony with your panther, it will be because your wills are one. You can't break her, nor do you want to. You are human. You have the unique gift of empathy. Use it to communicate with her."

"Val wants to go to the Catskills this weekend, just the two of us. Do you think I'm ready?"

"Look in the mirror. The answer is written all over your face. Follow your instincts." Malcolm's phone beeped once. "That would be my three o'clock. I'm afraid I will have to end our meeting here." Surprisingly, I heard a hint of genuine regret in his voice. He escorted Karma and me to the door, but lay a hand on my shoulder before I could cross the threshold.

"Know this. We are currently allied with the vampires because it is expedient and pragmatic. But there are significant philosophical rifts between the factions. You would do well to remember that, and take it into account when making future decisions."

His admonition, though delivered quietly, rang with gravitas.

When I nodded, he turned back to his desk, leaving me to ponder just how naïve I'd been, to believe that I could stay out of the politics of this world.

CHAPTER NINETEEN

I woke to the sensation of the car coming to a stop. Blinking the sleep from my eyes, I reached automatically for Val. She twined our fingers together and leaned over for a lingering kiss.

"Good morning, sleepycat."

I stretched. "Some navigator I was. Sorry about that."

Val shook her head as she curled a stray lock of hair behind my ear. "You needed the rest." Her concerned expression morphed into a smile. "Come on. Let's get our stuff inside."

We stepped out onto packed snow. I inhaled deeply, breathing in the scent of pine on the crisp winter air and the sound of a woodpecker drilling off in the distance. From the depths of my brain, the panther raised her head, curious. And then I felt something I'd never experienced before. Contentment. Even a sort of alien happiness. If she had been dominant, she would have been purring.

"What is it?" Val was staring at me from a few feet away. That worried expression was back, contorting her beautiful face into a frown. "Alexa?"

"She's...happy," I said, hearing the wonder in my own voice.

"Oh?" The bridge of Val's nose wrinkled adorably as she thought this over. "Maybe she's glad to be out of the city?"

"Makes sense." I popped the trunk and grabbed the two duffels that we'd packed full of sweaters and sweats. Val was juggling grocery bags and trying to fit the key into the lock at the same time. When she finally shouldered open the door, I was right behind her. We dumped everything onto the floor and looked around the small room, our breaths steaming in the crisp air.

A wooden table and two chairs sat in the middle of the room. Along the left wall were a stove, a sink, and some cabinets, while the right wall held a large brick fireplace. There was a frayed rug on the floor and a couch directly facing the hearth. A narrow ladder led up to a loft along the far side of the house, and I didn't resist the urge to climb up for a look. It held only a queen-sized bed and a nightstand.

"How is it?" Val said from just behind me. I shifted my feet on the rung to make room for her, smiling when she encircled my waist with one arm. "Oh, nice. Very cozy."

"Mmm-hmm." I kissed her neck, sucking lightly. When I heard her breathing stutter, I pulled away. I shouldn't have been tempting fate at all, of course, but something about being all alone with her, so far from the City and the Consortium, made resisting impossible.

"While it suddenly feels hot in here," she said, grinning, "I can still see my breath. I'll make you a deal: you take care of the groceries and I'll make a fire."

"Deal." This time I gave her a quick peck on the lips before descending back to the first floor. We worked in companionable silence for a while. I arranged several days' worth of food and drink in the cabinets while Val piled firewood both into and next to the hearth. Within twenty minutes, a broad column of flame was reaching for the shadows of the chimney, and I was heating snow on the gas stove so we'd have usable water later on.

Although she was just across the room, Valentine felt too far away. I sat on the couch, testing out the cushions and watching her make a few last adjustments to the blaze. Finally, she took a seat on the opposite end, reclining against the armrest, and beckoned. I slid into her embrace, sighing in pleasure as her arms encircled me. I tucked my face into the curve of her neck and smiled against her skin.

"This is so nice," I mumbled.

"Yeah, isn't it?" She was stroking my back with slow, feather-light touches. I could feel my body relaxing, molding itself to hers. The snaps and pops of the fire were comforting, and its heat was making me sleepy again despite my earlier nap.

"Sleep, my love," Val whispered.

"Want to…go explore," I said, even as I snuggled in closer. I felt more than heard the laughter rumble in her chest.

"Later. Rest now. We both need it."

She was right. Even the panther was in agreement, wordlessly urging me back into slumber. I caught the briefest of visions from her: tall grass, warm sun, the chatter of birds in a tree nearby. Halfhearted tail-flick at a buzzing fly. A lazy afternoon on the savannah.

Smiling, I let the warmth lull me under.

❖

We managed to nap for an hour before the urge to explore trumped the warmth of the fireplace. As we hiked up the mountain, the sun arced gently overhead on its way to slumber in the west, muting the sharp winter whites into mellow shades of pastel blue and purple. We began to see a few signs of wildlife: a hawk perched high on a naked tree branch; the occasional squirrel ferreting out its buried nut; even a snowshoe rabbit, darting away with one powerful push of its hind legs.

"I'm curious," Val said as we watched the rabbit zigzag around trees before disappearing into its hole. "What do you feel when you see something like that? I mean…does the panther want to take control? Do you get territorial? Hungry?"

I smiled at her stream of questions. "Sort of," I said as we continued on. "She definitely perks up. A few weeks ago, I might have had to struggle not to change. But her instincts are muted when I'm…me."

Val nodded thoughtfully. "You know," she said after a quiet moment, "She's—well, she's beautiful." At my surprised look, she hurried to explain. "You feel opposed to her a lot—I get that. Believe me, I do. But she suits you, too."

Tears pricked my eyes at her declaration. I didn't know what to say. "I'm glad," I finally whispered. I wondered if it was normal for her to be able to reach acceptance of my other half sooner than I could. And then I wondered whether I could lean on Val more than I had been—to draw strength from her instead of trying to shield her.

"Well, what about you?" I said a few minutes later, in an effort to lighten the mood between us. The path had broadened just enough for us to walk together again, and I caught her hand. "What do you feel when you see me? Does your thirst want to take control? Do you get territorial? Hungry? Hmm?"

Her eyes darkened immediately. A thrill of adrenaline surged into my blood at that look: love and need and thirst, braided together. "You know the answer," she said, and I could hear the roughness in her voice, the strain that it took to keep herself in check. I wanted that tension to disappear.

Hand in hand, we reached the spine of the mountain. While the trail had been steep and narrow in some places, this ridge was wide enough for both of us. The late-afternoon sunlight glittered off small mounds of windswept snow. The path opened up ahead and as I approached the edge of the overhang, I felt my heart catch in my chest. I hadn't realized how high an altitude we were hiking until I looked out at the entire valley below, spread out like a banquet of the vanities at our feet. Val pulled up alongside me and sucked in a sharp whistling breath.

"My God, it's gorgeous."

Trees were sparse here, affording us a panoramic view of the other mountains in the range, and the valleys weaving sinuously between them. The landscape rolled out before us like a tapestry of riotous color. Even in winter, the deep green of the spruces punctuated the snow-blanketed mountainsides like silent sentinels of spring. Speckled granite, glazed with ice and wetness, reflected the daylight rays in shining gold and crimson. The bright azure of the sky above met its dark twin in the inky indigo streams that snaked their way lazily through the heart of the valley.

I breathed in deeply, enjoying the crispness of the air and the crunching sounds that my snowshoes made at every step as we hiked the final feet to the pinnacle of the mountain. Instead of feeling small and insignificant, I soaked in the nearness of Valentine and the calmness of the winter and felt larger than life. Wrapping my arms around her, I savored the triumph in this moment. "It's incredible up here. I almost don't want to go back."

"I know," she said, a soft reverence tinting her words. "We're on top of the world."

Eternity, above and below. I turned to Val and gazed upon her face: so familiar, so beloved. She smiled at me, free and clear and pure. I looked into her eyes, a blue truer than the azure of the sky or the indigo of the water, a blue that sang of love and the promise of forever. My eternity, in those eyes.

I ran my hands up her sides, over her shoulders, and behind her neck. With a gentle tug, I pulled her lips to mine. The kiss steamed as we breathed into each others' mouths. And in that moment, I could feel the stress and tension of the last few months begin to leave me, dissipating into the air, soaking into the rock. It didn't matter that Valentine was a vampire or that I was a Were. We were alive, and together.

Soul mates.

Gradually, our mouths gentled until I shifted my lips away from Val's to press light, warm kisses on the cool skin of her jaw, her throat. She kneaded my back muscles through my jacket, and I suddenly ached to feel her hands on me with no barriers between us. But part of me didn't want to descend back into the woods—the openness and sense of space up here felt so good. Liberating.

"We should probably go," I finally said, "if we want to be back before dark."

"Yeah." She took a step backward and spun in a slow circle, trying to imprint the memory onto her brain. To savor it. I loved her for that impulse. I took her hand and tugged her toward the path. We were walking away from this magical ledge overlooking the world, but I knew we weren't leaving it behind.

❖

We made it back to the cabin just as the last tinges of red and gold were fading from the sky. Val reawakened the fire, while I began to prepare a simple dinner—spaghetti and garlic bread. When she came over to help, I couldn't keep my hands off her, and for the next half hour, we giggled like teenagers as we tried to fix a meal without ever letting go of each other. We ate on the couch, legs touching, and I regaled her with stories about my family's cabin in the northern woods of Wisconsin. When I got to the one about my oldest brother, lake leeches, and my middle sister's hair products, Val laughed so hard that she doubled over, tears streaking down her cheeks.

We ended up spooning, Val's face pressed against my neck as I stared into the fire, her fingers idly tracing the outer thigh seam of my sweats. And then, slowly, she pushed her hand beneath my sweater to rest her palm on my stomach. My entire body jolted at the sensation. I tensed automatically. The panther stirred, sensing my unrest.

"Shh," Val whispered. "I just need to touch you a little. It'll be okay. Relax."

Her voice was warm and loving, not sad or desperate or angry at my reaction. I closed my eyes, giving in to the urge to mold my body to hers. "You feel so good."

Her fingers traced aimless patterns across my skin for what felt like hours, until I was blazing in empathy with the flames in the hearth. Val's lips had been quiescent but now they were in motion, sliding back and forth across my neck. When she shifted up to lightly flick my earlobe with her tongue, a small needy sound escaped me.

I wasn't chagrined, and I didn't think to be afraid. Tugging at her shirt, I pulled her on top of me, blindly seeking out her mouth with my own. I was hungry but she was gentle—kissing me chastely, lingering at the corners of my lips. Beads of sweat rose to my skin, an homage to our rising passion. She felt them.

"Can I take this off?"

I arched in response, and she stripped off my shirt first, then her own. "Valentine," I gasped as our bodies reconnected. The exquisite softness, the delicate points of hardness, and the heat, oh God, the heat. My head spun. Val's hands roamed my torso, and although she was still being so gentle, I could feel the need behind her tenderness. I tensed again when she began to work my sweats over my hips, but for once, the panther didn't feel threatened. Instead she was almost…curious.

Naked now, our limbs twined together of their own volition. I clutched at the strong muscles of Val's back, urging her even closer. "I love you, Alexa," she murmured, rising up to slip one hand between us. "I love you. Every part of you. So much."

She was liquid need against my thigh and I, I was open as the skies during the monsoon, heavy rains pouring down on parched earth. I forced my eyes open to the stunning sight of Val moving above me, inside me, teeth bared in passion and thirst as she watched the ripples of emotion and sensation that crossed my face. I could feel the agonizing ecstatic energy gathering in me, coalescing. This was the essence of freedom.

"Val, please!" I gasped with my last coherent breath, and she heard the truth ringing in my stuttered words and the promise offered in the pulsing heat of my skin. Bending her head, she slid her teeth into the juncture between my neck and shoulder and took me fully. She drank gently but insistently. Warmth radiated from the pulse point in my neck where her lips met my skin. Every pull sent waves of pleasure through my body, coalescing in a knot of fierce desire deep within. Blindsided, the panther began to enrage—but I relentlessly fused our wills together, forcing her to feel the power and beauty of the ecstasy that ripped through my body and shook my very soul. Remarkably, the panther's resistance gentled and faded and soon I could feel nothing at all except the exquisite pleasure of Valentine touching me everywhere—her teeth in my skin, her fingers in my body, the heat of her, sliding frantically along my thigh.

Half a heartbeat later, she shuddered against me and her back arched as her teeth pulled cleanly away from my neck. I held her tightly as she rode out her release. When she finally began to come down, I took a long, deep breath, glorying in our triumph. She collapsed beside me, panting. I combed her damp hair back from her forehead and smiled. She looked dazed, satisfied, exhausted. A swell of love and joy and tenderness welled up in me.

"The ointment is in the side pocket of my backpack." I gestured lazily toward our luggage.

Val started to get up and then stopped. She leaned in closer to my neck. I thought she might have changed her mind and decided she wasn't done feeding yet, so I tilted my head to give her access to more. Instead, she stroked the site of the puncture tenderly, almost reverently. I moaned involuntarily and shivered under her touch. "It stopped bleeding. On its own." There was wonder and joy in her voice.

I reached my hand up and replaced her fingers with mine. Sure enough, the wound was dry and smooth, the way it usually felt a day after a feeding. "Wow." I smiled up at Val and she grinned exultantly in return.

I wrapped my hand around the back of her neck and pulled her lips to mine. The kiss was slow and deep and warm, full of promise and potential and passion. "Bed," I finally managed, breathing heavily as I pulled away. I rose from the couch and tugged her toward the ladder. When I threw back the sheets, she burrowed between them, immediately reaching for me. I crawled into her arms, peppering her face with light kisses.

"Incredible," she whispered. "So…incredible. Love. You."

"Yes. I love you back." I shifted onto my side to rub slow circles over her stomach. "Sleep now."

Within seconds, she was snoring lightly. I lay there for a long time, watching her and marveling at the miracle that was us. So many had said this was impossible, but we had overcome. Was there any force on earth that could stand between us now?

Contentment suffused me, but I didn't want to sleep. I wanted to run. I had contained the panther during our lovemaking, but she was still there, simmering just beneath my skin. She hadn't enraged, but she wasn't entirely comfortable with the pain yet. I might have managed to rein her in, but her first instinct would always be survival. At least I now knew that for the time being, a détente could be reached so long as I kept my vigilance and control.

I didn't want to leave Val, but the urge to be outdoors was too compelling. Silently, I left the bed and slipped out of the cabin. The night breeze wrapped itself around my nakedness, but I felt no chill. I started slowly, placing my feet carefully between the rocks and ruts of the path leading away from the cabin. The further I got, the bolder I became until I was no longer looking but feeling the ground as it passed beneath my feet. Faster and faster, my muscles stretched and my skin warmed. Branches and vines conspired to catch and slow me. I pulled past them without a thought, reveling in the sting as I tore free from their frustrated grasp. I laughed out loud into the night and the stars winked back at me.

The panther woke inside me, stretching like a cat out of slumber. I felt her heart quicken to mine and her awareness sharpening with every stride. I could share this with her, the joy that we both felt out here in the open. In this, we had perfect understanding, and I dared to believe that someday we could achieve the same peace when it came to Valentine. I reminded myself that there is always the carrot, in addition to the stick. I needn't always dominate my other self. Sometimes, I could give in. She pushed gently but insistently at the threshold of my consciousness like a friend—like family—asking to be let in. Before me, the path opened up to a large clearing. The night sky and its velvety darkness floated above and a lush carpet of grass and snow cradled my steps below. The panther asked and I acquiesced. I dropped to my knees, gazing up at the brilliant mass of stars that crowned the mountains, and willingly surrendered my body to her for the first time.

CHAPTER TWENTY

The morning sunlight, weak but cheerful, filtered down through the pine trees to form shifting chiaroscuro patterns along the ground and across the gleaming body of the car. I stood at the back, breaths puffing whitely in the crisp air, contemplating the arrangement of our bags in the trunk. We had plenty of room, but that didn't stop me from wanting to fit every piece together in the most efficient way possible, like a puzzle.

Val was inside, double-checking that we hadn't left anything. I looked at the cabin fondly. On impulse, I fished my phone out of my jeans pocket to take a picture. This place would always be special to me, given what we'd accomplished here. Maybe we could make a point of coming back, once a year. Or maybe someday, when we'd amassed enough money simply by being alive for so long, we could buy this piece of land.

When I turned my gaze to the mountains, the panther stirred. I feasted my eyes on the smooth rise of the wooded slopes and the jagged spire of a distant summit. How strange, to know that I had the potential to live longer than these mountains could survive the persistent whittling force of the wind and the rain. Deep inside, the panther pushed lightly, not content with just looking. She wanted to run. I shook my head in regret. Not now. *Home.* The shining city of last week's dream moved into the forefront of my mind, and I smiled. *Yes.* She pushed again but I tamped her down. It was getting easier to hold on to the upper hand while I was in human form. She hadn't made anything more than a halfhearted attempt to buck my authority as alpha since that first night. We were going to be fine, even back in the confines of New York.

I closed the trunk, started the car, and slid into the passenger seat. This newfound confidence was exhilarating, and I didn't feel tired at all; it was amazing how much energy I had regained simply by not having to struggle constantly against the desires of the panther. For the first time in weeks, I was looking forward to the coming hours, not dreading them. Val had been invited to a charity gala tonight that would be attended by a host of political bigwigs, and while I had despaired of being her date, I was now eager to go. In the absence of fear, I had begun to crave a social scene that didn't revolve around the Consortium. After my tête-à-tête with Malcolm, interacting with the Washington elite would be a cakewalk.

Val stepped outside and my entire body jolted at the sight of her: low-slung jeans clinging to her slim hips, green sweater poking out beneath the shell of her winter jacket, bright gold hair sparkling in the wintry sunlight. There was nothing palpably different about her appearance, and yet she seemed to radiate love and joy and peace in a frequency that only I could perceive. I had never seen her happier.

Suddenly giddy, I rolled down the window and reached over to honk the horn. She looked up quickly in alarm, but at the sight of me leaning out the door, a smile burst over her gorgeous face.

"What are you doing in there, Count Dracula?" I called. "Let's get a move on! Places to be!"

She pretended to look indignant, and tossed a pair of black lacy boyshorts through the window. I had put those on earlier this morning. They hadn't lasted long.

"I believe these are yours, Panthro," she scoffed.

Her teasing elated me. Finally, it seemed like the darkest times might actually be behind us. We had plenty of challenges still on the horizon, of course, but now, we could face them as a strong, united front.

"Dude," I said as she started the car, enjoying the easy banter. "Panthro was a guy."

She paused, palm hovering over the gear shift. "Did you just call me 'dude'?"

"So what if I did? That wouldn't be the first time someone's called you a dude. Got a problem?" When I leaned toward her, she automatically curled a stray lock of hair behind my ear. The graze of her fingers against my skin provoked a shiver. I hadn't thought it possible, but we were even more physically attuned now than when we had both been human.

"Dudes can't kiss like this," she said, just before closing the gap and devouring me. I clutched her hair with both hands, and when she pulled back to take a breath, I didn't let her put more than an inch of space between us.

"You're so right." I had already homed back in on her lips, but Val slid one finger between us before I could pounce.

"If you want to leave, then hit the pause button." Her words were warm against my face. I didn't want to move, but she was right—we had already delayed our departure by several hours.

"All right, all right." Begrudgingly, I untwisted my fingers and sat back in my seat, fastening the belt.

She revved the engine. "All set?"

My elation bubbling over, I planted one hand high on her leg, snapped down my sunglasses, and pointed toward the pine trees. "ThunderCats, ho!"

"Who are you calling a ho?" she said as she began to guide the car down the spiraling drive.

I thought back to our very first encounter in the Niagra—to the smoothness with which she had come on to me—and laughed. "Oh please. You were very much a ho before I came along."

Val struggled between amusement and indignation for the second time in five minutes. Consternation looked so darn cute on her. "'Ho' is slang for 'whore,' genius girl. I was not a whore. No one ever paid me for my services. I was a player."

"And I suppose I'm the sweet Midwestern girl who reformed you?"

"Reformed? Hell no." Val glanced over at me quickly, her expression suddenly serious, before turning her attention back to the road. "Neither of us was ever meant to be tamed. You're my match, babe."

My heartbeat stuttered at the depth of emotion in Val's voice. I squeezed her thigh in response, and she shifted restlessly. "Maybe...uh, maybe we should pull over."

I laughed again. It felt so good. "We just left!" I let my fingers dance up the seam on her leg, glorying in the ability to tease her without reservation, without guilt. "I'm instituting a rule. No sex until after the party."

"What? You're not going to have mercy on me when we get home?"

I stilled my hand temporarily. "We have a big gala to go to in a matter of hours. A black tie event. The first thing I'm doing when we get home is take a shower. And then I'm going out to get my hair done."

"You could do me in the shower," she pointed out.

"I could. But I won't. Patience, grasshopper."

She rolled her eyes, evidently deciding to change the subject. "So…you actually seem excited about this party. You do realize that my mother, and my father, and at least three of my asshat cousins will all be there, right? Maybe we should make a contingency plan in case World War Three breaks out."

"They'll be fine and you know it," I chided. "No one gets into a confrontation at a charity gala." When Val continued to look skeptical, I gently patted her knee. Not for the first time, I wished that I could eliminate the stress she felt over her family. Only now, I suddenly realized, the difference was that they didn't cow me, either.

"Maybe I'm eager to see them all again because they used to intimidate me," I thought aloud. "You know—wealthier than I could ever hope to be, politically connected at the highest level, parents of my lover…"

"Mmm. Lover." Val smiled and rested her hand on mine, lacing our fingers together. "So what's changed, then?"

"Now I can transform into a gigantic cat."

She laughed. "You definitely win. I am such the Robin to your Batman."

I cocked my head and looked her up and down. "You should wear tights."

"Oh, no. No, I really shouldn't."

"But you have fantastic legs—"

"What I have, lover, are terrifying memories of my mother stuffing me into tights and a dress every day during my elementary school years."

I didn't know whether to burst into laughter or make sympathetic noises. It was impossible for me to conceive of Valentine in a dress without thinking of the scenario as drag. "Clearly, we need to get on a better footing with her so that I can see those pictures."

"Well," she said, reaching over to turn on the iPod, "if you can convince hell to freeze over, then you have a right to them."

I didn't answer. Instead, I leaned back against the headrest and watched the countryside pass slowly by as Val guided the car toward the highway. Sometimes, it seemed as though Val had forgotten about our immortality. Her family, their money, and their contacts were simply a blip on the radar of history. They would rise and fall, but she and I would remain constant. Every chip they had ever held against her, against us, was meaningless in the face of our persistence against Time itself.

Maybe she still felt so human because of her fragility, her cravings. But she didn't have to feel weak—not now that I was in control of my beast. She had me to feed her, protect her, sustain her. This partnership was like nothing her family, the Consortium, or the world had ever seen.

Together, we were going to be a force to be reckoned with. I just knew it.

❖

Six hours later, we were on Park Avenue. "Up at the corner is fine," Val called to the cabbie, who obligingly pulled the taxi over to the curb.

I frowned as she paid. "The hotel isn't on this block."

She waited to answer until she had helped me from the car. I was wearing my new favorite dress: strapless and red, flowing from a knee-length height in the front to calf-length in the back. I'd always lamented "naturally clashing" with red, but that wasn't a problem anymore.

"I didn't want us to roll up to the Waldorf-Astoria in a yellow cab," Val explained, taking my elbow. She had already commented twice on how impressed she was at my ability to walk in such high heels—we were nearly the same height when I wore these shoes. "You deserve to make an impressive entrance, not to be jeered at."

I gave her my best skeptical look. "Val. I'm sure cabs frequent the Waldorf just as much as any other hotel in this city. The bellman wouldn't blink an eye."

"Pritchard would do a lot more than blink."

"Hmm." Sensing her discomfort, I pressed a little closer. "Maybe I should rid Pritchard of his right hand."

"Down, kitty," she murmured, smiling. Once we reached the entrance, she guided me into the lavish lobby and toward the bank of elevators. When we emerged on the third floor, a low, persistent hum greeted us. The panther stirred, startled by the nearness of strangers. Anxiety crawled uncomfortably across my skin. This was natural, I told myself. These people always made me feel uncomfortable. But I knew that the feral tinge to my discomfort was feline through and through. I threaded one arm through Val's and held her close.

"Listen to all those socialites," she said, leading me toward the Grand Ballroom. We collected our nameplates, and as we headed toward our table, I prayed that Fate—or whoever had done the seating arrangement—would be kind, for Val's sake.

The first Darrow we saw was her father, who was having a very serious-looking conversation with the secretary of state. "Let's not interrupt them," Val said.

"Yes, let's definitely not," I replied. "Oh—table fourteen. Two o'clock."

As soon as she turned in the right direction, she let out a sigh of relief. Already seated at our table was her cousin Holly, who worked as a healthcare lobbyist in D.C. When I had first met Val's family a few months ago, she had pointed out Holly as the sole member of Clan Darrow who hadn't treated Val's coming out as akin to her developing leprosy.

"Hey, Holly," Val said as she put down our nameplates.

"Valentine." Holly stood to kiss her cheeks. "And…Alexa, correct?"

"That's right." When I leaned over Val to shake Holly's hand, I couldn't help inhaling Val's candied scent. As always, she grounded me and excited me at the same time.

"You're looking well, Val. Feeling okay?"

"Almost back to a hundred percent," she said, reaching out to stroke my arm. Only then did I realize that I had unconsciously bristled at Holly's mention of the so-called "accident." The panther bared her teeth, snarling in aimless fury.

"Thanks again for the flowers," Val continued. "Where's Martin?"

Holly gestured in the direction of one of the bars, where a knot of men in their mid-thirties appeared to be collectively flirting with the bartender like a pack of scavenger dogs. Lovely. I would be staying the heck away from that particular corner, but fortunately there were three others to choose from.

"Can I get either of you a drink?" I asked, wanting to give them some time to catch up.

Martin was apparently taking care of Holly's beverage, and Val wanted a whiskey sour. I planted a light kiss on her cheek as I left, knowing that she'd be in decent hands.

I was waiting in line, watching some old, clearly Republican senator—or maybe congressman—flirt with one of the waitstaff, when someone put a hand on my elbow. I turned quickly and felt surprise. Olivia.

"Alexa, hi," she said. If I hadn't seen her a month and a half ago lying swaddled in a hospital bed, I never would have guessed that she had been the victim of a brutal beating. Her tan skin glowed against the black and gold fabric of her jacket and skirt. She looked vibrant and healthy and wholly human.

"Hello, Olivia." I tried to embrace her quickly, but she held me at arm's length.

"I almost didn't recognize you—that hair color looks fantastic on you. What made you decide to dye it?"

I shrugged, struggling to suppress a smile. "I just decided it was time for a change," I said, wishing that Val was next to me to get the pun. "But how are you feeling? You look great."

She waved off the compliment. "I'm still working out the kinks. I convalesced in Bermuda."

I nodded, uncertain of what to say next. I wondered whether, when Val saw Olivia, she would be jealous of Olivia's humanity. I hoped not. Then again, just because I was starting to reconcile my two halves didn't mean that Valentine was in the same mental space. She still wanted justice; there would be no peace for her until the rogue vampire was either in prison, or dead.

"And how is Val?" Olivia was asking. "I know she was having some lingering health problems. Is everything okay?"

"I'm getting her a drink right now," I said. "Come back with me, if you like. We can all get caught up." When the person in front of us moved away, drink in hand, I gestured for Olivia to go first and was surprised when she ordered only for herself.

"You came stag?" I asked as the man behind the counter poured Val's drink.

"No." She pointed to a petite blonde across the room, who was chatting animatedly with the Secretary of State's son. "Roselle Gibson. Consummate social climber. I expect to be dumped before I leave tonight."

At my look of horror, she rolled her eyes. "I knew what I was getting into when I asked her. Aston and I have a bet going about how long it'll take her to get rid of me." She flashed that wicked grin that had undoubtedly assured her of many a conquest since she and Val had been in boarding school together. "I'm going to win."

"You two should be honorary Darrows," I said, turning back toward the center of the room. "Val's cousins make those kinds of wagers all the time. They're probably suckering Martin into some asinine bet as we speak."

Olivia's perfect eyebrows shot up into her hair line, and I wondered how long it had been since someone had dared to challenge her in any way. "Don't think badly of me," she said, the words coming out more like a plea than she had intended, I was certain. Val was right—despite her aloofness, Olivia was attracted to me. The way her body vibrated and threw off heat when she was near me was obvious now with my panther-enhanced senses. And then there was the smell: sharp and pungent like that boy in the antitrust lecture who had been drooling over Christopher Blaine. Olivia Wentworth Lloyd wanted me. The panther inside me purred. The sense of power was heady.

"I don't," I said as we approached my table. I met Val's eyes as I handed over her drink, trying to wordlessly reassure her that she didn't need to feel jealous. Remarkably, she seemed calm, and I turned back to Olivia. "So tell me, what's the latest from the DA's office these days?"

We conversed for a while until Holly stood with the intention to drag Martin away from whatever trouble Val's cousins had gotten him into. Once it was just the three of us, Olivia rested her elbows on the table, gesturing for us to lean in. I took the opportunity to caress Val's shoulders and neck as I shifted.

"Did Detective Foster tell you about the latest mugging?"

Val and I shared a brief, shocked glance. "There's been another?" she asked.

"We've been up in the mountains for a few days," I explained. "No cell signal."

"Do either of you know Abigail Lonnquist?"

I shook my head, but Val frowned. "I know an Alexander Lonnquist. The ambassador to China."

Olivia nodded. "Abby is his daughter."

"And Foster thinks that whoever got to us is behind this latest one, too," Val said.

"It's a hunch, of course, but yes. Abby was beaten and mauled to within an inch of her life."

"What does she do?" Val asked. "Is she in politics, like her father?" Under the table, she reached for my hand and squeezed hard.

"Not at all. She's an up-and-coming screenwriter. Lives out in LA, but came to New York for the holidays. And now she's in the hospital."

Val fidgeted, her leg quivering under the table. I squeezed her hand again. "Does she remember any useful details?" she asked, her voice quiet and taut.

"She has no memory of the attacker," Olivia said, "but she does remember being put in a car after she was mugged." She looked at Val. "You were moved, too, weren't you?"

She nodded stiffly. "But I have no memory of it. At all."

Olivia nodded empathetically. "Whoever this perp is, he's clearly targeting people who have significant funds at their disposal. I've been encouraging everyone I know to only go out in pairs, and to carry very little cash on them."

"That sounds like good advice," I said as the rapid bouncing of Val's leg became even more pronounced. She nodded, but said nothing. What was going on in her head? Something she wanted to tell me, but not Olivia? Or was she just stressed out by this conversation, on top of being at this particular event?

"Oh. My mother is signaling me." Olivia got to her feet with a sigh. "Time to go make nice with the vice president. Talk to you both later?"

"Take care," I said. Val mumbled a good-bye. I was about to ask her why she was behaving so oddly when Pritchard's voice rang out behind us.

"Val-en-tine," he said, drawing out the syllables of her name. We simultaneously turned around to the sight of him, Martin, Collin, and an apologetic-looking Holly, drinks in hand. Pritchard's face was already flushed; he was well on his way to getting drunk. "Jesus. Look at you. Could you have dressed any less like a woman?"

I stiffened, but the twitching in Val's leg stopped. I didn't know whether that was a good or a bad sign. The panther raised her head at my sudden spike of anxiety and started to reach for control, but I pushed her back firmly. I kept my attention on Pritchard, trying to convey the disgust that I felt whenever I looked at him. *Bully,* I thought, knowing it would have no meaning to the panther but hoping that my emotions were clear enough. She snarled, and uncoiled into alertness. I leashed her in again. I was playing with fire here, goading my beast and feeding off her primal fury.

"Hello, Pritchard," Val said, keeping her voice even and baring her sharp teeth in a smile. A swell of pride washed over me. If he thought he was going to rattle her by insulting her androgynous appearance, he was sadly mistaken. Val could pass for a hotter guy than he'd ever be, and she knew it. Deep down, he probably did, too.

"The same cannot be said, however, about your companion here," he continued, leering at me. "How is it that we haven't met before?"

"Oh, we have," I said, as disdainfully as I could manage. The panther pushed again, hackles raised, and I almost gave in. Valentine was ours. No one could threaten her with impunity. "It was a few months ago. I'm not surprised that you can't remember. You were highly intoxicated then, as well." I rose smoothly to my feet and held out my hand to Val. "I think I see your mother, sweetheart," I said, leaning in to kiss her jaw. "Let's go say hello. Please excuse us, everyone."

And just like that, we were walking away. I managed to catch a glimpse of Holly's impressed expression before our backs were to them. Tucking my arm into Val's, I led us straight for the door. Only when we reached a deserted corridor on the far side of the elevators did I stop and face her. I had to unclench my jaw; the effort of holding back the panther was starting to give me a migraine.

"He infuriates me," I growled. The panther was pushing a little more insistently now. She didn't like that we had turned tail. She wanted to teach him a lesson. Maybe someday, when I had perfected my control, we could give Pritchard the scare of his life.

Val slid her arms around my waist and kissed my temple. "Did you almost transform, back there?"

I shook my head. "It was close, but I kept it together. We were both riled up and that made it a little harder."

She tightened her grip on me. "Oh, baby. I love you. But believe me, what he said didn't hurt. He's been delivering those kinds of potshots for years. They bounce right off. Why should I care what a jackass like him thinks anyway?"

"I know. I know that in my head. But it makes me crazy to hear him talk like that."

This time she kissed my lips, briefly but passionately. "You're my knight in shining armor. Or should I say sleek black fur."

I laughed softly, the last of the tension leaving me. About Pritchard, at least. We had much larger issues to worry about. I threaded my arms around Val's neck, twining my fingers in the short, wispy hairs at the base of her scalp. "What Olivia said really keyed you up. Did you remember something else?"

Val turned to look up and down the hallway. We were still alone. She put her mouth close to my ear, anyway. "I have a theory about why Abby and I were both moved after we were attacked."

"Oh?"

Val pressed even closer. "What if the rogue vamp has been deliberately moving his victims to places near hospitals where a Consortium doctor like Clavier is on staff?"

A thrill of fear rippled under my skin, bringing gooseflesh to the surface. I quashed it, trying to think this through. "Why would he do something like that?"

"I don't know. To send a message to the Consortium, maybe?"

"Or just to make sure that there's someone at the hospital who will recognize what he did to you."

Hearing the anxious note in my voice, Val squeezed my hips lightly. "In that case, why does this guy want to create more vampires so desperately?"

"I have no idea." I sighed against her neck in frustration. "You know…why are we even feeling compelled to sleuth this way? Shouldn't he be in Helen's custody already? What's her team doing—twiddling their thumbs?"

Val took a deep breath. "I don't think we should wait any longer. Foster's completely handicapped and the Consortium doesn't appear to have a clue. It's past time for me to hit the Red Circuit again."

I pulled back, frowning. Did she really think that I was going to let her go alone? I was the one with claws, teeth, and regenerative abilities, not her.

"You mean us."

"But—"

She reached out to gently smooth her thumbs across my cheeks. "It's violent—gory, even. Remember? People die, sometimes."

I couldn't believe I was hearing this. I was the one who could turn into a cat and maul people, and she was worried about my ability to handle violence? "You're the one who can't watch *28 Days Later* without freaking out," I reminded her.

"That's not what I meant. What if the panther reacts to the brutality? What if you lose control?"

I shook my head, refusing to let her write me out of this plan. "Nothing is more difficult for a Were than physical pain. You know that. So stop giving me the runaround. We're partners, Val. In this and all things."

A moment passed while we stared stubbornly into each other's eyes. Her resolution and determination mirrored my own. Deep inside, I felt the panther silently bare her teeth, as though daring Valentine to even try to stop us.

"You're right," she said finally, breaking the staring match to look over her shoulder toward the entrance of the hallway. "I know you're right."

Mollified, I pressed a lingering kiss to her cheek. "So. Since Kyle won't take us back, what's your plan for figuring out where and when the Circuit meets next?"

At that, she smiled—a dangerous smile that showed her teeth. "I was thinking," she said, pulling me close again, "that's it's time to pay a visit to Sebastian Brenner."

CHAPTER TWENTY-ONE

I wasn't used to feeling animosity toward a man for how he looked at my girlfriend, but the way Sebastian's gaze roved Val's body made me want to unleash my literal claws. Of course, he would utterly destroy me. Since my first transformation, I had become even more attuned to those kinds of things—the subtle gradations of power conveyed by a glance, a single step, a roll of the shoulders. I now understood why animals circle each other when they met. The evaluation was still a process for me. It took time. For him, I was certain, it was instantaneous: he was an alpha, and I, a nobody, was beneath his regard.

For now.

Val was wearing a heather green sweater and khaki cargo pants. She looked youthful. Boyish. I watched her play it cool with Sebastian; she kept her tone nonchalant and her movements deliberate. This was Valentine's public persona, stripped of the puppyish enthusiasm that only I ever saw. She was smooth, smart, slightly aloof. And it was turning him on. But while Val was adept at realizing when a woman was interested in her, she seemed completely oblivious to the desire in Sebastian's attention.

That frustrated me. And my frustration, in turn, frustrated me. This prickling jealousy was new—Sebastian's desire for Val had amused me when first we'd met. Now he felt like a rival. But how could he be? Who was he to her? An interesting new acquaintance, nothing more. Whereas I—I was the world.

"I'll talk to his agent," Sebastian was promising her. I had been listening to the subtext, rather than the conversation itself. "He seems like exactly the sound my weekend clientele is looking for."

Music. Probably some obscure DJ. Val did love her electronica. The entire genre was too repetitive for me, but Valentine thrived on a strong, fast beat. I wondered if she had noticed that whenever we were with Sebastian, he very effectively cut me out of the conversation, even now that I was also a shifter. That was fine with me. I wanted a chance to observe him unnoticed. The panther agreed; uneasy in the presence of such a powerful alpha, she wanted to watch from the shadows.

"So," I spoke into the brief pause, hoping to move this conversation along. "We have a bit of an ulterior motive in coming to see you today, Sebastian."

He raised one eyebrow. "Of course."

What a condescending bastard. I struggled to remain calm. He was probably baiting me on purpose, to see if he could needle me into a transformation. I wasn't about to give him any kind of satisfaction. At all. Very slowly and deliberately, I ran my palm from Valentine's left knee to the slight concavity between her leg and pelvis. Her muscles rippled beneath my hand and I could hear her breathing change. I knew he could, too. *Choke on that, Sebastian Brenner.*

"Why don't you tell him, love?" I said sweetly.

"All—all right." Val sucked in a deep breath when I let my fingers ghost over her inner thigh. She squared her shoulders and cleared her throat in what I knew was a desperate attempt to focus. When it came to me, Valentine had no defenses.

"We want to go to a Red Circuit party," she said, looking Sebastian straight in the eyes. "Can you get us an invitation?"

Sebastian didn't answer right away. He cocked his head, looking from Val to me and back again. Did this request change the way he thought of us? Would that be a good thing, or a bad thing? Or was he merely trying to decide whether we were serious, or tourists? Whatever he saw must have intrigued him, because he sat back in his chair and steepled his fingers beneath his chin. I snorted softly. Oh so pretentious. No one pulled that move naturally.

"Why?" he asked.

"Well, you know what they say about curiosity," I jibed.

Val jerked and glared at me. "Don't even fucking joke!"

I kissed her neck in apology, continuing to placate her by circling two of my fingers slowly against the seam of her pants. "We've been before, as guests of a regular, but that option's not available anymore. We need to get in another way."

Sebastian appeared to be lost in thought, presumably making up his mind. "I can help you," he said finally. "But you'll owe me one."

I stiffened, not liking the sound of that one bit. The longer we played in this secret world, the more people we owed. But Val just shrugged. "Fair enough," she said. She was vibrating with a nervous tension now that had nothing to do with my touch and everything to do with the promise of hunting down her quarry. As much as I didn't like being beholden to Sebastian, Val's peace of mind was more than worth it.

"There's an 'abandoned' theater in Hell's Kitchen, on the corner of Forty-seventh and Eleventh." He bared his teeth briefly. "In the old red light district."

"The party's there?" I asked, feeling disappointed at the simplicity. After being spoiled by the grand theatricality of the Steiner Studios location of the first Red Circuit party we'd gone to, this was a definite letdown.

"Oh, no." He laughed softly. "Every Monday, the marquee on the theater changes. It announces the date, time, and location of the next party. In code."

Against my will, my eyebrows arched. That was more like it. Val's excitement was palpable—she seemed to like the cloak-and-dagger aspect. "How do we decipher it?" she asked eagerly.

Sebastian shrugged and sipped from his cognac. "I'm not allowed to say."

"What do you mean?" Val said. I remained passive, allowing her to prompt him, hoping that he'd let more slip than if I were the one interrogating him.

"If you can't break the code, then you can't be on the Circuit."

Val frowned. "You won't even give us a hint?"

I nudged her with an elbow, then got to my feet. "Where's your pride, babe? We're smart girls, remember? We'll figure it out. No problem." Sebastian just sat there with a smirk on his face. I disliked him more with each passing second. "Thank you for your help," I told him as politely as I could manage. When Val stood, I curled my index finger through one of her belt loops. "Come on, lover. Let's crack this code and then go out to dinner."

She grinned and kissed me swiftly before raising her hand to Sebastian. "Thanks again. See you 'round."

"Good luck," he called after us, sounding certain that we'd need it.

❖

"What. The. Fuck." Val glowered at the marquee of the Vixen theater, a squat building made of brick that was almost completely obscured by black graffiti scrawlings. The windows were boarded up with wooden planks, and the marquee, tilted about thirty degrees, looked like it could fall off its hinges at any moment.

CLUB NIGHT AT THE VIXEN, it proclaimed. FEATURING: CAT CLAWS, FORKNIFE, AND DJ 010.

"How the hell are we supposed to make sense of that?" she said, scuffing the toe of one Doc Marten against the sidewalk in frustration. "I've never heard of any of those musicians in my life. Have you?"

"No," I said absently, wondering about the rules of the puzzle. The first order of business was to figure out what kind it was in the first place. An anagram? Some kind of cipher? Maybe, since the last word was actually a digit…

I met Val's frustrated gaze. "Hey, will you do something for me?"

"Yeah, of course."

"Do you have a way of writing down the numbers of each of those letters"—I pointed to the marquee—"in the alphabet? Let's see if they make an interesting sequence, or combine into something meaningful."

"Sure, all right." Val seemed happy to have something to do that didn't involve trying to solve a brainteaser directly.

While she pulled out her phone and started tapping numbers into it, I tried to rearrange the letters of each word mentally. This would have been a lot easier with a pen and some scratch paper so I could write down permutations and cross out letters as I used them. I was just about to suggest that we go to a drugstore so I could pick up a cheap little notebook, when—

"Cat Claws," Val mused, still staring at her phone as she punched in the numbers. "That reminds me of you. How about you use me as your scratching post when we get home from this goose chase, hmm?"

I felt the barest stirring of a realization, subtle and shifting like an underwater current. What do cat claws do? They scratch. Maybe Val's first suggestion had been closer to the right method—to look at each word or phrase as an entity instead of breaking them up into pieces.

"You may be on to something," I murmured, frowning even harder at the marquee.

"Seriously? I was just teasing you."

"Shh." I tuned out the sounds of the city around me. Cat Claws, Forknife, DJ 010. Okay. We were looking for a location—a place to hold what promised to be a highly illegal event. The venue would have to lend itself to discretion. Cat Claws. Cat claws scratch. But what about "Forknife"? Fork, knife…spoon? Scratch and spoon. Both began with the letter "s." I shook my head slightly. I was going to get nowhere fast on that line of thinking—plenty of words began with "s." So back to "Forknife." Funny looking word. The interesting part about it was that it was missing the extra "k" in the middle—in between "fork" and "knife."

In the depths of my brain, a spark leapt brazenly across the synapse separating me from interpretation. In between fork and knife. Of course! On a table, the space between a fork and knife was occupied by a plate. Plate. Scratch. Plate.

Scratchplate.

"I've got it," I said, hearing the surprise in my own voice. The panther raised her head, curious about the source of my sudden excitement. "Val…sweetheart, I've got it."

She raised her head eagerly, slipping her phone into her pocket. "Yeah?"

"Scratchplate. It's a grunge club on the Upper East Side."

Val leaned in to kiss me swiftly, triumphantly. Her eyes were bright and sparkling in excitement. "How on earth did you figure it out? And what the hell is a scratchplate?"

Laughing, I wrapped my arms around her waist, pressing against her long, lean body. "A scratchplate is a piece of metal or plastic on a guitar that protects its surface from being scratched by a pick."

The bridge of Val's nose scrunched up adorably as she pondered that. "Huh," she said finally. "I always thought that part was just for show."

"Nope. So, Scratchplate the club is famous for two reasons. First, it was started by one of the master guitar builders at Fender in the early nineties—supposedly the same guy who made Kurt Cobain's hybrid 'Jagstang' guitar."

Val was staring at me, slack-jawed. "How do you even know this stuff?"

"My high school grunge phase."

"You had a grunge phase?"

I smiled at the note of disbelief in her voice. It was easy to forget that Val didn't know all of me, because it sure felt like she did. I had to actively remind myself that she had met a carefully cultivated version of Alexa Newland—cosmopolitan, sophisticated, urbane. Light-years away from the restless teenage farm girl who had dreamt of the neon lights and sky-scraping towers of the sleepless city.

"It was my freshman year. In hindsight, I think I was trying to get attention. Big family, remember?"

"I must see those pictures." She curled a stray lock of hair behind my left ear, and I shivered lightly as her fingers trailed down my neck. "What's the second reason?"

"Hmm? Oh." I rolled my eyes at her smug grin. "Apparently, the club has been shut down by the police at least a dozen times, but always finds a way to reopen."

"Color me not surprised on either count." Val looked back up at the marquee. "So, what about 'DJ 010'? DJ-ten…could ten o'clock be the starting time?"

"Makes sense," I said, nodding. "That zero in front of the one bothers me, though."

"Why?"

"It's not necessary. All you need to express a time is two digits. Four if you're using military. But never three."

"Good point."

Val's warm breaths stirred my hair as we both stared at the last obscure element of the code. Zero. Why was it a zero? Maybe it would be helpful to think about what information we still needed. We had the time and the venue, but not a date. Not that we needed a date per se, since Sebastian had implied that these were weekly events...but we did need a day of the week.

"Oh!" Val said suddenly. "What if it's binary?" Just as quickly as it had come, though, her excitement faded. "Fuck. Even if it is, we don't know what the two options are."

But she was wrong. An event like this wasn't going to happen on a weeknight. "Yes, we do. Friday and Saturday."

"Nice!" Val hugged me tightly. "Think Friday is zero and Saturday is one?"

I stepped out of the circle of her arms and reached for her hand. "There's only one way to find out."

CHAPTER TWENTY-TWO

We meant to leave at ten o'clock on Friday, but it ended up being closer to eleven before we were walking toward the subway. I blamed Val's leather pants. And her black tank top. And the black leather cuff that adorned her left wrist. Val blamed my skintight T-shirt and ripped jeans—the closest outfit I could muster to what I'd worn routinely back when I was fourteen. Our lovemaking had been fierce, almost desperate, born of anxiety and the need for closeness.

We rode the train uptown to 110th Street and turned toward the river. As we walked, we huddled together for warmth, my left hand and Val's right cupped together in one of her jacket pockets. The other held her gun. Val was hoping that she wouldn't have to check it at the door. I didn't know whether I'd feel better or worse if that happened.

A few months ago, our conversation on the way to a party would have been light and animated, banter and flirtation. On this walk, both of us withdrew into our own thoughts. I was trying to mentally prepare myself for what awaited us. Blood. Violence. The thought of seeing someone die again forced bile into my throat, but I couldn't afford to fool myself: it would probably happen tonight. I was torn between revulsion and a morbid curiosity that made me avoid meeting my own eyes in the storefront windows. The panther was very surface today, as if she could tell that something was going to happen. If I was going to have any chance of keeping control tonight, I would have to pull it together. Beside me, Val fairly vibrated with tension. I could only imagine how she felt, knowing that tonight she might see the face of her attacker.

She caught sight of the club before I did. Red letters arched over a set of concrete stairs leading down into a recessed doorway. A large sign on the sidewalk declared that Scratchplate was closed for a private event. Val squeezed my hand.

"Ready?"

Given the fairly public nature of this place, I had expected some kind of security outside—a bouncer at the very least. But there was no one leaning against the plain black door, and when Val grabbed the handle and pulled, it swung open onto a hallway painted entirely black. Fluorescent lights embedded into the ceiling lent the corridor a glossy, metallic look. For a second, I hung back, hoping that Val might change her mind. She didn't.

We felt rather than heard the music after a few steps down the hall; it pulsed through the walls until it seemed that the club itself had a heartbeat, and we were caught in its bowels. Twenty feet later, we descended a set of spiral stairs that opened into a narrow atrium. Straight ahead was a tall metal gate—the revolving kind that were still in use at certain subway stops—and directly in front of it, a metal detector. I glanced at Val in time to see her jaw clench.

A Hispanic woman, her face and arms covered in sinuous tattoos, stood gracefully from a stool at the side of the metal detector. "Coats," she said in a husky voice, pointing to a rack crammed mainly with leather items. Clearly, Val was going to fit right in. "Weapons," she continued, pointing to a skinny man in a recessed alcove that I assumed was normally Scratchplate's coat check. Ironic.

Val handed over her gun while I hung our jackets on the same hanger. When I turned, she was pushing her claim slip into one of the narrow front pockets of her pants. The sight of her long fingers moving beneath the leather would have turned me on if I hadn't been so anxious.

"Welcome," the woman said as we approached the arch of the metal detector. She was holding, of all things, a spool of raffle tickets—the same kind that I recalled Monique rejecting offhand last time. I wondered what they were for. This woman could have been a very twisted version of my mother standing at the door of the gym during a soccer booster event. And then she took three hip-swaying steps to stand directly in front of Valentine. I tensed. When she leaned in so that her mouth was barely an inch from Val's neck, I couldn't help the growl that bubbled up from my throat. The panther pushed in harmony with my spike of jealousy, and I had to work at forcing her down as the woman inhaled deeply, then moved back. She was smiling slightly, as though amused by my response.

"One for you," she told Val, handing her a ticket. Val didn't thank her. Very wise.

The woman came to stand in front of me next, but barely leaned forward before nodding once. "She almost fooled me," she said, indicating Val with one hand. "Your musk is all over her."

I smiled tightly. *And don't you forget it.*

"Hang on to that ticket," she told Val, gesturing for us to proceed through the revolving door. "If your number is called, you'll be in for a treat." Her tone made the hair rise on the back of my neck; I really didn't want to think about why the tickets were only distributed to vampires. "I guess only your kind is eligible for door prizes?" I said, once we were both through.

Val rubbed the ticket between her fingers, regarding it thoughtfully. "Whatever this is for, I guarantee you I won't want it."

We hadn't even gone ten feet before the hallway bent at a ninety-degree angle, abruptly spilling out into a large, low-ceilinged room. The bar, a perfect square, took up the center. A few tables and chairs lined the walls, but most of them were vacant. The music blared from a DJ station in the corner closest to us, but the crowd was thickest near the far side of the room, between the bar and a stage. At the moment, it featured two completely naked women, their bodies glistening with sweat as they undulated their hips in an elaborate bellydancing routine. As I watched, one of them curled herself lasciviously around a tall metallic pole set in the center of the stage. I let out a relieved sigh; this was so much better than the dogfighting arena.

"Let's stick with the DJ this time, okay?"

Val nodded and took my hand. Hers was hot and moist with sweat. I looked up at her, but her gaze was darting around the room, eyes constantly roving in a search for him. "Let's get a drink," I shouted over the pounding beat. She nodded and set off for the bar, drawing me behind her through the thick crowd. We threaded our way past a group of men who all had identical haircuts and the same white wolf's head tattoo on their right forearms. A pack, clearly. I found myself feeling disdain and wondered whether it came from me or from the solitary feline who lurked under my skin. The uncertainty was still disconcerting.

Val slid into a small open space at the bar and pulled me in beside her. "Two whiskeys, neat," she called to the bartender—a huge, barrel-chested man with a shaggy brown mane that fell to his shoulders. His arms were as thick as my thighs, and covered in dark hair. He looked like a bear. I wondered if he was one.

"Any sign?" I asked, taking the opportunity to draw her arms around my waist.

"No," she said, resting her head against my shoulder. And then I felt her entire body stiffen. "Holy shit."

I followed her line of sight to the bar immediately opposite us, where a thin, pale woman wearing a dog collar was digging her fingernails into the pockmarked wooden surface, bracing herself as a chiseled man penetrated her from behind. I squeezed Val's hand hard as shock and arousal streaked down my spine. My involuntary gasp came out more like a groan. And then the man grinned ferally at his audience before leaning forward to sink his teeth into the snow-white skin at the juncture of his victim's neck and shoulder.

A rivulet of blood wended its way down her upper arm, but before it could pool in the dip of her elbow, one of the female bystanders leaned over to catch the stream on her tongue. The male vampire growled into the broken skin from which he still drank.

Valentine's breathing was ragged in my ear, and her fingers dug into the skin above my hips. "Does that turn you on?" she whispered harshly. "Does it?"

I couldn't stop staring at the erotic scene before me. The woman's eyes were glazed and a keening sound escaped her lips. She would come soon. I was throbbing in time with each thrust. I wanted Val's thigh between my legs, but she refused to let me turn around.

"Do you want me to take you that way when we get home?" she said. "Strap it on and bend you over the bed and impale you on my teeth and my cock?"

A violent shudder seized me at her words, and then again as the woman finally screamed out her pleasure in a descant over the music. The vampire was right behind her, the cords in his neck standing out in sharp relief as he slid into ecstasy. My skin felt hot and tight and sensitive, and when Val slipped one hand beneath my T-shirt to run her palm over my stomach, I had to bite down hard on my lower lip to keep from crying out. Despite our lovemaking less than two hours before, I needed her again.

Now.

Desire stripped away self-consciousness. But just as I was about to coax her fingers beneath the waistline of my jeans, the music faded into the background and a microphone crackled to life.

"It's time," whispered a sibilant, disembodied voice as two pools of light coalesced onto the stage. One of them encircled the large post. "Time to test the Record."

The words were taken up by the audience. *The Record, the Record,* they chanted, distracting both Val and me long enough to break the spell between us. This time, when I tried to turn she let me. I threaded one hand into her hair and wrapped the other around her waist. Her eyes were still hazy with desire.

"Baby," she began, the word heavy with need.

I kissed the soft skin beneath her ear. "Later, my love. I promise."

The balance of people in the room was shifting even more dramatically toward the front, and they hadn't stopped murmuring about "the Record," whatever that was.

"Do you know what they're talking about?"

"No."

The microphone channel opened again and the sound of soft, rhythmic breathing filled the room. A hush fell.

"Gwendolyn was reborn in India, one hundred and seventeen years ago. She believes that she can break the Record."

Gwendolyn. The crowd took up the name, scattering it around the room like leaves on the autumn wind. I frowned impatiently at the twin golden circles of light on the stage floor. The unknown emcee of this event was doing an excellent job of whipping the mob into a frenzy. The cadence of his words inspired a fierce need in me to see him—to know the face behind such a bewitching voice.

A figure stepped out of the shadows, dressed from head to toe in black and holding a cat-o'-nine-tails. Long blond hair cascaded down to her waist, but her face was obscured by a mask shaped like a falcon's head, the sharp beak ending just above the red slash of her lips. A small holster hung from the left side of her belt, which hung low across her curvaceous hips. Even before she took a bow, the room erupted in screams and cheers.

Two men entered from the wings, then—also dressed in black, but their faces were visible. They led out a naked woman, presumably Gwendolyn, by a chain clipped to a collar around her neck. Despite her captivity, she carried herself like royalty. Her aura of calm assurance did not falter—not even when she was secured to the post and her tormenter snapped the cat in anticipation.

"The Record," hissed that eerie, tantalizing voice, "is fifty-seven lashes."

Someone brought down the house lights so that the room was completely black, save for those two brilliant circles onstage. At the same time, the DJ began spinning a dark, throbbing beat.

And then the whip struck for the first time. High above her head, it cracked like summer thunder before smacking against Gwendolyn's bronze shoulders. I flinched, but she didn't. Instead, she smiled. The room went absolutely insane. Again, the cat rose and fell, this time on her back. And this time, it broke skin. The crowd surged at the sight and scent of blood on the air. Gwendolyn's smile wavered.

I pressed instinctively closer to Val. Each crack of the whip made me shiver, as though I were the one feeling the knotted leather cords bite into my own skin. Of course, if it had been me up there, I probably would have shifted as soon as my blood had been spilled, out of instinctual self-defense. Even though the panther and I had reached some sort of understanding over Valentine's feedings, I was sure that a vicious attack from a complete stranger would trump the measure of control I had fought so hard for.

"Oh my God," I said, realization dawning. "The Record—it must be how many lashes a shifter can take before she transforms."

I tipped my head back to meet Val's look of horror. "That's… that's sick," she whispered, clutching me even tighter, trying to shield me with her body. "Don't watch. Or better yet—let's just go."

"No," I said forcefully, twisting just enough in Val's embrace so that I could continue watching the tableau. "It's…it's not that bad. We're staying." The panther growled inside me, disagreeing, but I had made up my mind and she wasn't riled enough to wrest control just yet.

"Not that bad?" Val echoed me skeptically. But my resolve must have been apparent, because she didn't say anything else.

By now, I had lost count. The crowd hadn't, though. *Thirty-eight,* they chanted. *Thirty-nine.* Gwendolyn's back was covered in blood; I couldn't even see any skin left between her shoulders and hip bones. The urge to vomit came on strong, and I buried my face in Val's bicep, breathing in her familiar, comforting scent. No, I had to keep it together. I was getting seriously stressed out, and that would only end badly. Besides, how ironic would it be if I succumbed to the urge to protect myself before Gwendolyn did?

Val was rhythmically stroking the long muscles of my back. "It's okay, baby," she kept saying. "It's okay." I forced myself to stand still and watch as Gwendolyn took her strokes. Valentine's arms around me kept me grounded, kept me human.

Forty-six! Forty-seven!

And then Gwendolyn began to shudder. I felt a strange kind of admiration as I watched her fight the impulse—her fingertips scraped against the pole, and her face contorted in an expression of extreme concentration mingled with agony. But she was losing this battle. Her other self was determined to take over, now, pulled from hibernation by the call of the cat.

I expected the wielder of the whip to hightail it out of there at the first sign of a transformation, but she only continued to raise her arm—up, down. Up, down. *Fifty.* God, she was strong. *Fifty-one.*

Gwendolyn's spine arched into an impossible bow. Her scream as she folded in on herself was abruptly cut off, only to reemerge as a long, low, snarling growl. Where once a broken, bloodied woman had fought to remain upright against the pole, now a huge Bengal tiger crouched, her attention fixed on the perpetrator of her torture. Deep inside my brain, the panther howled in triumph, urging her sister-tiger to take vengeance on her tormenter.

Those red lips lifted in a cruel smile. With one powerful contraction of its haunch muscles, Gwendolyn the tiger leapt—only to be jerked back by the chain around her neck. The tiger whined and snarled in frustration.

The woman wielding the whip calmly drew the gun at her left side, firing into the belly of the beast she had summoned. Gwendolyn lurched forward several times before she finally collapsed. I bit down hard on Val's arm to stifle my own scream of horror. My brain rebelled even as a surge of adrenaline prepared my body for a fight. The panther pushed hard against my control and I barely held her back. The shifters would never stand for this, never.

"Oh, thank God," Val breathed suddenly. Her voice was relieved, which didn't make sense to me at all. "Tranquilizer." She slumped slightly against the bar.

Tranquilizer? Tamping down my panic, I focused on the immaculate snow-white fur of Gwendolyn's belly. I expected a red stain to be growing beneath her by now, but there was no blood at all—only the feathered end of a dart protruding from her pristine coat. Val had been right. There would be no bloodbath, after all.

I stepped back into her embrace just as she signaled the bartender for two additional much-needed whiskeys. The crowd was still wild; Gwendolyn hadn't broken the record, but she had come very close. I watched the dominatrix take her last bow before exiting stage right, while from stage left, the two men dragged the dead weight of the tiger into the wings.

"That was royally fucked up," Val muttered. When she looked down at me, contrition and guilt warred on her face. "I am so sorry for subjecting you to that."

"You didn't." Only when the words were out of my mouth did I realize just how true they were. I was as responsible for what had happened onstage as Gwendolyn and her anonymous tormenter. I had invited in the animal that now cohabited my body, and she had her own needs, her own agenda. I could still feel her pushing at the boundaries of her prison, instinctively longing to be free in this room that reeked of rage and blood. The atmosphere suited her far better than it did me. Val had been right to question my ability to control my beast tonight.

She handed me my second whiskey and I took a long, grateful sip. Maybe the dancing would start up again. The crowd was slowly beginning to settle down, and I imagined that Val would want to walk around, to leave no metaphorical stone unturned. I didn't relish the thought of trying to maneuver through such a dense pack of people, but I also didn't see an alternative. Regardless, until the house lights came back up, she didn't have a chance of finding him.

"Ladies and gentlemen," crooned the voice. "I do hope you've kept your raffle tickets. The main event is about to commence."

Val and I exchanged a look. The main event? Whatever she saw in my face galvanized her, and she drained the last of her glass. "Come on. Let's get out of here."

I shook my head. "I'm staying." When Val glared at me, I lost my temper. "Stop being so patronizing, Valentine! I'm not some helpless flower of femininity who's going to fall apart at the seams, here."

The passion drained from her face, frustration turning to contrition. "You're right," was all she said before turning to hail the bartender again. God, I hated making her feel bad. But I also wasn't going to put up with her Sir Lancelot routine.

The stage was still empty, and I wondered whether our emcee would ever show himself. All around us, vampires were holding on to their raffle tickets as though each was the Holy Grail. Val hadn't looked at hers, so I moved in until our thighs were brushing and stuck two fingers into her pocket. She shivered. I looked away from my hand and up into her dark, apologetic eyes, allowing my touch to smooth over the tense moment.

I dug out her ticket. "Three-oh-four. Maybe you'll get luck—"

"Look."

The two men were back, this time parading in a gaunt naked male twentysomething who couldn't seem to walk in a straight line. He was either drunk or high—the manacles on his hands didn't seem to faze him, and he smiled at the crowd, swaying on his feet while the stage crew secured him to the post just as they had Gwendolyn. He would have been handsome if he'd had a little more meat on his bones. I frowned, trying to figure out the name of this particular game. He was human—I had no doubt of that.

"This is Craig," said the voice, slicing through the crowd's buzzing murmur. "We found Craig on the corner of Thirty-Sixth Street and Eighth Avenue lying in a pool of his own urine, with one dollar and seventy-eight cents in his pocket. He was in withdrawal when we found him but, as you can see, he's buzzing quite nicely now!" The crowd roared in approval.

Dread pierced me, cold darkness slowly chilling my blood. Craig was clearly one of New York's many homeless. If he disappeared, no one would miss him. Now I understood why the vampires were the only ones holding tickets.

"Who will have the honor of the first taste?" mused the voice. "Could it be...could it be number two-hundred and seventy?"

A high-pitched scream of exultation echoed throughout the room as a thin, blonde vampire ascended to the stage, waving her ticket. It was checked by one of the black-coated men, who then allowed her to approach Craig. She smiled. He blinked at her in a mixture of confusion and lust.

I gasped as she dropped to her knees and took his semi-hard cock into her mouth. His mouth opened in pleasure as she deep-throated him expertly, all the while walking her ruby-tinted fingers along the muscles of his pelvis. And then, without a warning, she replaced her mouth with one hand and snapped forward like a cobra to sink her teeth into the flesh of his upper thigh.

"Number sixty-eight," said the voice as Craig jerked and came all over the stage. Spontaneous applause burst from the audience. I expected the first vampire to leave as a tall man approached to take his taste, but she remained on her knees, throat pulsing greedily. Craig's hands were in her hair now, but whether to pull her closer or push her away, I couldn't tell. The man circled behind both of them and licked from Craig's shoulder to the crook of his elbow before sinking in his teeth. He cried out quietly. The crowd hummed.

I turned to Val. Her teeth were clenched and her hands balled into fists. At first, I thought she was angry—but when I gently reached up to tilt her head toward mine, I realized that the tension in her body was born of equal parts thirst and the fierce need to fight it. "We have to do something," I said urgently. "They're killing him."

Val shook her head as though breaking out of a daze. She scanned the room, but her face was grim. "What can we do? These guys will tear us to shreds if we try to interfere."

The voice called out another number. Craig swayed on his feet, weakening fast. I wondered if he had realized that he was going to die. Behind me, Val was vibrating with tension. Did she see herself in the vampires bleeding him dry? Or in him, a victim at the nonexistent mercy of these monsters? I would never have told her this, but he reminded me of my weaker, human self on that fateful night when she had taken too much.

I fished my phone out of my jeans pocket. "I have Detective Foster's cell on speed dial. Maybe—" The announcer cut me off with the next winner.

"Number three-hundred and four."

The noise level of the room dipped as the crowd waited for the next winner to come forward. But there was no ripple of movement toward the stage, and after a few seconds, the voice repeated the number.

Val frowned suddenly. "What did you say my number was again?"

The masses began to chant. *Three-oh-four! Three-oh-four!* I looked down at the ticket in my hand. "Oh my God."

"No!" Val grated, her arms tightening around me so fiercely that I winced. It was almost as though she expected to be dragged up to the stage, kicking and screaming, and be forced to drink from Craig's fading body.

And then I realized that her thirst was doing just that. Karma had once called a Were's psychic battle "epic," but watching Valentine's face, I knew that the same description applied to the effort required from any vampire who fought against their compulsion. Cupping her face in my hands, I forced her to focus on me instead of on the horrific spectacle unfolding onstage. "You're mine," I whispered urgently. "I'm yours. And I'm not sharing you with anyone."

It must have been what she needed to hear, because she sucked in a deep, shuddering breath. "Yeah," she murmured, not looking away despite the clamor of the crowd. "Yeah."

"No three-oh-four?" the voice sounded surprised. "Very well, then. Congratulations, number one hundred sixty-eight—yours is the privilege of last blood."

As the last vampire was greeted with raucous cheers and whistles, the crowd surged around us like a starving beast. They were chanting in unison for last blood. I realized then that I couldn't call Foster. I couldn't call anybody. It would be like leading lambs to the slaughter.

I watched a bead of sweat snake down Val's neck, sliding directly over the pulse point that throbbed visibly beneath her skin. This lottery had blindsided her, and she was suffering. It was clearly time for us to get out of here.

"Come on, love," I said, reaching for her hand. "Let's go."

She didn't protest. We made our way slowly toward the hallway through the jam of people. I looked over my shoulder once; Craig was unconscious, held up only by his chained hands. A few seconds later, a loud roar shook the foundations of the club.

He was dead.

"Leaving already?" the Hispanic woman asked as we returned to the atrium. Neither of us answered her. "Fresh meat, so sensitive," she teased as Val collected her gun and I grabbed our jackets. "You'll be back."

Unfortunately, I suspected that she was right. We still hadn't made any progress in our search for the rogue vampire. Val hurried through the passageway to the outside door. She didn't speak until we emerged into the night air.

"We need to go see Helen. Right now."

"She's the Master of this city, Val. Don't you think she knows?"

"I don't care whether she knows or not. I won't be able to sleep tonight if I don't do something." She shook her head, hard. "That wasn't a shifter who knew exactly what the fuck he was doing, even if it was insane. That was some poor, drugged-up human SOB who died just because he didn't have a home!"

I squeezed her hand tightly, able to hear what she wasn't saying. Not to bring this to Helen's attention—not to try at all—would make Valentine feel like she was jeopardizing her own humanity.

Val was quiet for the entire train ride. Her internal struggle was palpable, and I wished that I could read her mind. I kept one hand on her knee the entire time, knowing that she would derive some measure of comfort from my nearness. I needed that closeness, too. I had watched a man die for sport again tonight. To most of the people in that room, Craig's demise had been a titillating game, designed to stimulate and satiate their most primal desires: to hunt, to feed, to grow stronger.

I leaned back in the plastic bucket seat and stared unseeing at the ads that checkered the walls of the train. Unlike our first foray into the Red Circuit, the carnage made a kind of sense now. To my panther half, hunting down and consuming prey that was weak seemed like the most natural impulse in the world. It was natural selection at its simplest; only the strong would survive, and Craig had been wasting away before the vampires ever found him.

What had happened tonight was inexcusable to a part of me. But to the other part, it was natural. Even…right.

When we arrived at the Consortium, Val didn't so much as pause before marching up to the receptionist. "We need to see Helen as soon as possible," she said, her tone brooking no arguments. I wondered if she really felt so black and white about what had just happened, or whether there was some piece of her that, like me, could justify it. Then again, if that was the case, perhaps it was her disgust at that aspect of herself that drove her now.

The receptionist looked Val up and down. I ground my teeth. She pretended not to notice. "You can have five minutes. But don't you dare push it, or I'll never let you in to see her without an appointment again."

I expected Val to bristle at this woman's patronizing tone, but she merely nodded. We rode the elevator up to Helen's penthouse office in silence. We didn't even have to knock; we were still a few feet shy of Helen's door when she called for us to come in.

She was seated behind her desk before the floor-to-ceiling windows, untinted now that it was night. The windows revealed an impressive view of the U.N. building swathed in spotlights. Her lips curved slightly when she saw us. "Valentine. Alexa. You look like you've been enjoying your Friday evening."

"We went to the Red Circuit," said Val, ignoring Helen's gestured invitation to sit in the lavish leather chairs arrayed before her desk.

"And you want to know why I haven't put a stop to it." Helen didn't seem surprised. It was comforting to know that we weren't the first members of our community to come to her with these concerns.

Val's jaw was clenched tightly, the small muscles beneath her jaw all bunched together. "A man died tonight, Helen. A nonconsensual, human murder. That never has to happen."

Helen leaned forward, sliding her folded hands along the polished wood surface. "What you're carefully not asking is indeed possible. I could shut down the Red Circuit. But I never have, and I will not, for the simple reason that it is a known evil. And the unknown evil would be much more dangerous."

Val opened her mouth to speak, but Helen didn't let her. "Consider the benefits of the current system. The Circuit knows that I am watching, and that knowledge puts a check on its controversial practices. Yes, humans die. But, as you no doubt saw tonight, they are carefully culled from the ranks of the weak and pitiful."

It was disconcerting to hear Helen vocalizing my thought process from earlier. She stood then, and turned her back to us, hands hanging loose at her sides. "Picture, in contrast, a Circuit without traditions, determined to flout the tyrannical policing that is always one step behind them. That would be anarchy. Infinitely more destructive."

A wave of anger swept through me at her dismissive justification. "That logic is ridiculous. Val is right. No one ever has to die. You told her that yourself, at the beginning of all of this—vampires have to feed, but they don't have to kill."

Helen turned her cold gray eyes on me, and it was a struggle not to take a step back. "If it bothers you so much," she said quietly, voice tinged with menace, "then why did you go back?"

I shouldn't have been surprised, but I was. And hiding it was impossible. I looked to Val, expecting her to answer—it was her show, after all. But instead of explaining to Helen that we had gone in pursuit of the rogue vampire that her task force still had not apprehended, Valentine hesitated. In the pause, I began to wonder. If Helen condoned the Circuit as a necessary evil, then what else did she know about that she was similarly overlooking? What if catching Val's attacker wasn't one of her top priorities? Malcolm had insinuated as much, and more. Maybe she considered Valentine—and almost Olivia—to be affordable or unavoidable casualties. The thought made me bristle, and I bit down on my lip to stifle the growl that wanted release.

"Monique only showed us the dogfighting," Val said smoothly. "We got curious about the rest of it." Which wasn't a lie per se, just not nearly the full truth.

"And now you don't have to be any longer." Helen returned to her chair, opened a manila folder, and began to read the document inside. Clearly, our five minutes were up. As we walked slowly back toward the elevator, I felt the first twinges of fatigue. It had been a long, emotional night. All I wanted was to climb inside the cocoon of our cool sheets, snuggle into the curve of Val's naked body, and fall into sleep. I wondered if I'd be able to shut my eyes without seeing Craig's face. Or Gwendolyn's.

"I'm glad you didn't tell her the whole truth," I said as the doors dinged behind us. "I'm starting to suspect that she doesn't really give a crap about catching him."

Val nodded, standing just close enough so that our arms brushed.

"You may be right." I watched her left hand tighten on the railing. "Damn it. I trusted her."

The doors opened and we hurried out into the chill night. Thankfully, we caught a cab almost immediately. I tucked one arm around Val's waist and rested my head in the dip between her neck and shoulder as the taxi pulled away from the curb.

"I guess…when you've been alive as long as she has, your priorities change. You forget how to be human."

"I don't want to forget," Val whispered. She sounded absolutely terrified, like a little girl afraid of the dark. It was, I realized, a much more immediate fear for her than for me. My blood was holding the advance of her parasite in check. Without me, so the legend went, she would lose the tether that kept her connected to humanity.

But I would never allow that to happen.

I gently kissed her neck. "You won't. We won't. We'll never forget, as long as we're together."

"Forever." Her voice held a note of forlornness, the single word half statement, half question. I thumbed open the bottom button of her coat and rubbed my palm in gentle circles over the light swell of her stomach, hoping to comfort her.

"Yes, my love. Forever."

CHAPTER TWENTY-THREE

I ran. The long grass of the savannah bent before me, paying homage to the speed of my passage. Ahead, my prey soared in leaping bounds, zigzagging gracefully around the occasional stunted tree. I maintained my pace easily. The young gazelle would tire before I did, and then she would be mine. I could almost taste her now: the hot spurt of her blood against my tongue, the sharp crack of her bones between my teeth, her moist, tender flesh sliding down my throat.

The wind blowing off the distant desert flowed around me, carrying with it a renewed burst of her enticing scent. I ran faster, now, restless for the kill. And then, she stumbled.

It was the barest misstep, the slightest imaginable pause, but it was enough. Mid-stride, I coiled every muscle and sprang. My claws pierced through her light coat of fur, tearing into the muscle beneath. She screamed and went down. I shifted my weight as she fell, pinning her to the earth. She struggled beneath me, but my weight held her easily. I took a moment to savor my triumph—her wild, rolling eyes, the pulse racing in her throat, the fragrant scent of her blood.

Flicker.

The body beneath me blurred, becoming human. Skin and bones and lanky brown hair. Craig. He looked up at me in terror, too frightened even to tremble.

Flicker.

The bluest eyes. I snarled into Valentine's face as she tried desperately to pull away. My paws held down her shoulders, claws digging into her skin. She flinched. And yet, I hesitated. This didn't feel right. Her expression was panicked, just like my usual quarries. She didn't want to die. She thrashed against my grip and almost managed to pull free. I dug my claws in harder and she whimpered in pain and fear. A thread of saliva dangled from my curled lips; she was the most delectable creature I'd ever hunted, and finally, finally I was going to sate my hunger. Her eyes rolled wildly I as I tensed for the lunge that would break her neck...

I sat up in bed, dizzy and sweating and nauseous. The dream. Again. *God damn you,* I thought at my internal beast, fighting to control my breathing. *Get out of my head!* Nearly a month had passed since our trip to the Catskills, and the progress I had made there was in jeopardy. The panther, strengthened by the blood and violence of the Red Circuit, was steadily gaining confidence and pushing the boundaries of my tenuous control. It was a vicious cycle; the harder she pushed, the less sleep I got. The less sleep I got, the stronger she became.

I turned to focus on Val, who was thrashing a little on the edge of wakefulness. She was having a nightmare, too; she must have cried out and woken me, sparing me the sensation of my razor teeth slicing through her spinal cord.

I shivered, determined to return the favor and free her from whatever horrors gripped her brain. Slowly, so as not to startle her, I caressed the warm skin of her stomach and began to rub in gentle circles. "Val, wake up. You're having a bad dream." I shifted so that my lips were grazing the shell of her ear. "Come on, sweetheart. Wake up. You're okay."

Her body jerked once as she woke. I slid my palm up to rest between her breasts, over her heart. It was racing. She swallowed, blinked, and looked at me. Terror cast a dark shadow over the brilliance of her eyes.

"Flashback?"

"Yeah," she said hoarsely.

We really had to stop going to these parties. Val had been dreaming of her attacker frequently, and I was back to fighting my panther tooth and nail. We'd returned to the Circuit twice since, but had come away empty-handed each time.

"You're all sweaty," Val murmured as she pulled me flush against her. "Were you dreaming, too?"

"Mmm." I kissed her forehead.

"Same one?"

"Mmm-hmm." I had told Valentine everything about my recurring nightmare up until the part when the gazelle-turned-Craig morphed into her. Knowing Val, she'd find a way to feel guilty. I held her close, running my fingers through her hair, and turned my attention inward. *I'll never let you hurt her. Never.* I didn't know whether my inner feline could actually catch the meaning of my thoughts, of course, but the mantra couldn't hurt. These days, I often wondered whether I would ever feel that peace we had so briefly found again, or whether our wills would be irrevocably at odds.

"I don't really want to go back tonight," Val said quietly, her hands ghosting up and down my spine.

"Me, neither." I wished there was some kind of alternative, but there simply wasn't.

"I just don't know what else we can do," said Val, echoing my thoughts. "Foster or Olivia would have told us if their investigation had come up with something, right?"

"And if she hadn't before, by now Helen seems to have completely forgotten that he even exists." Her reaction—or lack thereof—continued to grate on me. It seemed to me that the rogue vampire was a danger not just to humans, but to the continued secrecy of the Consortium. Wouldn't it make sense for her to be even more concerned than the police?

"God, I wish we could just get off square one." Val sighed against my neck before drawing away reluctantly. She leaned over to look at the alarm clock: 6:07. "Might as well get up. Maybe if I review my notes before class, I can impress the hell out of my Histology prof today."

I grabbed her hand before she could leave the bed. "It's early yet. We have some time."

She smiled for the first time since waking and leaned in to grant my unspoken request. Her lips were soft but firm against mine, her tongue hot in my mouth. God, could Val kiss. I twined my fingers into her hair to pull her closer. Everything else—the beginning of our daily routine, school, the rogue vampire—could wait for just a few minutes. This was what we had fought and were still struggling for, after all: the right to love each other for every second of forever.

❖

The Angel Orensanz Foundation was in our neighborhood. Just off East Houston on Norfolk Street, it looked like a cathedral, had once been a synagogue, and was now one of New York's preeminent cultural centers. The Foundation hosted banquets and balls, all held in the name of the arts. But tonight, its lofty neo-gothic frame housed the carnage of the Red Circuit.

Val and I stood on the balcony, sipping drinks and watching the seething crowd. Whenever there was a lull in the music, the snarls and growls from the dogfights in the basement filtered into the main hall. How they were going to get the blood off the walls, I had no idea. When I shuddered at the mental image, Val stroked my arm gently. But she never stopped watching the people below.

On the dais, just in front of the steps that had once led to the Holy of Holies, a St. Andrew's cross had been erected. Apparently, this particular Red Circuit party was a special occasion; I had seen people pointing to the cross and whispering about someone called "the Missionary" since we arrived. We had already suffered through this week's attempt to break the record (a failure after forty-two lashes), as well as the murder of a homeless meth addict found in the Bronx. Her two children, the disembodied voice told the crowd, had been adopted into loving families. I could only presume that they would grow up to be just like Kyle. The thought made it hard to swallow.

"You have all been very patient," the voice said finally. "But you don't have to be any longer. The Missionary has arrived." An expectant murmur rose in the room, a hot breeze before the storm. "Three lovely pets have been selected to compete tonight," the voice continued, low and hypnotic. The lights in the hall dimmed and a spotlight enclosed the dais in a cocoon of light. "Please welcome the first contestant, Jillian."

One of the crew, dressed completely in black as always, led a petite, red-haired woman out of the shadows. She was wearing a blue silk teddy with sequins at the neck that caught the light. He positioned her with her back to the giant "X" of the cross and secured her wrists, ankles, and waist to the frame. The teddy rode up a few inches on her thighs. She looked nervous, but not afraid.

"The Missionary is very, very thirsty," whispered the voice.

And then, several things happened at once.

A man stepped into the spotlight, clad only in black leather pants. His torso was heavily muscled and rippled with scars, his head shaven so cleanly that it shone. When he appeared on the dais, the masses cheered and screamed. But despite their reaction, he didn't smile. He didn't wave. He stood still, surveying them impassively, hands at his sides. My gaze was drawn to the knuckles of his left, where some kind of tattoo crept sinuously across his skin.

"Alexa!" Val choked out my name in a way that I'd never heard before. She was hanging on to the railing with a white knuckled grip, staring wide-eyed at the formidable figure of the Missionary. She had gone very pale. Her lips were drawn back in a snarl. And that's when I knew.

Rage clawed up my spine. The room turned red. Immediately, I closed my eyes and took a slow, deep breath. Another. And another. I wanted so badly to comfort Valentine in this terrible moment, but first I had to control myself. Val's hand closed over mine compulsively, but while her touch usually would have driven back the angry tide, the sensation of her fingernails digging into my skin only made it harder for me to force down the panther.

"It's him. God damn it, it's him!"

"I know," I said, hearing the strain in my own voice. "I know, just—just give me a second, here…" It was proving particularly difficult for me to regain my inner calm this time because for once, the panther and I were in agreement. She wanted to kill him. So did I. *Not now,* I silently pleaded with her. *Not now, not here. Wait.* Now was the time to be quiet and stealthy—to observe and stalk. Not to hunt.

For a moment, nothing happened…and then, so gradually that it was barely perceptible at first, she began to back down. Maybe we could speak the same language, after all.

I opened my eyes to the sight of Val looking between the scene below and the doorway behind us. "I have to go down there," she muttered. "Have to stop him."

Panic obliterated the anger. A vision streaked through my mind of Val confronting him in front of these hundreds of people, the vast majority of whom had been eagerly chanting his moniker. They would tear her apart, limb from limb. Literally.

I squeezed her hand even harder. "No!"

"Look what he's doing!" she retorted, flinging out an accusatory finger toward the Missionary. He was bent over Jillian, sucking greedily on her neck. I could only imagine what this scene was doing to Val, the helplessness and pain that she was remembering. Her head was back in that alleyway, when he had cornered her, beaten her, bitten her. But she wasn't there, and there was no way to stop him here.

I stepped forward to slide my arms around her waist, holding her stationary as much as I was holding her close. "We can't go after him here. We'll get ourselves killed. You know that, Valentine."

"I can't let him get away again! I won't!" She struggled against my grip, but she and I were well matched in strength now. I didn't back down.

"We're not going to let him get away," I said urgently. "He'll be there for a while. I'll call Foster right now, okay? We won't let him out of our sight."

The tension didn't ease from Val's body, but she nodded once. Digging my phone out of my pocket, I turned my face away from the scene below but kept my other arm securely around her. I had Detective Foster on speed dial, but after one ring, a male voice answered.

"NYPD dispatch. How may I help you?"

Crap. Why the heck was Foster having her calls routed to dispatch? And why tonight, of all nights? I squeezed my eyes shut and did my best to stay calm.

"My name is Alexa Newland. I need to speak with Detective Devon Foster immediately about one of the cases she's investigating."

"She's unavailable at the moment, ma'am," said the man on the other end of the line. "Are you in an emergency situation?"

"No," I said quickly, hoping that they couldn't trace this call to my location. Squad cars and ambulances showing up here tonight would be a fiasco of untold proportions. The Consortium would probably have to burn this place to the ground to cover up the ensuing massacre. A shiver ran under my skin like an electric shock, and I felt Val pull me closer automatically.

"I'm a family member of one of the victims and I have a question for the detective," I elaborated, hoping to evade any kind of suspicion. "Could you have her call me back as soon as possible?"

"Yes, ma'am. We've logged your number."

I hung up. My brain was racing in time with the visible pulse at Val's throat. I was pretty sure that I had kept that conversation under a minute in duration. Wasn't that how long they needed to trace a call?

"What the hell was that?" Val muttered, never taking her eyes off the Missionary as he pulled away from Jillian and stood at one side of the cross. She hung limply from her bonds, chin resting on her sternum, head lolling. A thin trail of blood trickled down her white skin to stain the collar of the teddy as we watched.

"Oh God," I whispered. "Is she—"

"No." Val spoke through gritted teeth. "I've been listening to the crowd, and apparently, the name of this game is to see which 'pet' can manage to stay conscious the longest while the Missionary sucks on them. He's a legend for being able to drain three or four victims in a night." Her jaw flexed as the two stage crew workers reappeared to carry a limp Jillian out of the circle of light. "Couldn't get hold of Foster?"

"The call went to dispatch." I could feel the adrenaline soaking into my bloodstream. It compelled me to act, but I had no idea what to do. The panther was growling and pushing continuously at the doors to my brain. "She must be on some operation or mission or something. I asked them to have her call us as soon as she could."

Val pulled away from my grip to brace herself against the railing. I was surprised that the metal didn't cut into her palms, the way she was squeezing it. Anger, fear, frustration—the emotions moved over her face like clouds before a hurricane.

Below us, a young man had taken Jillian's place. The Missionary, his torso shimmering with sweat from the hot lights above, bowed once to the crowd before turning to his next victim. Grasping the beams of the massive cross just above the man's wrists, he flexed the prodigious muscles of his back before he struck. The man shouted as the Missionary's teeth pierced his neck—whether in pleasure or pain, it was impossible to tell.

My stomach twisted. Yes, the mechanics of Val drinking from me were identical to what was happening on that dais. But qualitatively, the two acts were entirely different. When Valentine sheathed her teeth in my skin, it was an act of love. The scene playing out below was about domination and nothing more. Whenever Val fed from me, we shared our most desperate, most needy, most vulnerable sides with each other. She needed my blood to live, and I needed her to crave me that deeply. We met each other as equals; I gave and she took, I took and she gave, and we both became stronger.

These human "pets" might have been well cared for, but if their masters were willing to offer them up to the monstrous figure of the Missionary simply for the sake of a game, then those relationships were not founded on love. They did not and could not share a fraction of the bond that Valentine and I enjoyed. She was mine, and I was hers, and I would let nothing come between us for the rest of eternity.

"If Foster doesn't call before this is done, we have to follow him." Val was looking at me defiantly, as though she expected disagreement. But how could I block her now, when we had the chance to finally put her nightmare to rest?

"You're right," I said. "If she can't get here by the time he leaves, then we should track him to his daytime resting place. Then we can keep an eye on him until the police arrive."

A change came over Val then, determination replacing anxiety. "Yes. Okay. Good."

"We'll have to be careful, though," I warned her. "He has those full-vampire super senses. It won't be easy to track him and stay hidden."

"Mmm." Val turned back to the spectacle below, frowning in thought. My brain was racing again. How could we be certain that he wouldn't catch us? If I transformed, I'd be able to track him easily, but then I'd be a loose cannon of epic proportions. We were just going to have to be—

"Hang on a second," Val said suddenly. "You may be wrong, for once. Look. I think he's getting…drunk."

I followed her line of sight in time to see him stagger slightly as he moved away from his second victim. Was it possible that he was actually becoming intoxicated by their blood?

"Is it the amount that's doing that to him? Or is he picking up the effects of the drugs or alcohol in their bloodstreams?"

Val shook her head. "Not sure. Both, I think." Her voice was clipped, eager. "But this is going to work to our advantage."

The crowd roared as the third "pet"—a tall blonde who probably could have been a supermodel in a different life—was secured to the cross. I stared past the spectacle, into the shadowed wings of the hall. The main entrance to the Foundation was at the back of the synagogue, but a small set of stairs leading both to the ground floor and to the basement were tucked away into an alcove to the left of where the altar must have stood. The floor swarmed with people; we weren't going to be able to move quickly down there.

"We need a plan for how to pick him up as he leaves," I murmured. "What if you stay up here to maintain the bird's-eye view, and I shadow him—using your directions by phone, if necessary—on the ground. You can meet me outside."

Val pushed away from the rail, drawing herself up to her full height. "But—"

Having expected this protest, I pressed my index finger to her lips. "He knows what you look like. He doesn't know me from Eve. I should be on the ground."

Her jaw worked soundlessly before she finally sighed in acquiescence. I hefted my phone. "I'm going to call you right now, and keep it on until we meet back up, okay? That way you'll always know what's going on around me, in case we get temporarily separated."

Val heard what I wasn't saying—that this was a dangerous mission to undertake, especially here and especially now. That the vampire standing on the dais below might be our enemy, but to the crowd he was a celebrity. That he was strong and cruel, a veteran of violence. She crushed me to her and kissed me fiercely before pulling just as suddenly away. Her pupils had all but swallowed her irises.

"Be careful. See you soon."

"See you soon," I replied, before jogging down the balcony's spiral staircase. When I reached the floor of the hall, I hit a wall of people. Painstakingly, I moved through them toward the edge of the dais. I punched number one on speed dial, and Val answered immediately.

"He's still up there," she said without preamble. "But the woman's on the verge of collapsing already."

I raised my free arm to make myself thinner and pressed forward with more urgency. A few seconds later, a bestial roar sliced through the buzz of the crowd. Through a momentary gap between tightly packed bodies that gave me line of sight to the dais, I saw the Missionary, his lips stained dark, fists clenched as he bellowed in intoxicated triumph. An answering roar went up in response from the crowd. No one seemed to care which "pet" had been victorious. The Missionary's merciless draining had whipped the masses into a frenzy, and they surged onto the dais, enveloping him.

Carried forward on the crest of the wave, I clutched my phone tightly and tried to stay on my feet. The Missionary had completely disappeared from my view, and as much as I could, I tried to change course toward the edge of the hall. I glanced up once and saw Valentine, her head shifting back and forth desperately. She'd lost me. And probably him. Damn it!

Even as I was pushed nearer to the stage, I swept my gaze around the room, knowing that he could be anywhere. A sudden break in the forward momentum allowed me to dart to the left side of the hall, where the crowd was much thinner.

And that's when I saw the side door, standing open just a crack. I didn't allow myself a moment of doubt. The door led to a narrow staircase that spiraled down one flight to a small foyer and what was clearly the Foundation's back door, before continuing down into the basement. Growls and snapping barks floated up to me from the bowels of the former synagogue. Would he have gone down to watch the dogfights? Or out to the streets?

The streets, I decided, knowing that even the slightest hesitation could be the difference between success and failure. I pushed the door open as quietly as I could and looked both ways down the dark, narrow side street, just in time to watch a shadowy figure stumble around the corner onto Stanton Street.

I breathed a sigh of relief, checking my phone as I moved after him. The call had disconnected. I hit speed dial again, flinching at the chanting and screaming of the crowd that assaulted my ear as soon as Val picked up.

"Are you okay?" she shouted. "Where are you?"

"Going west on Stanton," I whispered, trailing a good thirty feet behind the Missionary. "Oh, wait, he just turned left onto Essex. And I'm fine. Get out of there, okay? It's a madhouse."

"Call if anything changes," was all she said before hanging up. I flicked my phone to vibrate mode in case Val or Detective Foster called me back. I didn't want anything drawing the Missionary's attention to me, even though he was exhibiting all the signs of a drunkard: stumbling, weaving, even occasionally propping himself up against a building while he waited for traffic to pass.

A few moments later, I heard quick footsteps behind me. Resisting the impulse to turn—just to be sure—I sighed in relief when Val twined my fingers with her own. She squeezed hard enough to make me wince.

"We've got him," I murmured, trying to offer her some comfort. I couldn't even imagine how she felt, stalking the Missionary as he had once stalked her. But soon, so soon, this whole nightmare would be over: Foster would call back, and soon afterward she'd show up and arrest him, and then finally, finally we would have peace.

"I could finish this," Val said, her voice curiously hollow. "Right now."

When I glanced at her, I noticed that her left hand was in her jacket pocket. Where she kept her gun. Our quarry had stopped at a busy intersection to wait for the signal, and I jerked her into the shadow of a nearby building.

"No," I whispered urgently. "He committed a crime, Val. This is not about vengeance—it's about justice!"

I wanted her to look at me, but she wouldn't focus on anything but the back of his bald head. "Don't you think the Consortium has people in the courts?" she said, still in that disconcerting, detached monotone. I wondered if she sounded that way because she was trying so hard to stay calm.

"Don't you think the Consortium wants to see him brought in, too?" I countered. "He's endangering the secret."

Val shrugged. The helplessness of the gesture made my heart ache. "Sometimes I don't know."

The light changed and she took off after him, forcing me to break into a brief jog to catch up. I took her hand again, not knowing what else to do and wanting a physical tether to her.

He was heading toward the river; I could smell damp and mold ahead. Modest warehouses—some abandoned, some not—were plentiful in this neighborhood. So were prostitutes. Some of them, lounging in doorways or reclining on stoops, dared to look Val up and down. She didn't notice, but even now, in the middle of this madness, I did.

The Missionary paused to talk to one of them, an anorexic-looking woman whose blond hair clearly came from a bottle. I watched her stroke his bald head with bright red fingertips. She giggled at something he said, and fell in step with him. She was going to die, but not until after he had his way with her sexually. Considering how turned on Val got while feeding, it was a wonder that he could walk home at all after gorging on three victims earlier. Maybe, since he'd glutted himself, he'd just sleep with her and let her go.

But maybe not.

A few blocks farther south, he paused at a massive steel door that led into a waterfront warehouse. He unlocked some kind of chain that held the door down before yanking it up in an impressive display of strength.

"You live here?" I faintly heard the hooker ask. He drew her inside and the door clanged shut behind them, a modern-day portcullis.

Val pulled me into a nearby alleyway. "He might see us from the windows." Never looking away from the building, she lowered her body into a crouch. "Do you think we dare go around the other side, just to make sure there's not a back way out?"

I didn't have a good answer for her, so it was a relief when my phone buzzed. "Foster," I breathed. Val sighed, her shoulders slumping in relief. "Detective, hello."

"Alexa, I just got your message, I'm sorry." She sounded harried. "Is everything—"

"We know where he lives," I said simply.

A moment of silence. "Are you there right now?"

"Yes, in front of the building. Both of us."

"How the—" She cut herself off. "Tell me your address." When I told her the cross street, she exhaled sharply. "Okay. Stay right there. Don't move a muscle until I arrive. It won't be more than twenty minutes."

"Okay." She hung up, and I lowered the phone from my ear. Val looked at me, scuffing her foot against the asphalt impatiently. I couldn't believe that things had moved so fast—that we had actually found him, successfully tracked and cornered him. That soon, he would be in police custody.

I could barely remember life before this bastard had changed everything. My former self seemed like a character in a book I'd read long ago, vague and distant. I knew that we could never go back to the way it had been, but maybe, maybe now we could relax. Settle. Ease into our shared immortal existence without being haunted by the trauma, the nightmares, the guilt. Maybe now, we could start to heal.

"She's on her way."

CHAPTER TWENTY-FOUR

I shivered violently in the wintry night air. It had to be in the twenties, and I was only wearing a tank top beneath my coat. Any minute now, I told my twitching muscles. It had been at least a quarter of an hour since Foster had hung up the phone.

Even with her gaze locked on the warehouse, Val noticed my chill. "Come here," she said, opening her arms and unzipping her jacket. I wanted to be close to her, so I didn't resist. Nestling my back to her chest, I sighed as she wrapped her arms and her coat around me. Every once in a while, a fine tremor ripped through her body, too, but I knew it wasn't from the cold. Her stance was rigid, her muscles taut.

"I love you," I whispered, out of truth and habit and comfort, all at once.

We heard the footsteps at the same time. Val tensed up even further, but she continued to look straight ahead, trusting me to tell her if there was danger. I swung my head in the direction of the sound and let out a long breath when I recognized Detectives Foster and Wilson.

"Valentine, Alexa," Foster said as they ducked into the alley. "I apologize for being inaccessible earlier. The president is in town, so the whole force is out chasing after bomb threats."

I opened my mouth to say something about how awful that job sounded, but Val spoke first. "He's in there," she said, jerking her chin toward the warehouse. I bit back a sigh, wishing that she could use a little more tact when dealing with the police. But Foster didn't bat an eye.

"How did you find him?"

In the intervening minutes between Foster's call and her arrival,

Val and I had discussed this. We agreed that it wasn't a good idea to mention the Angel Orensanz Foundation at all, lest Foster send a unit to stumble into the Red Circuit like cattle to the slaughterhouse. "We were walking home from a club and saw him on the street," I said. "It was crazy, so random…and then Val started flashing back."

I watched Foster's face closely as I spoke, triumph thrilling through me when she glanced sympathetically toward Valentine as soon as I mentioned her flashback. I knew that Foster had seen Val in the throes of remembering the night of the attack. She would believe me, certainly. She might not even ask as many questions as she otherwise would have.

"We called you, but when we couldn't get through, we decided to follow him ourselves."

"I'm glad you're safe," Foster said. Val hissed, so softly that only I could hear. I shifted my weight to step on her right foot—now was not the time for a display of ownership. Honestly. Why did she even feel threatened by Devon Foster?

"All right," Foster said. "Detective Wilson will take you both home—he can get a statement from you there. I appreciate your being willing to take a risk in following this guy when you saw him."

For the first time since we'd ended up in the alley, Val looked away from the warehouse. "You're going in after him alone?"

Foster shook her head. "I can't go in at all, until we get a warrant. I've already called for backup, though, and we'll continue to stake him out until that happens."

Val's eyes darkened and her breaths grew quick and shallow. She was getting angry, or frustrated, or both. I squeezed her hand, trying to keep her calm. "He's got someone in there with him right now," she said, her voice strained. "A hooker—he picked her up on the street a few blocks back. She could be in danger."

"Damn it." Foster rocked back on her heels, looking uncertain. "Did you hear him threaten her in any way?"

"No," Val admitted reluctantly.

Foster sighed. "Looks like I'm still going to have to wake up a judge. Once backup gets here, they can surround the premises to—"

A high-pitched scream. The faint tinkling sound of shattering glass. Movement at one of the warehouse windows. Val's arms tightened reflexively around me.

"Let's go!" Foster barked to Wilson, her gun already in hand. She looked directly at me. "Stay right here. Wait for the backup. Tell them we have an emergency situation inside."

"Okay." I was shivering again, but not from the cold. I felt a little dazed as I watched Foster and Wilson run across the street. Everything was happening so fast. At a sign from her partner, Foster took a few steps away from the door. The sharp report of his gun as he shot off the lock echoed down the street. Val and I shared a glance. The police had just announced their presence.

Foster and Wilson disappeared into the cavernous entrance of the warehouse. They left the door open behind them. Val immediately began to fidget. "It's making me crazy, not to be in there with them."

I linked my fingers through hers. "I know. Me, too." The Missionary was outnumbered, but he would also have the jump on them. I wondered how old, how experienced he was. And whether his drunkenness would cancel out the benefits from having glutted himself on blood. I hoped Foster was a good shot.

We waited. Down here, the sounds of the city were muted. The unfamiliar hush was eerie. I could make out the soft lapping of the water against the edge of a nearby pier, the rustle of a shutter against brick in the breeze. I leaned forward, straining to hear something from inside the warehouse…

…and pushed back hard against Val's body in alarm as a series of gunshots suddenly pierced the quiet.

"Shit, shit, shit." Val was openly clutching her own gun now. "We should—"

"Hell, no," I said, as firmly as I could. My hands were shaking. "Maybe—maybe they got him."

She nodded, starting to pace back and forth across the narrow mouth of the alley. I waited, breaths coming quickly, for some sign of life. *Foster took him out,* I told myself. She had taken him down and was either inspecting the corpse, or reading him his rights. This was over.

And then a flash of red fabric appeared in the shadows of the entrance. The prostitute staggered out, arms clutched around her waist, crying uncontrollably. Val and I started forward at the same time. The woman was white as a sheet and couldn't manage to walk in a straight line. Her skimpy skirt had a jagged slit that hadn't been there before, and a thin stream of blood was trailing slowly down her leg. I saw Val's nostrils flare.

"Valentine—"

"It's okay," she murmured as we crossed over onto the opposite sidewalk. The hooker noticed us then, and started to back away in dazed alarm. "It's okay," Val said again, this time to the prostitute. Thankfully, Val had put her gun back in her pocket. "We're here to help."

The woman just stared at her, continuing to sob. I wondered if she was going into some kind of shock, but Val would obviously know that better than I would. "Can you tell us what happened?" Val asked quietly.

When the prostitute sank to her knees, shivering, Val immediately crouched down beside her. She made no move to touch the woman. "How did he hurt you?"

"S-so rough," she choked out. "Strong."

Oh, God. The sex was so brutal she had bled. The panther howled inside me, wanting his neck between her teeth. I concentrated on breathing slowly, steadily, through the swell of anger.

"You're safe now," Val continued, her steady voice betraying none of the horror and rage that she surely must be feeling. "Did you see the police officers who came inside?"

The prostitute nodded, but began to rock back and forth on her knees. It sounded to me like she might be hyperventilating. Words finally escaped her in a garbled river of speech.

"They t-tried but it didn't even stop him they're dead I'm sure they're dead oh God…"

Didn't even stop him? What didn't? Had Foster hit him? But then why would she think they were dead? Of course, if they weren't at least seriously injured, they would have been out here by now.

Val looked up at me, her face a mask of cold determination. "We have to go in." When I started to shake my head, she rose to her feet so quickly that I took a step backward. "He'll think the danger's past. We'll catch him off guard. I can't let him get away. I can't. Not now."

My protest died at the pained urgency in her voice. I wasn't going to argue anymore. This had to end. Clenching my trembling hands, I eased my psychological grip on the panther just enough to let her silent snarls goad me into bravery.

"I'm going first. My night vision is better than yours."

Our gazes locked. Love, determination, shared purpose—they flowed silently between us in an instant. And then I stepped over the threshold, into the gloom. My eyes adjusted almost immediately, revealing a curving staircase that spiraled up to the second floor. Rising up onto the balls of my feet, I ascended quickly but quietly. Val, not quite as surefooted, trailed behind.

The stairs opened onto a small landing. The door ahead was ajar. Several pairs of boots were clustered around a coarse foot mat, and a heavy jacket hung from a hook in the wall. I reached for the doorknob and pulled as swiftly as I could to minimize any noise. It swung toward us without a squeak. My first impression of the large chamber beyond was a maze: rows upon rows of steel shelves illuminated only by the light of the moon. I was about to step inside when a movement to the right caught my eye. I couldn't suppress the gasp that rose in my throat at the sight of the Missionary, naked and hunched over two bodies on the floor. He must have heard my breath, because he looked up, blood dribbling darkly over his chin.

Oh, God. Foster. He'd been feeding on Foster. Next to her, Wilson lay motionless, a knife handle protruding from his throat. In that instant, I barely fought down the urge to vomit. And then all hell broke loose.

Valentine's right arm crashed into my chest, pushing me back. In the same movement, she fired her gun. I dropped into a crouch just as the bullet embedded itself into the insulation that covered the walls, point blank where the Missionary's head had been just a split second before. Time slowed. I could taste the sharp tang of gunpowder on the air. Val shifted her feet, brought her second hand up to the handgrip, and fired again. The Missionary, riding the blood high of four feedings, moved at an unearthly fast pace. His body was a blur against the drab walls as he acrobatically dodged between the clutter in the room.

He dove behind the nearest shelf. When she fired a third time, the bullet ricocheted off the metal and whined past my ear. "Val!" I screamed. Damn it, she was going to get us both killed this way!

But she was beyond hearing. Striding forward, she reached the gap between the shelves and took another shot. I wanted to move, to help her somehow, but the panther was fighting hard for control in the wake of my panic. She wanted to leap, to claw, to bite until the Missionary was as still as his victims. We were in agreement on the ends, but not the means.

"Stop it!" I hissed, wrapping both arms around myself as she made another play for power, as though I could physically hold her inside of me. Up ahead, Val fired yet another shot. I peered into the gloom, trying to make him out. Had she hit him yet, or had he managed to dodge all of her bullets? I watched her look to the right and then to the left, clearly confused.

And then he appeared directly in front of her, a pale, looming mass. Val lifted her gun, but he was faster. I watched in horror as he raised his arm and backhanded her viciously across the face, sending her flying into the first row of shelves. She lost her grip on the gun as she hit the floor and it skidded somewhere out of sight. Val pulled herself determinedly to her feet and wiped at the blood trickling down her forehead. She dropped into a defensive stance, her fists balled tightly in front of her.

The Missionary plowed his way through the debris that separated him from Val. He ducked her first punch, but her second caught him squarely in the chin. He barely flinched as he reached past Val's guard and grabbed her throat. In one effortless motion, he lifted her from the ground. She managed to kick him twice in the groin but her dangling legs couldn't generate enough leverage to hurt him. With a mighty heave, he threw her across the room into the rusted scaffolding along the back wall. The side of her head crashed into one of the crossbars with a sickening clang.

My scream became one with the panther's enraged howl. As the Missionary moved slowly toward her—limping heavily, I now saw, from a bullet wound in his left thigh—I stopped resisting. My alter ego was our only hope of survival now. I closed my eyes and bowed my head, willing her forth.

She came with speed, faster than ever before. The pain was sharp but brief, the disorientation still present, but far less jarring than usual. I welcomed the muscle slide, the color shift, the piercing hunger. *Hurry,* I urged her, watching as Val lay bleeding on the floor. The Missionary's mouth was twisted in a rictus of bloodlust and glee.

"Valentine Darrow. What a surprise." Despite his injury, he kicked Val in the ribs. When she groaned feebly, he laughed. "I don't care who you are or why they wanted you. I'm going to kill you tonight, and drain your girlfriend dry."

One final shiver rode up the panther's spine. I would have laughed in triumph if my voice had been my own. We were one. Whole. He stood only twenty feet away, so weak and unsuspecting. We crouched low, tail lashing, glorying in our coiled strength. When the Missionary finally lunged toward Val, we pounced, knocking him to the ground.

We sank our claws into his skin, for purchase as much as for pain. He grunted, swinging an elbow toward our jaw. With his blood-heightened reflexes, he almost caught us, but we dodged and his bare arm passed within millimeters of our face. It was beautiful, this single-minded purpose. This oneness. He tried to roll, to shake us off, but we sheathed our claws even deeper. Switching tactics, he grabbed us around the torso and rolled, to pin us against the ground. Scrambling, we pushed away from him, raking bloody furrows in his chest as we separated. He snarled then, in anger rather than pain, and lunged toward us.

We couldn't sidestep in time and his shoulder hit us squarely in our flank, momentarily knocking the wind from our lungs. Our claws slipped against the smooth concrete floor as we scrambled. He wrapped his arm around our neck and as he tightened his grip against our windpipe, we sank our teeth into his shoulder. He cried out then, but he still had one arm free and his hold tightened. We couldn't breathe through the crushing force against our throat and so we clamped down harder, our teeth tearing through muscle and grinding against bone. But it was a losing battle; as the oxygen in our blood dwindled, darkness seeped in the edges of our vision. Slowly, our grip on his shoulder loosened. Val, I thought and suddenly our thrashing intensified as we fought for our life. But his hold was sure and the darkness became absolute. *Val, I'm so sorry. Please be okay. I love you. I—*

A bright sharp crack and we were falling. We hit the floor in a crouch as air scorched through our lungs. It smelled like chalk and burning paper. Just a foot away, the Missionary lay twitching in a growing pool of blood. There was a gaping hole where his right eye used to be. Instinctively, we took a step toward the body, drawn by the scent of the fresh kill.

Starving, we tore into him, shredding the meat from his bones, savoring the warm rush of energy that seeped into our muscles. And then, from the periphery, a sudden movement. Sound. We raised our head, crouching defensively over the remains of our prey.

Valentine. She was leaning against the scaffolding, the smoking gun gripped loosely in her right hand. I could hear the rattling of her breath whenever she inhaled, and wondered whether the Missionary had broken something. *Oh, Val. You need a doctor!*

But the panther snarled, taking one step forward. And then another. She could smell the blood that drenched Val's scalp, neck, shirt. This was easy prey—irresistible.

No! I shouted silently, willing her to stop in her tracks. *Not her!*

But my pleas went unheard. She sank down into a stalk, belly brushing the floor. A menacing growl. The unsheathing of teeth. So much hunger, still. She wanted to sate it. Valentine's face filled her vision. Even distorted through her strangely monochromatic eyes, Val's expression was odd—proud and loving, not taut with fear. Sensing this strangeness, the panther paused, ears pricking forward.

"Alexa," Val rasped. "We did it. You did it. Without you, I'd be dead."

From the depths of the beast's chaotic brain, I asserted myself. *Stop. Not prey. She is our mate.* And then I let the memories flow from me, a river of sensations and images trickling through the link between us. Waking up next to Val on a lazy Saturday—reclining on my elbow as I watched the sun dapple her pale skin. Slipping my arms around her waist and inhaling her sweet scent as she stirred dinner on the stove. Arching under her passionate touch, succumbing to the ecstasy wrought by her elegant fingers. *She is our mate. We protect her. Forever.*

The panther blinked once, slowly…and then the tension began to flow from her muscles. I would have sighed in relief if I could have. She extended her massive paws in a long stretch, regarding Valentine with curiosity now, instead of hunger.

Val smiled. The movement must have hurt her bruised face, because she winced a little, too. "Hi," she whispered.

The need to be back in my own body was overwhelming, and I let that impulse carry me into the momentum of the change. *Sleep,* I told the panther—and for once, she did not balk. It was exhilarating, this cooperation. The shift and grind of my emerging bones was barely noticeable over my euphoria. I echoed my feline half and stretched into the transformation, feeling a smile spring to my lips at the familiar pull of my own shoulder and back muscles.

I opened my eyes to find Valentine looking at me like I was some kind of goddess.

"Babe. My God. It's never…it's never looked like that before."

I cocked my head slightly, still reveling in the feel of my own skin. "What hasn't?"

"The change."

She sank to the ground then, clutching her right side. The parts of her face not covered in blood were shining with sweat. She was in bad shape. I took a step forward—and paused in surprise. I was standing. Usually, the transformation left me curled in the fetal position, jaw clenched against the agony.

I was going to have to ask Karma about that. But right now, there were far more important matters at hand. We had to get out of here. Val was clearly in a lot of pain, and maybe even bleeding internally. And the police back-up would be here soon.

I knelt at Val's side. "Where's your phone, love? We need to call Helen."

She shook her head. "Smashed."

She looked so weak, so exhausted. I briefly cupped my palm against an unbloodied part of her face before moving across the room to sift through the remains of my torn clothing. There.

"This is Alexa Newland," I said when the receptionist answered. "Put me through to Helen. It's an emergency."

"Ms. Lambros is in a very important meeting. What is the nature of your—"

I clenched my free hand and spoke over her, vehemently. "The police are on the verge of discovering a very messy crime scene, involving the mutilated corpse of the vampire implicated in all of the recent muggings. We need an intervention. Now."

"Please hold."

I fidgeted, glancing from the window to Val and back again. Helen's sudden voice in my ear startled me.

"Where are you?"

I'd never heard her sound so agitated. "South of the Bowery. A warehouse off Water Street, near Market. Can you head off the police?"

"Stay exactly where you are. I'll be there within minutes."

I ended the call and returned to Val's side. She was breathing shallowly, and her face was even paler than usual. I dropped to my knees, shivering for the first time as the adrenaline wore off enough for me to feel the cool air against my bare skin, and gently wrapped one arm around her shoulders.

"Hey. How are you feeling?"

Her mouth twitched. "You're naked."

I pressed my lips to her uninjured temple, wishing that I could heal her with a kiss, just like in the fairy tales. "And your powers of deductive reasoning are staggering."

She coughed, then groaned. "Don't…make me laugh. One broken rib. At least."

"Helen will be here soon," I soothed her. "What about your head?"

"Concussion, I bet. Hurts. Dizzy. Don't let me sleep."

She was probably nauseous, too. When I rested one palm lightly over her stomach, she sighed. I let my gaze travel along the blood-streaked floor, over to the mangled body of the Missionary. I felt no guilt—only a grim satisfaction.

"It's over," I whispered. "You did it. You got him."

"I couldn't have done it without you. You bought me enough time to find my gun." Val's eyes were dark like fresh bruises, and clouded by pain. Even so, she tried for another smile. "I make a pretty good punching bag, too."

I opened my mouth to retort, but shut it again at the sound of footsteps below. For a moment, I thought about trying to find something to cover up with. But the idea of putting on anything that had belonged to the Missionary made me feel ill. Squeezing my knees to my chest, I turned just enough to see the door.

Two men, one of them Darren, entered first—guns at the ready. I relaxed when I saw them. They surveyed the scene for a moment, then lowered their weapons. "Clear," called out the one I didn't know. Darren walked toward us, taking off his jacket. He handed it to me without a word.

"Thanks."

He nodded, looking at the remains of the Missionary. "You really did a number on him."

"Bastard had it coming." Val tightened her grip on the gun reflexively.

The clicking sound of heels on the metal floor made us both turn in time to see Helen step over the threshold, her long, dark coat swirling around her ankles. She went directly to the corpse, not even acknowledging me or Val. She stood over it for a several seconds. Her jaw tightened once, then relaxed.

Finally she turned, her face impassive. Her steely gaze raked over me before focusing in on Valentine. We must have been a pathetic sight—Val slumped over and covered in blood, me trying to fold as much of my body as possible into Darren's huge jacket.

"Tell me what happened."

Val opened her mouth, but I jumped in first. I explained everything, beginning with the Missionary's appearance at the Angel Orensanz Foundation earlier tonight. When I got to the part about calling Detective Foster, Helen stiffened.

"What do the police know?"

I looked over at the two bodies near the door, my heart aching. I couldn't help but feel the sour twist of guilt in my stomach, either. We had sent them to their deaths. "Just that Val recognized him on the street and that we followed him here. I don't know what they told dispatch. They must have seen the hooker, but I don't think they got to talk to her."

"We're detaining the prostitute outside. What did she see?"

"All we got out of her was that the police were in danger, and that they'd managed to injure him."

"She did say he was 'strong,'" Val chipped in, trying to be helpful. I rested one hand on her leg. She looked even paler now. We really needed to get out of there.

Helen pointed to the corpse of the Missionary. "And him? What did he say to you?"

I frowned. Why did that matter? He was dead now. Finally. "Mostly just threats. He recognized Val, of course." I paused, a worrying thought poked at the edges of my memory. "Oh, and somehow he knew that I was Val's girlfriend. He threatened me."

Helen exhaled dismissively. "Most vampires are aware of your feeding arrangement with Valentine. That's nothing unusual."

I opened my mouth for a sharp retort but Val groaned beside me, clutching her side. I immediately shifted to give her more support to lean on. "We need to get her to a hospital."

"Very well." Helen gestured toward Darren. "Get them into the car. Call ahead for Clavier."

"What are you going to do?" Val asked hoarsely.

Helen dropped gracefully into a crouch and traced the side of Val's face with one red-tipped finger. She didn't so much as look at me. Don't worry," she murmured tenderly. "I'll take care of it."

Deep inside, the panther's hackles rose. I agreed with her. Helen could be really creepy sometimes. She wasn't Val's mother, and she certainly wasn't her lover, but she was acting like both.

She stood then, and Darren moved in. His movements were gentle as he helped Val stand, but as soon as she was upright, she leaned forward and vomited, barely missing his shoes.

"S-sorry," she gasped. "It's m-my head."

I grabbed my torn tank top off the floor and wiped her mouth with the ruined fabric. Seeing her suffer like this was awful, but at least we both knew that the one responsible would never hurt her again.

"I'll carry you," Darren rumbled, lifting her easily into his arms. She sagged against his chest as he walked toward the door.

I looked over my shoulder once. Helen was talking softly with the other man, indicating various corners of the room. I wondered what she was going to do with the crime scene and the bodies, and what she had told the police to stop them from coming. I wondered what would happen to the prostitute.

Most of all, I wondered whether this was really all over. And whether we could finally now find peace.

EPILOGUE

I woke to an empty bed. Heart trying to claw its way out of my chest, I threw off the covers and ran to the doorway...only to stop, sighing in relief at the sight of Valentine reclining on the couch, swaddled by the afghan that my mother had knit for me when I went off to college. The television was on, its volume turned down low. A thick white bandage slanted from just above her right eye to halfway across her scalp.

She looked up slowly, wincing. "Hey. Did I wake you?"

"No, not at all. I was just worried when you weren't in bed."

"I woke up two hours ago with the mother of all headaches." She wiggled her toes under the blanket. "Come sit?"

I crouched next to her head and placed a gentle kiss on her lips. "I'm going to make some tea. Did you take something for the pain? Can I get you anything?"

Val pointed to an empty glass. "More juice?"

She said it almost plaintively, like a small child. My heart thumped hard in sympathy. "Of course." I leaned in to kiss her again before heading for the kitchen. It was close to noon now. We hadn't gotten home until almost five in the morning. Val had sustained two broken ribs, a concussion, and a good deal of blood loss. It had taken a while to get her cleaned and stitched up. The whole time, she had grumbled about being infirm again.

I had worried about whether she was going to be able to sleep, but exhaustion pulled her under as soon as we were in bed. I hadn't been so lucky. The sensation of my teeth ripping into the Missionary's shoulder had haunted me for several hours, yanking me back from the brink of welcome oblivion whenever I started to fall into sleep. I had been keeping my distance from Val, so as not to hurt her if I moved in the night, but finally I gave in and aligned my body with hers. Breathing in her scent gave me the peace I so desperately needed. On a positive note, the fact that I couldn't sleep made it easy for me to wake Val every two hours as a precaution due to her concussion.

I was just firing up the teakettle when Val shouted my name. The panic returned full force, and I was through the doorway in an instant. But she was only pointing at the television. "Look!"

I sat near her feet and rested one hand on her leg over the blanket, willing my heartbeat to slow as I focused on the TV. One of the local news anchors was just introducing a story about three fatalities in a mysterious fire on the Lower East Side last night. She cut to a reporter who was stationed outside the Missionary's warehouse. Or rather, what was left of it.

Warped metal rebars twisted up out of still-smoldering ruins, reaching futilely for the sky. Yellow crime scene tape fenced off the sidewalk behind the reporter. "Apparently, a resident of the neighborhood dialed nine-one-one at three thirty this morning to report a fire," he was saying. "The investigation has only begun, but police tell us that the remains of three people have been discovered in the ruins. Two of them are presumed to be Detective Devon Foster and her partner Jared Wilson."

I squeezed Val's leg as the station flashed photos of Foster and Wilson on the screen. Devon was smiling in hers. And now she was dead. Val reached out from beneath the blanket to twine our fingers together.

"The third body has not yet been identified," the reporter continued. "The police believe this to be a case of arson, but have no leads yet as to what the motive might have been."

Val turned down the volume as the anchor switched to another story. I reached over to cup the uninjured side of her face, drawing my thumb gently across her lips. "See? It really is over."

She kissed my finger. "Yeah. It really is. I just…God, I wish we could have stopped him from killing them."

There was nothing I could say—the guilt was eating at me, too. But what could we have done? We'd had no options that would both preserve the secret and keep the police safe. Besides, it wasn't as though we had expected the Missionary to be able to overpower two of them. Despite what I had told Val about this being over, I was still curious about him. Helen had to know something. Maybe she would confide in Val, someday.

Val's eyes fluttered closed, and I withdrew my hand. "Sleep, love." I went back into the kitchen and poured myself a cup of tea, sipping it slowly as I stared out the window. The street below looked quiet—peaceful. Weak sunlight filtered down through the bare branches of the trees to coalesce in pools on the chipped sidewalk. A woman walking her dog—a miniature Schnauzer wearing its own sweater—paused to chat with a man who was salting the steps of his walk-up. It was a quiet scene. Peaceful. After everything that had happened over the past few months, that world looked alien.

And yet, I was still a part of it. I had an exam in three days that I desperately needed to study for, and a legal brief due by the end of the week. I also needed to work on finding a summer internship. That prospect had once been exciting, but now it just seemed like one more hoop to jump through on the way to getting my degree. It was disconcerting, this new realization that what had once been my intellectual passion now paled in comparison to my fascination with the animal that lurked inside me.

I wanted to experience again that wholeness and unity that we had discovered in the warehouse. I wanted that effortless transformation and perfected communication. I had believed that I was destined to forever struggle against the desires of the panther, but after last night, I dared to hope that we could be at perfect peace with each other. Someday.

The sound of the doorbell pulled me out of my introspection. "Don't get up, sweetheart," I called, hurrying out of the kitchen. When I looked through the peephole, I felt my eyebrows arch in surprise. "It's Helen."

She swept into our apartment regally, making it seem dingier than it really was. As usual, she wore an immaculately tailored pantsuit. The dark red color of this one made my skin crawl. The panther bared her teeth.

"Helen," Val said, and I went to the couch to help her sit up. She looked in confusion from Helen to the window and back again. It was broad daylight. "How are you here? Are you all—"

"I'm fine," she interrupted smoothly. "And I have my ways of moving about in daylight if necessary. I'll be out of town for a time, and wanted to check on you before leaving."

Val looked surprised. "Thank you. But you didn't need to come yourself."

Even Helen's shrug was elegant. I sat next to Val and put my hand on her knee to keep myself from fidgeting. It was logical for Helen to care about Valentine, I knew, but she took it further than my reason could justify and that made me nervous.

"I've taken care of last night's…problem," she continued. "There is no evidence that can be linked to either of you."

Val nodded solemnly. "We saw on the news. Thank you."

Helen looked at me for the first time since entering. "I'd like to speak with Valentine alone now, please."

Internally, I bristled at the request, wishing that Val would say something to keep me in the room. Helen cowed her far too easily. Then again, I reflected as I walked back into the kitchen, I wouldn't exactly have the impulse or inclination to buck Malcolm. I busied myself with pouring another cup of tea, and then washing the dishes in the sink. My hearing was effectively superhuman now, but even so, I couldn't catch more than a word or two of what they were discussing.

After about a minute, Val said something about Helen having a good trip, which was all the license I needed to reemerge. As I walked out, I saw Val pocket a small black box. It was the perfect size for a ring.

"Thanks again," she said as Helen went to the door. "Take care."

Helen nodded once before stepping outside. I bolted the door behind her, then took my place at Val's side. She was sipping thirstily at her juice, and I wondered whether she needed to feed, having lost so much blood last night. I hoped so. We needed that kind of intimacy right now.

"So?" I said, tracing my fingertips up and down along her thigh. "What was that all about?"

Val put down her empty glass and carefully rested her head on my shoulder. "She just wanted to ask me a few more questions about the Missionary, that's all."

"What did she give you?"

If our bodies hadn't been pressed up together, I would have missed the momentary tensing of Val's muscles that subsided as soon as it had appeared. "Just something I left at the Consortium," she said lightly.

She was clearly leaving something unsaid, but now didn't seem like the time to push. I brought my other arm across her body to pull her closer. She sighed, burrowing her face into my neck, and I kissed her temple. Whatever it was, I knew that she would tell me in due time.

We had forever, after all.

About the Authors

NELL STARK grew up predominately on the East Coast of the USA, attended Dartmouth College, and is now pursuing a doctorate in medieval English literature at the University of Wisconsin–Madison. When she is not teaching, writing, or teaching in the university's Writing Center, she enjoys cooking, sailing, reading, and most sports.

TRINITY TAM is a marketing executive in the music industry and an award-winning writer/producer of film and television. She lives, works, and parents a rambunctious toddler in New York City.

Books Available From Bold Strokes Books

The Pleasure Planner by Larkin Rose. Pleasure purveyor Bree Hendricks treats love like a commodity until Logan Delaney makes Bree the client in her own game. (978-1-60282-121-7)

everafter by Nell Stark and Trinity Tam. Valentine Darrow is bitten by a vampire on her way to propose to her lover Alexa Newland, and their lives and love are placed in mortal jeopardy. (978-1-60282-119-4)

Summer Winds by Andrews & Austin. When Maggie Turner hires a ranch hand to help work her thousand acres, she never expects to be attracted to the very young, very female Cash Tate. (978-1-60282-120-0)

Beggar of Love by Lee Lynch. Jefferson is the lover every woman wants to be—or to have. A revealing saga of lesbian sexuality. (978-1-60282-122-4)

The Seduction of Moxie by Colette Moody. When 1930s Broadway actress Violet London meets speakeasy singer Moxie Valette, she is instantly attracted and her Hollywood trip takes an unexpected turn. (978-1-60282-114-9)

Goldenseal by Gill McKnight. When Amy Fortune returns to her childhood home, she discovers something sinister in the air— but is former lover Leone Garoul stalking her or protecting her? (978-1-60282-115-6)

Romantic Interludes 2: Secrets edited by Radclyffe and Stacia Seaman. An anthology of sensual lesbian love stories: passion, surprises, and secret desires. (978-1-60282-116-3)

Femme Noir by Clara Nipper. Nora Delaney meets her match in Max Abbott, a sex-crazed dame who may or may not have the information Nora needs to solve a murder—but can she contain her lust for Max long enough to find out? (978-1-60282-117-0)

The Reluctant Daughter by Lesléa Newman. Heartwarming, heartbreaking, and ultimately triumphant—the story every daughter recognizes of the lifelong struggle for our mothers to really see us. (978-1-60282-118-7)

Erosistible by Gill McKnight. When Win Martin arrives at a luxurious Greek hotel for a much-anticipated week of sun and sex with her new girlfriend, she is stunned to find her ex-girlfriend, Benny, is the proprietor. Aeros Ebook. (978-1-60282-134-7)

Looking Glass Lives by Felice Picano. Cousins Roger and Alistair become lifelong friends and discover their sexuality amidst the backdrop of twentieth-century gay culture. (978-1-60282-089-0)

Breaking the Ice by Kim Baldwin. Nothing is easy about life above the Arctic Circle—except, perhaps, falling in love. At least that's what pilot Bryson Faulkner hopes when she meets Karla Edwards. (978-1-60282-087-6)

It Should Be a Crime by Carsen Taite. Two women fulfill their mutual desire with a night of passion, neither expecting more until law professor Morgan Bradley and student Parker Casey meet again…in the classroom. (978-1-60282-086-9)

Rough Trade edited by Todd Gregory. Top male erotica writers pen their own hot, sexy versions of the term "rough trade," producing some of the hottest, nastiest, and most dangerous fiction ever published. (978-1-60282-092-0)

The High Priest and the Idol by Jane Fletcher. Jemeryl and Tevi's relationship is put to the test when the Guardian sends Jemeryl on a mission that puts her not only in harm's way, but back into the sights of a previous lover. (978-1-60282-085-2)

Point of Ignition by Erin Dutton. Amid a blaze that threatens to consume them both, firefighter Kate Chambers and property owner Alexi Clark redefine love and trust. (978-1-60282-084-5)

Secrets in the Stone by Radclyffe. Reclusive sculptor Rooke Tyler suddenly finds herself the object of two very different women's affections, and choosing between them will change her life forever. (978-1-60282-083-8)